The Ice House

'Terrific first novel with a high Rendellesque frisson count'
The Times

The Sculptress

'A devastatingly effective novel'
Observer

The Scold's Bridle

'A gothic puzzle of great intricacy and psychological power'
Sunday Times

The Dark Room

'A marvellous, dramatically intelligent novel. It shimmers with suspense, ambiguity and a deep unholy joy'
Daily Mail

The Echo

'It grips like steel . . . Passion, compassion, intelligence and romance are what Walters offers with no quarter for squeamish cowards'
Mail on Sunday

The Breaker

'Stands head and shoulders above the vast majority of crime novels . . . Existing fans will love *The Breaker*, new readers will be instant converts'
Daily Express

The Shape of Snakes

'Breaking all the rules of popular fiction, Minette Walters asks as much of her readers as many literary novelists, and yet she offers them a book as gripping as any thriller'
Times Literary Supplement

Acid Row

'Humane intelligence enables Walters to twist and turn her plot . . . *Acid Row* is a breathtaking achievement'
Daily Telegraph

Fox Evil

'Fox Evil is the work of a writer at the peak of her confidence and supreme ability'
The Times

Disordered Minds

'A powerful, acute and vivid work from a staggeringly talented writer'
Observer

The Tinder Box

'If there wasn't a recognised school of crime writing called Home Counties noir before, there is now. Minette Walters invented it and remains the undisputed Head Girl'
Birmingham Post

The Devil's Feather

'One of the most powerful yet nuanced practitioners of the psychological thriller . . . always keeps the narrative momentum cracked up to a fierce degree'
Daily Express

Chickenfeed

'A marvellous little story, thoroughly intimate with human nastiness'
Evening Standard

The Chameleon's Shadow

'No wonder Minette Walters is the country's bestselling female crime writer. But even this label does not exactly do justice to the scope and breadth of her gripping, terrifying novels . . . *The Chameleon's Shadow* is another classic'
Daily Mirror

The Echo

With her debut, *The Ice House*, Minette Walters won the Crime Writers' Association John Creasey Award for the best first crime novel of 1992. Rapidly establishing a reputation as one of the most exciting crime novelists writing today, her second novel, *The Sculptress*, was acclaimed by critics as one of the most compelling and powerful novels of the year and won the Edgar Allan Poe Award for the best crime novel published in America in 1993. In 1994 Minette Walters achieved a unique triple when *The Scold's Bridle* was awarded the CWA Gold Dagger for best crime novel of the year. Her following five novels, *The Dark Room*, *The Echo*, *The Breaker*, *The Shape of Snakes* and *Acid Row* were also published to further critical acclaim throughout the world and her ninth novel, *Fox Evil*, won the 2003 CWA Gold Dagger for Fiction. Her short novel *Chickenfeed* was written for World Book Day to encourage emergent readers and was voted the 2006 Quick Reads Readers' Favourite.

Minette Walters lives in Dorset with her husband and two children.

By the same author

The Ice House

The Sculptress

The Scold's Bridle

The Dark Room

The Breaker

The Shape of Snakes

Acid Row

Fox Evil

Disordered Minds

The Tinder Box

The Devil's Feather

The Chameleon's Shadow

and

The Tinder Box

Chickenfeed
(Quick Reads)

MINETTE WALTERS

The Echo

PAN BOOKS

First published 1997 by Macmillan

First published in paperback 1998 by Pan Books

This edition published 2008 by Pan Books
an imprint of Pan Macmillan, a division of Macmillan Publishers Limited
Pan Macmillan, 20 New Wharf Road, London N1 9RR
Basingstoke and Oxford
Associated companies throughout the world
www.panmacmillan.com

ISBN 978-0-330-45503-9

1 3 5 7 9 8 6 4 2

A CIP catalogue record for this book is available from
the British Library.

Typeset by SetSystems Ltd, Saffron Walden, Essex
Printed and bound in Great Britain by
CPI Group (UK) Ltd, Croydon, CR0 4YY

For Frank and Mary

The echo began in some indescribable way to undermine her hold on life . . . it had managed a murmur, 'Pathos, piety, courage – they exist, but are identical, and so is filth. Everything exists, nothing has value.'

E. M. FORSTER (1879–1970)

O Rose, thou art sick!
The invisible worm
That flies in the night,
In the howling storm,

Has found out thy bed
Of crimson joy:
And his dark secret love
Does thy life destroy.

WILLIAM BLAKE (1757–1827)

Chapter One

IT WAS THE smell that Mrs Powell noticed first. Slightly sweet. Slightly unpleasant. She sniffed it on the air one warm June evening as she parked her car in her garage, but she assumed it came from her neighbours' dustbin on the other side of the low wall that divided the properties, and did nothing about it. The next morning the smell of decay eddied out from inside when she pulled open the garage doors, and curiosity led her to poke among the stack of boxes at the back after she had reversed her car on to the driveway. Certainly, she didn't expect to find a corpse. If she expected anything, it was that someone had abandoned their rubbish in there, and it shocked her badly to find a dead man huddled on sheets of flattened cardboard in the corner, his head slumped on his knees.

There was a flutter of media interest in the story, largely because of where the man was found – within the boundaries of an exclusive private estate bordering the Thames in London's old docklands – and because the pathologist gave cause of death as malnutrition. That a man should have died of starvation in one of the wealthiest parts of one of the wealthiest capitals of the world as the twentieth century drew to a close was irresistible to most journalists, the more so when they learned from the police that he had passed away beside a huge chest freezer filled with food. The rat-pack arrived in force.

But they were to be disappointed. Mrs Powell was a reluctant interviewee and had already vanished from her house. Nor was there anyone to flesh out the dead man's life and make it worth writing about. He was one of the army of homeless who haunted the streets of London, an alcoholic without family or friends, whose fingerprints were recorded under the name of Billy Blake as a result of a handful of convictions for petty thieving. Among London's policemen he had a small reputation as a street preacher from his habit of shouting aggressively at passers-by about forthcoming doom and destruction whenever he was drunk, but as none of them had ever listened closely to his incoherent ramblings, nothing was added to their knowledge of the man through what he had preached. The only curious fact about him was that he had lied about his age when first arrested in 1991. The police had him on file as sixty-five; while the pathologist's estimate, as officially recorded at the inquest, was forty-five.

Mrs Powell's involvement in this bizarre tragedy was that she owned the garage in which Billy had died. However, he preyed upon her mind following her return two weeks later after the morbid press interest had died down and, because she could afford it, she put up the money for his cremation when the coroner finally released the body. She had no need to do it – as in other areas of social welfare, the trappings of death were covered by a state benefit – but she felt an obligation to her uninvited guest. She chose the second cheapest package offered, and presented herself at the crematorium on the due date at the due time. As she had expected, she and the vicar were the only people there, the undertaker's men having left after depositing the coffin on the rollers. It was a somewhat harrowing service, conducted to the accompaniment of taped music. Elvis Presley sang 'Amazing Grace' over the sound system at the beginning, the vicar and she struggled through the service and the responses together (while worrying independently if Billy Blake had even been a Christian), and a Welsh male voice choir gave a harmonious rendition of 'Abide with Me' as the coffin rolled through to the burners and the curtains closed discreetly behind it.

There was little more to be said or done and, after shaking hands and thanking each other for being there, Mrs Powell and the vicar went their separate ways. As part of the package, Billy Blake's ashes were placed in an urn in a small corner of the crematorium with a plaque giving his name and date of death. Sadly, neither piece of information was accurate, for the dead man had not been christened Billy Blake and the pathologist had miscalculated his temperature readings and underestimated the time of death by a few hours.

Whoever Billy Blake was, he died on Tuesday, 13 June 1995.

*

The two visitors who came to view Billy Blake's plaque a few days later went unnoticed. The older man jabbed a stubby finger at the words and made a derisory noise in his throat. 'See, what did I tell you? Died twelfth of June 1995. The frigging Monday. Okay? Happy now?'

'We ought to've brought some flowers,' said his young companion, looking at the profusion of wreaths that other mourners had left in last respects to the recently cremated.

'There'd be no point, son. Billy's dead and I've yet to meet a corpse 'oo appreciates floral arrangements.'

'Yeah, but—'

'But nothing,' said the old man firmly. 'I keep telling you, the bugger's gone.' He pushed the youngster forward. 'Satisfy yerself I'm right, and then we'll be off.' He glanced around with a look of distaste creasing his weathered face. 'I never did like these places. It ain't 'ealthy thinking too much on death. It comes soon enough as it is.'

Despite having her garage cleansed three times in six weeks by three different cleaning companies, Mrs Powell disposed of her chest freezer, shopped rather more frequently and started parking her car in the driveway. Her neighbour remarked on it to his wife, and said it was a pity there was no Mr Powell. No *man* would allow a perfectly serviceable garage to go to waste simply because a tramp had died in it.

(Extract from *Unsolved Mysteries of the Twentieth Century* by Roger Hyde, published by Macmillan, 1994)

missing persons

Precisely how many people leave home for good every year in Britain remains a mystery, but if we define 'missing' as 'whereabouts unknown', then the figure is believed to run into hundreds of thousands. Only a tiny percentage ever hit the headlines, and these are usually children who are abducted and subsequently murdered. Adults rarely attract attention. The most famous missing person of recent years is the Earl of Lucan, who vanished from his estranged wife's house on 7 November 1974, following the brutal murder of Sandra Rivett, his children's nanny, and the attempted murder of Lady Lucan. He was never seen again, nor was his body found, but there seems little mystery about why he chose to vanish. Less explicable were the disappearances of two other 'missing persons': Peter Fenton, OBE, a Foreign Office 'high flyer', and James Streeter, a merchant banker.

† † †

The Case of the Vanishing Diplomat – Peter Fenton, OBE

The disappearance of Peter Fenton during the evening of 3 July 1988, only hours before his wife's body was discovered in the bedroom of their Knightsbridge home, created a sensation in the British press. The house was less than a mile from where the terrible Lucan tragedy had been played out nearly fourteen years before, and the parallels between Peter Fenton and Lord 'Lucky' Lucan were startling. The two men had moved in similar social circles and both were known to have loyal friends who would help them; each man's car was later found abandoned on the south coast of England, leading to speculation that they had fled across the Channel to France; there was even a bizarre similarity in their appearance, both being tall, dark and conventionally handsome.

But comparisons with the Lucan case ended when the police revealed that, following detailed forensic examination of the house and body, they were satisfied that Verity Fenton had committed suicide. She had hanged herself from a rafter in the attic some time during the evening of 1 July while Peter Fenton was on a five-day visit to Washington. A reconstruction of the evidence suggested that, on his return from America during the afternoon of 3 July, he had found her suicide note on the hall table and then searched the house for her. There seems no doubt that it was he who cut her down and he who laid her out on the bed. Nor is there any doubt that he phoned his stepdaughter and asked her to come to the house that evening with her husband. He did not warn her of what she would find, nor did he mention that he wouldn't be there, but he told her he would leave the door on the latch. She described him as sounding 'very tired'.

Unlike Lord Lucan, who was formally committed for trial at the Central Criminal Court after the inquest into the death of Sandra Rivett, Peter Fenton was effectively absolved of blame for the death of his wife, Verity. A verdict of 'suicide while the balance of her mind was disturbed' was recorded, following evidence from her daughter that she had been unnaturally depressed while her husband was away. This was borne out by her suicide note which said simply: 'Forgive me. I can't bear it any more, darling. Please don't blame yourself. Your betrayals are nothing compared with mine.'

However, the question remained: why did Peter Fenton vanish? It seemed logical to many columnists that 'betrayals' referred to love affairs, and there was much speculation that he had run to the comforting arms of a mistress. But this did not explain why his car was found abandoned near a cross-Channel ferry port, nor why he continued in hiding after the inquest verdict had been published. Interest began to centre on his job in the Foreign Office and the two postings he had held in Washington (1981–3 and 1985–7), where he was thought to have had access to highly secret information about NATO.

Was it coincidence that Fenton had vanished only weeks after the arrest of Nathan Driberg* in America? Why had he made the five-day trip to Washington alone when it must have been clear to him that his wife was deeply depressed? Could it have been a desperate attempt to find out if Driberg was going to talk in order to then reassure Verity that he was safe? For why had she written of 'betrayals' before hanging herself unless she had known that her husband was a spy? Parallels were now drawn, not with Lord Lucan, but with Guy Burgess and Donald Maclean, the notorious Foreign Office spies of the 1930s and 1940s, who disappeared in 1951 after being warned by Kim Philby

* Nathan Driberg (b. 1941, Sacramento, California) joined the CIA from Harvard in 1962. Although a man of high intellect he failed to make progress within the CIA and is said to have become increasingly angry with the system. Some time during the early 1980s he conceived the idea of a syndicated spying ring whose aims would be purely profit-making and whose members would be known only to him. Information was supplied by syndicate members and sold on to a selected buyer. Purchasing countries are said to have included Russia, China, South Africa, Colombia and Iraq. The syndicate is believed to have contained other CIA agents, members of Congress, foreign diplomats, journalists and industrialists, but, as Driberg has consistently refused to name any other person, their identities remain a secret. The syndicate's activities were only discovered when one of its members, Harry Castilli, a CIA agent, began to adopt an overly lavish lifestyle. In return for immunity, he led investigators to Driberg and testified against him at his trial. Shortly after Driberg's arrest, a French diplomat and a prominent US Congressman both committed suicide. A UK diplomat, Peter Fenton, vanished.

that a counter-intelligence investigation by British and American agencies was closing in on them. Had Peter Fenton, like Donald Maclean, used his position of trust in our Washington Embassy to betray his country?

Sadly, we shall probably never know because, if Peter Fenton *was* a traitor, then he did it for the money and he is unlikely to resurface as Burgess and Maclean did in Moscow in 1956, claiming a long-standing allegiance to communism. With the sort of wealth that the Driberg syndicate is said to have made, he could have had millions stashed away in Switzerland with which to fund a new identity for himself. But, according to his step-daughter, Marilyn Burghley, it would be wrong to assume that he benefited from his treachery. 'You have to understand that Peter adored my mother. I never believed that "betrayals" meant he'd had affairs. Which means, I suppose, that I have to accept he was betraying his country, and that she knew about it. Perhaps he asked her to run away with him, and when she refused, he accused her of not loving him. I think they must have had a terrible row for her to kill herself like that. Whatever the truth, life without her would have been something he couldn't bear. My mother's death was a far worse punishment than anything the courts could have given him.'

An examination of Peter Fenton's earlier life and background sheds little further light on the mystery. Born on 5 March 1950, he was the adopted son of

Jean and Harold Fenton of Colchester, Essex. Jean always described him as her 'little miracle' because she was forty-two at the time of the adoption and had given up hope of a child. She and her husband were both teachers and lavished time and effort on their son. Their reward was a gifted child who won scholarships first to Winchester and then to Cambridge, where he read classics. However, he became gradually estranged from his parents during his teenage years, spending fewer vacations in Essex and preferring whenever possible to stay with friends in London. There is evidence that he resented his humble background and set out to rise above it. He showed little love for his adoptive parents.

In a letter to his brother in 1971, Harold Fenton wrote: 'Peter has broken Jean's heart and I shall never forgive him for it. When I tackled him about his gambling, he asked me if I'd rather he stole to buy his way out of our lives and our house. He's ashamed of us. Apparently, he intends joining the Foreign Office when he leaves Cambridge and he wanted to "warn" us that we will see very little of him once that happens. His career must come first. I asked him if he had any explanation for why God saw fit to bless us with so objectionable a child and he said: "I made you proud. What more did you want?" I would have struck him had Jean not been present.'

Peter Fenton joined the Foreign Office from Cambridge in 1972, and was spotted early by Sir

Angus Fraser, then ambassador in Paris. With Fraser's backing, Fenton seemed set for a glittering career. However, his marriage to Verity Standish in 1980 was seen by many as a mistake, and his meteoric rise looked like faltering. Verity, a widow with two teenage children, was thirteen years older than Fenton and, because of her age, was considered an unsuitable wife for a future ambassador. Interestingly, in view of what he had said to his father ten years earlier, Fenton chose to put his love for Verity before his career, and his decision would seem to have been vindicated when he won his first posting to Washington in September 1981.

There followed seven years of apparently blameless marriage and dedicated work. Fenton was awarded the OBE in 1983 for services to Her Majesty's Government during the Falklands War, and Verity proved a loyal wife and much-sought-after hostess for official functions. Her children, who spent their vacations with the couple in whichever part of the world they were, remember Fenton with affection. 'He was always very kind to us,' said Verity's son, Anthony Standish. 'He told me once that he always thought money and ambition were the only things that mattered in life until my mother showed him how to love. That's why I don't believe he was a traitor. The money wouldn't have attracted him. If you want my opinion, it was she who was having the affair. She was the sort of woman who needed constant demonstrations of love, probably because my real father was a womanizer and their marriage had been an unhappy one. Perhaps she felt neglected because Peter was working so hard at that time, and she slid into infidelity by default. If Peter found out about it and threatened to leave her, it would explain why she hanged herself.'

But, unfortunately, it explains nothing else. Why did Peter Fenton vanish? Is he alive or dead? Was he a spy, a philandering husband or a cuckold? Can we really believe that love for Verity transformed him from ambitious materialist to loving husband and stepfather? And, if he loved her as much as his stepchildren claim he did, what did he do before he left for Washington that sent his wife into such a spiral of despair that she killed herself? More intriguingly, in view of its anonymity and the absence of an envelope, was Verity's suicide note addressed to him or to someone else?

The truth may well lie in what Jean Fenton wrote in her diary on his fifth birthday: 'How Peter does love acting. Today he's playing the part of the perfect child. Tomorrow it will be the devil. I wish I knew which of these various Peters is the *real* one.'

† † †

The Case of the Absconding Merchant Banker – James Streeter

James Streeter was born on 24 July 1951, the elder son of Kenneth and Hilary Streeter of Cheadle Hulme in Cheshire. He was educated at Manchester Grammar School and Durham University, where he read modern languages. On graduation, he took a job in Paris with Le Fournet, a French merchant bank, where he remained for five years before moving to a sister bank in Brussels. While there, he met and married Janine Ferrer, but the marriage lasted less than three years and, following his divorce in 1983, he returned to Britain to take a job with Lowenstein's Merchant Bank in the City of London. In 1986 he married a promising young architect who was seven years his junior. Kenneth and Hilary Streeter describe the marriage as a stormy one. 'They had very little in common,' admits Hilary, 'which led to rows, but it's ridiculous to suggest that depression over his marital problems prompted James to become a thief. In any case, if the police are to be believed, he began embezzling a year before his marriage, so the facts don't even add up. It makes us so angry that our son's reputation can be destroyed like this simply because the police have taken everything at face value. It's his murderer who deserves to be reviled, not James.'

Taken at face value, James Streeter's disappearance is as self-explanatory as Lord Lucan's for, within days of deserting his desk at Lowenstein's Merchant Bank on Friday, 27 April 1990, and in his absence, he was charged with defrauding his employers of £10 million. The case against him appears a strong one. Only weeks before he vanished, certain irregularities were noticed by the bank's auditors and were drawn to the attention of the board. At issue was a £10 million discrepancy which seemed to stem from Streeter's department and, worse, to stretch back over a period of five years. In simple terms, the theft involved the creation of fraudulent accounts which were set up as conduits for large international transactions and then creamed of interest. Their operation relied on the bank's failure to introduce proper security functions into its computer system, with the result that the false accounts went unnoticed and the interest creamed over the years was substantial.

The board's decision, a mistaken one as events proved, was to authorize a clandestine in-house investigation in order to avoid panicking the bank's customers. It was badly handled, with its secrecy compromised from the start, and the outcome was a failure to identify the responsible employee, while at the same time alerting him/her to the existence of the investigation. When James Streeter chose to run on the night of 27 April, the conclusion drawn was that he had 'got away' with a fortune, particularly as his abrupt departure followed within hours of the board's reaching its belated decision to turn the investigation over to the police.

However, despite lengthy questioning of his wife and a prolonged investigation into his financial affairs, no trace of Streeter or the stolen money has ever been found. Sceptics argue that his escape route was in place for weeks, months or even years, and that the £10 million were transferred out of the country into a safe haven abroad. Supporters, most notably his parents and brother, argue that James was a scapegoat for someone else's criminal activity and that he was murdered to shield the real culprit from further investigation. In defence of their position, they quote a handwritten facsimile that was sent from James's office at 3.05 p.m. on Friday, 27 April 1990, to his brother's office in Edinburgh.

> Dear John [it reads], Dad's pushing me to book a room for the Ruby Wedding 'do'. He's suggesting the Park Lane, but I remember Mum saying that if they ever celebrated a major anniversary she'd like to go back to the hotel in Kent where they had their reception. Am I imagining this? And did she ever mention the name of the hotel to you? Dad says it was somewhere in Sevenoaks but, needless to say, can't remember details. He claims his memory's going but I suspect he was pissed as a rat the whole day and <u>never</u> knew where he was! I've tried the aunts and uncles, but none of them can remember either. Failing all else, I think we'll have to blow the

surprise and ask Mum. You know what she's like. It'll offend her Puritan soul if we spend a fortune on something she doesn't really want, and then she won't enjoy herself. I know it's still a long way off, but the earlier we book the less likely we are to be disappointed. I shall be home all weekend, so give me a bell when you can. I've told Dad I'll call back Sunday lunchtime. Cheers. James.

'Whatever the police may argue,' says John Streeter, 'my brother would not have written that fax if he was planning to leave the country the same evening. There were a hundred better ways of allaying official suspicion about his alleged intentions. More likely he'd have referred to the visit that I and my family were making to him in May. "See you in two weeks" would have been far more telling than "give me a bell when you can." And why mention Dad? He couldn't afford to have two members of his family worried about nonexistent phone calls.'

The police take a more sceptical view. They cite the climate of suspicion that already existed in Lowenstein's and James's need to neutralize concern about his movements that weekend. Despite the supposed secrecy of the bank's in-house investigation, most of the employees noticed that security had been stepped up and that reports and transactions were being closely monitored. Gossip was rife and at least two people in Streeter's department are on record as saying they knew *before* he disappeared that some kind of fraud had been discovered and that suspicion centred on them. If, as the police believe, Streeter was biding his time until the investigation became serious enough to force him to run, then the fax to his brother was merely part of the smoke-screen he threw up to confuse the Lowenstein investigation. Almost every telephone call in the weeks preceding his disappearance contained invitations to business colleagues to meet on dates in April, May and June. His wife told police that around the beginning of April James became uncharacteristically sociable, encouraging her to organize dinner parties and weekend visits from friends, work colleagues and relations until well into July.

According to the police, he was working to a hidden agenda. They point to the fact that his secretary was instructed very early on in the 'clandestine' investigation to keep his desk diary up to date with social engagements, including private ones, and it is noticeable that April, May, June and July 1990 are significantly fuller than in the previous year. His brother admits this behaviour was unusual. 'Yes, we were surprised when they invited us to stay because James always said he found entertaining boring. The police argue that it was a successful attempt to lull the investigators into believing he had no idea the fraud had been discovered and would still be available for questioning through to

July. But it is equally logical to argue that, because he was as worried by the rumours as everyone else at Lowenstein's he acted out of character in trying to prove his commitment and dedication. Certainly, he wasn't the only employee to up his work schedule during that period and most of those diary dates refer to business meetings.'

His family go on to quote Streeter's computer illiteracy as further evidence of his innocence in this unsolved mystery. 'James simply didn't have the skill to work that fraud,' says John. 'His complete aversion to modern technology became something of a joke over the years. He could use a calculator and a fax machine but the idea of him being able to reprogram the bank's computer is laughable. When and where did he learn how to do it? He had no computer at home, and no one has ever come forward claiming to have taught him.'

But others have raised doubts about Streeter's alleged ignorance. There is evidence that he had an affair with a woman called Marianne Filbert, who was employed as a computer programmer by Softworks Limited. Softworks was invited to produce a report on Lowenstein's computer security in 1986, but they failed to complete the task and the report was never presented. James Streeter's detractors point to Marianne Filbert's access to that half-completed report as the key to the fraud, while his supporters dispute that he even knew Filbert. Alleged or otherwise, the affair was certainly over before the fraud was discovered because Filbert moved to America in August 1989. However, James Streeter's secretary has stated that on several occasions she found him using her word processor for personal correspondence, and colleagues testify to his easy understanding of the computer spreadsheet function. 'It took him no time at all to find an error I'd made,' claimed one member of his department. 'He said any fool could work the system if someone told him which buttons to press.'

Nevertheless, there remain several unanswered questions about James Streeter's disappearance which, in the opinion of this author, have never been adequately addressed. If we assume he *was* guilty of embezzling £10 million from Lowenstein's Merchant Bank, how did he know that the decision to involve the police was taken by the board on 27 April? The police allege that he had always planned to abscond if his fraud came to light and it was mere coincidence that his escape was scheduled for the day of the decisive board meeting. But, if that were true, why did he wait out the six weeks of the in-house investigation? Unless he had access to board documents, which the police admit is unlikely, then he could not have known the investigation was failing. And isn't it pushing the bounds of coincidence a little far that the last weekend in April, as recorded in James's office diary, was also the only weekend in April when his wife would be away, fulfilling a long-standing engagement with her mother, thus giving James – *or someone else* – two whole days to 'make good' his disappearance before his absence was reported?

The police argue that he chose that weekend to run because his movements could not be monitored, and that he would have gone whatever decision the board had reached, but this is to ignore the relationship that existed between James and his wife. According to Kenneth, one of the reasons the marriage was stormy was because the two people involved had more commitment to their careers than they had to each other. 'If James had said he had to fly to the Far East on Friday for a business meeting the following Monday, his wife wouldn't have turned a hair. That was what their lives were like. He didn't need to choose the one weekend she was away. Her absence only becomes important if someone else chose it.'

The police argument also ignores the fax James sent to his brother: 'I shall be home all weekend, so give me a bell when you can. I've told Dad I'll call back Sunday lunchtime.' The fact that John did telephone, but wasn't worried when there was no answer, may, as the police claim, have been entirely predictable, but it was a strange gamble for a guilty man to take. If we put that beside Kenneth Streeter's claim, tested and verified by a lie detector, that James promised to phone him on the Sunday with John's contribution to the Ruby Wedding debate, then the gamble becomes entirely unnecessary. Had John and Kenneth followed up the promised telephone calls, then James's absence might have been discovered earlier.

The Streeters' defence of their son relies heavily on a conspiracy theory – someone more highly placed than James and with access to privileged information manipulated decisions and events to avoid exposure – but without evidence to prove their case, their campaign to clear their son's name seems a hopeless one. Sadly, conspiracy theories work better in fiction than they do in real life, and on any objective reading of the evidence the conclusion must be that James Streeter *did* steal £10 million before running away and leaving his family to reap the bitter harvest of his betrayal.

Despite the Streeters' claims to the contrary, both James Streeter and Peter Fenton would appear to be genuine abscondees. They were mature men with settled backgrounds whose disappearances were bound to cause a stir within their communities and so provoke exhaustive investigations. However this is not true of the next two 'missing persons': Tracy Jevons, a troubled fifteen-year-old with a known history of prostitution; and Stephen Harding, a backward seventeen-year-old with a string of convictions for car theft . . .

Chapter Two

SIX MONTHS later, in the middle of a cold, wet December when flaming June and its sweltering heat were a distant memory, Mrs Powell was telephoned by a journalist from the *Street*, a self-styled politically left-of-centre magazine, who was compiling a feature on poverty and the homeless and wondered if she would agree to do an interview about Billy Blake. He gave his name as Michael Deacon.

'How did you get this number?' she asked suspiciously.

'It wasn't difficult. Your name and address were all over the newspapers six months ago and you're in the telephone book.'

'There's nothing I can tell you,' she said. 'The police knew more about him than I ever did.'

He was persistent. 'I won't take up much of your time, Mrs Powell. How about if I came round tomorrow evening? Say, eight o'clock.'

'What do you want to know about him?'

'Whatever you can tell me. I found his story very moving. No one seemed to be interested in him except you. The police told me you paid his funeral expenses. I wondered why.'

'I felt I owed him something.' There was a short silence. 'Are you the Michael Deacon who used to be with the *Independent*?'

'Yes.'

'I was sorry when you left. I like the way you write.'

'Thank you.' He sounded surprised, as if compliments were a rarity. 'In that case, surely I can persuade you to talk to me? You say you felt you owed Billy something.'

'Except I don't have the same liking for the *Street*, Mr Deacon. The only reason someone from that magazine would want to interview me about Billy would be to score cheap political points off the government, and I refuse to be exploited in that way.'

This time the silence was at Deacon's end while he reassessed his strategy. It would be helpful, he thought, if he could put an age and a face to the quiet, rather controlled voice of the woman he was talking to, more helpful if he genuinely believed this interview would produce anything of value. In his view the whole exercise was likely to be a waste of time and he was even less motivated than she was to go through with it. *However* . . .

'I don't make a habit of exploiting people, Mrs Powell, and I am interested in Billy Blake's story. Look, what have you got to lose by seeing me? You have my word that we'll abandon the whole thing if you don't like the way the interview's going.'

'All right,' she said, with abrupt decision. 'I'll expect you tomorrow at eight.' She rang off without saying goodbye.

*

The *Street* offices were a tired reminder that its namesake, Fleet Street, was once the glorious hub of the newspaper industry. The building still carried the masthead above its front door, but the letters were faded and cracked and few passers-by even noticed them. As with most of the broadsheets which had moved into cheaper, more efficient premises in the Docklands, the writing was on the wall for the *Street*, too. A new dynamic owner with ambitions to become a media tycoon waited in the shadows with plans to revamp the magazine by achieving lower costs, improved production and a twenty-first-century image through one galvanizing leap into pristine property in an outer London suburb. Meanwhile the magazine struggled on with outmoded work practices in elegant but impractical surroundings under an editor, Jim Pearce, who hankered after the good old days when the rich exploited the poor and everyone knew where he stood.

JP, still ignorant of what awaited them in the first few weeks of the new year (in his case enforced early retirement) but increasingly worried about the present owner's refusal to discuss anything that smacked of long-term strategy, sought out Deacon in his office the following afternoon. The only concessions to modernity were a word processor and an answering machine; otherwise the room looked as it had done for thirty years, with purple walls, an oak-panelled door covered in sheets of cheap white hardboard to smooth out unsightly bumps, and orange floral curtains at the window, all of which were the height of interior design in the heady, classless days of the 1960s.

'I want you to take a photographer with you when you interview Mrs Powell, Mike,' said Pearce in the belligerent tone that grew more ingrained as each worrying day passed. 'It's too good an opportunity to miss. I want tears and breast-beating from a Thatcherite who's seen the light.'

Deacon kept his eyes on his computer screen and continued typing. At six feet tall and weighing over thirteen stone, he wasn't easily bullied. In any case, he'd lied to Mrs Powell, and he didn't particularly want her to know it. 'No way,' he said bluntly. 'She did a runner the last time photographers turned up looking for pictures, and I'm not giving up precious time to go out and interview the silly cow only to have her slam the door in my face when she sees a camera lens.'

Pearce ignored this. 'I've told Lisa Smith to go with you. She knows how to behave, and if she keeps the camera out of sight till she's inside, the two of you should be able to talk Mrs Powell round.' He cast a critical eye over Deacon's crumpled jacket and five o'clock shadow. 'And, for Christ's sake, smarten yourself up, or you'll give the poor woman the screaming habdabs. I want a rich, well-fed Tory weeping over the iniquities of government housing policy, not someone scared out of her wits because she thinks a middle-aged mugger's come through her door.'

Deacon tilted his chair back and regarded his boss through half-closed lids. 'It won't make any difference what her blasted political affiliations are because I'm not including her unless she has something pertinent to say. She's your idea, JP, not mine. Homelessness is too big a social problem to be cheapened by one fat Tory weeping into her lace handkerchief.' He lit a cigarette and tossed the match angrily into an already overfull ashtray. 'I've sweated blood over this and I won't have it turned into a slanging match by the subs. I'm trying to offer some solutions here, not indulge in yah-boo politics.'

Pearce prowled across to the window and stared down on a wet, grey Fleet Street where cars crawled bumper to bumper in the driving rain and the odd window showed an ephemeral gaiety with lighted Christmas trees and sprayed-on snow. More than ever he had a sense of chapters ending. 'What sort of solutions?'

Deacon searched through a pile of papers on his desk and removed a typed sheet. 'The consensus sort. I've taken views from politicians, religious leaders and different social lobby groups to assess how the picture's changed in the last twenty years.' He consulted the page. 'There's across-the-board agreement that the figures on family breakdown, teenage drug and drink addiction and teenage pregnancies are alarming, and I'm using that agreement as a starting point.'

'Boring, Mike. Tell me something new.' He watched a progression of raised black umbrellas pass below the window, and he was reminded of all the funerals he'd attended over the years.

Deacon took in a lungful of smoke as he studied JP's back. 'Like what?'

'Tell me you've got a statement from a government minister saying all single mothers should be sterilized. Then maybe I'll let you off your interview with Mrs Powell. Have you?' His breath misted the glass.

'No,' said Deacon evenly. 'Oddly enough, I couldn't find a single mainstream politician who was that stupid.' He squared the papers on his desk. 'How about this for a quote? The poor are always with us and the only way to deal with them is to love them.'

Pearce turned round. 'Who said that?'

'Jesus Christ.'

'Is that supposed to be funny?'

Deacon gave an indifferent shrug. 'Not particularly. Thought-provoking, perhaps. In two thousand years no one's come up with a better solution. Certainly no politician anywhere at any time has managed to crack the problem. Like it or not, even communism has its share of paupers.'

'We're a political magazine, not an apologist for born-again Christianity,' said JP coldly. 'If mud-slinging offends you so much, then you should have kept your job on the *Independent*. Think about that the next time you tell me you don't want to get your hands dirty.'

Thoughtfully, Deacon blew a smoke ring into the air above his head. 'You can't afford to sack me,' he murmured. 'It's my byline that's keeping this rag afloat. You know as well as I do that until the tabloids raided my piece on the health service for scare stories about chaos in the A. and E. departments 99.99 per cent of the adult population of this country had no idea the *Street* was still being published. I'm a necessary evil as far as you're concerned.'

This was no exaggeration. In the ten months since Deacon had joined the staff, the circulation figures had begun to show a modest increase after fifteen years of steady decline. Even so, they were still only a third of what they had been in the late seventies and early eighties. It would require something more radical to revitalize the *Street* than the occasional publicity that one writer could generate, and in Deacon's view that meant a new editor with new ideas – a fact of which JP was very aware.

His smile held all the warmth of a rattlesnake's. 'If you'd written that story the way I told you to, *we* would have benefited from the scare stories and not the sodding tabloids. Why the hell did you have to be so coy about identifying the two children involved?'

'Because I gave my word to their parents. *And*,' said Deacon with heavy emphasis, 'I do not believe in using pictures of severely damaged children to sell copy.'

'They were used anyway.'

Yes, thought Deacon, and it still made him angry. He had taken great pains to keep the two families anonymous, but cheque-book journalism had seduced neighbours and friends into talking. 'Not because of anything I did,' he said.

'That's mealy-mouthed crap. You knew damn well it was only a matter of time before someone sold out.'

'I *should* have known,' corrected Deacon, squinting through the smoke from his cigarette. 'God knows I've spent enough time listening to your views on the subject. You'd sell your granny down the river for one more reader on the mailing-list.'

'You're an ungrateful bastard, Mike. Loyalty's a one-way street with you, isn't it? Do you remember coming here and begging me for a job when Malcolm Fletter bad-mouthed you round the industry? You'd been out of work for two months and it was doing your head in.' He levelled an accusing finger at the younger man. 'Who took you on? Who prised you out of that flat and gave you something to think about other than the self-induced misery of your personal life?'

'You did.'

'Right. So give me something in return. Smarten yourself up, and go chase pictures and quotes off a fat Tory. Put some spice into this article of yours.' He slammed the door as he left.

Deacon was half-inclined to pursue his irascible little boss and tell him that Malcolm Fletter had offered him his job back on the *Independent* less than two weeks previously; however, he was too soft-hearted to do it.

JP wasn't the only one who had a sense of chapters ending.

Lisa Smith whistled appreciatively when Deacon met her outside the offices at seven thirty. 'You look great. What's the occasion? Getting married again?'

He took her arm and steered her towards his car. 'Take my advice, Smith, and keep your mouth shut. I'm sure the last thing you want to do is rub salt in raw wounds. You're far too sweet and far too caring to do anything so crass.'

She was a beautiful, boisterous 24-year-old with a cloud of fuzzy dark hair and an attentive boyfriend. Deacon had lusted after her for months, but was too canny to let her know it. He feared rejection. More particularly he feared being told he was old enough to be her father. At forty-two, he was increasingly aware that he'd been abusing his body far too long and far too recklessly. What had once been lean, hard muscle had converted itself into alcoholic ripples that lurked beneath his waistband and escaped detection only because pleated chinos disguised what skin-tight jeans had formerly enhanced.

'But you're a different man when you take a little trouble, Deacon,' she said with apparent sincerity. 'The *enfant terrible* image was quite sweet in the sixties, but hardly something to cultivate into the nineties.'

He unlocked the doors and waited while she stowed her equipment on the back seat before folding her long legs into the front. 'How's Craig?' he asked, climbing in beside her.

She displayed a diamond hoop on her engagement finger. 'We're getting married.'

He fired the engine and drew out into the traffic. 'Why?'

'Because we want to.'

'That's no reason for doing anything. I want to screw twenty women a night but I value my sanity too much to do it.'

'It's not your sanity that would crack, Deacon, it's your self-esteem. You'd never find twenty women who were that desperate.'

He grinned. 'I wanted to marry both of my wives until I'd gone through with it and discovered they paid more attention to my bank statements than they did to my body.'

'Thanks.'

'What for?'

'The congratulations and the good wishes for my future.'

'I'm merely being practical.'

'No, you're not.' She bared her teeth at him. 'You're being bitter – as usual. Craig is very different from you, Mike. For a start, he likes women.'

'I *love* women.'

'Yes,' she agreed, 'that's your problem. You don't like them but you sure as hell love them as long as you think there's a chance of getting them into bed.' She lit a cigarette and opened her window. 'Has it never occurred to you that if you'd actually been friends with either of your wives you'd probably still be married?'

'Now you're sounding bitter,' he said, heading towards Blackfriars Bridge.

'I'm merely being practical,' she murmured. 'I don't want to end up as lonely as you.' She held the tip of her cigarette to the crack in the window and let the slipstream suck out the ash. 'So what's the MO for this evening? JP says he wants me to capture this woman's emotions while you ask her about some dead wino she found in her garage.'

'That's the plan.'

'What's she like?'

'I've no idea,' said Deacon. 'The nationals ran the story in June but, bar her name, which is Mrs Powell, and her address, which is expensive, there were no other details. She did a vanishing act before the rat-pack arrived and, by the time she came back, the story was dead. JP's hoping for late fifties, immaculate grooming, strong right-wing political affiliations and a husband who's a stockbroker.'

Mrs Powell was certainly immaculately groomed but she was twenty years short of late fifties. She was also far too controlled ever to display the sorts of emotion that Lisa was hoping for. She greeted them with a brisk, professional courtesy before showing them into an impeccable sitting-room which smelt of rose-petal pot-pourri and had the clean, spare look of designer minimalism. She clearly liked space, and Deacon rather approved of the cream leather and chrome chairs and sofa that formed an island about a low glass coffee table in the middle of a russet-coloured carpet. Beyond them an expanse of window, framed by draped but undrawn curtains, looked across the Thames to the lights on the other side. There was very little else in the room: only a series of glass shelves above tinted glass cabinets which clearly contained a stereo system; and three canvases – one white, one grey and one black – which adorned the wall opposite the shelves.

He nodded towards them. 'What are they called?'

'The title's in French. *Gravure à la manière noire*. It means mezzotint in English. They're by Henri Benoit.'

'Interesting,' he said, glancing at her, although it wasn't clear if he was referring to the canvases or to the woman herself.

In fact he was thinking that her taste in interior design sat rather oddly with her choice of house. It was an uninteresting brick box on a new estate in the Isle of Dogs which would probably be billed in estate agents' jargon as 'an exclusive development of detached executive homes with views of the river'. He guessed the house to be about five years old, with three bedrooms and two reception rooms, and put its value at well outside an average price range. But why, he wondered, would an obviously wealthy woman with interesting taste choose something so characterless when, for the equivalent money, she could have had a spacious flat anywhere in the heart of London? Perhaps she liked detached houses, he thought rather cynically. Or views of the river. Or perhaps *Mr* Powell had chosen it.

'Do sit down,' she said gesturing towards the sofa. 'Can I get you something to drink?'

'Thank you,' said Lisa, who'd taken an instant dislike to her. 'Black coffee would be nice.' In the scheme of feminine competition, Mrs Powell oozed success. She appeared to have everything – even femininity – and Lisa looked around for something to criticize.

'Mr Deacon?'

'Do you have anything stronger?'

'Of course. Whisky, brandy, beer?'

'Red wine?' he suggested hopefully.

'I've a 1984 Rioja open. Would that do?'

'It would. Thank you very much.'

Mrs Powell disappeared down the corridor and they heard her filling the kettle in the kitchen.

'What's with black coffee, Smith,' murmured Deacon, 'when there's alcohol on offer?'

'I thought we were supposed to be behaving ourselves,'

she whispered. 'And, for Christ's sake, don't start smoking. There are no ashtrays. I've already looked. I don't want you putting her back up before she agrees to the photographs.'

He watched her critical appraisal of the room. 'What's the verdict?'

'JP was right about everything except her age and her husband. *She*'s the stockbroker. I'll bet the Mrs is a courtesy title to give her some status in a male-dominated world. There's no sign of a man living here. It's all too uncomfortable and it doesn't half stink of roses. She probably sprayed the room before we arrived.' She turned her mouth down. 'I hate women who do that. It's a kind of one-upmanship. They want to prove their house is cleaner than yours.'

He lifted an amused eyebrow. 'Are you jealous?'

'What's to be jealous of?' she hissed.

'Success,' he murmured, holding a finger to his lips as they heard Mrs Powell returning.

'If you want to smoke,' she said, passing a coffee cup to Lisa and a glass of red wine to Deacon, 'I'll find you an ashtray.' She put her own wine glass on the table near an armchair and looked at them both.

'No, thank you,' said Lisa, thinking of JP's instruction.

'Yes, please,' said Deacon, doubting he could stand the scent of rose petals for an hour. He wished Lisa hadn't mentioned them. Once noticed, the smell was cloying, and he was reminded of the second Mrs Deacon who had plundered his very mediocre fortune in order to dowse herself in Chanel No. 5. It had been the shorter of his two marriages, lasting a mere three years before

Clara had cleared off with a twenty-year-old toyboy and rather too much of her husband's capital. He took the china saucer Mrs Powell handed him, then placed a cigarette between his lips and lit it. The smell of burning tobacco immediately swamped the roses, and Deacon felt guilt and satisfaction in equal measures. He left the cigarette jutting from his mouth as he took a tape recorder and a notebook from his pocket and placed them on the table in front of him. 'Do you mind if I record what you say?'

'No.'

He set the tape in motion and reluctantly broached the subject of photographs. 'We'd like a small visual to accompany the piece, Mrs Powell, so have you any objections to Lisa photographing you?'

She stared at him as she sat down. 'Why would you want photographs of me if you're planning to write about Billy Blake, Mr Deacon?'

Why indeed? 'Because in the absence of pictures of Billy, which we've established don't exist,' he lied, transferring the cigarette to the ashtray, 'I'm afraid you're the next best thing. Is that a problem for you?'

'Yes,' she said flatly. 'I'm afraid it is. I've already told you I have no intention of being used by your magazine.'

'And, as I told you, Mrs Powell, I don't make a habit of using people.'

She had ice-blue eyes which reminded him of his mother's, and that was a shame, he thought, because in other respects she was quite attractive. 'Then surely you agree that it's absurd to illustrate an article on poverty and the homeless with a picture of a woman who lives in an expensive house in an expensive part of London.' She paused for a moment, inviting him to speak. When he didn't she went on: 'In fact, there *are* pictures of Billy Blake. I have two which I'm prepared to lend you. One is a mugshot from when he was first arrested and the other was taken in the mortuary. Either would illustrate poverty better than a photograph of me.'

Deacon shrugged but didn't say anything.

'You said you were interested in Billy.'

She sounded put out, he thought, and that made him curious, for he'd been a journalist long enough to recognize that Mrs Powell was keener to tell her story than he was to hear it. *But why now, when she had refused to talk to the press at the time?* That question intrigued him. 'No pictures of you, no story, I'm afraid,' he said, reaching forward to switch off the tape. 'Editor's instructions. I'm sorry to have wasted your time, Mrs Powell.' He looked with regret at his untouched wine. 'And your Rioja.'

She watched him as he began to gather his bits and pieces together, clearly weighing something in her mind. 'All right,' she said abruptly, 'you can take your photographs. Billy's story needs to be told.'

'Why?' He shot the word at her as he depressed the record button a second time.

It was a question she had prepared for. The words came out so fluently that he was sure she'd rehearsed the answer in advance. 'Because we're in terrible trouble as a society if we assume that any man's life is so worthless that the manner of his death is the only interesting thing about him.'

'That's a fine sentiment,' he said mildly, 'but hardly very newsworthy. People die in obscurity all the time.'

'But why starve to death? Why here? Why does nobody know anything about him? Why had he told the police he was twenty years older than he actually was?' She searched his face intently. 'Aren't you at all curious about him?'

Of course! Curiosity wormed like a maggot in his brain, but he was far more interested in her than he was in the man who had died in her garage. *Why, for example, did she take Billy's death so personally that she was prepared to be exploited in order to have his story publicized?* 'Are you sure you didn't know him?' he suggested with apparent indifference.

Her surprise was genuine. 'No. Why would I need answers if I'd known him?'

He opened his notebook on his lap, and wrote: *Why does anyone need answers about a complete stranger six months after his death?* 'Which would you prefer,' he asked, 'that Lisa takes her photographs before we talk or while we're talking?'

'While.'

He waited as Lisa unzipped her bag and removed her camera. 'Do you have a Christian name, Mrs Powell?'

'Amanda.'

'Do you prefer Amanda Powell or Mrs Powell?'

'I don't mind.' She frowned into the camera lens.

'A smile would be better,' said Lisa. She snapped the shutter. Click. 'That's great.' Click. 'Could you look at the floor? Good.' Click. 'Keep your eyes cast down. That's really touching.' Click, click.

'Go on, Mr Deacon,' said the woman curtly. 'I'm sure you don't want me to be sick over my own carpet.'

He grinned. 'I prefer Deacon or Mike. How old are you?'

'Thirty-six.'

'What do you do for a job?'

She glanced at him as Lisa took another photograph. 'I'm an architect.'

'On your own or with a firm?'

'I'm with W. F. Meredith.' Click.

Not bad, he thought. Meredith was about as good as you could get. 'What are your political affiliations, Amanda?'

'None.'

'How about off the record?'

She gave a faint smile which Lisa caught. 'The same.'

'Do you vote?' She caught him watching her, and he looked away.

'Of course. Women fought long and hard to give me that right.'

'Are you going to tell me which party you usually vote for?'

'Whichever I think will do the least damage.'

'You seem to have little time for politicians. Is there a particular reason for that or is it just *fin-de-siècle* depression?'

The faint smile again as she reached for her wine glass. 'Personally, I'd hesitate to qualify a huge abstract concept like *fin-de-siècle* depression with "just", but for the purposes of your article it's as truthful as anything else.'

He wondered what it would be like to kiss her. 'Are you married at the moment, Amanda?'

'Yes.'

'What does your husband do?'

She raised the glass to her lips, momentarily forgetting the camera lens pointing at her, then lowered it with a frown as Lisa took another photograph. 'My husband wasn't here when I found the body,' she said, 'so what he does is irrelevant.'

Deacon caught the look of amused cynicism on Lisa's face. 'It's human interest,' he countered lightly. 'People will want to know what sort of man a successful architect is married to.'

Perhaps she realized that his curiosity was personal, or perhaps, as Lisa had guessed, there *was* no Mr Powell. In either case, she refused to expand on the matter. 'It was I who found the body,' she repeated, 'and you have my details already. Shall we continue?'

The pale eyes, so like his mother's, rested on Deacon's craggy face too long for comfort, and his mild fantasy about kissing her shifted from harmless fun to sadistic revenge. He could imagine what JP's reaction was going to be to the paucity of information that he'd managed to drag out of her so far. *Name, rank and number.* And he had little optimism that the photographs would be any better. Her features were so controlled that she might as well be a poker-faced prisoner of war backed against a wall. He wondered if fires had ever burned in her cool little face, or if her life had been entirely passionless. Predictably, the idea excited him.

'All right,' he agreed, 'let's talk about finding the body. You said you were shocked. Can you describe the experience for me? What sort of thoughts went through your mind when you saw him?'

'Disgust,' she said, careful to keep her voice neutral. 'He was behind a stack of empty boxes in the corner and he'd covered himself in an old blanket. The smell was really quite awful once I'd pulled it away from him. Also, his body fluids had seeped out all over the floor.' Her mouth tightened in sudden distaste and she blinked as the flash of the camera stung her eyes. 'Afterwards, when the police told me that he'd died of self-neglect and malnutrition, I kept wondering why he'd made no attempt to save himself. It wasn't just that I found him beside my chest freezer' – she gestured unhappily towards the window – 'everyone's so affluent on this estate that even the dustbins have perfectly edible food in them.'

'Any ideas?'

'Only that he was so weak by the time he found my garage that he hadn't the energy to do more than crawl into the corner and hide himself.'

'Why would he want to hide?'

She studied him for a moment. 'I don't know. But if he wasn't hiding, why didn't he try to attract my attention? The police think he must have entered the garage on the Saturday, because his only opportunity to get inside was when I went to the shops that afternoon and left the doors unlocked for half an hour.' In so far as she was capable of showing emotion, she did. Her hand flickered nervously towards her mouth before she remembered the camera and dropped it abruptly. 'I found his body on the following Friday and the pathologist estimated he'd been dead five days. That means he was alive on the Sunday. I could have helped him if he'd called out and let me know he was there. So why didn't he?'

'Perhaps he was afraid.'

'Of what?'

'Being turned over to the police for trespass.'

She shook her head. 'Certainly not that. He had no fear of the police or of prison. I understand he was arrested quite regularly. Why should this time have been any different?'

Deacon made shorthand notes on his pad to remind himself of the nuances of expression that crossed her face as she talked about Billy. *Anxiety. Concern. Bewilderment even.* Curiouser and curiouser. *What was Billy Blake to her that he could inspire emotion where her husband couldn't?* 'Maybe he was just too weak to attract your attention. Presumably the pathologist can't say if he was conscious on the Sunday?'

'No,' she said slowly, 'but I can. There was a bag of ice-cubes in the freezer. Someone had opened it, and it certainly wasn't me, so I presume it must have been Billy. And one corner of the garage had been urinated in. If he was strong enough to move around the garage, then he was strong enough to bang on the connecting door between the garage and my hall. He must have known I was here that weekend because he could have heard me. The door's not thick enough to block out sound.'

'What did the police make of that?'

'Nothing,' she said. 'It made no difference to the pathologist's verdict. Billy still died of malnutrition whether through wilful self-neglect or involuntary self-neglect.'

He lit another cigarette and eyed her through the smoke. 'How much did the cremation cost you?'

'Does the amount matter?'

'It depends how cynical you believe the average reader to be. He might think you're being coy about the figure because you want everyone to assume you spent more.'

'Five hundred pounds.'

'Which is a great deal more than you would have given him alive?'

She nodded. Click. 'If I'd met him as a beggar in the street, I'd have thought I was being generous if I gave him five pounds.' Click. Click. She glanced with irritation at Lisa, looked as if she were about to say something, then thought better of it. Her face took on its closed expression again.

'You said yesterday that you felt you owed him something. What exactly?'

'Respect, I suppose.'

'Because you felt he hadn't been shown any in life?'

'Something like that,' she admitted. 'But it sounds ridiculously sentimental when it's put into words.'

He wrote for a moment. 'Do you have a religion?'

She turned away as another flash exploded in her eyes. 'Surely she's taken enough by now?'

Lisa kept the camera lens on her face. 'Just a couple more shots with the eyes cast down, Amanda.' Click.

'Yes, that's really nice, Amanda.' Click. 'More compassion maybe.' Click. 'Great, Amanda.' Click, click, click.

Deacon watched increasing irritation gather in the woman's eyes. 'All right, Smith. Let's call a halt, shall we?'

'How about a few more in the garage?' suggested the girl, reluctant to waste the end of the film. 'It won't take a minute.'

Mrs Powell stared into the blood-red depths of her glass before taking a sip. 'Be my guest,' she said without raising her head. 'The keys are on the table in the hall, and the light comes on automatically when the garage door is lifted. I don't use the connecting door any more.'

'I meant a few more of you,' said Lisa. 'I'll need you to come with me. If it's cold and damp out there, a few atmospheric shots could be really good. More in tune with a wino dying of starvation.'

The woman's stillness following this remark persuaded Lisa she hadn't been listening. She tried again. 'Five minutes, Amanda, that's all we'll need. You might like to stand near where you found him, look a bit upset, that sort of thing.'

The only sound in the room was the ticking of a clock on the mantelpiece, and it grew louder as Mrs Powell's silence lengthened. She seemed to Deacon to be waiting for something, and he held his breath and waited with her. It startled him to hear her speak. 'I'm sorry,' she said to the girl, 'but you and I are very different animals. I could no more pose weepy-eyed over where Billy died than I could wear your fuck-me clothes or your fuck-me make-up. You see, I'm neither so vulgar nor so desperate to be noticed.'

There were too many sibilants in the last sentence, and her careful diction abandoned her. With a slight shock, Deacon realized she was drunk.

Chapter Three

IT WAS dangerous to allow a silence to go on too long. The impact of her words did not diminish in a vacuum; instead they grew and gained in authority. Deacon was drawn to see Lisa through her eyes, and he was struck by how appropriate her description of the girl was. Compared with the snow queen in the chair opposite, Lisa's outlined pouting lips and bottom-hugging skirt were blatantly provocative, and he felt himself belittled to have lusted after her so long in silence when lust was what she was inviting. He saw himself as one of Pavlov's dogs, lured into salivating every time his greed was stimulated, and the idea offended him.

He took his keys from his pocket and suggested that Lisa use the car to drive herself back to the office with her equipment. 'I'll grab a taxi when I'm through,' he said. 'Leave the keys with Glen at the front desk and I'll pick them up from him.'

She nodded, glad of an excuse to leave, and immediately he regretted his perfidy. It wasn't a crime to display bright plumage; rather it was a celebration of youth. She left the camera out as she repacked the case, then with a curt nod in the older woman's direction let herself out of the sitting-room door.

They both heard the rattle of garage keys being lifted from the hall table. Amanda sighed. 'I was rude to her. I'm sorry. I find it hard to treat Billy's death quite as casually as you and she do.' She examined her glass for a moment, as if aware that she'd given herself away, then abandoned it on the coffee table.

'You certainly seem to take it very personally.'

'He died on my property.'

'That doesn't make you responsible for him.'

She looked at him rather blankly. 'Then who is responsible?'

The question was simplistic – it was what a child would ask. 'Billy himself,' said Deacon. 'He was old enough to make his own choices in life.'

She shook her head then leaned forward, searching his face earnestly. 'You said yesterday that you were moved by Billy's story, so could we talk about his life instead of his death? I know I said there was nothing I could tell you, but that wasn't strictly accurate. I know at least as much as the police do.'

'I'm listening.'

'According to the pathologist, he was forty-five years old, six feet tall and although his hair was completely white when he died, it would have been dark. He was first arrested four years ago for stealing some bread and ham from a high-street supermarket, and he gave his name as Billy Blake and his age as sixty-one, which, if the pathologist is right, was twenty years older than his actual age.' She spoke quickly and fluently, as if she had spent a long time preparing the facts for just such a presentation. 'He said he'd been living rough for ten years, but refused to give any other information. He wouldn't say where he came from and he wouldn't say if he had a family. The police checked Missing Persons in London and the South-East, but nobody of his description had been reported missing in the previous ten years. His fingerprints, such as they were, weren't in the police files and he had nothing on him that could establish his identity. In the absence of any other information, the police recorded the details he gave them and for the next four years he lived and subsequently died as Billy Blake. He spent a total of six months in prison for stealing food or alcohol, with each sentence amounting to a one- or two-month stretch, and he preferred to doss down as near to the Thames as possible when he was out. His favourite pitch was a derelict warehouse about a mile from here. I've talked to some of the other old men who use it, but none of them admitted to knowing anything about Billy's history.'

Deacon was impressed by the extent of her interest and effort. 'What did you mean by "his fingerprints, such as they were"?'

'The police said he'd burnt his hands in a fire at some time and left them to heal on their own. Both were so badly scarred that his fingers were like claws. They think he may have mutilated himself deliberately to avoid some previous crime catching up with him.'

'Shit!' he said unguardedly.

She stood up and walked over to the glass cabinet on the far wall. 'As I said earlier, there *are* photographs of him.' She took an envelope from a shelf inside and came back with it, slipping the contents into her hand. 'I persuaded the police to give me two of them. This is the best they had out of the batch the pathologist took. It's not very pleasant and they say it's doubtful anyone would recognize him from it.' She handed it across. 'His face is very shrunken from lack of food, and because his forehead and jaw were so pronounced, it's likely that he was much fuller faced when he was healthy.'

Deacon examined the picture. She was right. It wasn't very pleasant. He was reminded of the corpses piled high inside Bergen-Belsen when the Allies liberated it. The face was almost fleshless, so tightly was the skin drawn across the bones. She handed him the other photograph. 'That's the one that was taken four years ago when he was first arrested. But it's not much better. He was skeletal even then, although it gives a slightly clearer idea of what he might have looked like.'

Could this really be the face of a 41-year-old? Deacon wondered. Old age had scored itself into deep lines round the mouth, and the eyes that looked into the camera were faded and yellow. Only the hair had any vitality where it sprang up from the high forehead, although its whiteness was startling against the sallowness of the complexion. 'Could the pathologist have been wrong about his age?' he asked.

'Apparently not. I understand he took a second opinion when the police didn't believe him. It did occur to me,' she went on, 'that someone with the right computer software might be able to build on the images, but I don't know anyone who specializes in that area. If your magazine could do it, it would make a far better visual accompaniment to your article than the picture of me.'

'Why haven't the police done that?'

'He didn't commit a crime before he died, so they're not interested. I believe they put his description on to a missing persons computer file but it didn't match with anyone, so they've written him off.'

'Can I borrow these? We'll have some negatives made and then I can let you have them back.' He tucked the photographs between the pages of his notebook when she nodded agreement. 'Did the police ever come up with any other explanation for why he chose your garage, apart from the door being open on the day he went into it?'

She sat down again and folded her hands in her lap. Deacon was surprised to see how whitely her knuckles shone. 'They thought he might have followed me home from work, although they never produced a valid reason for why he might have wanted to do that. If he'd singled me out as someone worth following, then he'd have asked me for help. Would you agree with that?' She was appealing to him on an intellectual level, but Deacon was more inclined to respond to the tic of anxiety that fluttered at the corner of her mouth. He hadn't noticed it before. He was beginning to understand that her composure was a surface thing and that something far more turbulent was at work underneath.

'Yes,' he said. 'There's no sense in following you without a reason. So? Could there have been another reason?'

'Like what?'

'Perhaps he thought he recognized you.'

'As whom?'

'I don't know.'

'Wouldn't he have been even more likely to speak to me if he thought he knew me?' She darted the question at him so quickly that he guessed it was one she had asked herself many times.

Deacon scratched his jaw. 'Maybe he was too far gone by then to do anything other than collapse and die. Where exactly is your office?'

'Two hundred yards from the derelict warehouse where Billy used to doss. The whole area's up for redevelopment. W. F. Meredith rent office space in a warehouse which was refurbished three years ago during the first phase. The police felt the proximity of the buildings was too much of a coincidence, but I'm not sure I agree with them. Two hundred yards is a long way in a city like London.' She looked unhappy and he guessed she found this argument less convincing than she claimed.

He lifted the pages of his notebook to study the skull's-head photograph again. 'Was this house a Meredith construction?' he asked without looking up. 'Did you get a discount on it because you're part of the firm?'

She didn't answer immediately. 'I don't think that's any of your business,' she said then.

He gave a low laugh. 'Probably not, but a place like this costs a fortune, and you haven't exactly stinted on the furnishings. You're not short of a bob or two if you can afford all this and shell out five hundred pounds on an unknown man's cremation. I'm curious, Amanda. You're either a very successful architect or you have another source of income.'

'As I said, Mr Deacon, it's none of your business.' Briefly the drink slurred her words again. 'Shall we go back to Billy?'

He shrugged. 'Presumably you'd have noticed anyone like this watching you?' he asked her, tapping the celluloid face.

She straightened slowly, a troubled expression on her face. 'No, I don't think I would.'

'How could you have missed him?'

'By avoiding eye-contact,' she admitted reluctantly. 'It's the only way to escape being pestered. Even if I do give money to someone, I very rarely look at them. I certainly couldn't give a detailed description of them afterwards.'

Deacon reflected on the homeless youngsters he'd interviewed already for his article, and realized he'd have trouble describing any particular individual. It depressed him to admit it, but she was right. Through sheer embarrassment, one never looked too long on the destitute. 'All right,' he said, 'let's say it was pure coincidence that Billy chose your garage to die in. Then someone must have seen him. If he was walking along the road looking for a place to hide, particularly on an estate like this, he couldn't have gone unnoticed. Did any of your neighbours come forward as witnesses?'

'No one's mentioned it.'

'Did the police ask?'

'I don't know. It was all over in three or four hours. As soon as the doctor arrived and pronounced him dead, that was effectively it. The doctor said he'd died of natural causes, and the PC who answered my 999 call claimed they'd all known it was only a matter of time before Billy Blake turned up as a bundle of rags somewhere. His words were: "The silly old sod has been committing slow suicide for years. People can't live the way he did and expect to survive."'

'Did you ask him what he meant by that?'

'He said the only time Billy ate properly was when he was in prison. Otherwise he survived on a diet of alcohol.'

'Poor bastard,' said Deacon, eyeing her glass. 'I suppose life under anaesthetic was more bearable than life without.'

If she understood the personal import of his remark, she didn't show it. 'Yes,' was all she said.

'You suggested Billy Blake wasn't his real name, but one he adopted four years ago when he was first arrested. So where did he get the money to buy the alcohol? He'd need to register to get welfare payments.'

She shook her head again. 'I asked the old men in the warehouse about that, and they said he survived on charity rather than government hand-outs. He used to draw pavement pictures down on the embankment near the river cruisers, and he earned enough from the tourists to pay for his drink. It was only in the winter when the sightseers dried up that he resorted to stealing and, if you look at his prison record, you'll find that all his stretches were done during the winter months.'

'It sounds as though he had his life pretty well organized.'

'I agree.'

'What sort of things did he draw? Do you know?'

'He did the same picture each time. From the way the men describe it, he drew the nativity scene. He also used to preach to the passers-by about the damnation to come for all sinners.'

'Was he mentally ill?'

'It sounds like it.'

'Did he use the same pitch each time?'

'No. I gather he was moved on fairly regularly by the police.'

'But he only drew the one picture?'

'I believe so.'

'Was it any good?'

'The old men said it was. They described him as a real artist.' Unexpectedly she laughed, and mischief brightened her eyes. 'But they were drunk when I spoke to them, so I'm not sure how valid their artistic judgement is.'

The mischief vanished as quickly as it came, but once again Deacon fell prey to his fantasies. He persuaded himself that she was ignorant of real desire and that it needed an experienced man to release her passion . . . 'What else have you managed to find out?'

'Nothing. I'm afraid that's it.'

He reached forward to switch off his tape recorder. 'You said Billy's story needs to be told,' he reminded her, 'but everything you know about him will fit into two or three sentences. And if I'm honest, I'd say he doesn't justify even that much space.' He reflected for a moment, collating the information in his head. 'He was an alcoholic and a petty criminal who lied about his age and used an alias. He was running away from someone or something, probably a wife and an unhappy marriage, and he descended into destitution because he was either inadequate or mentally ill. He had some ability as an artist and he died in your garage because you live near the river and the door happened to be open.' He watched his abandoned cigarette expire in a long curl of ash in the saucer. 'Have I missed anything?'

'Yes.' The movement at the side of her mouth became suddenly more pronounced. 'You haven't explained why he was starving himself to death or why he burnt his hands to claws.'

He made a gesture of apology. 'That's what chronic alcoholics with severe depression do, Amanda. They drink instead of eating, which is why the pathologist included self-neglect as a cause of death, and they mutilate themselves as a way of externalizing their anguish about a life that holds no hope for them. I think your Billy was clinically ill and, because he drank to make himself feel better, he ended up dead in your garage.'

He could see from the resigned expression on her face that he hadn't told her anything she hadn't already worked out for herself, and his curiosity about her increased. Why this *idée fixe* about Billy Blake's life? There was something much deeper driving her, he thought, than simple compassion or high-minded sentiment about a man's value to society.

'I couldn't get anyone even remotely interested in trying to find out who he might have been,' she murmured, bending her head to the bowl of pot-pourri and sifting the petals idly between her fingers. 'The police were polite but bored. I've written to my MP and to the Home Office, asking for some attempts to be made to trace his family, and had replies saying it's not their responsibility. The only people who were at all sympathetic were the Salvation Army. They have his description on their files now and have promised to contact me if anyone tries to trace him, but they're not optimistic about it.' She looked very unhappy. 'I simply don't know what else to do. After six months I've reached a dead end.'

He watched her for several moments, fascinated by the play of expressions that crossed her face. He guessed that her look of unhappiness probably translated as deep despair for someone more demonstrative. 'If it's that important, why don't you hire a private detective?' he suggested.

'Have you any idea how much they charge?'

'You've explored the possibility then?'

She nodded. 'And I could never justify the expense. I was told it could take weeks, even months, and there's no guarantee of success at the end of it.'

'But we've already established that you're a rich woman, so who would you be justifying the expense to?'

A flicker of emotion – *embarrassment?* – crossed her face. 'Myself,' she said.

'Not your husband.'

'No.'

'Are you saying he wouldn't mind if you spent a fortune trying to trace a dead stranger's family?' The elusive Mr Powell intrigued him.

She didn't say anything.

'You've already recognized Billy's worth by paying for his funeral. Why isn't that enough for you?'

'Because it's life that matters, not death.'

'That's not a good enough reason, or not for the kind of obsession you've developed.'

She laughed again, and the sound startled Deacon. It was pitched far too high, but he couldn't decide if it was drink – *or fear?* – that had introduced the note of hysteria. She made a visible effort to bring herself under control. 'You know about obsession, do you, Mr Deacon?'

'I know there's something else to this story that you haven't told me. You seem to be going to extraordinary lengths to try and identify Billy Blake and trace his family. Almost,' he said thoughtfully, 'as if you felt under an obligation. I think you did speak to him, and I think he asked you to do something. Am I right?'

She stared through him with the same expression of disappointment that his mother had shown the last time he saw her. He had wished so often that he'd tried for a reconciliation then that he reached out now, in a strange, confused transposition, to do for a stranger what he hadn't done for Penelope. He put a sympathetic hand on Amanda's arm but her skin was cold and unresponsive to his touch, and if she noticed the gesture at all, she didn't show it.

Instead she leaned her head against the back of her chair to stare at the ceiling, and Deacon had a sense of doors closing and opportunities lost. 'Could you retrieve my garage keys when you return to your office?' she asked politely. 'Unless your friend is still out there, she's taken them with her.'

'What did he say to you, Amanda?'

She glanced at him for a moment but there was only boredom in her eyes. He was no longer of any interest to her. 'I've wasted your time and mine, Mr Deacon. I hope you find a taxi without too much trouble. It's usually easier if you turn left out of the entrance to the estate and walk up to the main road.'

He wished he was better at reading a woman's character. He was sure she was lying to him, but women had lied to him for years and he had never known when they were doing it.

There was a note with the two sets of keys at the front desk. *What a cow! Hope she didn't eat you alive after I left. I put her stupid keys in my pocket and forgot about them. Here they are with your car keys. Thought you should return them rather than me! If you're interested, I left the film with Barry. He said he'll develop it tonight. See you tomorrow. Love, Lisa.*

Deacon decided he was in no hurry, and wandered up to the third floor where Barry Grover doubled as film processor and archives' librarian. He was a somewhat pathetic character in his early thirties, very much a loner, short, pot-bellied and bug-eyed behind magnifying lenses, who pored over the picture cuttings in his library with the avidity of a collector and haunted the offices till all hours in preference to going home. The female staff avoided him whenever possible, and invented malicious gossip behind his back. Over the years they had described him variously, and always with conviction, as a paedophile, a Peeping Tom and a flasher, because it was the only way they could account for his infatuation with pictures. Deacon, who found him as unsympathetic as the women did, nevertheless felt sorry for him. Barry's was a peculiarly barren life.

'Still here?' he said with false bonhomie as he shouldered open the door and caught the man bent over a newspaper cutting on his desk.

'As you say, Mike.'

He propped a buttock on the edge of the desk. 'Lisa told me you were developing her film. I thought I'd drop in to see how it turned out.'

'I'll get the contact sheets for you.' Barry scuttled hurriedly out of the room like a fleshy white cockroach, and Deacon, watching him critically, decided it was the way he moved that set people's teeth on edge. There was something very effeminate about the rapid little steps he took, and he wondered, not for the first time, if Barry's problem had more to do with unresolved homosexuality than the heterosexual perversions of which the women accused him.

He lit a cigarette and turned the cutting that Barry had been reading towards himself.

The Guardian 6th May, 1990

Banker's Wife Released

Amanda Streeter, 31, was released without charge yesterday following two days of police questioning. 'We are satisfied,' said a police spokesman, 'that Mrs Streeter was not implicated in the theft of £10 million from Lowenstein's Merchant Bank, nor has any knowledge of her husband's whereabouts.' He confirmed that James Streeter, 38, is believed to have left the country some time during the night of 27 April. 'His description has been circulated around the world and we expect him to be found within days. As soon as we are notified of where he is, extradition procedures will begin.'

Amanda Streeter's solicitor issued the following statement to the press. 'Mrs Streeter has been deeply shocked by the events of the last eight days and has given the police as much assistance as she can in their search for her husband. Now that she has been ruled out of the investigation, she asks to be left in peace. There is nothing she can add to the information that is already in the public domain.'

The allegations against James Streeter are that, over a period of five years, he used his position at Lowenstein's to falsify accounts and steal over £10 million. The alleged irregularities came to light some six weeks ago but the details were kept in-house to avoid panicking the bank's customers. When it became clear that the bank's own investigation was going nowhere, the board decided to call in the police. Within hours of the decision being taken, James Streeter disappeared. Charges are being brought against him in his absence.

'I recognized her face.'

Deacon hadn't heard Barry return and was startled by the sudden, breathy voice in the silence. He watched the man's fat finger push the cutting to one side and point to a grainy photograph underneath.

'That's her with her husband before he ran. Lisa called her Mrs Powell, but it's the same woman. You probably remember the case. He was never caught.'

Deacon stared down at the photograph of Amanda Powell-Streeter, aged thirty-one. She was wearing glasses, her hair was shorter and darker and her face was in three-quarters profile. He wouldn't have recognized her, yet, knowing who it was, he saw the similarities. He looked thoughtfully at the husband for a moment or two, searching for a resemblance with Billy Blake, but nothing in life was ever that easy. 'How do you do it?' he asked Barry.

'It's what I'm paid for.'

'That doesn't explain how you do it.'

The other man smiled to himself. 'Some people say it's a gift, Mike.' He placed the contact sheets on the desk. 'Lisa's done a lousy job with these. There are only five or six that are good enough to pass muster. She needs to do them again.'

Deacon held the sheets to the light and examined them closely. They were uniformly bad, either out of focus or so poorly lit that Amanda Powell's face looked like granite. There were six perfect shots of an empty garage at the end of the sequence. He stubbed his cigarette out in an ashtray on Barry's desk which was placed beside a prominent notice saying: *In the interests of my health please don't smoke*. 'How the hell did she manage to produce crap like this?' he asked crossly.

Fastidiously, Barry emptied the ashtray into his waste-paper basket. 'Obviously there's something wrong with her camera. I'll call it in for service tomorrow. It's a shame. She's usually very reliable.'

Considering how bad Lisa's photographs were, it was even more extraordinary that Barry had been able to make the connection. Deacon fished his notebook from his coat pocket and isolated the two photographs of Billy Blake. 'I suppose you don't recognize him?'

The little man took the prints and placed them side by side on his desk. He examined them for a long time. 'Maybe,' he said at last.

'What do you mean, maybe? Either you do or you don't.'

Barry looked put out. 'You don't know anything about it, Mike. Supposing I played a bar of Mozart to you, you might be able to identify it as Mozart, but you'd never be able to say which of his works it came from.'

'What's that got to do with identifying a photograph?'

'You wouldn't understand. It's very complicated. I shall have to work on it.'

Deacon felt suitably put in his place. And not for the first time that night. But thoughts of Barry were less likely to haunt him than thoughts of a woman who reminded him of his mother. 'How about making some good negatives for me? The chances are he looked nothing like this when he was fit and healthy, but we might be able to do something on the computer to flesh the face out a bit. That would give you a better base to start from, wouldn't it?'

'Possibly. Where did the prints come from?'

'Mrs Powell. He died in her garage under the name of Billy Blake, but she doesn't think that was his real name.' He gave Barry a quick summary of what Amanda had told him. 'She has a bee in her bonnet about trying to identify him and trace his family.'

'Why?'

Deacon touched the newspaper cuttings. 'I don't know. Perhaps it has something to do with what happened to her husband.'

'I can make the negatives easily enough. When do you want them?'

'First thing tomorrow?'

'I'll do them for you now.'

'Thanks.' Deacon glanced at his watch as he stood up and saw with surprise that it was after ten o'clock. 'Change of plan,' he said abruptly, reaching Barry's coat from a hook behind the door. 'I'm taking you for a drink instead. Christ, man, this bloody magazine doesn't own you. Why the hell don't you tell us all to get stuffed occasionally?'

Barry Grover allowed himself to be drawn along the pavement by Deacon's insistent hand on his shoulder, but he was a reluctant volunteer. He had been on the receiving end of such spontaneous invitations before. He knew the routine, knew he had only been invited because Deacon's irregular conscience had struck, knew he would be forgotten and ignored within five minutes of entering the pub. Deacon's drinking cronies would be lining the bar and Barry would be left to stand at the side, unwilling to intrude where he wasn't wanted, unwilling to draw attention to himself by leaving.

Yet, as usual, he was prey to a terrible ambivalence as the pub drew closer, because he both feared and yearned to go drinking with Deacon. He feared inevitable rejection, yearned to be accepted as Deacon's friend, for Deacon had shown him more casual companionship since he'd arrived at the *Street* than Barry had known in years. He told himself that to be accepted just once would suffice. It was such a small ambition for a man to hold, after all. To feel part of a social group for a single night, to tell a joke and raise a laugh, to be able to say the next morning: 'I went for a drink with a mate.'

He stopped abruptly outside the pub and started to polish his glasses furiously on a large white handkerchief. 'After all, Mike, I think I'd better get home. I hadn't realized how late it was and, if I'm to do those negatives for you, I can't afford to oversleep.'

'You've time for a pint,' said Deacon cheerfully. 'Where's home? I'll drop you off afterwards if it's on my way.'

'Camden.'

'It's a deal then. I'm in Islington.' He clapped a friendly arm across Barry's shoulders and escorted him through the doors of the Lame Beggar.

But the fat little man's forebodings were well founded. Within minutes, Deacon had been subsumed into a raucous pre-Christmas drinking throng, while Barry was left to blink his embarrassment and his loneliness in feigned insouciance by the wall. It was when he realized that Deacon was too drunk to drive him home, or even to remember the offer, that a terrible sense of injustice began to grow in him. Confused feelings of hero-worship turned angrily to bitter resentment. Hell could freeze over, as far as he was concerned, before Deacon would ever learn from him who Billy Blake really was.

11.00 p.m. – Cape Town, South Africa

It was a warm summer night in the Western Cape. A well-dressed woman sat alone in the glass-fronted restaurant of the Victoria and Alfred Hotel, toying with a cup of black coffee. She was a regular customer, although little was known about her other than that her name was Mrs Metcalfe. She always ate and drank sparingly, and it was a mystery to the waiters why she came at all. She seemed to take little pleasure in her solitary meal, and preferred to turn her back as far as possible on her fellow diners. She chose instead to gaze out over the harbour where, had it been daylight, she would have seen the seals that play among the moored ships. The night held fewer diversions and, as usual, her expression was bored.

At eleven o'clock, her driver presented himself at reception and, after settling her bill, she left. Her waiter pocketed his customary handsome tip and wondered, not for the first time, what brought her here every Wednesday evening to spend three hours doing something she found so uncomfortable.

Had she been remotely friendly, he might have asked her, but she was a typical tight-lipped, skinny white woman and their relationship was a professional one.

Chapter Four

IF DEACON was surprised that Barry Grover left the pub without saying anything, he didn't dwell on it. He had walked out on too many drinking sessions himself to regard it as anything unusual. In any case he was relieved to be shot of the responsibility of driving the man home. He wasn't as drunk as Barry had believed, but he was certainly over the limit and chose to abandon his car at the office and take a taxi. He was renting an attic flat, and he slouched dejectedly in his seat as Islington drew closer. He and Barry had something in common, he thought, assuming Barry's long hours at work meant he shared Deacon's aversion to going home. The parallel intrigued him suddenly. What were Barry's reasons, he wondered? Did he, like Deacon, fear the emptiness of a flat that contained nothing of a personal nature because there was nothing from his past that he wanted to remember?

He sank deeper into maudlin gloom, indulging himself in drink-inspired self-loathing. He was to blame for everything. His father's death. His failed marriages. His family's bitterness and their ultimate rejection of him. (*God, how he wished he could get that damn woman's eyes out of his mind. Memories of his mother had been haunting him all evening.*) No children. No friends because they'd all taken his first wife's side. He must have been out of his mind to betray one wife, only to find the second wasn't worth the price he'd paid for her.

From time to time, the cab driver flicked him a sympathetic glance in the rear-view mirror. He recognized the melancholy of a man who drank to drown his sorrows. London was full of them in the run-up to Christmas.

Deacon woke with a sense of purpose, which was unusual for him. He put it down to the fact that his subconscious mind had been replaying the tape of his interview with Amanda Powell, further whetting his curiosity about her. Why should mention of Billy Blake, a stranger, produce an emotional reaction when mention of her husband, James Streeter, produced none? Not even anger.

He pondered the question in the solitary isolation of his kitchen while he stirred his coffee and looked with disfavour at the blank white walls and blank white units that surrounded him. Predictably, his thoughts turned inwards. Did either of *his* wives show emotion when *his* name was mentioned? Or was he just a forgotten episode in their lives?

He could die like Billy Blake, he thought, slumped in a corner of this wretched flat, and when he was found, days later, it would almost certainly be by a stranger. Who would come looking, after all? JP? Lisa? His drinking pals?

Jesus wept! Was his life really as empty – and worthless? – as Billy Blake's . . .?

He arrived at the office early, consulted the phone book and an *A to Z* of London, left a message at the front desk to say he would be back later, then retrieved his car and headed east along the river towards what had once been the thriving port of London. As in so many other ports around the world, the shipping fleets and working docks had long since given way to pleasure vessels, expensive housing and marinas.

He made his way down the western shores of the Isle of Dogs and located the refurbished warehouse where W. F. Meredith, architects, had their offices, then drove on towards a filthy, boarded-up building that bore no resemblance to its neighbours except in its rectangular lines and gabled roof. Not that it required much imagination on his part to picture what this sad relic of Victorian London could become. He had lived in the capital long enough to witness the transformation of the old docklands buildings into things of beauty, and he had only to look at the converted warehouses around him to remind himself of what was achievable.

He parked his car, took a torch and a bottle of Bell's whisky from the dashboard pocket and made his way through a gap in the fence to the front of the building. He tested the boarding on the doors and windows before making his way round to the back. Five or six metres of exposed scrubland separated the rear wall from the river, and he pulled his coat more tightly about him as a bitterly cold wind whipped across the surface of the Thames and flayed the skin of his face. How anyone could expose themselves to such conditions was beyond him, yet a small group of men, apparently impervious to the morning cold and damp, sat huddled about a brazier of burning wood in an open doorway in the warehouse wall. They regarded him with suspicion as he approached.

'Hi,' he said, squatting down in a gap in the circle with the bottle between his feet, 'my name's Michael Deacon.' He took out his cigarette packet and offered it around. 'I'm a reporter.'

One of the men, much younger than the rest, gave a short laugh and mimicked Deacon's educated diction. 'Hi. My name's R. S. Hole. I'm a bum.' He took a cigarette. 'Ta. I'll save it for drinkies before dinner if you've no objections.'

'None at all, Mr Hole. Seems a shame to wait for dinner, though.'

The lad had a thin, washed-out face beneath a crudely shaven head. 'The name's Terry. What are you after, you bastard?'

He really was very young, thought Deacon, but there was street wisdom in the aggressive tilt of his jaw and a terrible cynicism in the narrowed eyes. With a slight shock, it occurred to him that Terry thought he was a middle-class homosexual in search of a rent-boy. 'Information,' he said matter-of-factly. 'About a man called Billy Blake who used to doss here when he wasn't in prison.'

'Who says we knew him?'

'The woman who paid for his funeral. She tells me she came here and got answers to some of her questions.'

'*Aye*-mander,' said one of the others. 'I remember 'er.

Saw 'er on the corner not so long ago and she gave me a fiver.'

Terry cut him off with an impatient hand. 'What does a reporter want with Billy? He's been dead six months.'

'I don't know yet,' said Deacon honestly. 'Maybe I just want to prove that Billy's life had value.' He clamped his hands over the bottle. 'Whichever one of you can tell me something useful gets the whisky.'

The older men watched the bottle; Terry watched Deacon's face. 'And what exactly does useful mean?' he asked with heavy irony. 'I know he couldn't give a shit about anything. Is that useful?'

'I could have guessed that, Terry, from the way he died. Useful means anything I don't know already, or anything that will lead me towards someone who might have information on him. Let's start with his real name. Who was he before he became Billy Blake?'

They shook their heads.

''E did pavement pictures,' said one old man. ''Ad a pitch down near the cruisers.'

'I know about that. Amanda tells me he always drew the same nativity scene. Does anyone know why?'

More shakes of heads. They were like something out of a *Star Wars* film, thought Deacon irrelevantly. Wizened little monkey-men, swathed in overcoats that were too big for them, but with bright, beady eyes that spoke of a cunning he would never possess.

'It were just a picture of a family that everyone would recognize,' said Terry. 'He weren't stupid, and he needed money. He wrote "Blessed are the poor" underneath, then lay beside it. He looked so fucking ill most of the time that people felt guilty when they saw the painting and read the message. He did pretty well out of it and he were only aggressive when he'd had a skinful and started preaching at the punters. But that just frightened them off, and he'd come home skint those days and have to sober up.'

The faces around him split into grins of reminiscence.

''E was a good artist when 'e was sober,' said the old man who'd spoken before. 'Bloody awful when 'e was drunk.' He cackled to himself, his leathery skin creasing inside the frame of a matted balaclava. 'Drew 'eaven when 'e was sober and 'ell when 'e was pissed.'

'You mean he did two different pictures?'

''E did 'undreds, s'long as 'e could get the paper.' The old head jerked towards the office blocks. 'Used to take piles of old letters out of the bins of an evening, draw his pictures all night on the backs, then abandon 'em in the morning.'

'What happened to them?'

'We burned 'em the next day.'

'Did Billy mind?'

'Nah,' said another. 'He needed to keep warm like the rest of us. Matter of fact, it used to make him laugh.' He screwed his finger into his forehead. 'He was mad as a sodding hatter. Always screaming about hell-fire and being cleansed by the devil's flames. Stuck his hand in the middle of a mound of blazing paper once and kept it there for ages before we dragged him off.'

'Why did he do that?'

A shrug of indifference rippled round the group like a

muted Mexican wave. There was no logic to the actions of a madman seemed to be their common thinking.

'He were always doing it,' said Terry. 'Sometimes it were both hands, more often just the right. It really used to bug me. There were days when he couldn't move his fingers at all because the blisters were so bad, but he'd still draw his sodding pictures. He'd stick the crayon between two fingers and move his whole hand to do the drawing. He said he needed to feel the pain of creation.'

'Young Terry reckoned 'e was schizo,' declared the leathery-faced ancient in the balaclava. 'Told 'im 'e should get medication, but Billy weren't interested. 'E said 'e didn't suffer from anyfing mental and 'e weren't going near no doctors. Death was the only cure for what ailed 'im.'

'Did he ever try to kill himself?'

Terry gave another short laugh and gestured around him. 'What d'you call this? Living or dying?'

Deacon acknowledged the point with a nod. 'I meant did he make specific attempts on his life?'

'No,' said the boy flatly. 'He said he hadn't suffered enough and needed to die slowly.' He drew his coat about his spare frame as another blast of wind whistled across the water and drew sparks from the blazing wood. 'Listen, mate, the poor bastard had galloping schizophrenia, just like Walt here.' He nudged the muffled shape beside him who sat, much as Billy must have done when Amanda Powell found him, with head slumped on knees. 'Walt gets medication, but half the time he forgets to take it. By rights he should be in hospital but there ain't no hospitals any more. He stayed with his old mum for a while when the doctors said he was okay to live on the out, but he scared the poor old biddy out of her wits and she barred the door on him.' He turned to look into the warehouse. 'There's twenty more like him inside. It's us sane ones who're looking after them, and it's a bloody joke, if you ask me.'

Deacon agreed with him. What was society coming to when it was the down-and-outs who offered care in the community to the mentally ill? 'Did Billy ever mention being in a hospital?'

Terry shook his head. 'He never talked much about the past.'

'Okay. How about prison? Do you know which one he did his time in?'

Terry nodded towards the leathery-faced old man. 'Tom and him did a month in Brixton once.'

'Where did they keep him?' Deacon asked Tom. 'On the hospital wing or in a cell?'

'Cell, same as me.'

'Was he given any medication?'

'Not that I remember.'

'So he wasn't diagnosed schizophrenic in prison?'

Tom shook his head. 'The screws ain't got the time or the inclination to worry about a wino doing four weeks in the nick. It'd take 'im that long to dry out so, if 'e screams 'is 'ead off on a regular basis, they just put it down to DTs or anything else they fancy.'

'Did he act as crazy inside as he did on the out?'

Tom made a rocking motion with his hand. 'Bit up and down, got depressed every so often, but otherwise 'e was okay. Went to chapel like a good'un and be'aved 'isself. Reckon it was the drink made 'im mad. 'E was only ever off his 'ead when 'e'd 'ad a skinful. Sane as you an' me when 'e was sober.'

Deacon offered his cigarettes round a second time, then raised his coat flap against the wind to light one for himself. 'And none of you knows where he came from, or who he might have been, or why he called himself Billy Blake?'

'What makes you think it wasn't his real name?' asked Terry. This time he chose to smoke his cigarette, pulling a brand from the fire to light it.

Deacon shrugged. 'I'm guessing.' He drew heavily on his cigarette in order to keep the tip alight. 'How did he speak? Did he have an accent?'

'Not so's you'd notice. I asked him once if he was an actor because he sounded pretty classy when he was raving. But he said no.'

'What did he do when he was raving?'

'Shouted anything that came into his head. Some of it rhymed, but I don't know if he was making it up himself or if he was quoting someone else. I remember some of it – and one bit more or less because he said it over and over again. It was bloody weird stuff, all about his mother groaning, his father weeping and demons leaping out of clouds.'

'Can you quote it?'

Terry looked at the others for inspiration. 'Not really,' he said when he didn't find any. 'He always began with "My mother groaned, my father wept" but I forget what came after.'

Deacon cupped his cigarette in his hands and dredged deep into his memory. '"My mother groaned, my father wept,"' he murmured, '"Into the dangerous world I leapt;/Helpless, naked, piping loud,/Like a fiend hid in a cloud."'

'Yeah,' said the young man with surprised respect. 'How the hell did you know that?'

'It's a poem entitled "Infant Sorrow" by a man called William Blake. I wrote a thesis on him years ago. He was an eighteenth-century poet and artist who was considered off the wall by his contemporaries because he claimed to see visions.' Deacon gave a faint smile. 'William wrote some wonderful poetry, but lived and died in virtual poverty because no one recognized his genius until after he was dead. I suspect your friend knew William and his work rather well.'

'Yeah,' said Terry with quick intelligence. 'William Blake, Billy Blake. What else did this guy write?'

'"Tyger! Tyger! burning bright/In the forests of the night" . . .' Deacon paused, inviting the lad to finish it.

'"What immortal hand or eye/Could frame *thy* fearful symmetry?'" said the youngster in triumph. 'Yeah, Billy were always spouting that one. I told him it didn't rhyme properly, and he said you had to stress "thy", which was where the rhyme was.'

Deacon nodded. Had Billy Blake been a teacher? he wondered. 'There's a line in the next verse that goes: "What the hand dare seize the fire?" Was he thinking of that, do you suppose, when he tried to burn his own hand?'

'I dunno. It depends what it means.'

'The tiger represents power, energy and cruelty. The poem describes this beautiful but uncontrollable creature being forged in flames and then goes on to question why his creator was brave enough to manufacture anything so dangerous.' Deacon could see he'd lost the others but there was keen interest still in Terry's face. 'It's the creator's hand that dared "seize the fire", so perhaps Billy thought he'd started something that he couldn't control.'

'Maybe.' A far-away look came into the young man's eyes as he stared across the river. 'Is the creator God?'

'*A* god. Blake doesn't specify which one.'

'Billy reckoned there were loads of gods. Gods of war. Gods of love. Gods of rivers. Gods of every-bloody-thing. He used to swear at them all the time. "It's your fault, you buggers," he used to shout, "so let me alone and let me die." I said he should just stop believing that the gods were there, then he wouldn't have to hate them. Makes sense, doesn't it?' The pinched face turned back towards the brazier.

'What did he think was the gods' fault?'

'It's not what he *thought*,' said Terry with careful emphasis, 'it's what he *knew*.' He reached out and gripped the air with his fingers. 'He strangled someone because the gods wrote it into his fate. That's why he stuck his hand in the fire. He called it the "offending instrument" and said "such sacrifices were necessary if the gods' anger was to be directed somewhere else." Poor bastard. He didn't know his arse from his elbow most of the time.'

*

On Terry's instructions, Deacon gave the bottle of Bell's whisky into the care of the old man in the balaclava before following Terry into the warehouse to see where Billy had slept. 'It's a waste of time,' the lad grumbled. 'He's been dead six months. What are you expecting to find?'

'Anything.'

'Listen, there've been a hundred dossers in his space since he kicked it. You won't find nothing.' But despite this he led Deacon into the gloom. 'You nuts or what?' he said in amusement as Deacon lit a small pool of light at their feet with his torch. 'That's not going to help you see a damn thing. Just wait, okay. Your eyes'll soon adjust. There's enough light comes through the door.'

A grey lunar landscape slowly developed in front of Deacon, a wasteland of twisted metal, piled bricks and abandoned warehouse wreckage. It was the aftermath of war where nothing recognizable existed any more, and only the acrid smell of urine suggested human presence. 'How long have you been here?' he asked Terry, as he began to pick out sleeping bodies among the rubble.

'Two years on and off.'

'Why here? Why not a squat or a hostel?'

The young man shrugged. 'I've done them. This ain't so bad.' He led the way past a pile of bricks and gestured to a makeshift structure, made out of polythene and old blankets. He pulled one of the blankets aside and reached in to light a battery-operated hurricane lamp. 'Take a look,' he invited. 'This is my pitch.'

Deacon experienced a strange sort of envy. It was a cobbled-together tent in the middle of a urine-smelling bomb site, but it had personality in a way his flat did not. There were posters of semi-nude women pinned to the polythene walls, a mattress on the floor with a handmade patchwork quilt, ornaments on a metal filing cabinet, a wicker chair with a dressing-gown on it, and a jam-jar of plastic red roses on a small painted table. He went in and sat on the chair, carefully folding the dressing-gown on to his lap. 'This is good. You've done it up well.'

'*I* like it. Got most of this stuff off the council tip. It's fucking amazing what people chuck out.' Terry squeezed in beside him and lay on the bed. He looked younger in repose than he did in tense concentration against the wind. 'It's freer than a hostel and not so cramped as a squat. People can get on your nerves in a squat.'

'Don't you have any family?'

'Nah. Been in and out of homes since I was six. One bloke told me once that my mother went to prison which is why I ended up in care, but I've never tried to find her. She's a loser, so it'd be a waste of time looking. I get by.'

Deacon made a point of examining the young face in order to remember it afterwards. But there was nothing memorable about the lad. He was like a hundred shaven-headed boys of the same age, uniformly colourless, uniformly unattractive. He wondered why Terry hadn't mentioned a father, but guessed the father was anonymous and therefore irrelevant. He thought of all the women he himself had slept with over the years. Had one of them fallen pregnant by him and given birth to a Terry whom she subsequently abandoned?

'Still, it can't be much fun living rough like this.'

'Yeah, well, I'm not the first to do it, and I sure as hell won't be the last. Like I said, I get by. Whatever man has done, man can do.'

The expression seemed an unlikely one for a youngster like Terry to use. 'Is that something Billy used to say?'

The lad gave an indifferent shrug. 'Maybe. He were always fucking preaching at me.' His voice took on a more refined tone. '"You cannot have rights without responsibility, Terry. Man's greatest sin is pride because he dethrones God at his peril. Be prepared – the Day of Judgement is closer than you think."' He reverted to his own, rougher accent. 'I'm telling you, it did your head in to listen to him. He were a right nutter most of the time, but he meant well and I reckon I learnt a thing or two off of him.'

'Like what?'

Terry grinned. 'Like, fools ask questions that wise men cannot answer.'

Deacon smiled. 'How old are you?'

'Eighteen.'

Somehow Deacon doubted that. For all Terry's readiness of speech and mind, which allowed him to dominate the derelict old men he was living with, the fluff on his chin was still downy and he was growing too fast for his thin frame to keep pace. His great bony hands hung out of his sleeves like paddles, and it would be a while yet before maturity bulked his chest and shoulders. It made Deacon all the more curious about the preacher – *and teacher?* – who had befriended him.

'How long did you know Billy?' he asked.

'A couple of years.'

Since he'd been in the warehouse then. 'Was his doss as good as this?'

Terry shook his head. 'He wanted to suffer. I told you, he was a real head-case. I found him prancing around in the fucking nude this time last year. You wouldn't believe how cold it was. He was blue from head to toe. I said, what the fuck are you doing, you fucking idiot, and he said he was mortifying the flesh – ' he paused, unsure if he'd used the right word – 'or something like that. He never built himself a place, just used to roll in an old blanket and doss down by the fire. He didn't have nothing, you see, didn't want nothing, didn't see the point in making himself comfortable. He knew the gods would get him in the end, and he reckoned he'd make it as easy for the rotten bastards as he could.'

'Because he was a murderer?'

'Maybe.'

'Did he say if it was a man or a woman that he killed?'

Terry linked his hands behind his head. 'I don't remember.'

'Why did he tell you and not the others?'

'How do you know he didn't tell them?'

'I was watching their faces.'

'They're so drunk most of the time they don't remember nothing.' Terry closed his eyes. 'It might come back for a tenner.'

Deacon's snort of laughter fanned the corner of one of the posters. 'I wasn't born yesterday, sunshine.' He took a card from his wallet and flipped it on to Terry's chest. 'Give me a ring any time you can come up with something I can verify, but don't ring me with crap. And the information had better be good if you want money for it.' He stood up and looked down on the youthful face. 'How old are you really, Terry?' Sixteen was his guess.

'Old enough to recognize a tight-fisted bastard when I meet one.'

On his return to the office, Deacon found a note from Barry Grover on his desk with the original prints of Billy Blake in a transparent plastic envelope. *I cannot trace this man in my files*, he'd written, *but I've passed the negatives and fresh prints to Paul Garrety. He is seeing what he can do with them on the computer. B. G.*

Paul Garrety, the art editor, shook his head when Deacon sought him out and asked him how he was getting on with the Billy Blake pictures. JP had been persuaded to invest heavily in computer equipment for the art department on the promise that technology could do for *Street* style and design, and therefore improved sales, what an army of graphics artists had previously failed to do. But he was too attached to the old look of the magazine to give Paul free rein with the equipment, and Garrety, like Deacon, spent most of his working day at loggerheads with his boss.

'You need an expert, Mike,' he said now. 'I can give you a hundred different versions of him, but it'll take someone with a knowledge of physiognomy to tell you which is the most accurate.' He pointed to his computer screen. 'Watch this. You can have a fuller face, which is just fattening up the whole thing. You can have fuller cheeks, which is puffing up the lower half. You can have double chins, you can have fleshy eyes, you can have thicker hair. The permutations are endless, and every one looks different.'

Deacon watched the alternatives appear on the screen. 'I see what you mean.'

'It's a science. Your best bet is to find yourself a pathologist or an Identikit artist who specializes in faces. We could choose any one of these variations but the chances are it'll look nothing like your dead guy.'

'Any hope of JP running the original alongside my copy?'

Garrety laughed. 'None at all, and for once I'd agree with him. It'd put the punters right off their breakfast. Be fair. Who wants to eat cornflakes looking at a shrivelled old wino who died of starvation?'

'He was only forty-five,' said Deacon mildly. 'Three years older than I am, and ten years younger than you. It's not so funny when you think of it in those terms, is it?'

Michael Deacon's feature on poverty and homelessness appeared in that week's *Street* without any mention of Amanda Powell or Billy Blake. Indeed, the final draft was precisely as he had envisaged at the outset. A thoughtful analysis of changing social trends which concentrated on causes and long-term solutions. JP doubted it would appeal to their readers ('It's bloody boring, Mike. Where's the human interest, for God's sake?'), but, without a decent photograph of either Billy or Mrs Powell, there seemed little point in going with the uninspired statements that Mrs Powell had made on the subject of homelessness in general. JP repeated his threats about the non-renewal of Deacon's contract if he didn't recognize that political mud-slinging was the magazine's stock in trade, and Deacon answered sarcastically that if the sales figures were anything to go by, the *Street* readership enjoyed having its intelligence insulted about as much as the rest of the electorate did.

Amanda Powell, who had received her garage keys and the two photographs of Billy through the post with an anonymous *Street* compliments slip, was disappointed, but not surprised, to find herself and Billy excluded from Deacon's article. But she read it with interest, particularly the paragraph describing a derelict warehouse and its community of mentally disturbed residents who were being cared for by a handful of old men and a young boy.

There was a look of relief in her eyes as she laid the magazine aside.

Chapter Five

A LITTLE research during a quiet afternoon produced the names and addresses of James Streeter's parents and brother, plus some imaginative – *and deliberately libellous?* – press releases from the Friends of James Streeter Campaign which was based at the brother's address in Edinburgh. The last one was dated August 1991.

Despite twelve months of determined lobbying, not a single newspaper has followed up the claims of the Friends of James Streeter Campaign that James was murdered on the night of Friday, 27 April 1990, in order to protect a member of Lowenstein's board and save the bank from the catastrophic collapse that would inevitably result from loss of confidence in its management.

In the interests of justice, the following facts must be investigated:

- James Streeter did not have the knowledge to work the fraud of which he is accused. It is alleged that he gained his computer skills while abroad in France and Belgium.

The FoJSC has collected witness evidence from his previous employers and his first wife that he did not. (See enclosures.)

- James Streeter had no access either to the progress of Lowenstein's in-house investigation or to board decisions, therefore he could not have known the 'ideal' date to leave the country. The FoJSC has witness statements to this effect from his secretary and members of his department. (See enclosures.)
- James Streeter made reference to friends and colleagues in the six months before his disappearance about the incompetence of Nigel de Vriess, his line manager, who was a member of the Lowenstein board in 1990 and who has since left the bank. The FoJSC has three sworn statements which testify that James said in January 1990 that Mr de Vriess was 'at best incompetent and at worst criminally motivated'. (See enclosures.)
- Much reliance has been placed on the damaging allegations made by Amanda Streeter against her husband in a written statement to police. They were: (1) That James was having an affair with a woman who worked for a computer software company – name, Marianne Filbert, whereabouts unknown. (2) That he once remarked, 'Any fool could work the system if someone told him which buttons to press.' (3) That he was obsessed with wealth.
- The FoJSC refutes all three allegations. (1) and (3) depend entirely on the word of Amanda Streeter. (2) refers to a statement made by one of James's colleagues who has since admitted that he wasn't sure even in 1990 if it was James who made the remark.

Further:

- The FoJSC has obtained proof that it was Amanda herself who was having the affair and that her lover was Nigel de Vriess. We have photocopies of bills and eye-witness statements which refer to two secret meetings the couple had in 1986 and 1989 at the George Hotel, Bath. The first occurred only weeks before her marriage to James, the second three years after it. (See enclosures.)

We accuse Amanda Streeter and Nigel de Vriess.

- James Streeter's murder has gone unpunished. Unless the press shakes off its apathy and acts now, the guilty will continue to profit from an innocent man's death. The FoJSC urges, indeed demands, a proper enquiry into the activities of Nigel de Vriess and his lover, Amanda Streeter. Please fax or phone on the above numbers for assistance and/or further information. John and Kenneth Streeter are available for interview at any time.

Two evenings later, and because he had nothing better to do, Deacon dialled John Streeter's number in Edinburgh. A woman answered.

'Hello,' she said in a soft Scottish accent.

Deacon introduced himself as a London-based journalist who was interested in talking to a spokesman from the Friends of James Streeter Campaign.

'Oh, lord!'

He waited a moment. 'Is this a problem for you?'

'No, it's just – well, to be honest, it's over a year since – look, just hang on a moment, will you?' A hand went over the receiver. 'JOHN! JO-OHN!' The hand was removed. 'It's my husband you need to talk to.'

'Fine.'

'I'm sorry I didn't catch your name.'

'Michael Deacon.'

'He'll be here in a minute.' The hand again, and this time her voice was muffled. 'For God's sake, hurry. It's a journalist and he wants to talk about James. His name's Michael Deacon. No, you must. You promised your father you wouldn't give up.' She came back, louder. 'Here's my husband.'

'Hello,' said a man's much deeper voice. 'I'm John Streeter. How can I help you?'

Deacon flicked the trigger on his biro and pulled forward his notepad. 'Does the fact that it's three and a half years since you sent out your last press release mean you've now accepted your brother's guilt?' he said bluntly.

'Are you with a national newspaper, Mr Deacon?'

'No.'

'Then you're freelance?'

'As far as these questions are concerned, yes.'

'Have you any idea how many freelancers I've spoken to over the years?' He paused, but Deacon didn't rise to the bait. 'Approximately thirty,' he went on, 'and the number of column inches I've had out of them is nil because no editor would take the story. I'm afraid I'd be wasting both our time if I answered your questions.'

Deacon tucked the telephone more firmly under his chin and drew a spiral on his pad. 'Thirty is nothing, Mr Streeter. I've known campaigns like yours approach hundreds of journalists before they get anywhere. That apart, most of what you allege in your press releases is actionable. Frankly, you're lucky to have avoided a libel suit this far.'

'Which proves something in itself, don't you think? If what we're claiming is defamatory, why does no one challenge us?'

'Because your targets aren't that stupid. Why give your campaign the adrenalin of publicity when it's dying a death of its own accord? It would be a different matter if you managed to persuade an editor to go against his better judgement. Are you saying nothing has ever been published in defence of your brother?'

'Only a grudging piece in a compilation of unsolved mysteries that came out last year. I spent two days talking to Roger Hyde, the author, only to have him write a bland summary which ended with his own half-baked conclusion that James was guilty.' He sounded angry and frustrated. 'I'm growing rather tired of beating my head against a brick wall.'

'Then perhaps you're less persuaded of your brother's innocence than you were five years ago?'

There was a smothered obscenity. 'That's all you lot ever want, isn't it? Confirmation of James's guilt.'

'Except I'm giving you an opportunity to defend him which you don't seem very keen to take.'

John Streeter ignored this. 'My brother came from an honest, hard-working background, just as I did. Have you any idea what it's done to my parents to have their son labelled a thief? They're decent, respectable people and they can't understand why journalists like you won't listen to them.' He drew another angry breath. 'You're not interested in facts, only in trying to further destroy a man's reputation.'

'Aren't you playing the same game?' Deacon murmured unemphatically. 'Unless I've misread your releases, your defence of James rests entirely on blackening Nigel de Vriess and Amanda Streeter.'

'With reason. There's no proof of her assertion that James was having an affair, but we've found evidence of hers with de Vriess. He stripped the bank of ten million and she aided and abetted him in pushing the blame on to her husband.'

'That's some accusation. Can you prove it?'

'Not without access to their bank and investment accounts, but you only need to look at their respective addresses to realize there was an injection of cash from somewhere. Amanda bought herself a £600,000 house on the Thames within months of James's disappearance and de Vriess bought himself a mansion in Hampshire shortly afterwards.'

'Do they still see each other?'

'We don't think so. De Vriess has had at least five lovers in the last three years, while Amanda's kept herself to herself and remained celibate.'

'Why do you think that is?'

Streeter's voice hardened. 'Probably for the same reason she's never sought a divorce. She wants to give the impression that James is alive somewhere.'

Deacon consulted some photocopies of the press releases. 'Okay, let's talk about James's alleged affair with – ' he isolated a paragraph – 'Marianne Filbert. If there's no proof of its existence why did the police accept Amanda's word on it? Who is Marianne Filbert? Where is she? What does she say about it?'

'I'll answer those questions in order. The police accepted Amanda's word because it suited them. They needed a computer expert in the frame, and Marianne fitted the bill. She was part of a research-and-development team working for Softworks Limited in the mid-eighties. Softworks was commissioned to prepare a report for Lowenstein's Bank in '86, although no one knows if Marianne Filbert was involved with that. She went to America in '89.' He paused briefly. 'She was employed for six months by a computer software company in Virginia before moving on to Australia.'

'And?' prompted Deacon, when he didn't continue.

'There's no trace of her after that. If she went to Australia, which now seems doubtful, she was using another name.'

'When did she leave the Virginian company?'

'April 1990,' said the other reluctantly.

Deacon felt sorry for him. John Streeter wasn't a fool, and blind faith clearly made him uncomfortable. 'So the police see a connection between your brother's disappearance and hers? He told her when to run, in other words.'

'Except they haven't established that James and Marianne even knew each other.' Streeter's furious indrawn breath was audible down the wire. 'We believe it was de Vriess and Amanda who gave her the green light to disappear.'

'A three-way conspiracy then?'

'Why not? It's just as plausible as the police theory. Look, it was Amanda who gave them Marianne Filbert's name and Amanda who told them she'd gone to America. Without that evidence, there'd have been no computer link and no way that James could have worked the fraud. The entire police case rests on James having access to expert knowledge, but Amanda's testimony about his alleged affair with Marianne has never been independently substantiated.'

'I find that hard to believe, Mr Streeter. According to the newspapers, Amanda spent two days answering police questions, which means she was high on their list of suspects. It also means she must have had something more convincing than just a name to give them. What was it?'

'It wasn't proof of anything,' said John Streeter stubbornly.

Deacon lit a cigarette while he waited.

'Are you still there?' demanded Streeter.

'Yes.'

'She couldn't prove a relationship between them. She couldn't even prove they knew each other.'

'I'm listening.'

'She gave the police a series of photographs, most of which were pictures of James's car parked outside the block of flats in Kensington where Marianne Filbert lived before she went to the States. There were three blurred shots of a couple kissing who, she claimed, were Marianne and James but frankly could have been anybody, and there was a back view of a man, wearing a coat similar to James's, entering the front door of the building. As I say, it proves nothing.'

'Who took the photographs?'

'A private detective hired by Amanda.'

The same one she consulted about Billy Blake? 'Were they dated?'

'Yes.'

'From when to when?'

'January to August '89.'

'You say most of the pictures were of James's car. Was he in it when they were taken?'

'Someone was, but the quality of the photographs isn't good enough to say whether or not it was James.'

'Perhaps it was Nigel de Vriess,' murmured Deacon with an irony that was lost on the other man. He was beginning to think that John Streeter's obsession to prove his brother innocent was even greater than Amanda's to establish Billy Blake's true identity. Did the seeds of paranoia find fertile ground in the aftermath of betrayal?

'We certainly believe the man to have been de Vriess,' said Streeter.

'So they were deliberately setting your brother up as a fall-guy?'

'Yes.'

'That's one hell of a conspiracy theory, my friend.' This time Deacon ladled the sarcasm into his voice. 'You're saying these people worked out a year in advance of the event how they were going to murder a completely innocent man, irrespective of anything that might happen in the intervening period. And you feel happy with that scenario?' Ash dropped from the cigarette in his mouth, powdering the lapel of his jacket. 'Is your sister-in-law a monster, Mr Streeter? She would need to be, I think, to share a house indefinitely with a man whose murder she'd already planned. So? Who are we talking about here? Medusa?'

Silence.

'And what sort of idiot would rely on a status quo existing indefinitely? James was a free agent. He could have walked out on his wife or his job at any time, and where would the conspiracy have been then?' He paused, inviting the other to speak, but went on when he didn't: 'The obvious explanation is the one the police have accepted. James was having an affair with Marianne Filbert and Amanda put a stop to it by having him followed and photographs taken. She then brought pressure to bear which resulted in Marianne banishing herself, or being banished, to the States.'

'How could she tell the police where to find Marianne?'

'Because she's not stupid. Part of the deal for rescuing the marriage would be proof that Marianne was out of harm's way. And the only proof worth having would be something verifiable, like an address or a legal contract with a company's name on it.'

'Have you spoken to her?'

'Who?'

'Amanda.'

'No,' lied Deacon. 'You're my first contact on this,

Mr Streeter. I came across your press releases and they interested me enough to make this call. Tell me,' he went on with the easy fluency of practised deceit, 'what set you looking for a connection between Amanda and de Vriess in the first place?'

'She met James through de Vriess at some official function. De Vriess was married then, but it was an open secret that he was planning to leave his wife for Amanda. He used to parade her whenever his wife was away. It seemed logical, once we realized de Vriess was behind the fraud, that Amanda was involved too, so we set out to find evidence that the affair was an on-going one.'

'Except your evidence seems to be as flawed as your logic.' He pulled the relevant photocopies towards him. 'You have a hotel bill, signed by de Vriess and dated 1986, plus a description of a woman who *might* have been Amanda Streeter. Your 1989 witness account is even vaguer.' He moved the top copy aside and ran his pen down the one underneath. 'A waiter claims to have taken champagne to a couple in Room 306 who, he says, were the same two people, but there's no signed bill to back it up. You can't even prove the man was de Vriess, let alone that the woman was Amanda.'

'He paid cash the second time.'

'What name was on the bill?'

'Mr Smith.'

Deacon stubbed out his cigarette. 'And you're surprised that no one's prepared to publish? None of your allegations is sustainable.'

'We've limited funds and limited influence. We need

a reporter on a national newspaper to wield a bit of clout. We've been told there's more in the hotel files if we're prepared to pay for it.'

'It'll be an expensive ride with nothing at the end of it.'

'I'd back my brother's honesty any day against his wife's.'

'Then you're deluding yourself,' said Deacon bluntly. 'His *dis*honesty isn't in doubt. He was cheating on his wife and she was able to prove it, and you've allowed your anger over that to cloud your judgement. Your starting point should have been recognition that James played a part in his own destruction.'

'I knew this would be a waste of time,' said the other angrily.

'You keep firing at the wrong targets, Mr Streeter. That's where you've been wasting your time.'

The line went dead.

Deacon's enquiries of the Isle of Dogs police about Billy Blake had produced little of value, despite his suggestion that Billy might have been a murderer. This elicited the surprising response that the police had investigated just that possibility at the time of Billy's first arrest.

'I went through his file for the coroner,' said the uniformed constable who had overseen the removal of Billy's corpse. 'He was first arrested in 1991 for a series of food thefts from supermarkets. He was starving even then, and there was a bit of debate over whether to charge him or get him into supervised care. In the end a decision was made to have him remanded for psychiatric reports because he'd burnt off his fingerprints. Some bright spark decided he'd done it on purpose to beat a murder charge, and people started getting twitched about whether he constituted a danger to society.'

'And?'

The PC shrugged. 'He was interviewed in Brixton, and was given the all-clear. The psychiatrist's view was that he was more of a danger to himself than to anyone else.'

'What was his explanation for the burnt fingerprints?'

'As far as I remember, he called it a morbid interest in mortification. He described Billy as a penitent.'

'What does that mean?'

Another shrug. 'Maybe you should ask the psychiatrist.'

Deacon took out his notebook. 'Do you know his name?'

'I can find out.' He came back in ten minutes and handed Deacon a piece of paper with a name and address on it. 'Is there anything else?' he asked, keen to get on with something more pressing than a dead wino.

Reluctantly, Deacon stood up. 'The information I had was fairly specific.' He tucked the notebook back into his pocket. 'I was told that Billy Blake said he'd strangled someone.'

The PC showed mild interest until Deacon admitted that his informant had no details beyond what Billy had screamed one drunken night when the snakes of alcohol were writhing and squeezing in his brain. 'Would that someone be a man or a woman, sir?'

'I don't know.'

'Can you give me a name?'

'No.'

'Where did this murder happen?'

'I don't know.'

'When?'

'I don't know.'

'Then I'm sorry, sir, but I don't think we can be of any assistance.'

Deacon had visited Westminster Pier where the cruisers docked, but had looked in vain for someone to question about a pavement artist who had once earned charity there. He was impressed by how hostile the river seemed in winter, how stealthily its water lapped the hibernating pleasure cruisers, how black and secretive its depths. He remembered what Amanda Powell had said: '. . . *he preferred to doss down as near to the Thames as possible.*' But why? What was the bond that tied Billy to this great sinew at the heart of London? He leaned forward and stared into the water.

An elderly woman paused in her progress along the walkway. 'Premature death is never a solution, young man. It raises far more questions than it answers. Have you taken into account that there may be something waiting for you on the other side, and that you may not be prepared yet to face it?'

He turned, unsure whether to be offended or touched. 'It's all right, ma'am. I'm not planning to kill myself.'

'Not today perhaps,' she said, 'but you've thought about it.' She had a tiny white poodle on a lead which wagged its stumpy tail at Deacon. 'I can always tell the ones who've thought about it. They're looking for answers that don't exist because God has not chosen to reveal them yet.'

He squatted down to scratch the little creature's ears. 'I was thinking about a friend of mine who killed himself six months ago. I was wondering why he didn't drown himself in the river. It would have been a less painful way to die than the one he chose.'

'But would you be thinking about him if he hadn't died painfully?'

Deacon straightened. 'Probably not.'

'Then perhaps that's why he chose the method he did.'

He took out his wallet and removed the first photograph of Billy. 'You might have seen him. He was a pavement artist here in the summers. He used to draw pictures of the nativity with "Blessed are the poor" written underneath. Do you recognize him?'

She studied the thin face for several seconds. 'Yes, I think I do,' she said slowly. 'I certainly remember a pavement artist who drew pictures of the Holy Family, and I think this was the man.'

'Did you speak to him?'

'No.' She returned the photograph. 'There was nothing I could say to him.'

'You spoke to me,' Deacon reminded her.

'Because I thought you'd listen.'

'And you didn't think he would?'

'I *knew* he wouldn't. Your friend wanted to suffer.'

On the off-chance that Billy had been a teacher, and in the absence of a national register, which he had established did not exist, Deacon wined and dined a contact at NUT headquarters, told him what he knew and asked him to search the union backlist for any English teachers whose subscriptions had lapsed in the last ten years without good reason.

'You're pulling my leg, I hope,' said his acquaintance with some amusement. 'Have you any idea how many teachers there are in this country and what the turnover is? At the last count there were upwards of four hundred thousand full-time equivalents in the maintained sector alone, and that's excluding the universities.' He pushed his plate to one side. 'And what does "without good reason" mean anyway? Depression? That's very common. Physical disability inflicted by fifteen-year-old thugs? More common than anyone wants to admit. At the moment, I'd guess there are more inactive teachers than active ones. Who wants the hell of the classroom if there's something more civilized on offer? You're asking me to search for the needle in the proverbial haystack. You have also, and rather conveniently, forgotten the Data Protection Act, which means I couldn't give you the information even if I could find it.'

'The man's been dead six months,' said Deacon, 'so you won't be betraying any confidences, and his subscription was probably stopped at least four years before that.

You'll be looking at lapsed membership between say, 1984 and 1990.' He smiled suddenly. 'All right, it was a long shot, but it was worth a try.'

'I can give you several more apt descriptions than long shot. Try damp squib, non-starter or absolute no-no. You don't know his name, where he came from or even if he was a member of the NUT. He might have belonged to one of the other teachers' unions. Or to no union at all.'

'I realize that.'

'Matter of fact, you don't even know if he was a teacher. You're guessing he might have been because he could recite poems by William Blake.' The man smiled amiably. 'Do me a favour, Deacon, go boil your head in cooking oil. I'm an overworked, underpaid union official, not a ruddy clairvoyant.'

Deacon laughed. 'Okay. Point taken. It was a bad idea.'

'What's so important about him, anyway? You didn't really explain that.'

'Maybe nothing.'

'Then why the pressure to find out who he was?'

'I'm curious about what drives an educated man to self-destruct.'

'Oh, I see,' said the other sympathetically. 'It's a personal thing then.'

THE STREET, FLEET STREET, LONDON EC4

Dr Henry Irvine,
St Peter's Hospital,
London SW10

10th December 1995

Dear Dr Irvine,
Your name has been given to me in connection with a prisoner you interviewed at Brixton Prison in 1991. His name was Billy Blake and you may have read about his death by starvation in a garage in London's docklands in June of this year. I have become interested in his story, which seems a tragic one, and I wonder if you have any information that might help me establish who he was and where he came from.

I believe he chose the alias William Blake because there were echoes of the poet's life in his own. Like William, Billy was obsessed with God (and/or gods), and while he preached their importance to anyone who would listen, his message was too arcane to be understood; both men were artists and visionaries, and both died in poverty and destitution. It might interest you to know that I wrote my MA thesis on William Blake, so I find these echoes particularly interesting.

From the little information I have been able to gather so far, Billy was clearly a tortured individual who may or may not have been schizophrenic. In addition one of my informants (not very reliable) says that Billy confessed to strangling a man or woman in the past. Is there anything you can tell me that would confirm or refute that statement?

Whilst I fully accept that your interview(s) with Billy were of a confidential nature, I do believe his death demands investigation, and anything you can tell me will be greatly appreciated. I have no desire to compromise your professional reputation and will only use what you send me to further my research into Billy's story.

You may already know my work but, in case you do not, I enclose some examples. I hope they will give you the confidence to trust me.

Yours sincerely,

Michael Deacon

Dr Henry Irvine MB, FRCP,
St Peter's Hospital,
London

17th December 1995

Dear Michael Deacon,
Thank you for your letter of 10th December. My report on Billy Blake has been in the public domain since 1991 so I cannot see that it's a breach of confidence to give you the information you want. Also, I agree that his death demands investigation. I was upset when my access to him was denied after I advised that Billy's self-mutilation was more likely the result of private trauma than criminal offence, because I firmly believe that further sessions would have allowed me to help him. While I offered him free treatment when he left prison, I could not force him to accept it and, inevitably, I lost touch with him. Your letter is the only follow-up on his case that I have ever had.

To put my role into perspective, the police were not satisfied that Billy Blake's first crime was the theft of bread and ham from a supermarket. They recognized that he was using an alias, and they were suspicious of his mutilated hands which defied fingerprint analysis. However, despite lengthy questioning, they failed to 'break' him and fell back on the charge of shoplifting to which he had already admitted. I was asked to write a psychological report prior to sentencing because of the bizarre nature of the man. In simple terms my brief was to discover if Billy was a danger to the community, the argument being that he would not have scarred his fingers so badly unless he was afraid of a previous, violent crime being brought home to him.

Despite having only three meetings with him, Billy made an extraordinary impact on me. He was desperately thin with a shock of white hair and, though clearly suffering acute alcohol-withdrawal symptoms, he was always in command of himself. He had a powerful presence and considerable charm, and the best description I can give of him is 'fanatic' or 'saint'. These may seem strange epithets in the London of the nineties, but his commitment to the salvation of others while suffering torment himself makes any other description invalid once the more obvious mental disorders were ruled out. He was rather a fine man.

I enclose the concluding paragraphs of the psychiatric report and a transcript of part of a conversation I had with him, which may interest you. I confess to having missed the William Blake association, but Billy's conversation was certainly of a visionary nature. If I can be of any further assistance please don't hesitate to contact me.

With best wishes,

Henry Irvine

Henry Irvine

P.S. Re: the transcript – it was, of course, the answers Billy declined to give that tell us most about him.

Psychiatric Report
Subject: Billy Blake * */5387
Interviewer: Dr Henry Irvine

- page 3 -

In conclusion:
Billy has a fully developed understanding of moral and ethical codes, but refers to them as 'ritual devices for the subjugation of individual to tribal will', from which I infer that his own morality is in conflict with social and legal definitions of right and wrong. He exhibits extraordinary self-control and gives no insight into his background or history. Billy Blake is almost certainly an alias, although questions about specific crimes elicit no reaction from him. He has a high IQ and it is difficult to assess his reasons for refusing to talk about his past. He has a morbid interest in hell and mortification, but poses more of a threat to himself than to the community. I can find no evidence of a dangerous mental disorder. He seems to have a clear rationale for his choice of lifestyle – I would describe it as a penitent's life – and I consider it far more likely that some private trauma, unrelated to any crime, motivates him.

He presents himself as a passive individual although I have noticed signs of agitation whenever he is pressed about where he was and what he was doing before he first came to police attention. I agree that there may be a crime in his past – he is quite single-minded enough to mutilate himself to achieve a purpose – but I think it unlikely. He quickly developed a strong resistance to my questions on the matter, and it is doubtful that further sessions will persuade him to be more forthcoming. It is my considered opinion, however, that he would benefit from therapy as I believe his 'exile' from society, involving as it does an almost fanatical desire to suffer through starvation and deprivation, will result in his unnecessary and premature death.

Henry Irvine

Henry Irvine

Transcript of taped interview with Billy Blake – 12.7.91 (part only)

IRVINE: Are you saying that your personal code of ethics is of a higher order than the religious codes?
BLAKE: I'm saying it's different.
IRVINE: In what way?
BLAKE: Absolute values have no place in my morality.
IRVINE: Can you explain that?
BLAKE: Different circumstances demand different codes of ethics. For example, it isn't always sinful to steal. Were I a mother with hungry children, I would think it a greater sin to let them starve.
IRVINE: That's too easy an example, Billy. Most people would agree with you. What about murder?
BLAKE: The same. I believe there are times and occasions when murder, premeditated or not, is appropriate. (Pause) But I don't think it's possible to live with the consequences of such a crime. The taboo against killing a member of our own species is very strong, and taboos are difficult to rationalize.
IRVINE: Are you speaking from personal experience?
BLAKE: (Gave no answer)
IRVINE: You seem to have inflicted severe punishment on yourself, particularly by burning your hands. As I'm sure you already know, the

police suspect a deliberate attempt to obscure your fingerprints.

BLAKE: Only because they can conceive of no other reason why a man should want to express himself upon the only thing that truly belongs to him – namely his body.

IRVINE: Self-mutilation is normally an indication of a disordered mind.

BLAKE: Would you say the same if I had disfigured myself with tattoos? The skin is a canvas for individual creativity. I see the same beauty in my hands as a woman sees when she paints her face in a mirror. (Pause) We assume we control our minds when we don't. They're so easily manipulated. Make a man destitute and you make him envious. Make him wealthy and you make him proud. Saints and sinners are the only free-thinkers in a governed society.

IRVINE: Which are you?

BLAKE: Neither. I'm incapable of free thought. My mind is bound.

IRVINE: By what?

BLAKE: By the same thing as yours, doctor. By intellect. You're too sensible to act against your own interests, therefore your life lacks spontaneity. You will die in the chains you've made for yourself.

IRVINE: You were arrested for stealing. Wasn't that acting against your own interests?

BLAKE: I was hungry.

IRVINE: You think it's sensible to be in prison?

BLAKE: It's cold outside.

IRVINE: Tell me about these chains I've made for myself.

BLAKE: They're in your mind. You conform to the patterns of behaviour that others have prescribed for you. You will never do what you want because the tribe's will is stronger than yours.

IRVINE: Yet you said your mind is as constrained as mine, and you're no conformist, Billy. If you were, you wouldn't be in prison.

BLAKE: Prisoners are the most diligent of conformists, otherwise places like this would be in perpetual riot and rebellion.

IRVINE: That's not what I meant. You appear to be an educated man, yet you live as a derelict. Is the loneliness of the streets preferable to the more conventional existence of home and family?

BLAKE: (Long pause) I need to understand the concept before I can answer the question. How do you define home and family, doctor?

IRVINE: Home is the bricks and mortar that keeps your family – wife and children – safe. It's a place most of us love because it contains the people we love.

BLAKE: Then I left no such place when I took to the streets.

IRVINE: What *did* you leave?

BLAKE: Nothing. I carry everything with me.

IRVINE: Meaning memories?

BLAKE: I'm only interested in the present. It's how

we live our present that predicts our past and our future.

IRVINE: In other words, joy in the present gives rise to joyful memories and an optimistic view of the future?

BLAKE: Yes. If that is what you want.

IRVINE: Isn't it what *you* want?

BLAKE: Joy is another concept that is incomprehensible to me. A destitute man takes pleasure in a butt-end in the gutter, while a wealthy man is disgusted by the self-same object. I am content to be at peace.

IRVINE: Does drinking help you achieve peace?

BLAKE: It's a quick road to oblivion, and I would describe oblivion as being at peace.

IRVINE: Don't you like your memories?

BLAKE: (Gave no answer)

IRVINE: Can you recall a bad memory for me?

BLAKE: I've found men dead of cold in the gutter, and I've watched men die violently because anger drives others to the point of insanity. The human mind is so fragile that any powerful emotion can overturn its precepts.

IRVINE: I'm more interested in memories from before you took to the streets.

BLAKE: (Gave no answer)

IRVINE: Do you think it's possible to recover from the kind of insanity you've just described?

BLAKE: Are you talking about rehabilitation or salvation?

IRVINE: Either. Do you believe in salvation?
BLAKE: I believe in hell. Not the burning hell and torment of the Inquisition but the frozen hell of eternal despair where love is absent. It's difficult to conceive how salvation can enter such a place unless God exists. Only divine intervention can save a soul condemned for ever to exist in the loneliness of the bottomless pit.
IRVINE: Do you believe in God?
BLAKE: I believe that each of us has the potential for divinity. If salvation is possible, then it can only happen in the here and now. You and I will be judged by the efforts we make to keep another's soul from eternal despair.
IRVINE: Is saving that other soul a passport to heaven?
BLAKE: (Gave no answer)
IRVINE: Can we earn salvation for ourselves?
BLAKE: Not if we fail others.
IRVINE: Who will judge us?
BLAKE: We judge ourselves. Our future, be it now or in the hereafter, is defined by our present.
IRVINE: Have you failed someone, Billy?
BLAKE: (Gave no answer)
IRVINE: I may be wrong but you seem to have judged and condemned yourself already. Why is that, when you believe in salvation for others?
BLAKE: I'm still searching for truth.
IRVINE: It's a very bleak philosophy, Billy. Is there no room for happiness in your life?
BLAKE: I get drunk whenever I can.

IRVINE: Does that make you happy?
BLAKE: Of course, but then I define happiness as intellectual absence. Your definition is probably different.
IRVINE: Do you want to talk about what you did that makes stupefied oblivion your only way of coping with your memories?
BLAKE: I suffer in the present, doctor, not the past.
IRVINE: Do you enjoy suffering?
BLAKE: Yes, if it inspires compassion. There's no way out of hell except through God's mercy.
IRVINE: Why enter hell at all? Can you not redeem yourself now?
BLAKE: My own redemption doesn't interest me.
(Billy refused to say anything further on the subject and we talked for several minutes on general subjects until the session ended.)

Chapter Six

THERE WERE two Christmas cards on Deacon's desk one morning. The first was from his sister, Emma. *Hugh keeps seeing your byline in the* Street *so we're assuming this will find you*, she had written. *We are none of us getting any younger, so isn't it time we called a truce? At least ring me if you won't ring Ma. Surely it's not* that *difficult to say sorry and start again.* The other was from his first wife, Julia. *I bumped into Emma the other day and she said you're working for the* Street. *Apparently your mother's been very ill this last year but Emma has promised she won't tell you because Penelope doesn't want you coming back out of guilt or pity. As I've made no such promise, I thought you should know. However, unless you've changed radically in the last five years, you'll probably tear this up and do nothing about it. You were always more stubborn than Penelope.*

As Julia had predicted he tore up her card, but stood Emma's on his desk.

Despite spending long hours on Paul Garrety's computer in an attempt to make a match between Billy Blake's image and James Streeter's, Deacon got nowhere. Paul pointed out that it would always be a waste of time unless he could find a better picture of James. 'You're not comparing like with like,' he explained. 'Billy's shots are full-face and the one of James is three-quarters. You need to go back to his wife and see what she's got in the way of old snapshots.'

'It's a waste of time, full stop,' said Deacon in disgust, tilting back his chair and staring at the faces. 'They're two different men.'

'Which is what I've been telling you for the last three days. Why can't you accept it?'

'Because I don't believe in coincidences. It makes sense if Billy was James and none at all if he wasn't.' He ticked the points off on his fingers. 'James had a reason to seek out his wife – a stranger didn't. Amanda paid for his funeral out of guilt, but her guilt is only logical if she was burying her husband – illogical if she was burying a stranger. She's obsessed with finding out who Billy was, but why, if he was completely unknown to her?' He rapped out a tattoo on his desk. 'I think she's telling the truth when she says she didn't know he was there. I also think she's telling the truth when she says she didn't recognize him. But I'm convinced she rapidly came to the conclusion *afterwards* that the man who died in her garage was James.'

Paul was doubtful. 'Why didn't she tell the police?'

'Out of fear that they'd think she locked him in the garage on purpose.'

'Then why get you interested? Why not let the story die?

Deacon shrugged. 'I can think of two reasons. The first, simple curiosity. She wants to know what happened to James after he walked out of her life. The second, freedom. Until he's declared officially dead, she'll always be tied to him.'

'She could divorce him tomorrow on the grounds of desertion.'

'But as far as everyone else was concerned he'd still be alive, which means people like me would always be turning up on her doorstep asking questions.'

Paul shook his head. 'That's a crap argument, Mike. Now if you'd said she wanted him declared dead for mercenary reasons, I'd probably go along with you. Let's say he spoke to her before he died and told her how to lay her hands on his fortune. As his widow she'd inherit the lot. Think on that, my friend.'

'My theory only works if she *didn't* speak to him,' declared Deacon mildly. 'We're into a whole new ball game if she *did*. In any case, it looks to me as if she got her hands on the fortune a long time ago.'

'You've never been in the ball game, chum. That guy – ' he tapped the photograph of Billy Blake – 'is not James Streeter.'

'Then who was he and what the hell was he doing in her garage?'

'Get Barry on to it. He's your best bet.'

'I've tried already. He doesn't know. Whoever Billy was he's not in Barry's files.'

Paul Garrety looked surprised. 'Did he tell you that?' Deacon nodded. 'Then how come he strings me along for weeks before he'll admit defeat?'

'Perhaps you've upset him,' said Deacon with unconscious irony.

With time on his hands the weekend before Christmas, Deacon telephoned Kenneth Streeter, mentioned his conversation with John and asked if he could drive out to Bromley and have a chat with James's parents. Kenneth was friendlier and more amenable than his younger son, and made an appointment for the Sunday afternoon.

They lived in a tired-looking terraced house in an unfashionable road, and Deacon was struck by the contrast between this and Amanda's house. *Where had her money come from?* He rang the doorbell and smiled pleasantly at the elderly man who opened the door. 'Michael Deacon,' he said, offering his hand.

Kenneth ignored the hand but gestured him inside. 'You'd better come in,' he said ungraciously, 'but only because I don't want our neighbours listening to what I have to say.' He closed the door but kept Deacon pinned behind it in the dark hallway. 'I don't take kindly to being tricked, Mr Deacon. You gave me to understand that John would approve of my talking to you, but I spoke to him this morning and discovered that the opposite is true. I will not allow the press to drive a wedge between me and my remaining son, so I'm afraid this has been a wasted trip for you.' He reached for the door handle again. 'Good day to you.'

'Your son misunderstood me, Mr Streeter. He assumed that because I said James played a part in his own destruction I was referring to the theft of the £10 million when in fact I was referring to his wife's rejection of him.' He moved forward as the door met his back. 'In simple terms, if you want your wife to stand by you when the chips are down, you don't lose her trust by having affairs.'

'She's the one who was having the affair. She never gave de Vriess up,' said the other bitterly.

'Are you sure about that? The evidence is very flimsy.' He hurried on when the pressure on his back relaxed slightly. 'I suggested to John that he's been firing at the wrong targets, which is not the same as saying that James was guilty of theft. Let's say he was murdered, as you and John believe, how will you get at the truth if you keep denying that James had an affair with Marianne Filbert? If the evidence was strong enough to convince the police, then it ought to be strong enough to convince you.'

A tear glittered in the other man's eye. 'If we give in on that point, we have nothing left except our knowledge of James. And what use is a father's word about his son's honesty? Who would believe me?'

'No one that matters,' said Deacon brutally. 'You'll have to prove it.'

'In this country it's guilt that must be proved, not innocence,' said the old man obstinately. 'I fought for that right fifty years ago and it's outrageous that James has been condemned without any proper hearing of the evidence.'

'I agree with you, Mr Streeter, but to date his defence has been poorly focused. You can't fight a campaign based on a lie. If nothing else, you've alienated the one person who's best placed to help you.'

'Meaning Amanda?'

Deacon nodded.

'We believe she was party to his murder.'

'But you've no proof that he was murdered.'

'He never contacted us. That's proof enough.'

Deacon took the mugshot of Billy Blake from his breast pocket. 'Does this man remind you of James at all?'

Bewilderment furrowed Kenneth's brow. 'How could he? He's too old.'

'He was in his mid-forties when this photograph was taken six months ago.'

Streeter pulled the door wide to examine the picture in daylight. 'This isn't my son,' he said. 'What on earth made you think it was?'

'He was a down-and-out, using an alias, and he died in your daughter-in-law's garage. He didn't speak to her or reveal that he was there, but she paid for his funeral and she's been trying to find out who he was ever since. The only obvious explanation for her interest is that she's afraid he may have been James.'

There was a long silence while Streeter stared at Billy Blake's face. 'It can't be,' he said at last, but there was less certainty in his tone. 'How could he have aged so much in five years? And why would he live as a down-and-out when he was always welcome here?'

'He would have been arrested if he came here. You couldn't have kept him hidden from your neighbours.'

'Are you trying to tell me that this *is* James?'

'Not necessarily,' said Deacon. 'I'm saying that for your daughter-in-law to think it might have been, she had to believe he was still alive when this man turned up dead in her garage in June. And that means she can't have been a party to James's alleged murder five years ago.'

'Then what happened to him?' asked the older man in despair. 'He wasn't a thief, Mr Deacon. He was brought up to earn money honestly, and it simply wouldn't have occurred to him to take short cuts. You see, he wanted the status that wealth brings, just as much as he wanted wealth itself, so theft and the danger of imprisonment would never have attracted him.' He gave another bewildered frown. 'At the time he disappeared, he and Amanda had just sunk all their capital into an old school on the Thames at Teddington, which they were planning to develop into luxury flats, and James was as excited about it as she was. They stood to make a handsome profit if the project went through. But why would he be excited by half a million if he was already sitting on ten?'

Because it represented a legitimate way to start laundering the rest, thought Deacon cynically. 'What happened to the project?'

'It was completed in '92 by a construction firm called Lowndes, but we can't find out if Amanda saw it through herself or whether Lowndes bought the property from her. We've written several letters of enquiry, but we've never had an answer. Either way, we'd like to know how she put together enough money to buy her present house in '91. If she sold the school first, she couldn't have raised more than the four hundred thousand she and James put towards the purchase of it. But it was probably a great deal less after nine months' interest on bank loans, and certainly not enough to buy into an expensive estate on the Thames. If she didn't sell the school but saw the project through, then she'd have had no capital at all in '91.' He smiled unhappily. 'You see now why we're so suspicious of her.'

'Perhaps she and James had other investments which they never told you about.'

But Kenneth wouldn't accept that. Four hundred thousand was already more spare capital than most young couples could lay their hands on, he pointed out, and it was honestly earned. James had cashed in his stocks and shares to support the project. Deacon acknowledged the point with a smile while his mind pursued its own line of thought. That would explain why Amanda hadn't wanted a divorce. If the investments were jointly owned, she had access to everything as long as she didn't dissolve the partnership before he could be legally presumed dead seven years after his disappearance. And if there were other investments in James's name – *dishonestly earned?* – then she still had another two years to wait before she could inherit as his widow.

How much simpler if he'd died in her garage six months ago . . .

'Do you have a photograph of James that you could lend me, Mr Streeter? Preferably a full-face one. I can let you have it back by Tuesday.'

. . . and how frustrating if she couldn't prove it . . .

'The police must have searched James's bank accounts

at the time he disappeared,' he said, taking the snapshot Kenneth Streeter produced for him. 'Did they find anything that shouldn't have been there?'

'Of course not. There was nothing to find.'

'Have you told them your suspicions about Amanda's new-found wealth?'

A look of weariness crossed the older man's face. 'So regularly that I've had an official caution for wasting police time. It's harder than you think to prove a man's innocence, Mr Deacon.'

He phoned an old colleague, now retired, who had spent most of his working life on the financial desks of different newspapers, and arranged to meet him that evening in a pub in Camden Town. 'I'm supposed to be off the bloody booze,' Alan Parker had growled down the wire, 'so I can't invite you here. There's not a drop worth drinking in the house.'

'Coffee won't kill me,' said Deacon.

'It's killing *me*. I'll see you in the Three Pigeons at eight o'clock. Make mine a double Bell's if you get there first.'

Deacon hadn't seen Alan for a couple of years and he was shocked by the sight of his old friend. He was desperately thin and his skin had the yellow tinge of jaundice. 'Should I be doing this?' Deacon asked him as he paid for their whiskies.

'You'd better not tell me I look like death, Mike.'

He did, but Deacon just smiled and pushed the Bell's

towards him. 'How's Maggie?' he asked, referring to Alan's wife.

'She'd have my guts for garters if she knew where I was and what I was doing.' He raised the glass and sampled a mouthful. 'I can't get it through to the silly old woman that I'm a far better judge of what's good for me than the blasted quacks.'

'So what's the problem? Why have they ordered you off the booze?'

Alan chuckled. 'It's the newest form of tyranny, Mike. No one's allowed to die any more, so you're expected to live out your last months in misery. I mustn't smoke, drink or eat anything remotely tasty in case it kills me. Apparently, dying of boredom is politically correct while succumbing to anything that gives you pleasure isn't.'

'Well, don't peg out here, for God's sake, or Maggie will have *my* guts for garters. Where does she think you are, as a matter of interest? Church?'

'She knows exactly where I am, but she's a tyrant with a soft centre. I'll be hauled over the coals for this when I get back, but in her heart of hearts she'll be glad I was happy for half an hour. So? What did you want to talk to me about?'

'A man called Nigel de Vriess. The only information I have on him is that he lives in a mansion in Hampshire which he bought in '91, and was on the board of Lowenstein's Merchant Bank, which he's since left. Do you know him? I'm interested in where he got the money to buy the mansion.'

'That's easy enough. He didn't buy it because he already owned it. If I remember right, his wife took the marital home in Hampstead and he took Halcombe House, although I can't recall now if it was his first divorce or his second. Probably the second because it was a clean-break settlement. It was the first marriage that produced the kids.'

'I was told he bought it.'

'He did, when he made his first million. But that was twenty-odd years ago. He came something of a cropper in the eighties when he invested in a transatlantic airline that went bust during the cartel war, but he managed to hang on to the properties. The only reason he joined Lowenstein's was to buy a period of stability while the market recovered. In return for a damn good salary, he expanded their operations in the Far East and gave them footholds round the Pacific rim. He did well for them, too. They owe their place on the map to de Vriess.'

'What about this guy James Streeter, who ripped them off for ten million?'

'What about him? Ten million's chicken feed these days. It took eight *hundred* million to bring down Baring's Bank.' Alan swallowed another mouthful of whisky. 'The mistake Lowenstein's made was to force the guy to run and bring the whole thing into the open. They recouped their ten million within forty-eight hours' trading on the foreign-exchange markets but the bad publicity set them back six months in terms of credibility.'

Deacon took out his cigarette packet and proffered it to Alan with a lift of his eyebrows. 'I won't tell Maggie if you don't.'

'You're a good lad, Mike.' He placed a cigarette reverently between his lips. 'The only reason I stopped was because the silly old cow kept crying. Would you believe that? I'm dying in misery so she won't be miserable watching me die. And she always said I was the most selfish man alive.'

Deacon found a laugh from somewhere – though God only knew where. 'She's right,' he said. 'I'll never forget that time you invited me out to dinner, then made me pay because you claimed you'd left your wallet at home.'

'I had.'

'Bullshit. I could see the bulge it was making in your jacket.'

'You were very young and green in those days, Mike.'

'Yes, and you took advantage of it, you old sod.'

'You've been a good friend.'

'What do you mean, *been* a good friend? I still am. Who bought the whisky?' He saw a cloud pass over Alan's face and changed the subject abruptly. 'What's de Vriess doing now?'

'He bought a computer software company called Softworks, renamed it de Vriess Softworks or DVS, sacked half the staff and turned the damn thing round in two years by producing a cheaper version of Windows for the home computer market. He's an arrogant SOB, but he has a knack for making money. He started with a paper round at thirteen and he's never looked back.'

'You said he came a cropper in the eighties,' Deacon reminded him.

'A temporary blip, Mike, hence the job with Lowenstein's. Now he's back to where he was before the crash.

Shares have recovered, and he's found a nice little earner in DVS.'

'There was a woman who used to work for Softworks called Marianne Filbert. Does that name mean anything to you?'

Alan shook his head. 'What's the connection with de Vriess?'

Briefly, Deacon explained John Streeter's theory about the conspiracy against James. 'I suspect his whole argument is based on wishful thinking, but it's interesting that de Vriess bought the company where James Streeter found his computer expert.'

'It's highly predictable if you know de Vriess. I imagine Softworks was put under a microscope to see if the bank's money had found its way into their books, and in the process de Vriess spotted an opportunity. He's as sharp as a bloody ferret.'

'You sound as if you admire him.'

'I do. The guy has balls. Mind, I don't like him much – few people do – but he doesn't lose sleep over trifles like that. Women love him, which is all he cares about. He's a randy little toad.' He gave another chuckle. 'Rich men often are. Unlike the rest of us, they can afford to pay for their mistakes.'

'You always were a cynical bastard,' said Deacon affectionately.

'I'm dying of liver cancer, Mike, but at least my cynicism remains healthy.'

'How long have you got?'

'Six months.'

'Are you worried about it?'

'Terrified, old son, but I cling to Heinrich Heine's dying words: "God will forgive me. It's his job."'

Barry Grover held the snapshot of James Streeter under the lamplight and examined it carefully. 'It's a better angle,' he said grudgingly. 'You'll have more chance of making comparisons with this than with the other one.'

Deacon perched casually on the edge of the desk, looming over Barry in a way the little man hated, and planted a cigarette in the corner of his mouth. 'You're the expert,' he said. 'Is that Billy or not?'

'I'd rather you didn't smoke in here,' muttered Barry, poking fussily at his *In the interests of my health please don't smoke* notice. 'I have asthma and it's not good for me.'

'Why didn't you say so before?'

'I assumed you could read.' He shoved a folder against Deacon's hip in an attempt to dislodge him from the desk, but Deacon just grinned at him.

'The smell of cigarette smoke is preferable any day to the smell of your feet. When did you last buy yourself a new pair of shoes?'

'It's none of your business.'

'The only colour you ever wear is black and, believe me, if I've noticed that, then the whole damn building's noticed it. I'm beginning to think you only have one pair, which probably explains your asthma.'

'You're a very rude man.'

Deacon's grin broadened. 'I suppose you were out on the razzle last night? Hence the lousy mood.'

'Yes,' lied the little man bitterly. 'I went for a drink with some friends.'

'Well, if it's a hangover, I've got some codeine in my office, and if it's not, then buck up, for Christ's sake, and give me an opinion on this picture. Does it look like Billy to you?'

'No.'

'They're pretty alike.'

'The mouths are different.'

'Ten million buys a lot of plastic surgery.'

Barry took off his glasses and rubbed his eyes. 'If you want to identify someone, you don't just compare a couple of photographs and dismiss anything that doesn't fit as plastic surgery. It really is a little more scientific than that, Mike.'

'I'm listening.'

'Lots of people look like each other, particularly in photographs, so you have to examine what you know about them as well. It's quite pointless finding similarities in faces if one belongs to a man in America and the other to a man in France.'

'But that's the whole point. James went missing in 1990 and Billy didn't surface at a police station until '91 with his fingers like claws because he'd been burning off his prints. It's certainly possible that they're one and the same.'

'But highly improbable.' Barry looked at the photograph again. 'What happened to the rest of the money?'

'I don't follow.'

'How could he become a penniless derelict within

months of having his face altered by plastic surgery? What happened to the rest of the money?'

'I'm still working on that.' Deacon interpreted Barry's expression correctly as one of scathing disbelief, although as usual it looked rather silly on the owlish face. 'Okay, okay. I agree it's improbable.' He stood up. 'I promised to send that snapshot back today. Do you have time to make a negative for me?'

'I'm busy at the moment.' Barry shuffled pieces of paper around his desk as if to prove the point.

Deacon nodded. 'No problem. I'll find out how Lisa's placed. She can probably do it for me.'

After he'd gone, Barry drew his own full-face photograph of James Streeter from his top drawer. If Deacon had seen this version, he thought, there'd have been no stopping him. The likeness to Billy Blake was extraordinary.

Purely out of curiosity, Deacon phoned Lowndes Building and Development Corporation and asked to speak to someone about a block of flats they had converted on the Thames at Teddington in 1992. He was given the address of the flats, but was told there was no one available to discuss the mechanics of the conversion. 'To be honest,' said a flustered secretary, 'I think it may have been Mr Merton who saw it through, but he was sacked two years ago.'

'Why?'

'I'm not sure. Someone said he was on cocaine.'

'Any idea how I can contact him?'

'He emigrated somewhere, but I don't think we have his address.'

Deacon pencilled Mr Merton in as someone to follow up after Christmas, alongside Nigel de Vriess.

It was the twenty-first of December. Deacon was crawling in a slow-moving traffic jam and his mood grew blacker as the compulsory office party drew nearer. God, how he loathed Christmas! It was the ultimate proof that his life was empty.

He had spent the afternoon interviewing a prostitute who, under the guise of 'researcher', claimed to have had regular access to the Houses of Parliament for paid sex romps with MPs. *Good God almighty! And this was news?* He despised the British thirst for sleaze, which said more about the repressed sexuality of the average Briton than it ever did about the men and women whose peccadilloes were splashed across the newspapers. In any case, he was sure the woman was lying (if not about the paid sex sessions, then certainly about the regular access) because she hadn't known enough about the internal layout of the buildings. He was equally sure that JP, who was of the 'never let the facts get in the way of a good story' school of journalism, would have him chasing the sordid little allegations for weeks in the hopes there was some truth in them. Ah, Jesus! Was this all there was?

He put his depression down to Seasonal Adjusted Disorder – SADness – because he couldn't face the alternative of inherited insanity. Every damn thing that had ever gone wrong in his life had happened in bloody

December. It couldn't be coincidence. His father had died in December, both his wives had abandoned him in December, he'd been sacked from the *Independent* in December. And why? Because he couldn't steer clear of the booze at Christmas and had punched his editor during a disagreement over copy. (If he wasn't careful, he was going to punch JP over the very same issue.) In the summer he was objective enough to recognize that he was caught in a vicious circle – things went wrong at Christmas because he was drunk, and he got drunk because things went wrong – but objectivity was always in rare supply when he most needed it.

He abandoned a congested Whitehall to drive up past the Palace. The bitter east wind of the past few days had turned to sleet, but beyond the metronome clicking of his windscreen wipers was a London geared for festivity. Signs of it were everywhere, in the brilliantly lit Norwegian spruce that annually supplanted Nelson's domination of Trafalgar Square, in the coloured lights that decorated shops and offices, in the crowds that thronged the pavements. He viewed them all with a baleful eye and thought about what lay ahead of him when the office shut for Christmas.

Days of waiting for the bloody place to reopen.

An empty flat.

A desert.

JP decided the prostitute's story had 'legs' and told him to rake as much muck as he could.

*

If there was any gaiety about the office party, then it was happening in another room. Feeling like a trespasser at some interminable wake, Deacon made a half-hearted pass at Lisa and was slapped down for his pains.

'Act your age,' she said crossly. 'You're old enough to be my father.'

With a certain grim satisfaction, he set out to get very drunk indeed.

Chapter Seven

IT WAS NEARLY midnight. Amanda Powell would have ignored the ringing of her doorbell if whoever was doing it had had the courtesy to remove his finger from the buzzer, but after thirty seconds she went into the hall and peered through the spyhole. When she saw who it was, she glanced thoughtfully towards her stairs as if weighing the pros and cons of retreating up them, then opened the door twelve inches. 'What do you want, Mr Deacon?'

He shifted his hand from the bell to the door and leaned on it, pushing it wide, before lurching past her to collapse on a delicate wicker chair in the hall. He waved an arm towards the street. 'I was passing.' He made an effort to sound sober. 'Seemed polite to say hello. It occurred to me you might be lonely, what with Mr Streeter being away.'

She looked at him for a moment, then closed the door. 'That's an extremely valuable antique you're sitting on,' she said evenly. 'I think it would be better if you came into the drawing-room. The chairs in there aren't quite so fragile. I'll call for a taxi.'

He rolled his eyes at her, making himself ridiculous.

'You're a beautiful woman, Mrs Streeter. Did James ever tell you that?'

'Over and over again. It saved him having to think of anything more original to say.' She put a hand under his elbow and tried to lift him.

'It's really bad, what he did,' said Deacon, oblivious to the sarcasm. 'You probably wonder what you did to deserve him.' Whisky gusted on his breath.

'Yes,' she said, drawing her head away, 'I do.'

Tears bloomed in his eyes. 'He didn't love you very much, did he?' He put his hand over hers where it lay on his arm and stroked it clumsily. 'Poor Amanda. I know what it's like, you see. It's very lonely when no one loves you.'

With an abrupt movement, she curled the fingers of her other hand and dug her sharp nails in under his chin. 'Are you going to get up before you break my chair, Mr Deacon, or am I going to draw blood?'

'It's only money.'

'Hard-earned money.'

'That's not what John and Kenneth say.' He leered at her. 'They say it's stolen money and that you and Nigel murdered poor old James to get it.'

She kept up the pressure under his chin, forcing him to look at her. 'And what do you say, Mr Deacon?'

'*I* say you'd never have thought Billy was James if James was already dead.'

Her face became suddenly impassive. 'You're a clever man.'

'I worked it out. There are five million women in London, but Billy chose you.' He wagged a finger at her.

'Now why did he do that, Amanda, if he didn't know you? That's what I'd like to know.'

Without warning, she got going with her nails again, and he focused rather unsuccessfully on the frosty blue eyes.

'You're so like my mother. She's beautiful too.' He struggled upright under the painful prodding of her fingers. 'Not when she's angry, though. She's horrible when she's angry.'

'So am I.' Amanda drew him through the sitting-room door, then pushed him unceremoniously on to the sofa. 'How did you get here?'

'I walked.' He curled up on the sofa and laid his head on the arm.

'Why didn't you go home?'

'I wanted to come here.'

'Well, you can't stay. I'll call a cab.' She reached for the telephone. 'Where do you live?'

'I don't live anywhere,' he said into the cream leather. 'I exist.'

'You can't exist in my house.'

But he could and he did because he was already unconscious, and nothing on earth was going to wake him.

He opened his eyes on grey morning light and stared about him. He was so cold that he thought he was dying, but lethargy meant he did nothing about it. There was pleasure in passivity, none at all in action. A clock on a glass shelf gave the time as seven thirty. He recognized the room as somewhere he knew but couldn't remember whose it was or why he was there. He thought he could hear voices – *in his head?* – but the cold numbed his curiosity, and he slept again.

He dreamt he was drowning in a ferocious sea.

'Wake up! WAKE UP, YOU BASTARD!'

A hand slapped his cheek and he opened his eyes. He was lying on the floor, curled like a foetus, and his nose was filled with the putrid smell of decay. Bile rose in his throat. 'Devourer of thy parent,' he muttered. 'Now thy unutterable torment renews.'

'I thought you were dead,' said Amanda.

For a moment, before memory returned, Deacon wondered who she was. 'I'm wet,' he said, touching the saturated neck of his shirt.

'I threw water over you.' He saw the empty jug in her hand. 'I've been rocking you and pushing you for ten minutes and you didn't stir.' She looked very pale. 'I thought you were dead,' she said again.

'Dead men aren't frightening,' he said in an odd tone of voice, 'they're just messy.' He struggled into a sitting position and buried his face in his hands. 'What time is it?'

'Nine o'clock.'

His stomach heaved. 'I need a lavatory.'

'Turn right and it's at the end of the hall.' She stood aside to let him pass. 'If you're going to be sick, could you make sure you wipe the bowl round afterwards with the brush? I tend to draw the line at cleaning up after uninvited guests.'

As Deacon weaved along the corridor, he sought for explanations. *Dear God, what the hell was he doing here?*

She had opened the windows and sprayed the room with air freshener by the time he returned. He looked slightly more presentable, having dried his face and straightened his clothes, but he had the shakes and his skin was the queasy grey of nausea. 'There's nothing I can say to you,' he managed from the doorway, 'except sorry.'

'What for?' She was sitting in the chair she'd sat in before and Deacon was dazzled by how vibrant and colourful she was. Her hair and skin seemed to glow, and her dress fell in bright yellow folds about her calves, tumbling like a lemon pool on to the autumn leaves of the russet carpet.

Too much colour. It hurt his eyes, and he pressed on his lids with his fingertips. 'I've embarrassed you.'

'You may have embarrassed yourself but you certainly haven't embarrassed me.'

So cool, he thought. *Or so cruel?* He longed for kindness. 'That's all right then,' he said weakly. 'I'll say goodbye.'

'You might as well drink your coffee before you go.'

He longed for escape as well. The room smelled of roses again and he couldn't bring himself to intrude his rancid breath and rancid sweat into the scented air. *What had he said to her last night?* 'To be honest, I'd rather leave now.'

'I expect you would,' she said with emphasis, 'but at least show me the courtesy of drinking the coffee I made for you. It will be the politest thing you've done since you entered my house.'

He came into the room but didn't sit down. 'I'm sorry.' He reached for the cup.

'Please' – she gestured towards the sofa – 'make yourself comfortable. Or perhaps you'd prefer to have another go at breaking the antique chair in the hall?'

Had he been violent? He gave a tentative smile. 'I'm sorry.'

'I wish you wouldn't keep saying that.'

'What else can I say? I don't know what I'm doing here or why I came.'

'And you think *I* do?'

He shook his head gently in order not to incite the nausea that was churning in his stomach. 'This must seem very odd to you,' he murmured lamely.

'Good *lord*, no,' she said with leaden irony. 'What on *earth* gives you that idea? It's quite the norm for me these days to find middle-aged drunks slumped in heaps on my floors. Billy chose the garage, you chose the drawing-room. Same difference, except that you had the decency not to die on me.' Her eyes narrowed, but whether in anger or puzzlement he couldn't tell. 'Is there something about me and my house that encourages this sort of behaviour, Mr Deacon? And will you sit *down*, for Christ's sake?' she snapped in sudden impatience. 'It's very uncomfortable having you towering over me like this.'

He lowered himself on to the arm of the sofa and tried to reknit the fabric of his tattered memory, but the effort was too much for him and his lips spread in a ghastly smile. 'I think I'm going to be sick again.'

She took a towel from behind her back and passed it over. 'I find it's better to try and hang on, but you know where to go if you can't.' She waited in silence for several seconds while he brought his nausea under control. 'Why did you say you'd devoured your parents and that your unutterable torment was renewing? It seems an odd comment to make.'

He looked at her blankly as he wiped the sweat from his forehead. 'I don't know.' He read irritation on her face. 'I don't KNOW!' he said, with a surge of anger. 'I was confused. I didn't know where I was. Okay? Is that *allowed* in this house? Or does everyone have to be in control of himself at all bloody times?' He bent his head and pressed the towel over his eyes. 'I'm sorry,' he said after a moment. 'I didn't mean to be rude. The truth is, I'm struggling a bit here. I can't remember anything about last night.'

'You arrived about twelve.'

'Was I on my own?'

'Yes.'

'Why did you let me in?'

'Because you wouldn't take your finger off the doorbell.'

Sweet Jesus! What had he been thinking of? 'What else did I say?'

'That I reminded you of your mother.'

He lowered the towel to his lap and set about folding it carefully. 'Is that the reason I gave for being here?'

'No.'

'What reason did I give?'

'You didn't.' He looked at her with so much relief in his strained, sweaty face that she smiled briefly. 'Instead you called me Mrs Streeter, talked about my husband, my brother-in-law and my father-in-law, and implied that this house and its contents came from the proceeds of theft.'

Hell! 'Did I frighten you?'

'No,' she said evenly, 'I'm long past being frightened by anything.'

He wondered why. Life itself frightened him. 'Someone at the magazine recognized your face from when you were questioned at the time of James's disappearance,' he said by way of explanation. 'I was interested enough to follow it up.'

The tic above her lip started working again, but she didn't say anything.

'John Streeter seemed an obvious person to talk to, so I telephoned him and heard his side of the story. He has – er – reservations about you.'

'I wouldn't describe calling your sister-in-law a whore, a murderer and a thief as "having reservations", but perhaps you're more worried about being sued than he is.'

Deacon put the towel to his mouth again. He was in no condition for this conversation, he thought. He felt like something half-alive on a dissecting bench, waiting for the scalpel to slice through its gut. 'You'd win huge damages if you took him to court,' he told her. 'He has no evidence for his accusations.'

'Of course not. None of them is true.'

He drained his coffee cup and put it on the table.

'"Devourer of thy parent, now thy unutterable torment renews" is a line from William Blake,' he said suddenly, as if he had been thinking about that and nothing else. 'It's in one of his visionary poems about social revolution and political upheaval. The search for liberty means the destruction of established authority – in other words, the parent – and the push for freedom means every generation suffers the same torment.' He stood up and looked towards the window and its view of the river. 'William Blake – Billy Blake. Your uninvited guest was a fan of a poet who's been dead for nearly two hundred years. Why is this house so cold?' he asked abruptly, drawing his coat about him.

'It isn't. You've got a hangover. That's why you're shivering.'

He stared down at her where she sat like a radiant sun in her expensive designer dress in her expensive scented environment. But the radiance was skin deep, he thought. Underneath the immaculate façade of her and her house, he sensed despair. 'I smelt death when I woke up,' he said. 'Is that what you're trying to mask with the pot-pourri and the air spray?'

She looked very surprised. 'I don't know what you're talking about.'

'Perhaps I imagined it.'

She gave a ghost of a smile. 'Then I hope your imagination returns to normal when the alcohol's out of your system. Goodbye, Mr Deacon.'

He walked to the door. 'Goodbye, Mrs Streeter.'

*

Outside the estate he found a small grassed area with a bench seat overlooking the Thames. He huddled into his coat and let the wind suck the poisonous alcohol out of his system. The tide was out, and on the mud bank in front of him four men were sorting through the debris that had been washed up overnight. They were of indeterminate age, muffled like him in heavy overcoats, with nothing to show who they were or what their backgrounds were, and whatever assumptions he made about them would probably be as wrong as their assumptions about him. Deacon was struck again, as he had been when he met Terry, by how unremarkable most faces were, for he realized that he would not recognize these men in a different setting. Ultimately the various arrangements of eyes, nose, ears and mouth had more in common than they had apart, and it was only adornment and expression that gave them individuality. Change those, he thought, and anonymity was guaranteed.

'So what's your verdict, Michael?' asked a quiet voice beside him. 'Are any of us worth saving or are we all damned?'

Deacon turned to the frail old man with silver hair who had slipped quietly on to the bench beside him and was studying the industry on the shore with as much concentration as he was. He frowned, trying to recall the face from his past. It was someone he'd interviewed, he thought; but he talked to so many people and he rarely remembered their names afterwards.

'Lawrence Greenhill,' prompted the old man. 'You did an interview with me ten years ago for an article on euthanasia called "Freedom to Die". I was a practising solicitor and I'd written a letter to *The Times* pointing out the practical and ethical dangers of legalized suicide both to the individual and to his family. You didn't agree with me, and described me unflatteringly as "a righteous judge who claims the moral high ground for himself". I've never forgotten those words.'

Deacon's heart sank. *He didn't deserve this, not when he'd been through one guilt trip already this morning.* 'I remember,' he said. *Rather too well in fact.* The old bugger had been so complacent about biblical authority for his opinion that Deacon had come close to throttling him. But then Greenhill hadn't known how touchy he was on the whole damn subject. *Suicide in any form is wrong, Michael . . . we damn ourselves if we usurp God's authority in our lives . . .*

'Well, I'm sorry,' he went on abruptly, 'but I still don't agree with you. My philosophy doesn't recognize damnation.' He stubbed out his cigarette, while wondering if he even believed what he was saying. *Damnation had been real enough to Billy Blake.* 'Nor does it recognize *sal*vation because the whole concept worries me. Are we being saved *from* something or *for* something? If it's the former, then our right to live by our own code of ethics is under threat from moral totalitarianism, and if it's the latter, then we must blindly follow negative logic that something better awaits us when we die.' He glanced pointedly at his watch. 'Now you'll have to excuse me, I'm afraid.'

The old man gave a quiet laugh. 'You give up too easily, my friend. Is your philosophy so fragile that it can't defend itself in debate?'

'Far from it,' said Deacon, 'but I have better things to do than stand in judgement on other people's lives.'

'Unlike me?'

'Yes.'

His companion smiled. 'Except I try never to judge anyone.' He paused for a moment. 'Do you know those words by John Donne? "Any man's death diminishes me because I am involved in mankind."'

Deacon finished the quote: '"Therefore never send to know for whom the bell tolls; it tolls for thee."'

'So tell me, is it wrong to ask a man to go on living, even though he's in pain, when his life is more precious to me than his death?'

Deacon experienced a strange sort of dislocation. Words hammered in his brain. *Devourer of thy parent . . . now thy unutterable torment renews . . . Is any man's life so worthless that the manner of his death is the only interesting thing about him* . . . He stared rather blankly at Lawrence. 'Why are you here? I remember going to Knightsbridge to interview you.'

'I moved seven years ago after my wife died.'

'I see.' He rubbed his face vigorously to clear his head. 'Well, look, I'm sorry but I have to go now.' He stood up. 'It's been good talking to you, Lawrence. Enjoy your Christmas.'

A twinkle glittered in the old man's eyes. 'What's to enjoy? I'm Jewish. Do you think I like being reminded that most of the civilized world condemns my people for what they did two thousand years ago?'

'Aren't you confusing Christmas with Easter?'

Lawrence raised his eyes to heaven. 'I talk about two

thousand years of isolation and he quibbles over a few months.'

Deacon lingered, seduced by the twinkle and the outrageous racial blackmail. 'Enjoy Hanukka then, or are you going to tell me that that's impossible, too, because there's no one to enjoy it with?'

'What else can a childless widower expect?' He saw hesitation in the younger man's face, and patted the seat. 'Sit down again and give me the pleasure of a few minutes' companionship. We're old friends, Michael, and it's so rare for me to spend time with an intelligent man. Would it relieve your mind if I said I've always been a better lawyer than I've been a Jew, so your soul is in no danger?'

Deacon persuaded himself that he only sat down out of curiosity but the truth was he had no weapons against Lawrence's frailty. Death was in the old man's face just as clearly as it had been in Alan Parker's, and Deacon's sensitivity to death was always more acute as Christmas drew nearer.

'In fact, I was thinking how alike we all are and how easy it would be to drop out of our boring lives and start again,' said Deacon, nodding towards the men on the shore. 'Would you recognize them, for example, if the next time you saw them was in the Dorchester?'

'Their friends would know them.'

'Not if they came across them in a different environment. Recognition is about relating a series of known facts. Change those facts and recognition becomes harder.'

'Is a new identity what you want, Michael?'

He scraped the stubble on his chin. 'It certainly has its attractions. Did you never think about dropping out and wiping the slate clean?'

'Of course. We all have mid-life crises. If we didn't, we wouldn't be normal.'

Deacon laughed. 'To be honest, Lawrence, I'd rather you'd said I was different. The last thing a red-blooded male with unrealized ambitions wants to hear is that he's *normal*. I've done damn-all with my life and it's driving me round the bend.'

'I tend to give Christmas a wide berth,' said Deacon, lighting a fresh cigarette. 'I'd rather be at work than pretending I'm enjoying myself.'

'What does giving it a wide berth usually involve?'

Deacon shrugged. 'Ignoring it, I suppose. Keeping my head down till it's all over and sanity's restored. I don't have any children. It might be different if I had children.'

'Yes, we suffer when we have no one to love.'

'I thought it was the other way round,' he said, watching one of the men tug at a piece of wood in the mud's embrace. *No woman had ever held on to him so tenaciously as the mud held the wood.* 'We suffer when no one loves *us*.'

'Perhaps you're right.'

'I know I'm right. I've had two wives and I fucked my brains out trying to express my love for both of them. It was a waste of time.'

Lawrence smiled. 'My *dear* fellow,' he murmured. 'So much fucking for so little result. How terribly exhausting for you.'

Deacon grinned. 'It clearly served some purpose if it amuses you.'

'It reminds me of the woman who gave her husband a DIY kit when he told her he wanted a good screw.'

'Is there a moral to this story?'

'Five or six at least, depending on whether it was a genuine misunderstanding or whether the wife was teaching her husband a lesson.'

'Meaning she thought he was taking her for granted? Well, I never took either of the Mrs Deacons for granted, or not until it was obvious the marriages were on the skids. It was they who took me' – he drew morosely on his cigarette – 'for every damn penny they could. I had to sell two bloody good houses to give them each a half of my capital, lost most of my possessions in the process and now I'm shacked up in a miserable rented flat in Islington. Is there anything in your morality tale to account for that?'

Lawrence chuckled. 'I don't know. I'm a little confused now about who was screwing whom. What was the purpose of these marriages, Michael?'

'What do you mean, what was the purpose? I loved them, or at least I thought I did.'

'I love my cats but I don't intend to marry any of them.'

'What *is* the purpose of marriage then?'

'Isn't that the question you need to answer before you try again?'

'Do me a favour,' said Deacon. 'I don't intend to have my balls chopped off a third time.'

'You sound as if you're sulking, Michael.'

'Clara – she was my second wife – kept accusing me of going through the male menopause. She said I was only interested in sex.'

'Naturally. Wanting babies isn't a female prerogative. I still want babies, and I'm eighty-three years old. Why did God give me sperm if it wasn't to make babies? Look at Abraham. He was geriatric when he had Isaac.'

Deacon's rugged face broke into a smile. 'Now you're sulking, Lawrence.'

'No, Michael, I'm complaining. But old men are allowed to complain because it doesn't matter how positive their mental attitude, they still have to persuade a woman under forty to have sex with them. And that's not as easy as it sounds. I know because I've tried.'

'I can't pretend it was anything other than lust. Clara was – is – beautiful.'

'Who am I to argue? I had to have my tomcat neutered six months ago because the neighbours kept complaining about his insatiable appetite for their pretty little queens.'

'I wasn't that bad, Lawrence.'

'Neither was my tom, Michael. He was only doing what God programmed him to do, and the fact that he preferred the pretty ones merely demonstrated his good taste.'

'I don't think I ever told Clara I wanted children. I mentioned it to Julia a couple of times, but she always said there was plenty of time.'

'There was, until you deserted her for Clara.'

'I thought you were trying to persuade me to feel less guilty about that. Didn't I do it out of desperation to keep the Deacon line going?'

'There's no excuse for inefficiency, Michael. If children are what you want, then you must find a woman who wants them too. Surely the moral of the DIY story is that people have different priorities in life.'

'So where do I go from here?' asked Deacon with wry amusement. 'Singles bars? Dating agencies? Or maybe I should try an ad in *Private Eye*?'

'I think it was Chairman Mao who said, "Every journey begins with the first step." Why do you want to make that first step so difficult?'

'I don't understand.'

'You need a little practice before you throw yourself in at the deep end again. You've forgotten how simple love is. Relearn that lesson first.'

'How do I do that?'

'As I said, I love my cats but I don't plan to marry them.'

'Are you telling me to get a pet?'

'I'm not telling you anything, Michael. You're intelligent enough to work this one out for yourself.' Lawrence took a card from his inside pocket. 'This is my phone number. You can call me at any time. I'm almost always there.'

'You might live to regret it. How do you know I won't take you up on it and drive you mad with endless phone calls?'

The old eyes twinkled with what looked to Deacon like genuine affection. 'I hope you will. It's such a rarity for me to feel useful these days.'

'You're the most dreadful old fraud I've ever met.'

'Why do you say that?'

'"It's such a rarity for me to feel useful these days,"' he quoted. 'I bet you say that to all the waifs and strays you pick up. As a matter of interest, does everyone get emotionally blackmailed or am I peculiarly privileged?'

The old man chortled happily. 'Only those who inspire me with hope. You can only feed the hungry, Michael.'

It was a startling trigger to Deacon's memory. Images of skeletal Billy Blake floated to the surface of his mind. He felt for his wallet and took out a print of the dead man's mugshot. 'Did you ever talk to him? He was a derelict who lived in a warehouse squat about a mile from here and died of starvation six months ago on that estate behind us. He called himself Billy Blake but I don't think it was his real name. I need to find out who he was.'

Lawrence studied the photograph for several seconds then shook his head regretfully. 'I'm afraid not. I'm sure I'd remember if I had. It's not a face you can easily forget, is it?'

'No.'

'I remember the story. It caused quite a stir here for a day or two. Why is he important to you?'

'The woman whose garage he died in asked me to find out who he was,' said Deacon.

'Mrs Powell.'

'Yes.'

'I've seen her once or twice. She drives a black BMW.'

'That's the one.'

'Do you like her, Michael?'

Deacon thought about it. 'I haven't decided yet. She's a complicated woman.' He shrugged. 'It's a long story.'

'Then save it for your phone call.'

'It may never happen, Lawrence. My wives would tell you I score very low on reliability.'

'One little call, Michael. Is that so much to ask?'

'But it's not one little call, is it?' he growled. 'You're after people's souls, and don't think for one moment I don't know it.'

Lawrence glanced at the back of the photograph. 'May I keep this? I know quite a number of the homeless community and one of them might recognize him.'

'Sure.' Deacon stood up. 'But it doesn't mean I'll phone you, so don't raise your hopes. I'm going to be very embarrassed about this tomorrow.' He shook the old man's hand. 'Shalom, Lawrence, and thanks. Go home before you freeze to death.'

'I will. Shalom, my friend.'

He watched the younger man walk away across the grass, then smiled to himself as he took out his address book and made a careful note of Deacon's name, followed by the address and telephone number of the *Street* which Barry Grover had thoughtfully stamped on the back of the photograph. Not that he expected to need them. Lawrence's faith in God's mysterious ways was absolute, and he knew it was only a question of time before Michael phoned him.

The old man turned his face upstream and listened to the wind and the waves rebuking each other.

Chapter Eight

THE FIGHT THAT broke out inside the warehouse was a bloody affair, started by one of the more aggressive schizophrenics who decided the man next to him wanted to kill him. He pulled a flick-knife from his pocket and plunged it into his neighbour's stomach. The man's screams acted on the other inmates like a strident alarm, bringing some to his rescue and driving the rest to stampede in fear. Terry Dalton and old Tom snatched up pieces of lead piping and waded in to try to break up the affray but, like a fighting dog, the aggressor ignored the rain of blows that descended on his back and concentrated his energy on his victim. It ended, as so many of these fights ended, only when the man's stamina ran out and he retired, bruised and battered, to nurse his wounds.

Tom knelt beside the pathetic, curled figure of the man who'd been stabbed. 'It's poor old Walter,' he said. 'That bastard Denning's done for 'im good an' proper. If 'e ain't dead now, 'e soon will be.'

Terry, who was shaking from head to toe in the aftermath of heightened adrenalin, flung his piece of pipe to the ground and stripped his coat from his thin body. 'Put this over Walt and keep him warm. I'm calling an ambulance,' he said. 'And get yourselves ready for when the Old Bill gets here. This time I'm having Denning put away good and proper. He's too fucking dangerous.'

'You can cut that kind of talk, son,' said Tom, laying the coat over the body. 'There's no one gonna thank you for dropping the law on us like a ton of bricks. We'll shift Walt out and let the coppers think it 'appened in the street. The poor bastard's leaking like a stuck pig, so there'll be enough blood on the pavement to persuade 'em it were a gang of louts what did for 'im.'

'No!' snapped Terry. 'If you shift him, you'll kill him quicker.' He clenched his fists. 'We have rights, Tom, same as everyone else. Walt's right is to be given his chance, and our right is to get shot of a psycho.'

'There ain't no rights in 'ell, son,' said Tom dismissively, 'never mind Billy filled your 'ead with claptrap about 'uman dignity. You bring the bizzies in 'ere and it won't be just Denning for the 'igh jump. You think about what's in your pockets before you go calling in the filth.' He touched a gnarled hand to the wounded man's face. 'Walt's had it anyway, so it won't make no difference where 'e dies. We'll get shot of Denning ourselves, send 'im back on the streets where 'e'll likely die of cold before too long. 'E's tired 'isself out with this, so 'e won't be no trouble.'

He spoke with the authority of a man who expected to be obeyed, for, despite Deacon's impression that Terry's quick mind allowed him to dominate the group, it was Tom who governed the warehouse, and there was no place in Tom's philosophy for sentiment. He'd seen too many derelicts die to care much about this one.

'NO!' roared the youngster, making for the doorway. 'You move Walt, and you'll answer to me. We're not fucking savages, so we don't fucking behave like them. YOU HEAR ME?' He pushed his way furiously through the crowd around the door.

The phone rang in Deacon's flat as he emerged from a shower. 'I need to speak to Michael Deacon,' said an urgent voice.

'Speaking,' he said, rubbing his hair dry with a towel.

'Do you remember that warehouse you came to a couple of weeks back?'

'Yes.' He recognized his caller. 'Are you Terry?'

'Yeah. Listen, are you still after information on Billy Blake?'

'I am.'

'Then get yourself down to the warehouse in the next half-hour and bring a camera with you. Can you do that?'

'Why the hurry?'

'Because the cops are on the way, and there's stuff in there that belonged to Billy. I reckon half an hour tops before the barricades go up. You coming?'

'I'll be there.'

Terry Dalton, muffled inside an old donkey-jacket and with a black bobble hat pulled down over his shaven head, was leaning against the corner of the building, watching for Deacon's arrival. As Deacon drew into the kerb in front of an empty police car, Terry pushed himself off the wall and went to meet him.

'There's been a stabbing,' he said in a rush, as the older man got out, 'and it was me called the coppers. I reckoned it wouldn't do no harm to have a journalist in on the act. Tom reckons they're going to use this as an excuse to evict us and maybe charge us with other offences, but we've got rights, and I want them protected. In return, I'll give you everything I've got on Billy. Is it a deal?' He looked down the road as another police car rounded the corner. 'Move yourself. We ain't got much time. Did you bring a camera?'

Confused by this babble of information, Deacon allowed himself to be drawn into the lee of the building. 'It's in my pocket.'

Terry gestured along the way. 'There's a way in through one of the windows which the Old Bill don't know about. If I get you inside, they'll think you were there all the time.'

'What about the policemen already in there?'

'There's just the two of them, and they didn't get here till after the medics. They won't have a clue who was inside and who wasn't. It's too bloody dark, and they were more interested in keeping Walt alive. They didn't start asking questions till five minutes ago when the ambulance left.' He eased aside a piece of boarding. 'Okay, remember this. It were Walter what got stabbed and a psycho called Denning what did it. It's something you'd know if you'd been here a while.'

Deacon put a hand on the boy's shoulder to restrain him as he prepared to climb through the window. 'Hang on a minute. I'm not a lawyer. What are these rights you're expecting me to protect? And how am I supposed to do it?'

Terry rounded on him. 'Take pictures or something. Jesus, I don't know. Use your imagination.' His expression changed to bitterness when Deacon gave a doubtful shake of his head. 'Look, you bastard, you said you wanted to prove that Billy's life had value. Well, start by proving that Walt, Tom, me and every other damn sod in here have value. I know it's a fucking shit-hole, but we've got squatters' rights over it and it's where we live. It was me as rung the police, not the police as had to come looking, so they've no call to treat us like scum.' His pale eyes narrowed in sudden desperation. 'Billy always said that press freedom was the people's strongest weapon. Are you telling me he was wrong?'

'Okay, you lot, out,' said a harassed police constable, pushing resistant bodies. 'Let's have you in the light where we can see you.' He caught at an arm and swung the man to face the doorway. 'Out! Out!'

The flash of Deacon's camera startled him, and he turned, open-mouthed, to be caught in a second flash. A sudden silence descended on the warehouse as the light popped several times in quick succession.

'They'll be mounted in a series across the front page,' said Deacon, swinging the camera towards another policeman whose foot was nudging a sleeping man, 'with a caption like "Police use concentration-camp tactics on the homeless".' He pointed the lens at the first policeman again, zooming in for a close-up. 'How about a repeat of the "*'Raus! 'Raus! 'Raus!*"? That should stir a few worrying memories among the great and the good.'

'Who the hell are you?'

'Who the hell are you, *sir*?' said Deacon, lowering the camera to offer a card. 'Michael Deacon, and I'm a journalist. May I have your name, please, and the names of the other officers present?' He took out his notebook.

A plain-clothes policeman intervened. 'I'm Detective Sergeant Harrison, sir. Perhaps I can be of assistance.' He was a pleasant-looking individual in his thirties, solidly built and with thinning blond hair, which lifted in the breeze from the warehouse doorway. His eyes creased in an amiable smile.

'You could begin by explaining what's going on here?'

'Certainly, sir. We are asking these gentlemen to clear the site of an attempted murder. As the only free area is outside, we have requested them to vacate the building.'

Deacon raised the camera again, pointed the lens the length of the warehouse and took a photograph of its vast interior. 'Are you sure about that, sergeant? There seems to be acres of free space in here. As a matter of interest, when did the police adopt this policy?'

'What policy's that, sir?'

'Forcing people to leave their homes when a crime's been committed inside. Isn't the normal procedure to invite them to sit in another part of the house, usually the kitchen, where they can have a cup of tea to calm their nerves?'

'Look, sir, this is hardly run-of-the-mill, as you can see for yourself. It's a serious crime we're investigating. There are no lights. Half these guys are comatose on drink or drugs. The only way we can find out what's been going on is to move everyone out and introduce some order.'

'Really?' Deacon continued to take pictures. 'I thought the more usual first step was to invite witnesses to come forward and make a statement.'

Briefly, the sergeant's guard slipped and Deacon's camera caught his look of contempt. 'These guys don't even know what co-operation means. However' – he raised his voice – 'a man was stabbed in here in the last hour. Would anyone who saw the incident or has information about it please step forward?' He waited a second or two, then smiled good-humouredly at Deacon. 'Satisfied, sir? Now perhaps you'll let us get on.'

'*I* saw it,' said Terry, sliding out from behind Deacon's back. His eyes searched the darkness for Tom. 'And I weren't the only one, though you'd think I was for all the guts the rest of them are showing.'

Silence greeted this remark.

'Jesus, you're pathetic,' he went on scathingly. 'No wonder the Old Bill treat you like dirt. That's all you know, isn't it? How to lie down in the gutter while anyone who wants to walks all over you.' He spat on the floor. 'That's what I think of men who'd rather let a psycho loose on the streets than stand up and be counted once in their fucking lives.'

'Okay, okay,' said a disgruntled voice from the middle of the crowd. 'Leave off, son, for Christ's sake.' Tom shouldered his way to the front and glared malignantly at Terry. 'Anyone'd think you were the Archbishop of flaming Canterbury the way you're carrying on.' He nodded at the sergeant. 'I saw it too. 'Ow's tricks, Mr 'Arrison?'

The demeanour of the detective sergeant changed. He gave a broad grin. 'Good God! Tom Beale! I thought you were dead. Your old lady did, too.'

Tom's face creased into lines of disgust. 'I might as well be for all she cares. She told me to bugger off the last time you got me sent down, and I never saw 'er or 'eard from 'er again.'

'Bull! She was on my back for months after you were released, pressuring me to find you. Why the hell didn't you go home like you were supposed to?'

'There weren't no point,' said Tom morosely. 'She made it clear she didn't want me. In any case the silly cow went and died on me. I thought I'd pay 'er a visit a couple of years ago, and there were a load of strangers in the 'ouse. I were that upset, you wouldn't believe.'

'That doesn't mean she's dead, for God's sake. The council moved her into a flat six months after you scarpered.'

Tom looked pleased. 'Is that right? You reckon she wants to see me?'

'I'd put money on it.' The DS laughed. 'How about we get you home for Christmas? God only knows why, but you're probably the present your old lady's been waiting for.' He turned his watch face towards the light. 'Better than that, if we can get this mess sorted out PDQ, we'll have you home in time for supper. What do you say?'

'You're on, Mr 'Arrison.'

'Okay, let's start with names and descriptions of everyone involved.'

'There were only the one.' Tom nodded towards the sleeping man and the policeman standing over him. 'That's the bastard you want. Name of Denning. 'E's out for the count at the moment because 'e wears 'isself out with 'is rages, but you want to be careful 'ow you tackle 'im. Like Terry says, 'e's a psycho and 'e's still got the knife on 'im.' He cackled again and produced a cigar from one of his pockets. 'We don't want no accidents, not when we're all getting along so well. I tell you what, Mr 'Arrison, I've never been so pleased to see the Old Bill in my life. 'Ere, 'ave a cigar on me.'

Because he was a professional, Deacon caught the presentation on film and made a few pounds out of the picture by selling it to a photographic agency. It appeared after Christmas in one of the tabloids with the caption **'Havana nice cigar'** and a sentimental version of Tom's reunion with his wife, together with Sergeant Harrison's part in the little drama. It was a parody of the truth, glossed up by a staff reporter to stimulate a New Year feel-good factor, for the facts were that Tom preferred the company of men, his wife preferred her cat and Sergeant Harrison was furious when he discovered the cigar was part of a consignment stolen from a hijacked lorry.

The whole episode left a sour taste in Deacon's

mouth. It offended him that police even-handedness should turn on the warmth that one sergeant felt for one destitute man. This wasn't reality. Reality was Terry's shit-hole of a warehouse where dereliction ruled and the manner of a man's death was the most interesting thing about him.

Terry caught up with him as he was unlocking his car door. 'They're saying I have to go down the nick and make a statement.'

'Is that a problem?'

'Yeah. I don't want to go.'

Deacon glanced beyond Terry to the policeman who had followed him. 'You can't have it both ways, you know. If you want your rights respected, then you have to show willing in return.'

'I'll go if you come with me.'

'There'd be no point. Lawyers are the only people allowed in interview rooms.' He searched the lad's anxious face. 'Why the change of heart? You were all fired up to make a statement twenty minutes ago.'

'Yeah, but not down the nick on my own.'

'Tom'll be there.'

A terrible disillusionment curled the boy's lip. 'He doesn't give a toss about me or Walt. He's only interested in licking the sergeant's arse and getting home to his missus. He'll drop me in the shit, quick as winking, if it suits him.'

'What does he know that the rest of us don't?'

'That I'm only fourteen, and that my name's not

Terry Dalton. I ran away from care at twelve and I ain't going back.'

Jesus wept. 'Why not? What was so bad about it?'

'The bastard in charge was a sodding shirt-lifter, that's what.' Terry clenched his fists. 'I swore I'd kill him if I ever got the chance, and if they send me back, that's what I'm gonna do. You'd better believe that.' He spoke with intense aggression. 'Billy believed it. It's why he watched out for me. He said he didn't want another murder on his conscience.'

Deacon relocked the car door. 'Why do I get the feeling my fate is inextricably linked with Billy Blake's?'

'I don't get you.'

'Does death by starvation sound familiar?' He cuffed the boy lightly across the back of the head. 'There's no food in my flat,' he grumbled, 'and I was planning to do all my shopping this afternoon. It'll be bedlam tomorrow.' He steered Terry towards the policeman. 'Don't panic,' he said more gently as he felt him tense, 'I won't abandon you. Unlike Tom, I have no desire to see either of my wives again.'

'Is that you, Lawrence? It's Michael – Michael Deacon . . . Yes, as a matter of fact, I do have a problem. I need a respectable lawyer to tell a couple of little white lies for me . . . Only to the police.' He held his mobile telephone away from his ear. 'Look, you're the one who told me to get a pet, so I reckon you owe me some support here . . . No, it's not a dangerous dog and it hasn't bitten anyone. It's a harmless little stray . . . I can't prove ownership, so they look like impounding him over Christmas . . . Yes, I agree. It's a shame . . . That's it. All I need is a sponsor . . . You will? Good man. It's the police station on the Isle of Dogs. I'll reimburse the taxi fare when you get here.'

Terry was hunched in the passenger seat of Deacon's car in an East End back street. 'You should've told him the truth. He'll blow a fuse when he gets here and finds I'm a bloke. There's no way he's going to tell lies for someone he doesn't know.' He put his fingers on the door handle. 'I reckon I should take off now while the going's good.'

'Don't even think about it,' said Deacon evenly. 'I promised Sergeant Harrison you'd be at the nick by five o'clock, and you're going to be there.' He offered the boy a cigarette and took one himself. 'Look, no one's forcing you to make this statement. You're volunteering it, so you won't be put through the third degree unless Tom decides to drop you in it. Even then, you'll be treated with kid gloves because children aren't allowed to be interviewed without an adult present. I guarantee it won't even come to that, but if it does, Lawrence will get you out.'

'Yeah, but—'

'Trust me. If Lawrence says your name's Terry Dalton and you're aged eighteen, then the police will believe him. He's very convincing. He looks like a cross between the Pope and Albert Einstein.'

'He's a fucking lawyer. If you tell him the truth, he'll have to pass it on to the Old Bill. That's what lawyers do.'

'No, they don't,' said Deacon with more conviction than he felt. 'They represent their clients' interests. But, in any case, I won't tell Lawrence anything unless I have to.'

Terry was grinning broadly as he left the interview room. 'You coming?' he asked Deacon and Lawrence as he passed them in the waiting-room on his way out.

They caught up with him in the street. 'Well?' demanded Deacon.

'No problem. It never crossed their minds I wasn't who I said I was.' He started to laugh.

'What's so funny?'

'They warned me off you and Lawrence because they reckoned you were a couple of chutney ferrets after my arse. Otherwise, why'd you be hanging around when all I was doing was making a statement?'

'God almighty,' snarled Deacon. 'What did you say?'

'I said they needn't worry because I don't do that kind of stuff.'

'Oh, great! So our reputations go down the pan while you come out smelling of roses.'

'That's about the size of it,' said Terry, retreating behind Lawrence for safety.

Lawrence chuckled joyfully. 'To be honest, I'm flattered anyone thinks I still have the energy to do anything so active.' He tucked his hand into Terry's arm and drew him along the pavement towards a pub on the corner. 'What was the term you used? Chutney ferret? Of course, I'm a very old man, and not at all in touch with modern idiom, but I do think gay is preferable.' He paused in front of the pub door, waiting for Terry to open it for him. 'Thank you,' he said, gripping the boy's hand to steady himself as he carefully mounted the step at the entrance.

Terry threw an anguished glance over his shoulder at Deacon which clearly said, *This old guy's got his hand in mine, and I think he's a fucking woofter*, but Deacon only bared his teeth in a savage smile. 'Serves you right,' he mouthed, following them inside.

Barry Grover looked up rather guiltily as the security guard opened the cuttings library door and stepped inside. 'All right, son, let's have you out of here,' said Glen Hopkins firmly. 'The office is closed and you are supposed to be on holiday.'

He was a blunt-spoken retired chief petty officer, and after much deliberation, and having listened to the vicious gossip about Barry that came from the women, he had decided to take the little man in hand. He knew exactly what his problem was, and it was nothing that practical advice and straight speaking couldn't put right. He had come across Barry's type in the Navy, although admittedly they were usually younger.

Barry covered what he was doing. 'I'm working on something important,' he said priggishly.

'No, you're not. We both know what you're up to, and it's not work.'

Barry took off his glasses and stared blindly across the

room. 'I'm afraid I don't know what you're talking about.'

'Oh, yes, you do, and it isn't healthy, son.' Glen moved heavily across the floor. 'Listen to me, a man of your age should be out having fun, not shutting himself away in the dark looking at snapshots. Now, I've a few cards here with some addresses and telephone numbers on them, and my best advice to you is to choose the one you like and give her a ring. She'll cost a bob or two and you'll need a condom, but she'll get you up and running, if you follow my drift. There's no shame in having a helping hand at the start.' He placed some prostitutes' cards on the desk, and gave Barry a fatherly pat on the shoulder. 'You'll find the real thing's a damn sight more fun than a boxful of pictures.'

Barry blushed a fiery red. 'You don't understand, Mr Hopkins. I'm working on a project for Mike Deacon.' He uncovered the pictures of Billy Blake and James Streeter. 'It's a big story.'

'Which explains why Mike's at the other desk helping you, I suppose,' said Glen ironically, 'instead of out on the tiles as per usual. Come on, son, no story's so important that it can't wait till after Christmas. You can say it's none of my business, but I'm a good judge of what a man's problems are and you're not going to solve yours by staying here.'

Barry shrank away from him. 'It's not what you think,' he mumbled.

'You're lonely, lad, and you don't know how to cure it. Your mum's the nosy type – don't forget it's me who answers the phone if she rings of an evening – and if you'll forgive the plain speaking, you'd have done better to get out from under her apronstrings a long time ago. All you need is a little confidence to get started, and there's no law that says you shouldn't pay for it.' His lugubrious face broke into a smile. 'Now, hop it, and give yourself the sort of Christmas present you'll never forget.'

Thoroughly humiliated, Barry had no option but to pick up the cards and leave, but the shame of the experience brought tears to his eyes and he blinked forlornly on the pavement as the front door was locked behind him. He was so afraid that Glen would quiz him on how he'd got on that he finally made his way to a phone box and called the first number in the pile that the man had selected for him. Had he known that, in the simplistic belief that sex cured all ills, Glen habitually passed prostitutes' cards to any male colleague whom he deemed to be going through a bad patch, Barry might have thought twice about what he was doing. As it was, he assumed his virginity would become common gossip if he didn't fulfil Glen's ambitions for him, and it was more in dread of being the butt of office jokes than in anticipation of pleasure that he agreed to pay £100 for Fatima, the Turkish Delight.

Chapter Nine

'NOW,' SAID LAWRENCE, when they were settled at a table with drinks in front of them, 'perhaps Terry would like to tell me why I'm here.'

Terry ducked the question by burying his nose in his pint of beer.

'It's quite simple—' began Deacon.

'Then I should like Terry to explain it,' said the old man with surprising firmness. 'I'm a lover of simplicity, Michael, but so far you've only confused me. I am very doubtful that Terry is who he says he is, which means you and I could be in the invidious position of accessories after the fact to a crime he committed previously.'

A resigned expression settled on Terry's face. 'I knew this were a bad idea,' he told Deacon morosely. 'For a kick-off, I don't understand a bleeding word he says. It's like listening to Billy. He were always using words the rest of us had never heard of. I told him once to speak fucking English, and he laughed so much you'd of thought I'd just told the best joke in the world.' His pale eyes fixed on Lawrence. 'People get hung up on names,' he said fiercely, 'but what's so important about a fucking name? If it comes to that, what's so important about a person's age? It's the age you act that matters, not the age you are. Okay, maybe my name isn't Terry and maybe I'm not eighteen, but I like 'em both because they give me respect. One day, I'm gonna *be* somebody, and people like you will want to know me whatever I'm calling myself. It's me that's important' – he tapped his chest above his heart – 'not my name.'

Deacon passed Terry a cigarette. 'There's no crime involved, Lawrence,' he said matter-of-factly.

'How do you know?'

'What did I tell you?' demanded Terry aggressively. 'Fucking lawyers. Now he's calling me a liar.'

Deacon made a dampening motion with his hand. 'Terry ran away from care two years ago at the age of twelve, and he doesn't want to be sent back because the man in charge is a paedophile. To avoid that happening he's added four years to his age and has been living under an alias in a squat. It's as simple as that.'

Lawrence clicked his tongue impatiently, unintimidated by Terry's seething anger beside him. 'You call it simple that a child has been living in dreadful circumstances without education or loving parental control during two of the most important years of his life? Perhaps I should remind you, Michael, that it's only five hours since you were telling me you wanted to be a father.' He raised a thin, transparent hand towards Terry. 'This young man is no harmless stray who can be left to his own devices now that you've prevented the police from exercising their responsibility towards him. He's in need of the care and protection that a civilized society—'

'There were Billy,' broke in Terry fiercely. 'He were caring.'

Lawrence looked at him for a moment, then took the photograph Deacon had given him from his wallet. 'Is this Billy?'

Terry glanced at the haggard face then looked away. 'Yeah.'

'It must have grieved you to lose him.'

'Not so's you'd notice.' He lowered his head. 'He weren't that bloody brilliant. Half the time he were off his head, so it were *me* looking after *him*.'

'But you did love him?'

The boy's hands clenched into fists again. 'If you're saying me and Billy were sodding poofs, I'll belt you one.'

'My dear boy,' murmured the old man gently, 'such a thing never crossed my mind. I dread to think what kind of world you inhabit where men are frightened to express their fondness for each other because of what others might think. There are a thousand ways to love a person, and only one of them is sexual. I think you loved Billy as a father and, from the way you describe him, he loved you as a son. Is that so shameful that you have to deny it?'

Terry didn't say anything and a silence developed. Deacon broke it eventually because it was becoming uncomfortable.

'Look, I don't know about anyone else,' he said, 'but I had a terrible night last night, and I wouldn't mind calling it a day. My personal view is that Terry's a streetwise kid with a hell of a lot going for him – he's certainly got more nous than I had at his age. There's a spare bed in my flat, I look like spending a miserable Christmas on my own, and I'd welcome some company. What do you say, Terry? My place or the warehouse for the next few days? You and I can enjoy ourselves while Lawrence does the worrying about the future.'

'I thought you said there was no food,' he muttered ungraciously.

'There isn't. We'll grab a takeaway tonight and go looking for turkey tomorrow.'

'Except you don't really want me. It's only because Lawrence reckons you'd make a lousy father that you thought of it.'

'Right. But I *have* thought of it, so what's the answer?' He looked at the bowed head. 'Listen, you miserable little sod, I haven't done badly by you so far today. Okay, I don't know the first damn thing about parenting but a small thank you for the efforts I have made wouldn't go amiss.'

Terry grinned suddenly and raised his head. 'Thanks, Dad. You've done good. How about we make it an Indian takeaway?'

There was a gleam of triumph in the lad's pale eyes which came and went too swiftly for Deacon to notice. But Lawrence saw it. Being older and wiser, he had been looking for it.

Lawrence refused Deacon's offer of a lift home but took the Islington address in case he was contacted by the police. He advised Terry to use his few days' grace to consider whether a return to the warehouse was in his best interests, warned him that his true age and identity would undoubtedly be discovered if and when he was required to give evidence against Denning in court, and suggested he think about regularizing his position voluntarily before he was forced into it. He then asked Terry to call him a taxi from the phone at the bar and, while the boy was out of earshot, he cautioned Deacon against naivety. 'Retain a healthy scepticism, Michael. Remember the kind of life Terry's been leading and how little you actually know about him.'

Deacon smiled slightly. 'I was afraid you were going to tell me to clutch him to my heart with expressions of love. Healthy scepticism I can cope with. It's what I know best.'

'Oh, I don't think you're quite so hardened as you think you are, my dear fellow. You've accepted everything he's told you without blinking an eyelid.'

'You think he's lying?'

Lawrence shrugged. 'We've had a conversation filled with references to homosexuality, and that troubles me. You'll be very vulnerable to a charge of attempted rape if you take him back to your flat. And that will leave you no option but to pay whatever he demands from you.'

Deacon frowned. 'Come on, Lawrence, he's completely paranoid on the whole subject. He'd never let me near enough to touch him, so how could he accuse me of rape?'

'*Attempted* rape, dear chap, and do please recognize

how effective his paranoia is. He's lulled you into thinking it's safe to take him home, which I'm bound to say is not something I would feel confident doing.'

'Then why were you pushing me into it?'

Lawrence sighed. 'I wasn't, Michael. I was hoping to persuade you both that Terry should be returned to care.' He was watching the boy as he spoke. The barman was trying to give him a telephone directory, which he seemed reluctant to take. 'Tell me, what will your reaction be when he screams and tears his clothes, and threatens to run to one of your neighbours with stories of imprisonment and sexual assault?'

'Why would he want to do that?'

'I would imagine because he's done it before and knows it works. You really mustn't go into this with your eyes closed, my dear chap.'

'Great,' said Deacon, lowering his head wearily into his hands. 'So what the hell am I supposed to do now? Tell the little bastard to get stuffed?'

Lawrence chuckled. 'Dear, dear, dear! What a fellow you are for losing heart. The least generous but probably most sensible course would be to hand him back to the police and let the social workers deal with him, but that would be very unkind when you've just offered him Christmas in your flat. Forewarned is, after all, forearmed. I think you must honour your invitation to the poor lad but keep one step ahead of him all the time.'

'I wish you'd make up your mind,' growled Deacon. 'Half a minute ago the *poor lad* was planning to con me out of thousands.'

'Why should the two be mutually exclusive? He's an

unloved, ill-educated, half-formed adolescent who, through living rough, will have learned some sophisticated tricks to keep him in clothes, food, drink and drugs. The truth may be that you're exactly the person he needs to bring him back into the fold.'

'He'll run rings around me,' said Deacon gloomily.

'Surely not,' murmured Lawrence, looking towards the bar where Terry had finally asked the barman to locate a minicab firm for him in the directory. 'At least you have the advantage of literacy.'

Barry experienced only humiliation at the hands of Fatima, who spoke very poor English. The light in her bed-sitting room was dim, and he looked in fastidious alarm at the tumbled bed, which still seemed to bear the imprint of a previous client. There was a strong Turkish atmosphere in the frowsty room which owed more to Fatima herself than to the array of joss sticks burning on a dressing-table.

She was a well-covered woman, somewhere in her middle years, with a routine that was well established and made no allowance for time-wasting. She recognized rapidly that she was dealing with a virgin and looked repeatedly at her clock while Barry stumbled through an inarticulate introduction of himself as he tried to work out how to extricate himself from this dreadful situation without offending her.

'One hunra,' she broke in impatiently, stroking her palm. 'And take zee trowse off. Who care you call Barree? *I* call you sweeties. What you like? Doggy-doggy? Oil?'

She pursed her full lips into a ripe rosebud. 'You nice clean boy. For a hunra and fifty Fatima do sucky-sucky. You like sucky-sucky? Sounds good, eh, sweeties?'

Terrified that she wouldn't let him go without some sort of payment, Barry fumbled his wallet out of his coat pocket and allowed her to remove five twenties. It was a mistake. Once the money had changed hands, and when Barry didn't immediately start shedding his clothes, she set about doing it for him. She was a strong woman and clearly expected to fulfil her side of the contract.

'Come on, sweeties. No need to be shy. Fatima, she know all the tricks. There, you see, no problem. You beeg boy.' With deft hands she plucked a condom from a nearby drawer, applied it with consummate artistry and proceeded to practise her Turkish delights at speed.

Barry was no match for her skill and matters reached a conclusion in seconds.

'There you are, sweeties,' she said, 'all done, all enjoyed. You really *beeg* boy. You come back any time as long as you have a hunra. Fatima always willing. Next time less talk, more fun, okay? You pay for good sex, and Fatima give good sex. Maybe you like doggy-doggy and fondle Fatima's nice round arse. Now put zee trowse back on and say bye-bye.'

She had the door open before he was properly dressed and, because he didn't know what else to do with it, he put the condom in his pocket. She called after him as he walked away: 'You come back soon, Barree,' and his heart swelled with loathing for her and all her sex.

*

'What was the old guy saying to you while I was on the phone?' demanded Terry suspiciously as he and Deacon made their way back to the car.

'Nothing much. He's concerned about your future and how best to handle it.'

'Yeah, well, if he does the dirty on me and goes to the police, he'd better watch his back.'

'He gave you his word he wouldn't. Don't you believe him?'

Terry kicked at the kerb. 'I guess so. But he's a bit fucking heavy on the hand-patting and calling everyone dear. D'you reckon he's bent?'

'No. Would it make a difference if he were?'

'Bloody right it would. I don't hold with poofs.'

Deacon inserted his key in the car door, but paused before turning it to look across the roof at his would-be passenger. 'Then why do you keep talking about them?' he asked. 'You're like an alcoholic who can't keep off the subject of booze because he's dying for his next drink.'

'I'm not a bloody poof,' said Terry indignantly.

'Then prove it by keeping off the subject.'

'Okay. Can we stop at the warehouse?'

Deacon eyed him thoughtfully. 'Why?'

'There's things I need. Extra clothes and such.'

'Why can't you come as you are?'

'Because I'm not a fucking tramp.'

After ten minutes of drumming his fingers on the steering wheel and with no sign of Terry's re-emergence from the dark building, Deacon wondered if he should go after him. He could hear Lawrence's voice in his ear: '*You think this is good parenting, Michael? You let a fourteen-year-old boy go into a den of thieves, and you call that responsible?*'

He postponed one difficult decision by making another. He picked up his mobile telephone and dialled his sister's number. 'Emma?' he said when a woman's voice answered at the other end.

'No, it's Antonia.'

'You sound like your mother.'

'Who is this, please?'

'Your Uncle Michael.'

'God!' said the voice at the other end in some awe. 'Listen, hang on, okay? I'll get Mum.' The phone clattered on to a table and he heard her shouting for her mother. 'Quick, quick! It's Michael.'

His sister's breathless voice came down the line. 'Hello, hello! Michael?'

'Calm down and get your breath back,' he said in some amusement. 'I'm still here.'

'I ran. Where are you?'

'In a car outside a warehouse in the East End.'

'What are you doing there?'

'Nothing of any interest.' He could see the conversation being hijacked by irrelevancies, for, like him, Emma was adept at postponing anything difficult. 'Look, I got your card. I also got one from Julia. I gather Ma's not well.'

There was a short silence. 'Julia shouldn't have told you,' she said rather bitterly. 'I hoped you'd rung because you wanted to end this silly feud, not because you feel guilty about Ma.'

'I don't feel guilty.'

'Out of pity then.'

Did he feel pity either? His strongest emotion was still anger. '*Do not bring that whore into my house*,' his mother had said when he told her he'd married Clara. '*How dare you sully your father's name by giving it to a cheap tart? Was killing him not enough for you, Michael?*' That had been five years ago and he hadn't spoken to her since. 'I'm still angry, Emma, so maybe I'm phoning you out of filial duty. I'm not going to apologize to her – or you for that matter – but I am sorry she's ill. What do you want me to do about it? I'm quite happy to see her as long as she's prepared to keep a rein on her tongue, but I'll walk out the minute she starts having a go. That's the only deal you or she will get, so do I come or not?'

'You haven't changed one little bit, have you?' Her voice was angry. 'Your mother's virtually blind and may have to have her leg amputated as a result of diabetes, and you talk about deals. Some filial duty, Michael. She was in hospital for most of September, and now Hugh and I are paying through the nose for private nursing care at the farm because she won't come and live with us. *That*'s filial duty, making sure your mother's being looked after properly even if it means hardships for yourself.'

Deacon looked towards the warehouse with a frown in his dark eyes. 'What happened to her investments? She had a perfectly good income five years ago, so why isn't she paying for the nursing care herself?'

Emma didn't answer.

'Are you still there?'

'Yes.'

'Why isn't she paying herself?'

'She offered to put the girls through school and used her capital to buy their fees in advance,' said Emma reluctantly. 'She left herself enough to live on but not enough to pay for extras. We didn't *ask*,' she went on defensively. 'It was her idea, but none of us knew she was going to be struck down like this. And it's not as if there was any point keeping anything for you. As far as the rest of us were aware, you were never going to speak to us again.'

'That's right,' he agreed coolly. 'I'm only speaking to you now because Julia was so damn sure I wouldn't.'

Emma sighed. 'Is that the only reason you phoned?'

'Yes.'

'I don't believe you. Why can't you just say sorry and let bygones be bygones?'

'Because I've nothing to be sorry for. It's not my fault Pa died, whatever you and Ma like to think.'

'That's not what she was angry about. She was angry about the way you treated Julia.'

'It was none of her business.'

'Julia was her daughter-in-law. She was very fond of her. So was I.'

'You weren't married to her.'

'That's cheap, Michael.'

'Yes, well, I can't accuse you of that, can I? Not when you and Hugh have scooped the pot,' said Deacon sarcastically. 'I've never taken a cent from Ma and don't intend to start now, so if she wants to see me, it'll have to be on my terms because I don't owe her a damn thing, never mind how many bloody legs she's about to lose.'

'I can't believe you said that,' snapped his sister. 'Aren't you at all upset that she's ill?'

If he was, he wasn't going to admit it. 'My terms, Emma, or not at all. Have you a pen? Okay, this is my telephone number at home.' He gave it to her. 'I presume you'll be at the farm for Christmas, so I suggest you talk this over with Ma and ring me with your verdict. And don't forget I promised to deck Hugh the next time I saw him, so take that into account before you reach a decision.'

'You can't hit Hugh,' she said indignantly. 'He's fifty-three.'

Deacon bared his teeth at the receiver. 'Good, then one punch should do it easily.'

There was another silence. 'Actually, he's been wanting to apologize for ages,' she said weakly. 'He didn't really mean what he said. It just sort of came out in the heat of the moment. He regretted it afterwards.'

'Poor old Hugh. It's going to be doubly painful then when I break his nose.'

Terry appeared from the warehouse with two filthy suitcases which he parked on the back seat. He offered the explanation that as the warehouse was full of fucking thieves, he was safeguarding his possessions by bringing them with him. Deacon thought it looked more like wholesale removal to what promised to be luxury living.

'Doesn't the endless "fucking" get a little boring after a while?' he murmured as he drew away from the kerb.

They ate their takeaway perched on the bonnet of Deacon's car. They were in danger of freezing to death in the night air, but he preferred that to having his upholstery splattered with red tandoori chicken dye. Terry wanted to know why they hadn't eaten in the restaurant.

'I didn't think we'd ever get served,' said Deacon rather grimly, 'not after you called them wogs.'

Terry grinned. 'What d'you call them then?'

'People.'

They sat in silence for a while, gazing down the street ahead of them. Fortunately it was well-nigh deserted, so they attracted little curiosity. Deacon wondered who would have been the more embarrassed, himself or Terry, had some acquaintance passed by and seen them.

'So what are we going to do next?' asked Terry, cramming a last onion bhaji into his mouth. 'Go down the pub? Visit a club maybe? Get stoned?'

Deacon, who had been looking forward to putting his feet up in front of the fire and dozing through whatever film was on the television, groaned quietly to himself. *Pubbing, clubbing or getting stoned?* He felt old and decrepit beside the hyperactivity of movement – fidgeting, scratching, position-changing – that had been going on beside him for over an hour now. This, in turn, meant that his mind toiled with the threats of fleas, lice and bedbugs, and the problem of how to get Terry into a bath and every stitch of his clothing into the washing-machine without having his motives misconstrued.

One thing was certain. He had no intention of giving house room to Terry's wildlife.

The row between Emma and Hugh Tremayne had reached stentorian levels and, as usual, Hugh had resorted to the whisky bottle. 'Have you any idea what it's like to be the only man in a houseful of domineering women?' he demanded. 'Don't you think I've been tempted to do what Michael did and walk out? Nag, nag, nag. That's the only thing you and your mother have any talent for, isn't it?'

'I'm not the one who called Michael a sack of worthless shit,' said Emma furiously. 'That was your wonderful idea, although what made you think you could order him out of his own house I can't imagine. The only reason you're in our family is because you married me.'

'You're right,' he said abruptly, replenishing his glass. 'And what the hell am I still doing here? I sometimes think the only member of your family I've ever really liked was your brother. He's certainly the least critical.'

'Don't be so childish,' she snapped.

He stared at her moodily over the rim of his glass. 'I never liked Julia – she was a frigid bitch – and I certainly didn't blame Michael for taking up with Clara. Yet I let myself get dragged into defending you and your mother when I should have told Michael to go ahead and smash the house up with you and Penelope in it. As far as I'm concerned, he was well within his rights. You'd been screaming at him like a couple of fishwives for well over an hour before he lost his temper, and you had the damn nerve to accuse his *wife* of being common as muck.' He shook his head and moved towards the door. 'I'm not interested any more. If you want Michael's help, then you'd better persuade your mother to treat him with a little respect.'

Emma was close to tears. 'If I try, she won't talk to him at all. It's Julia's fault. If she hadn't told him Ma was ill, he'd probably have rung anyway.'

'You're running out of people to blame.'

'Yes, but what are we going to do?' she wailed. 'She's got to sell the farm.'

'It's your blasted family,' he growled, 'so you sort it out. You know damn well I never wanted your mother's money. It was obvious she'd use it as a stick to beat us with.' He slammed the door behind him. 'And I'm not going to the farm for Christmas,' he yelled from the hall. 'I've done it for sixteen bloody years, and it's been sixteen years of undiluted misery.'

'This is how we're going to play it,' said Deacon, pausing outside the door to his flat after carrying a suitcase up three flights of stairs. 'You're going to remove everything washable from these cases out here on the landing. We will then put it all into black dustbin bags which I will empty into the washing-machine while you're having your bath. You will leave what you're wearing outside the bathroom door, and when you're locked inside, I will take your clothes away and replace them with some of my own. Are we agreed?'

In the half-light of the landing, Terry looked a great deal older than fourteen. 'You sound like you're scared of me,' he remarked curiously. 'What did that old bugger Lawrence really say?'

'He told me how unhygienic you were likely to be.'

'Oh, right.' Terry looked amused. 'You sure he didn't tell you about the rape scam?'

'That, too,' said Deacon.

'It always works, you know. I met a guy once who scored five hundred off of it. Some old geezer took him in out of the goodness of his heart, and the next thing he knew this kid was screaming rape all over the place.' He smiled in a friendly way. 'I'll bet Lawrence tore strips off you for inviting me back here – he's sharp as a tack, that one – but he's wrong if he thinks I'd turn on you. Billy taught me this saying: never bite the hand that feeds you. So you've got nothing to worry about, okay? You're safe with me.'

Deacon opened the front door and reached inside for the light switch. 'That's good news, Terry. It lets us both off the hook.'

'Oh, yeah? You had something planned just in case, did you?'

'It's called revenge.'

Terry's smile broadened into a grin. 'You can't take revenge on an under-age kid. The cops'd crucify you.'

Deacon smiled back, but rather unpleasantly. 'What makes you think you'd still be a kid when it's done or that I'm the one who'd do it? Here's another saying Billy should have taught you: revenge is a dish best eaten cold.' His voice dropped abruptly to sound like sifted gravel. 'You'll have a second or two to remember it when a psycho like Denning does to you what was done to Walter this afternoon. And, if you're lucky, you'll *live* to regret it.'

'Yeah, well it's not going to happen, is it?' muttered Terry, somewhat alarmed by Deacon's tone. 'Like I said, you're safe with me.'

Terry was deeply critical of Deacon's flat. He didn't like the way the front door opened into the sitting-room – 'Jesus, it means you've got to be well tidy all the time'; nor the narrow corridor that led off it to the bathroom and the two bedrooms – 'It'd be bigger without these stupid walls all over the place'; only the kitchen passed muster because it was attached to the sitting-room – 'I guess that's pretty handy for TV dinners.' Once all his underlying odours had been effectively soaked away, he prowled around it in a pair of overwide jeans and a jumper, shaking his head over the blandness of it all. He reeked strongly of Jazz aftershave ('Nicked from a chemist,' he said proudly), which Deacon had to admit introduced an exotic quality into the atmosphere that hadn't been there before.

The final verdict was damning. 'You're not a boring bloke, Mike, so how come you live in such a boring place?'

'What's boring about it?' Deacon was using a long-handled wooden spoon to poke Terry's patchwork quilt with infinite care into the washing-machine. He kept his eyes peeled for anything that looked like hopping, although as his only plan was to try to whack the offending parasites with the head of the spoon, it was fortunate they never emerged.

Terry waved an arm in a wide, encompassing circle. 'The only room that's even half-way reasonable's your bedroom, and that's only because there's a stereo and a load of books in there. You ought to have more bits and pieces at your age. I reckon I've got more fucking stuff – sorry – and I ain't been knocking around half as long as you.'

Deacon produced his cigarettes and handed one to the boy. 'Then don't get married. This is what two divorces can do to you.'

'Billy always said women were dangerous.'

'Was he married?'

'Probably. He never talked about it though.' He pulled open the kitchen cupboard doors. 'Is there anything to drink in this place?'

'There's some beer in the fridge and some wine in a rack by the far wall.'

'Can I have a beer?'

Deacon took two cans from the fridge and tossed one across. 'There are glasses in the cupboard to your right.'

Terry preferred to drink from the can. He said it was more American.

'Do you know much about America?' Deacon asked him.

'Only what Billy told me.'

Deacon pulled out a kitchen chair and straddled it. 'What did Billy say about it?'

'He didn't rate it much. Reckoned it'd been corrupted by money. He liked Europe better. He were always talking about commies. Said they took after Jesus.'

The phone rang, but as neither of them answered it, the tape went into action. '*Michael, it's Hugh,*' said his brother-in-law's tipsy voice over the amplifier. '*I'll be in the Red Lion in Deanery Street tomorrow at lunchtime. I'm not going to apologize now because it's only fair you break my nose first. I'll apologize afterwards. Hope that's okay.*'

Terry frowned. 'What was that about?'

'Revenge,' said Deacon. 'I told you, it's a dish best eaten cold.'

Chapter Ten

THREE MILES AWAY in Fleet Street, Barry Grover skulked in the shadows waiting for Glen Hopkins's shift to finish. Only when the replacement, Reg Linden, had been *in situ* for fifteen minutes did he scuttle across the road and let himself in. Reg, who as nightwatchman had very little contact with *Street* employees, had long since ceased to question Barry's nocturnal visits to the offices, even looked forward to them for the company they offered. He took as much interest in Barry's researches as Barry did himself, and his view – untarnished by female gossip – was that the little man's problem was a tendency to insomnia. In that peculiarly uncomplicated way reserved to men who don't seek to know too much about each other, he and Barry were friends.

He smiled affably. 'Still trying to identify your dead wino?' he asked.

Barry nodded. Had Reg been a little more perceptive, he might have wondered at the little man's agitation, he might even have questioned why Barry's fly was undone, but fate had ruled him an unobservant man.

'This might help,' he said, producing a paperback from under the desk. 'You want chapter five – missing persons. No pictures, I'm afraid, but some useful information on James Streeter. Mrs Linden came across it in a bookshop and thought you might like it. She's always been interested in your projects.' He waved Barry's thanks aside, and promised to bring him a cup of tea when he made one for himself.

Deacon emptied another bag of washing into the machine. 'You said there was stuff in the warehouse that belonged to Billy,' he reminded Terry. 'Was that a ploy to get me down there or was it true?'

'True, but you'll have to pay if you want to see it.'

'Where is it?'

Terry jerked his head towards the sitting-room, where the suitcases stood in a corner. 'In there.'

'What's to stop me going through the cases myself?'

'One of these.' The lad clenched his right hand into a fist. 'I'll lay you flat, and if you hit me back, I'll have proof of assault.' He smiled engagingly. 'Sexual or the other kind, depending on my mood.'

'How much do you want?'

'My mate got five hundred off of his old geezer.'

'Bog off, Terry. Billy can go hang for all I care. I'm bored with him.'

'Like hell you are. He's bugging you, same as he bugs me. Four hundred.'

'Twenty.'

'One hundred.'

'Fifty, and it'd better be good' – Deacon clenched his own hand into a fist – 'or *you*'ll be on the receiving end of one of these. And to hell with the consequences, frankly.'

'It's a deal. Give us the fifty.' Terry uncurled his palm. 'Cash only, or all bets are off.'

Deacon nodded towards the kitchen cabinets. 'Third cupboard along, biscuit tin on the second shelf, take five tens and leave the rest.' He watched the boy locate the tin, remove the wad of notes inside it and peel off £50.

'Jesus, but you're a weird bastard, Mike,' he said resuming his seat. 'There must be another two hundred in there. What's to stop me nicking it, now you've shown me where it is?'

'Nothing,' said Deacon, 'except it's mine, and you haven't earned it. Not yet, anyway.'

'What'd I have to do to earn it?'

'Learn to read.' He saw the cynical look in Terry's eyes. 'I'll teach you.'

'Sure you will, for two miserable days. And when I still can't read at the end of it, you'll get mad and I'll've wasted my time for nothing.'

'Why didn't Billy teach you?'

'He tried once or twice,' said the boy dismissively, 'but he couldn't see well enough to teach anything 'cept what was in his head. It were another of his punishments. He poked a pin into his eye one time, which meant he couldn't read very long without getting a headache.' He took another cigarette. 'I told you, he were a right nutter. He were only happy when he were hurting himself.'

*

They were the most meagre of possessions: a battered postcard, some crayons, a silver dollar, and two flimsy letters which were in danger of falling apart from having been read so often. 'Is this all there was?' asked Deacon.

'I told you before. He didn't want nothing and he didn't have nothing. A bit like you if you think about it.'

Deacon spread the items across the table. 'Why weren't these on him when he died?'

Terry shrugged. 'Because he told me to burn them a few days before he buggered off that last time. I hung on to them in case he changed his mind.'

'Did he say why he wanted them burned?'

'Not so's you'd notice. It was while he was in one of his mad fits. He kept yelling that everything was dust, then told me to chuck this lot on the fire.'

'Dust to dust and ashes to ashes,' murmured Deacon, picking up the postcard and turning it over. It was blank on one side and showed a reproduction of Leonardo da Vinci's cartoon of *The Virgin and Child with St Anne* on the other. It was worn at the edges and there were crease marks across the glossy surface of the picture, but it required more than that to diminish the power of da Vinci's drawing. 'Why did he have this?'

'He used to copy it on to the pavement. That's the family he drew.' Terry touched the figure of the infant John the Baptist to the right of the picture. 'He left this baby out' – his finger moved to the face of St Anne – 'turned this woman into a man and drew the other woman and the baby that's on her knee the way they are. Then he'd colour it in. It were bloody good, too. You could see what was what in Billy's picture whereas this one's a bit of a mess, don't you reckon?'

Deacon gave a snort of laughter. 'It's one of the world's great masterpieces, Terry.'

'It ain't as good as Billy's. I mean, look at the legs. They're all mixed up, so Billy sorted them. He gave the bloke brown legs and the woman blue legs.'

With a muffled guffaw, Deacon lowered his forehead to the table. He reached surreptitiously for a handkerchief from his pocket and blew his nose loudly before sitting up again. 'Remind me to show you the original one day,' he said a little unsteadily. 'It's in the National Gallery in Trafalgar Square and I'm not as convinced as you that the legs need – er – sorting.' He took a pull at his beer can. 'Tell me how Billy managed to do these paintings if he couldn't see properly.'

'He could see to draw – I mean, he were drawing every night on bits of paper – and, anyway, he made his pavement pictures really big. It were only reading that gave him a headache.'

'What about the writing that you said he put at the bottom of the picture?'

'He did it big like the painting, otherwise people wouldn't have noticed it.'

'How do you know what it said if you can't read?'

'Billy learned it to me so I could write it myself.' He pulled Deacon's notebook and pencil towards him and carefully formed the words across the page.

Blessed are the poor

'If you can do that,' said Deacon matter-of-factly, 'you can learn to read in two days.' He took up one of the letters and spread it carefully on the table in front of him.

Cadogan Square
April 4th

Darling,
Thank you for your beautiful letter, but how I wish you could enjoy the here and now and forget the future. Of course I am flattered that you want the world to know you love me, but isn't what we have more perfect because it is a secret? You say your glass shall not persuade you you are old, so long as youth and I are of one date, but, my darling, Shakespeare never named his love because he knew how cruel the world could be. Do you want me pilloried as a calculating bitch who set out to seduce any man who could offer her security? For that is what will happen if you insist on acknowledging me publicly. I adore you with all my heart but my heart will break if you ever stop loving me because of what people say. Please, <u>please</u>, let's leave things the way they are. Your loving V.

Deacon unfolded the second letter and placed it beside the first. It was written in the same hand.

Paris
Friday

Darling,
Don't think me mad but I am so afraid of dying. I

have nightmares sometimes where I float in black space beyond the reach of anyone's love. Is that what hell is, do you think? For ever to know that love exists while for ever condemned to exist without it? If so, it will be my punishment for the happiness I've had with you. I can't help thinking it's wrong for one person to love another so much that she can't bear to be apart from him. Please, please, don't stay away any longer than is necessary. Life isn't life without you. V.

'Did Billy read these to you, Terry?'

The boy shook his head.

'They're love letters. Rather beautiful love letters, in fact. Do you want to hear them?' He took Terry's shrug for assent and read the words aloud. He waited for a reaction when he'd finished, but didn't get one. 'Did you ever hear him talking about someone whose name began with a "v"?' he asked then. 'It sounds as if she was a lot younger than he was.'

The boy didn't answer immediately. 'Whoever she is, I bet she's dead,' he said. 'Billy told me once that hell was being left alone for ever and not being able to do nothing about it, and then he started to cry. He said it always made him cry to think of someone being that lonely, but I guess he was really crying for this lady. That's sad, isn't it?'

'Yes,' said Deacon slowly, 'but I wonder why he thought she was in hell.' He read through the letters again but found nothing to account for Billy's certainty about V's fate.

'He reckoned *he*'d go to hell. He kind of looked

forward to it in a funny sort of way. He said he deserved all the punishment the gods could throw at him.'

'Because he was a murderer?'

'I guess so. He went on and on about life being a holy gift. It used to drive Tom up the wall. He'd say' – he fell into a fair imitation of Tom's cockney accent – '"If it's so effing 'oly, what the fuck are we doing living in this soddin' 'ell of a cess-pit?" And Billy'd say' – Terry now adopted a classier tone – '"You are here by choice because your gift included free will. Decide now whether you seek to bring the gods' anger upon your heads. If the answer's no, then choose a wiser course."'

Deacon chuckled. 'Is that what he actually said?'

'Sure. I used to say it for him sometimes when he was too pissed to say it himself.' He returned to his mimicking of Billy's voice. '"You are here by choice because your gift included free will." Blah-blah-blah. He were a bit of a pillock really, couldn't see when he was annoying people. Or if he did, he didn't care. Then he'd get rat-arsed and start yelling, and that was worse because we couldn't understand what he was on about.'

Deacon fetched another two beer cans from the fridge, and chucked the empties into the bin. 'Do you remember him saying anything about repentance?' he asked, propping himself against the kitchen worktop.

'Is that the same as repent?'

'Yes.'

'He used to shout that a lot. "Repent! Repent! Repent! The hour is later than you think!" He did it that time he took all his clothes off in the middle of the fucking winter. "Repent! Repent! Repent!" he kept screaming.'

'Do you know what repentance is?'

'Yeah. Saying sorry.'

Deacon nodded. 'Then why didn't Billy follow his own advice and say sorry for this murder? He'd have been looking to heaven then instead of hell.' *Except that he'd told the psychiatrist his own redemption didn't interest him . . .*

Terry pondered this for some time. 'I get what you're saying,' he declared finally, 'but, see, I never thought about it before. The trouble with Billy was he was well noisy most of the time, and it did your head in to listen to him. And he only spoke about the murder once, when he were really worked up about something.' His eyes screwed in concentrated reflection. 'In any case, he stuck his hand in the fire straight afterwards and wouldn't take it out till we all pulled him off of it, so I guess no one thought to ask why he didn't repent himself.' He shrugged. 'I expect it's quite simple. I expect it was his fault his lady went to hell, so he felt he ought to go there too. Poor bitch.'

Deacon remembered his suspicions the first time he heard this story, when it was obvious to him that Terry was relating an incident that the other men at the warehouse knew nothing about. They had recalled the hand in the fire, but not the revelations of murder. 'Or maybe there was nothing to repent,' he suggested. 'Another way to go to hell is to destroy the gods' gift of life by killing *yourself*. For centuries, suicides were buried in wasteland to demonstrate that they had put themselves beyond the reach of God's mercy. Isn't that the path Billy was taking?'

'You asked me that one already, and I already told you, Billy never tried to kill himself.'

'He starved himself to death.'

'Nah. He just forgot to eat. That's different, that is. He were too drunk most of the time to know what he was doing.'

Deacon thought back. 'You said he strangled someone because the gods had written it in his fate. Were those the actual words he used?'

'I can't remember.'

'Try.'

'It were that or something like it.'

Deacon looked sceptical. 'You also said he burned his hand as a sacrifice to direct the gods' anger somewhere else. But why would he do that if he wanted to go to hell?'

'Jesus!' said Terry in disgust. 'How should I know? The guy was a nutter.'

'Except your definition of a nutter isn't the same as mine,' said Deacon impatiently. 'Didn't it occur to you that Billy was ranting and raving all the time because he was with a bunch of bozos who couldn't follow a single damn word he was saying? I'm not surprised he was driven to drink.'

'It wasn't our fault,' said the boy sullenly. 'We did our best for the miserable sod, and it wasn't easy keeping our cool when he were having a go at us.'

'All right, try this question. You said he was worked up about something just before he told you he was a murderer, so what was he worked up about?'

Terry didn't answer.

'Was it something personal between you and him?' said Deacon with sudden intuition. 'Is that why the others didn't know about it?' He waited for a moment. 'What happened? Did you have a fight? Perhaps he tried to strangle you and then thrust his hand in the fire out of remorse?'

'No, it were the other way round,' said the boy unhappily. 'It were me tried to strangle *him*. He only burned his bloody hand so I'd remember how close I came to murder.'

The awful irony of Barry's situation came home to him forcibly in the semi-darkness of the cuttings library when he realized he was no longer content to look at photographs of beautiful men and fantasize harmlessly about what they could do for him.

His hands trembled slightly as he separated out the photographs of Amanda Powell.

He knew everything about her, including where she lived and that she lived alone.

As far as Terry could remember, it had happened two weeks after his fourteenth birthday, during the last weekend in February. The weather had been bitter for several days, and tempers in the warehouse were frayed. It was always worse when it was cold, he explained, because if they didn't go daily to one of the soup kitchens for hot food, survival became impossible. More often than not, the older ones and the madder ones refused to emerge from whatever cocoon they had made for themselves, so Terry and Tom took it upon themselves to bully them into moving. But, as Terry said, it was a quick way to make enemies, and Billy was more easily riled than most.

'One of the reasons Tom didn't want me calling the coppers this afternoon was because of what's stashed away in that warehouse.' He produced a small wad of silver foil from his pocket and placed it on the table. 'I do puff' – he nodded to the wad – 'and maybe some E if I go to a rave. But that's kids' stuff compared to what some of them are on. There's bodies all over the shop most days, stoned on anything from jellies to H, and half the bastards don't even live there but come in off the streets for a fix because they reckon it's safer. And then there's the nicked stuff – booze and fags and the like – that people have hidden in the rubble. You have to be bloody careful not to go stumbling on someone's stash or you get a knife in the ribs the way Walter did. It can get pretty bad sometimes. This last week there's been two beatings and the stabbing. It gets to you after a while.'

'Is that why you called the police today?'

'Yeah, and because of Billy. I've been thinking about him a lot recently.' He returned to his story. 'Anyway, it were no different last February – worse, if anything, because it were colder than now, so there were more bodies than usual. If they slept on the streets, they froze where they lay, so Tom and the others let them doss inside.'

'Why didn't they go to the government-run hostels?

Surely a bed there has to be better than a floor in a warehouse?'

'Why'd you think?' said Terry scathingly. 'We're talking druggies and psychos who don't even trust their own fucking shadows.' He fingered the silver-foil wad. 'Tom was doing really well out of it. He'd let any sodding bastard in as long as he got something in exchange. He even took a guy's coat once because it was the only thing he had, and the poor bloke froze to death during the night. So Tom had him carried into the street – like he was going to do with Walter – in case the cops came in. And that's what made Billy flip his lid. He went ballistic and said it all had to stop.'

'What did he do?' prompted Deacon when the boy didn't go on.

'The worst thing he could've done. He started breaking people's bottles, and searching the rubble for stashes, and yelling that we had to get rid of the evil before it swallowed us up. So I jumped the silly bugger and tied him up in my doss before one of the psychos could kill him, and that's when he started on me.' Terry reached for another cigarette and lit it with a hand that shook slightly. 'Even you'd've said he was a nutter if you'd seen him that day. He was off his sodding rocker – shaking, screaming—' The boy pulled a wry face. 'See, once he got going he couldn't stop. He'd go on and on till he got so tired he'd give up. But he wouldn't give up this time. He kept spitting at me, and saying that I was the worst kind of scum, and when I didn't take no notice of that he started yelling out that I was a rent-boy and that anyone who wanted a bit of my arse should just come in the tent and take it.' He drew heavily on his cigarette. 'I wanted to kill him, so I put my hands round his neck and squeezed.'

'What stopped you?'

'Nothing. I went on squeezing till I thought he was dead.' He fell into a long silence which Deacon let drift. 'Then I got scared and didn't know what to do, so I untied him and pushed him about a bit to see if he really was dead, and the bugger opened his eyes and smiled at me. And that's when he told me about this bloke he'd killed, and how anger made people do things that could ruin their lives. Then he said he wanted to show the gods that it was his fault and not mine, so he went outside and stuck his hand in the fire.'

Deacon wished there had been a woman there to hear Terry's story, one who would have wrapped him in her arms and petted him, and told him there was nothing to worry about, for that most obvious course of action was denied to him. He could only look away from the tears that brightened the boy's eyes and talk prosaically about the mechanics of how to dry Terry's wet clothes overnight without the benefit of a tumble-drier.

Reg brought up Barry's tea and placed the mug on the desk beside the book his wife had bought. It was lying face down and he pointed to a quote on the back of it. '*Immensely readable.* Charles Lamb, THE STREET.'

'The wife is always happier with a recommendation,' he said, 'but, as I pointed out, it's surprisingly short for Mr Lamb. If he likes a book, he tends to go overboard.

Could "immensely readable" be the only words of praise in the review, I wonder? An example, perhaps, of a publisher's creative *dis*counting?'

One of the reasons why Reg enjoyed Barry's company so much was that Barry allowed him to practise his ponderous wit, and Barry chuckled dutifully as he picked up the paperback and turned to the imprint page. 'First published by Macmillan in 1994, so the review will have come out last year. I'll find it for you,' he offered. 'Consider it a small thank you for the book and the tea.'

'It could be interesting,' said Reg prophetically.

> ... Another mixed bag of a book is Roger Hyde's **Unsolved Mysteries of the Twentieth Century** (published by Macmillan at £15.99). Immensely readable, it nevertheless disappoints because, as the title suggests, it raises too many unanswered questions and ignores the fact that other writers have already shed light on some of these 'unsolved' mysteries. There are the infamous Digby murders of 1933, when Gilbert and Fanny Digby and their three young children were found dead in their beds of arsenic poisoning one April morning with nothing to suggest who murdered them or why. Hyde describes the background to the case in meticulous detail – Gilbert and Fanny's histories, the names of all those known to have visited the house in the days preceding the murders, the crime scene itself – but he fails to mention M. G. Dunner's book **Sweet Fanny Digby** (Gollancz, 1963) which contained evidence that Fanny Digby, who had a history of depression, had

> been seen to soak flypaper in an enamel bowl the day before she and her family were found dead. There is the case of the diplomat Peter Fenton, who walked out of his house in July 1988 after his wife Verity committed suicide. Again, Hyde describes the background to these events in detail, referring to the Driberg syndicate and Fenton's access to NATO secrets, but he makes no mention of Anne Cattrell's Sunday Times feature **'The truth about Verity Fenton'** (17 June 1990) which revealed the appalling brutality suffered by Verity at the hands of Geoffrey Standish, her first husband, before his convenient death in a hit-and-run accident in 1971. If, as Anne Cattrell claims, this was no accident, and if Verity did indeed meet Fenton six years earlier than either of them ever admitted, then the solution to her suicide and his disappearance lies in Geoffrey Standish's coffin and not in Nathan Driberg's prison cell . . .

Out of interest, Barry searched the microfiche files for the *Sunday Times* of 17 June 1990. He held his breath as Anne Cattrell's feature appeared with a full-face photograph of Peter Fenton, OBE.

He was as sure as he could be that he was looking at Billy Blake.

The truth about Verity Fenton
by Anne Cattrell

There have been few more effective smokescreens than that thrown up by Peter Fenton when he vanished from his house on 3 July 1988, leaving his wife's dead body on the marital bed. It began as a sensational Lucan-style murder hunt until Verity Fenton was found to have committed suicide. There followed a rampage through Peter's history, looking for mistresses and/or treachery, when it was discovered that he had access to NATO secrets. Interest centred on his sudden trip to Washington, and easy links were drawn with the anonymous members of the Driberg syndicate.

And where did Verity Fenton's suicide feature in all this? Barely at all is the answer because minds were focused on Peter's inexplicable disappearance and not on the reasons why a 'neurotic' woman should want to kill herself. The coroner's verdict was 'suicide while the balance of her mind was disturbed', relying largely on her daughter's evidence that she had been 'unnaturally depressed' while Peter was in Washington. Yet no real explanation for her depression was sought, as the assumption seems to have been that Peter's disappearance meant that her reference in her suicide note to his betrayals was true, and these were shocking enough to drive a woman to suicide.

Two years on from these bizarre events of July 1988, it is worth reassessing what is known about Peter and Verity Fenton. Perhaps the first thing to strike anyone researching this story is the complete lack of evidence to show that Peter Fenton was a traitor. He certainly had access to confidential NATO information during 1985–7, but sources within the organization admit that three different investigations have failed to trace any leakage of information to him or to his desk.

By contrast, there is a

wealth of evidence about his 'sudden' trip to Washington at the end of June, which was painted as a 'fishing' expedition to find out if Driberg was about to name his associates. The details of the trip were made available at the time by his immediate superior at the Foreign Office but they were ignored in the scramble to prove Fenton a traitor. The facts are that he was briefed on 6 June to attend high-level discussions in Washington from 29 June to 2 July. It is difficult now to understand how three weeks' notification came to be interpreted as 'sudden' or why, if he *were* part of the Driberg syndicate, he should have waited until eight weeks after Driberg's arrest to go 'fishing'.

The Fenton tragedy takes on a very different perspective if suggestions that Peter was a traitor are dismissed. The question that must then be asked is: what were the betrayals that Verity talked about in her suicide note? She wrote: '*Forgive me, I can't bear it any more, darling. Please don't blame yourself. Your betrayals are nothing compared with mine.*'

But why have Verity's own betrayals been so consistently under-examined? The simple answer is that, as the wife of a diplomat, she was always less interesting than her husband. What or who could a 'neurotic' woman possibly have betrayed that could compete with treachery in the Foreign Office? Yet it was imperative, even in 1988, that her betrayals be examined because she claimed they were worse than her husband's, and *he* was branded a spy.

Born Verity Parnell in London on 28 September 1937, she was brought up alone by her mother after her father, Colonel Parnell, died in 1940 during the evacuation from Dunkirk. She and her mother are believed to have spent the war years in Suffolk but returned to London in 1945. Verity was enrolled at a preparatory school before transferring to the Mary Bartholomew School for Girls in Barnes in May 1950. Although considered bright enough to go on to university, she chose instead to marry Geoffrey Standish, a handsome, 32-year-old stockbroker who was fourteen years her senior, in August 1955. The marriage caused an estrangement between herself and her mother, and it is not clear whether she saw Mrs Parnell again before the woman's death some time in the late fifties. Verity gave birth to a daughter, Marilyn, in 1960 and a son, Anthony, in 1966.

The marriage was a disaster. Geoffrey was described, even by close friends, as 'unpredictable'. He was a gambler, a womanizer and a drunk, and it soon became clear to those who knew him that he was taking out his frustrations on his young wife. There was a history of 'accidents', days of indisposition, a reluctance to do anything that might upset Geoffrey, an obsessive protectiveness towards her children. It is not surprising then that, according to one of her neighbours, Verity described her husband's death in March 1971 as a 'blessed relief'.

Like so much in this story the details surrounding Geoffrey's death are obscure. The only verifiable facts are these: he had arranged to spend the weekend alone with friends in Huntingdon; he phoned them at 5.00 p.m. on the Friday night to say he wouldn't be with them until the following day; at 6.30 a.m. on the Saturday, a police patrol recorded his car abandoned with an empty petrol tank beside the A11 near Newmarket; at 10.30 a.m. his bruised and battered body was found sprawled in a ditch some two miles up the road; his injuries were consistent with having been run over by a car.

On the face of it, it was a straightforward case of hit-and-run while Geoffrey was walking through the dark in search of petrol, but because of the last-minute alterations in his plans, the police attempted to establish why he was in the vicinity of Newmarket. They had no success with that line of enquiry, but in the course of their investigation they unearthed the unpalatable details of the man's character and lifestyle. Although they were never able to prove it, it is clear from the reports that the Cambridgeshire police believed he was murdered.

Verity herself had a cast-iron alibi. She was admitted to St Thomas's Hospital on the Wednesday before Geoffrey's death with a broken collar-bone, fractured ribs and a perforated lung, and was not discharged until the Sunday. Her children were being cared for by a neighbour, so there is some doubt about Geoffrey's whereabouts on the Friday. Certainly he did not go to work that day, and this led to police speculation that someone, whose sympathies lay with Verity, removed him from his house during the Thursday night and cold-bloodedly planned his murder over the Friday.

Unfortunately, from the police point of view, no such sympathizer could be traced, and the file was closed through lack of evidence. The coroner recorded a verdict of 'manslaughter by person or persons unknown', and Geoffrey Standish's premature death remains unpunished to this day.

Now, however, with our knowledge of the events of 3 July 1988 it is logical to look back from the suicide of a desperate woman and the disappearance of her second husband to Geoffrey's death in 1971, and ask whether the person whose sympathies lay with Verity was a young and impressionable Cambridge undergraduate called Peter Fenton. Newmarket is less than 20 miles from Cambridge, and Peter was known to make frequent visits to the family of a friend from his Winchester College days who lived ten doors away from Geoffrey and Verity Standish in Cadogan Square. There is no evidence to rebut Peter's and Verity's own claims that their first meeting was at a party at Peter's friend's house in 1978, but it would be curious if their paths hadn't crossed earlier. Certainly, the friend, Harry Grisham, remembers the Standishes being regular guests at his parents' dinner parties.

But, assuming Peter's

involvement, what could have happened seventeen years after Geoffrey's murder to drive Verity into killing herself and Peter into vanishing? Did one of them betray the other inadvertently? Had Verity been ignorant of what Peter had done, and learned by accident that she'd married her first husband's murderer? We may never know, but it is a strange coincidence that two days before Peter left for Washington the following advertisement appeared in the personal column of *The Times*:

'**Geoffrey Standish**. Will anyone knowing anything about the murder of Geoffrey Standish on the A11 near Newmarket 10.3.71 please write to Box 431.'

Chapter Eleven

TERRY WAS PUT out to discover that his clothes were still wet when he finally stumbled out of his bedroom in an old T-shirt and shorts of Deacon's, rubbing his shaven head and yawning sleep away. 'I can't go out in your God-awful stuff, Mike. I mean, I've got a reputation to consider. Know what I'm saying? You'll have to go shopping on your own while I wait for this lot to dry.'

'Okay.' Deacon consulted his watch. 'I'd better get moving then or I'll miss the chance to break Hugh's nose.'

'You really going to do that?'

'Sure. I was also planning to buy you some new gear for a Christmas present, but if you're not there to try it on—' He shrugged. 'I'll get you some reading books instead.'

Terry was back, fully dressed, in under three minutes. 'Where did you put my coat?'

'I chucked it in the bin downstairs while you were having your bath.'

'What you want to do that for?'

'It had Walter's blood all over it.' He took a Barbour from a hook on the wall. 'You can borrow this till we buy you a new one.'

'I can't wear that,' said Terry in disgust, refusing to take it. 'Jesus, Mike, I'll look like one of those poncy gits who drive around in Range Rovers. Supposing we meet someone I know?'

'Frankly,' growled Deacon, 'I'm more concerned about meeting someone *I* know. I haven't worked out yet how to explain why a foul-mouthed, shaven-headed thug is (A) staying in my flat and (B) wearing my clothes.'

Terry put on the Barbour with bad grace. 'Considering how much of my puff you smoked last night, you ought to be in a better mood.'

Barry lay in bed and listened to his mother's heavy tread on the stairs. He held his breath while she held hers on the other side of his door. 'I know you're awake,' she said in the strangulated voice that seemed to start somewhere in her fat stomach and squeeze up out of her blubbery mouth. The door handle rattled. 'Why have you locked the door?' The voice dropped to a menacing whisper. 'If you're playing with yourself again, Barry, I'll find out.'

He didn't answer, only stared at the door while his fingers gripped and squeezed her imaginary neck. He fantasized about how easy it would be to kill her and hide her body somewhere out of sight – in the front parlour, perhaps, where it could sit for months on end with no visitors to disturb it. Why should someone so unlovely and unloved be allowed to live? And who would miss her?

Not her son . . .

Barry fumbled for his glasses and brought his world back into focus. He noticed with alarm that his hands were trembling again.

'Why haven't you ever been arrested?' asked Deacon as Terry selected a pair of Levis, saying they'd be 'a doddle to nick'. (He made a habit of locating security cameras and staying blind-side of them, Deacon noticed.)

'What makes you think I ain't?'

'You'd have been sent back into care.'

The boy shook his head. 'Not unless I told them the truth about myself, which I ain't never done. Sure, I've been arrested, but I was always with old Billy when it happened so he took the rap. He reckoned I'd have trouble with poofs if I went into an adult prison, or be sent back to the shirt-lifter if I gave my right name, so it were him what did the time and not me.' His gaze shifted restlessly about the shop. 'How about a jacket then? They're on the far side.' He set off purposefully.

Deacon followed behind. Were all adolescents so ruthlessly self-centred? He had an unpleasant picture of this terrible child latching on to protectors like a leech in order to suck them dry, and he realized that Lawrence's advice about keeping one step ahead was about as useful as pissing in the wind. Any half-way decent man with a sense of moral duty was putty in Terry's hands, he thought.

'I like this one,' said Terry, taking a donkey-jacket off

a coat hanger and thrusting his arms into the sleeves. 'What d'you think?'

'It's about ten times too big for you.'

'I'm still growing.'

'I'm damned if I'll be seen walking around with a mobile barrage balloon.'

'You ain't got the first idea of fashion, have you? Everyone wears things big these days.' He tried the next size down. 'Tight stuff's what guys like you pranced around in in the seventies, along with flares and beads and long hair and that. Billy said it was good to be young then, but I reckon you must've looked like a load of poofs.'

Deacon lifted his lip in a snarl. 'Well, you've got nothing to worry about then,' he said. 'You look like a paid-up member of the National Front.'

Terry looked pleased with himself. 'I ain't got a problem with that.'

Barry stood in the doorway and watched the back of his mother's head as she was slumped on a chair in front of the television, her feet propped on a stool. Sparse, bristly hair poked out of her pink scalp and cavernous snores roared from her mouth. The untidy room smelt of her farts, and a sense of injustice overwhelmed him. It was a cruel fate that had taken his father and left him to the mercies of a . . .

his fingers flexed involuntarily.

. . . *PIG!*

*

Terry found a shop that was selling Christmas decorations and posters. He selected a reproduction of Picasso's *Woman in a Chemise* and insisted Deacon buy it.

'Why that one?' Deacon asked him.

'She's beautiful.'

It was certainly a beautiful painting, but whether or not the woman herself was beautiful depended on taste. It marked the transition between Picasso's blue and rose periods, so the subject had the cold, emaciated melancholy of the earlier period enlivened by the pink and ochre hues of the later. 'Personally, I prefer a little more flesh,' said Deacon, 'but I'm happy to have her on my wall.'

'Billy drew her more than anyone else,' said Terry surprisingly.

'On the pavements?'

'No, on the bits of paper we used to burn afterwards. He copied her off of a postcard to begin with but he got so good at it that he could do her out of his head in the end.' He traced his finger along the clear lines of the woman's profile and torso. 'See, she's real simple to draw. Like Billy said, there's no mess in this picture.'

'Unlike the Leonardo?'

'Yeah.'

It was true, thought Deacon. Picasso's woman was glorious in her simplicity – and so much more delicate than da Vinci's plumper Madonna. 'Maybe you should become an artist, Terry. You seem to have an eye for a good painting.'

'I've been up Green Park once or twice to look at the stuff on the railings, but that's crap. Billy always said he'd take me to a proper gallery but he never got around to it. They probably wouldn't've let us in anyway, not with Billy roaring drunk most of the time.' He was flicking through the poster rack. 'What d'you reckon to this? You reckon this painter saw hell the same way Billy's lady did? Like being alone and afraid in a place that doesn't make sense to you?'

He had pulled out Edvard Munch's *The Scream* with its powerful, twisted imagery of a man screaming in terror before the elemental forces of nature. 'You really do have an eye,' said Deacon in admiration. 'Did Billy draw this one as well?'

'No, he wouldn't have liked it. There's too much red in it. He hated red because it reminded him of blood.'

'Well, I'm not having that on my wall or I'll think about hell every time I look at it.' *And blood*, he thought. He wished he and Billy had less in common.

They settled on reproductions of the Picasso (for its simplicity), Manet's *Luncheon in the Studio* (for its harmonious symmetry – 'That one works real good,' said Terry), Hieronymus Bosch's *The Garden of Earthly Delights* (for its colour and interest – 'It's well brilliant,' said Terry) and finally Turner's *The Fighting Téméraire* (for its perfection in every respect – 'Shit!' said Terry. 'That's one beautiful picture').

'What happened to Billy's postcard of the Picasso?' asked Deacon as he was paying.

'Tom burned it.'

'Why?'

'Because he was well out of order. He and Billy were drunk as lords and they'd been having a row about women. Tom said Billy was too ugly ever to've had one, and Billy said he couldn't be as ugly as Tom's missus or Tom wouldn't've walked out on her. Everyone laughed and Tom was gutted.'

'What did that have to do with the postcard?'

'Nothing much, except Billy really loved it. He kissed it sometimes when he was drunk. Tom was that riled at having his missus insulted, he went for something he knew'd send Billy mad. It worked, too. Billy damn near throttled Tom for burning it, then he burst into tears and said truth was dead anyway, so nothing mattered any more. And that were the end of it.'

It was six years since Deacon had last visited the Red Lion. It had been his local when he and Julia had lived in Fulham and Hugh had been in the habit of meeting him there a couple of times a month on his way home to Putney. The outside had changed very little over the years and Deacon half-expected to find the same landlord and the same regulars inside when he pushed open the doors. But it was a room full of strangers where the only recognizable face was Hugh's. He was sitting at a table in the far corner, and he raised a tentative hand in greeting when he saw Deacon.

'Hello, Michael,' he said, standing up as they approached. 'I wasn't sure if you'd come.'

'Wouldn't have missed it for the world. It might be the only chance I ever get to flatten you.' He beckoned Terry forward. 'Meet Terry Dalton. He's staying with me for Christmas. Terry, meet Hugh Tremayne, my brother-in-law.'

Terry gave his amiable grin and stuck out a bony hand. 'Hi. How ya doing?'

Hugh looked surprised but shook the offered hand. 'Very well, thank you. Are we – er – related?'

Terry appraised his round face and overweight figure. 'I don't reckon so, not unless you were putting it about a bit in Birmingham fifteen years ago. Nah,' he said. 'I think my dad was probably a bit taller and thinner. No offence meant, of course.'

Deacon gave a snort of laughter. 'I think Hugh was wondering if you were related to my second wife, Terry.'

'Oh, right. Why didn't he say that then?'

Deacon turned to the wall and banged his head against it for several seconds. Finally he took a deep breath, mopped his eyes with his handkerchief and faced the room again. 'It's a touchy subject,' he explained. 'My family didn't like Clara very much.'

'What was wrong with her?'

'Nothing,' said Hugh firmly, afraid that Deacon was going to embarrass him and Terry with references to tarts and sluts. 'What are you both having? Lager?' He escaped to the bar while they divested themselves of their coats and sat down.

'You can't hit *him*,' said Terry. 'Okay, he's a pillock, but he's about six inches shorter than you and ten years older. What did he do, anyway?'

Deacon propped his feet on a chair and laced his hands behind his head. 'He insulted me in my mother's house and then ordered me out of it.' He smiled slightly. 'I swore I'd deck him the next time I saw him, and this is the next time.'

'Well, I wouldn't do it if I were you. It don't make you any bigger, you know. I felt well gutted after what I did to Billy.' He nodded his thanks as Hugh returned with their drinks.

There was a painful silence while Hugh sought for something to say and Deacon grinned at the ceiling, thoroughly enjoying his brother-in-law's discomfort.

Terry offered Hugh a cigarette, which he refused. 'Maybe if you apologized, he'd forget the beating,' he suggested, lighting his own cigarette. 'Billy always said it were harder to hit someone you'd had a natter with. That's why guys who do violence tell people to keep their mouths shut. They're scared shitless of losing their bottle.'

'Who's Billy?'

'An old geezer I used to know. He reckoned talking was better than fighting, then he'd get rat-arsed and start attacking people. Mind, he were a bit of a nutter, so you couldn't really blame him. His advice was good, though.'

'Stop meddling, Terry,' said Deacon mildly. 'I want some answers before we get anywhere near an apology.' He lowered his feet from the chair and leaned across the table. 'What's going on, Hugh? Why am I so popular suddenly?'

Hugh took a mouthful of lager while he weighed up his answer. 'Your mother isn't well,' he said carefully.

'So Emma told me.'

'And she's keen to bury the hatchet with you.'

'Really?' He reached for the cigarette packet. 'Would that explain the daily phone messages at my office?'

Hugh looked surprised. 'Has she?'

'No, of course she hasn't. I haven't heard a word from her in five years, not since she accused me of killing my father. Which is odd, don't you think, if she wants to bury the hatchet?' He bent his head to the match.

'You know your mother as well as I do.' Hugh sighed. 'In sixteen years I've never heard her admit to being wrong about anything, and I can't see her starting now. I'm afraid you're expected to make the first move.'

Deacon's eyes narrowed suspiciously. 'This isn't what Ma wants, is it? It's what Emma wants. Is she feeling guilty about stripping Ma of her capital? Is that what this is about?'

Hugh toyed unhappily with his beer glass. 'Frankly, I've had about as much of your family squabbles as I can take, Michael. It's like living in the middle of a war zone being married to a Deacon.'

Deacon gave a low chuckle. 'Be grateful you weren't around when my father was alive then. It was worse.' He tapped his cigarette against the ashtray. 'You might as well spit it out. I'm not going anywhere near Ma unless I know why Emma wants me to.'

Again, Hugh appeared to weigh his answer. 'Oh, to hell with it!' he said abruptly. 'Your father did make a new will. Emma found it, or should I say the pieces, when she was sorting through your mother's things while she was in hospital. She asked us to pay her bills and keep everything ticking over while she was off games. I suppose she'd forgotten that the will was still sitting there, although why she didn't burn it or throw it away—' He gave a hollow laugh. 'We stuck it back together again. His first two bequests were made out of duty. He left the cottage in Cornwall to Penelope plus enough investments to provide her with an income of ten thousand a year, and he left Emma a lump sum of twenty thousand. The third bequest was made out of love. He left you the farmhouse and the residue of the estate because, and I quote, "Michael is the only member of my family who cares whether I live or die." He made it two weeks before he shot himself, and we assume it was your mother who tore it up as she's the only one who benefited under the old will.'

Deacon smoked thoughtfully for a moment or two. 'Did he appoint David and Harriet Price as executors?'

'Yes.'

'Well, at least that vindicates poor old David.' He thought back to the furious row his mother had had with their then next-door neighbours when David Price had dared to suggest that Francis Deacon had talked about making a new will with him as executor. '*Show it to me*,' she had said, '*tell me what's in it*.' And David had had to admit that he had never seen it, only agreed in principle to act as executor should Francis revoke his previous will. 'Who drew it up?'

'We think your father did it himself. It's in his handwriting.'

'Is it legal?'

'A solicitor friend of ours says it's properly worded and properly witnessed. The witnesses were two of the librarians in Bedford general library. Our friend's only caveat was whether your father was in sound mind when he made it, bearing in mind he shot himself two weeks later.' He shrugged. 'But, according to Emma, he had been right as rain for months prior to his suicide and only became really depressed the day before he pulled the trigger.'

Deacon glanced at Terry who was wide-eyed with curiosity. 'It's a long story,' he said, 'which you don't want to hear.'

'You can shorten it, can't you? I mean, you know all about me. Seems only fair I should know a bit about you.'

It was on the tip of Deacon's tongue to say he didn't even know what Terry's real name was, but he decided against it. 'My father was a manic depressive. He was supposed to take drugs to control the condition, but he wasn't very reliable and the rest of us suffered.' He saw that Terry didn't understand. 'Manic depression is typified by mood swings. You can be high as a kite in a manic phase – it's a bit like being stoned – and suicidal in a depressed phase.' He drew on his cigarette then ground the butt out under his heel. 'On Christmas Day 1976, while depressed, my father put his shotgun in his mouth at four o'clock in the morning and blew his head away.' He smiled slightly. 'It was very quick, very loud and very messy, and it's why I try to forget that Christmas even exists.'

Terry was impressed. 'Shit!' he said.

'It's also why Emma and Michael are so difficult to live with,' said Hugh drily. 'They're both scared to death they've inherited manic depressive psychosis, which is why they resist feeling happy about anything and view mild *un*happiness as the onset of clinical depression.'

'It's in the genes then, is it? Billy were big on genes. He always said you couldn't escape what your parents programmed into you.'

'No, it's not in the genes,' said Hugh crossly. 'There's evidence suggesting hereditary predisposition but innumerable other factors would have to come into play to precipitate the same psychosis in Emma and Michael as occurred in Francis.'

Deacon laughed. 'That means I'm not a nutter yet,' he told Terry. 'Hugh's a civil servant, so he likes to be precise in his definitions.'

Terry frowned. 'Yeah, but why'd your mother accuse you of killing your dad if he topped himself?'

Deacon drank his lager in silence.

'Because she's a bitch,' said Hugh flatly.

Deacon stirred himself. 'She said it because it's true. He told me at eleven o'clock on Christmas Eve that he wanted to die, and I gave him the go-ahead to do it. Five hours later he was dead. My mother thinks I should have persuaded him out of it.'

'Why didn't you?'

'Because he asked me not to.'

'Yeah, but—' The boy's puzzled eyes searched Deacon's face. 'Didn't you mind if he died? I was well gutted every time Billy tried to hurt himself. I mean, you feel responsible like.'

Deacon held his gaze for a moment then looked down at his glass. 'It's a good expression – gutted. It's exactly how I felt when I heard the shot. And, yes, of course I minded, but I'd stopped him before, and this time he said he was going to do it anyway and would rather do it with my blessing than without. So I gave him my blessing.' He shook his head. 'I hoped he wouldn't go through with it, but I wanted him to know I wouldn't condemn him if he did.'

'Yeah, but—' said Terry again. He was more disturbed by the story than Deacon would have expected, and he wondered if there were resonances in it of his friendship with Billy. Had Terry lied about Billy not trying to kill himself? he wondered. Or perhaps, like Deacon, he had lost interest and had aided and abetted a suicide through apathy?

'But what?' he asked.

'Why didn't you say something to your mum, give her a chance like to stop him?'

Deacon looked at his watch. 'How about we leave that question till later?' he suggested. 'We've still got food to buy and I haven't settled what I'm going to do to Hugh's nose yet.' He lit another cigarette and studied his brother-in-law through the smoke for a second or two. 'Why didn't Emma throw the pieces of this will away when she found them?' He smiled rather cynically at Hugh's expression. 'Let me guess. She didn't realize he'd only left her twenty thousand until she'd stuck it back together again, by which time you and your girls had seen it too.'

'She was curious. She'd have brought it home anyway. But, yes, she hoped – we both hoped – that he'd left her enough to wipe out the debt we owe your mother. As things stand, Penelope's used money that's rightfully yours, so we're actually in debt to you. And I swear to you, Michael, it's not money we even asked for. Your mother went on and on and on about how she wanted to do something for the only grandchildren she was going to have, then I mentioned one day that we were worried about Antonia's poor grades, and that was it. Penelope set up an educational trust and Antonia and Jessica were in private boarding school within a couple of months.'

Deacon took that with a pinch of salt. Knowing Hugh and Emma, there would have been endless little hints until Penelope paid up. 'Are they doing well?'

'Yes. Ant's doing A levels and Jesse's doing GCSEs.' He rubbed a worried hand across his bald head. 'That trust was set up to pay the equivalent of twelve years' schooling – five years for Ant because she was two years older when it started, and seven for Jesse – and they've already had nearly ten between them. We're talking a lot of money, Michael. You've probably no idea how expensive private boarding education is.'

'Let me guess. Upwards of a hundred and fifty thousand so far?' He lifted an amused eyebrow. 'You obviously didn't read my piece on selective education. I researched the whole subject in depth, including cost. Has it been money well spent?'

Hugh shrugged unhappily, forced to consider his daughters' merits. 'They're very bright,' he said, but Deacon had the impression he would've liked to have said they were nice. 'We need to sort this out, Michael. Frankly, it's a nightmare. As I see it, the situation is this.

Your mother deliberately tore up your father's will and stole her children's inheritance, for which she will be prosecuted if the whole thing's made public. She has materially altered your father's estate by selling the cottage in Cornwall and by setting up a trust fund for the girls. Against that, had you inherited what Francis left you, presumably Julia would have taken half its value in her divorce settlement and Clara would have taken half of what was left in hers, leaving you with a quarter share of what you inherited. For all I know, they may still be entitled to do that.' He raised his hands in a gesture of despair. 'So where do we go from here? What do we do?'

'You've left out your resentment at paying through the nose for Ma's private nursing care,' murmured Deacon. 'Doesn't that play a part in this complicated equation?'

'Yes,' Hugh admitted honestly. 'We accepted the trust money in good faith, believing it to be a gift, but the quid pro quo seems to be that Emma and I must fork out indefinitely for a live-in nurse, which we can't afford. Your mother claims she's dying, which means the expenditure won't go on for very much longer, but her doctors say she's good for another ten years.' He pressed finger and thumb to the bridge of his nose. 'I've tried to explain to her that if we could afford that level of private nursing care, we wouldn't have had to use her money to pay the girls' school fees, but she won't listen to reason. She refuses to sell her house, refuses to come and live with us. She just makes sure the weekly bill is sent to our address.' His voice hardened. 'And it's driving me mad. If I thought I could get away with it, I'd have put a pillow over her face months ago and done us all a favour.'

Deacon studied him curiously. 'What do you expect me to achieve by talking to her? If she won't listen to you, she certainly won't listen to me.'

Hugh sighed. 'The obvious way out of the mess is for her to sell the farm, invest the capital and move into a nursing home somewhere. But Emma thinks she's more likely to accept that suggestion if it comes from you.'

'Particularly if I hold Pa's will over her head?'

Hugh nodded.

'It might work.' Deacon reached for his coat and stood up. 'Assuming I was remotely interested in helping you and Emma out of your hole. But I have a real problem understanding why you think you're entitled to so much of Pa's wealth. Here's an alternative suggestion. Sell your own house and pay Ma back what you owe her.' His smile was not a friendly one. 'At least it means you'll be able to look her in the eye the next time you call her a bitch.'

Chapter Twelve

DEACON SELECTED A frozen turkey and chucked it into the supermarket trolley. He had been like a bear with a sore head since they'd left the pub, and Terry had been careful not to antagonize him further since remarking in the car that it wasn't surprising Deacon's old man had shot himself if all the women in his family were such cows.

'What would you know about it?' Deacon had asked in an icy voice. 'Did Billy make life so difficult for you that no one wanted to know you? Would it have mattered anyway? You can't get much lower than the gutter in all conscience.'

They hadn't spoken for half an hour, but now Deacon leaned on the trolley bar and turned to the youngster. 'I'm sorry, Terry. I was out of order. It doesn't matter how angry I was, it was no excuse for rudeness.'

'It were true, though. You can't get no lower than the gutter, and it ain't rude to tell the truth.'

Deacon smiled. 'There's a lot lower than the gutter. There's the sewer and there's hell, and you're a long way from both.' He straightened. 'You're not in the gutter either, not while you're under my roof, so choose your favourite foods and we'll eat like kings.'

After five minutes he returned to something that had been nagging at him. 'Did Billy ever tell you how old he was?'

'Nope. All I know is he was old enough to be my grandfather.'

Deacon shook his head. 'According to the pathologist, he was somewhere in his mid-forties. Not much older than me, in fact.'

Terry was genuinely astonished. He stood open-mouthed with a packet of cornflakes in his hand. 'You've gotta be joking. Shit! He looked well ancient. I reckoned he was the same age as Tom, near enough, and Tom's sixty-eight.'

'But he said it was good to be young in the seventies.' He knocked the cornflakes out of the boy's hand into the trolley. 'And the seventies were only twenty years ago.'

'Yeah, but I wasn't born then, was I?'

'What's that got to do with anything?'

'It means it was a long time ago.'

'Why did Billy say truth was dead?' asked Deacon as they drove home after packing the boot with food. 'What's that got to do with a postcard?' He recalled a line from Billy's interview with Dr Irvine. '*I am still searching for truth.*'

'How the hell should I know?'

Deacon held on to his patience with difficulty. 'You

lived with the man for two years on and off but, as far as I can see, you never questioned a single damn thing he said. Where was your curiosity? You ask *me* enough bloody questions.'

'Yeah, but you answer them,' said Terry, smoothing the front of his donkey-jacket with satisfaction. 'Billy got really angry if I said "why" too many times, so I gave up asking. It wasn't worth the aggro.'

'Presumably he said it in the present tense?'

'What?'

'"Truth *is* dead so nothing matters any more."'

'Yeah, I already told you that.'

'Another word for truth is verity,' mused Deacon gnawing at it like a dog with a bone. 'Verity is a girl's name.' He glanced sideways. 'Do you think V stood for Verity? In other words when he said, "Truth is dead," did he mean "Verity is dead"?' *I am still searching for Verity?* 'And don't say, "How the hell should I know?" because I might be inclined to stop the car and ram the turkey down your throat.'

'I'm not a fucking mind reader,' said Terry plaintively. 'If Billy said, "Truth is dead," I reckon he meant, "Truth is dead."'

'Yes, but *why*?' growled Deacon. 'Which truth was he talking about? Absolute truth, relative truth, plain truth, gospel truth? Or was he talking about one particular truth – say, the murder – where the truth had never been uncovered?'

'How the—' Hastily Terry bit his tongue. 'He didn't say.'

'Then I'm going with V for Verity,' said Deacon

decisively. He drew up at some traffic lights. 'I'll go further. I'm betting she looked like the woman in Picasso's painting. Do you think that's a possibility? You said he loved the postcard and kissed it when he was drunk. Doesn't that imply she reminded him of someone?'

'Don't see why,' said Terry matter-of-factly. 'I mean, one of the guys has a picture of Madonna. He's always slobbering over her, but in his wildest dreams he never had a bird like that. I reckon it's the only way he can get a hard-on.'

Deacon let out the clutch. 'There's a difference between a photograph of a living woman who enjoys exploiting male fantasies and a portrait painted nearly a hundred years ago.'

'There probably wasn't at the time,' said Terry, after giving the matter some serious thought. 'I bet Picasso had a hard-on when he was painting his bird, and I bet he hoped other blokes'd get one, too, when they looked at her. I mean, you have to admit she's got nice tits.'

1.00 p.m. – Cape Town, South Africa

'Who *is* that woman?' asked an elderly matron of her daughter, nodding towards the solitary figure at a window table. 'I've seen her here before. She's always on her own, and she always looks as if she'd rather be somewhere else.'

Her daughter followed her gaze. 'Gerry was introduced to her once. I think her name's Felicity Metcalfe.

Her husband owns a diamond mine or something. She's absolutely rolling in it, anyway.' She looked with some dissatisfaction on her small solitaire engagement ring.

'I've never seen her with a man.'

The younger woman shrugged. 'Maybe she's divorced. With a face like that, she's almost bound to be.' She smiled unkindly. 'You could cut diamonds with it.'

Her mother subjected the lonely figure to a close scrutiny. 'She is very thin,' she agreed, 'and rather sad too, I think.' She returned to her food. 'It's true what they say, darling – money doesn't buy happiness.'

'Neither does poverty,' said her daughter rather bitterly.

While Terry decorated the flat that afternoon, Deacon sat at the kitchen table and made a stab at drawing conclusions from what little information he had. He threw out questions from time to time. Why did Billy choose to doss in the warehouse? *For the same reason as the rest of us, I guess.* Did he have a thing about rivers? *He never said.* Did he mention the name of a town where he might have lived? *No.* Did he mention a university or a profession or the name of a company he might have worked for? *I don't know any universities, so I wouldn't know, would I?*

'WELL, YOU BLOODY WELL SHOULD!' roared Deacon, losing his temper. 'I have never met anyone who knows as little about what matters as you do.'

Terry poked his head round the kitchen door with a broad grin splitting his face in two. 'You'd be dead in a week if you had to live the way I do.'

'Who says?'

'Me. Any guy who reckons the names of universities are more important than knowing how to graft for food ain't got a chance when the chips are down. What matters is staying alive, and you can't eat fucking universities. D'you want to see what I've done in here? It looks well brilliant.'

He was right. After two years, Deacon's flat had a homely feel about it.

Deacon simplified his notes down to names, ages, places and connecting ideas, and grouped them together logically on a page of A4 paper, putting Billy in the centre. He propped the sheet against the wine bottle. 'You're the artist. See if you can spot patterns. I'll help you with anything you can't manage.' He crossed his arms and watched the boy scrutinize the page, reading words out loud every time Terry pointed a questioning finger.

		The Thames (any river?)
Terry Dalton (14)		
Tom Beale (68)	Cadogan Square	Paris
The warehouse	HELL	(V) - Verity? - (45+)
SUICIDE	Billy Blake (45)	IDENTITY
	MURDER	
		James Streeter (44)
		Amanda Powell (36)
		MONEY
W.F. Meredith (architects)		Nigel de Vriess (?)
Teddington flats		Lowenstein's Bank
Thamesbank Estate		Marianne Filbert (?)

'What's this hang-up with rivers?' Terry asked.

'Amanda said Billy liked to doss down as near the Thames as possible.'

'Who told her that?'

Deacon checked through a transcript he'd made of his recorded conversation with her. 'The police presumably.'

'First I've heard of it. He really hated the river. He moaned about the damp getting into his bones, and said the water reminded him of blood.'

'Why on earth should it remind him of blood?'

'I dunno. It was something to do with the river being the cord between the mother and the baby but I can't remember its name.'

'The umbilical cord.'

'That's it. He said London's full of shit and she sends her shit along the river to infect the innocent places further down.'

'You said he had a thing about genes. Was he drawing an analogy?'

'If you speak English,' said Terry scathingly, 'then I might be able to give you an answer.'

Deacon smiled. 'Do you think he was talking about his own mother? Was he saying that his mother had passed on bad genes to him through the umbilical cord?'

'He only ever mentioned London.'

'Or maybe he meant all parents pass on bad genes?'

'He only ever mentioned London,' repeated Terry stubbornly.

'I heard you the first time. It was a rhetorical question.'

'Jesus! You're so like him. Lahdy-bloody-dah, and

never mind no one knew what the fuck he was talking about.' He pointed to the 45+ beside the name Verity. 'I thought you reckoned V was younger than Billy,' he said, 'so how come you've made her the same age?'

'I've added a plus sign,' said Deacon, 'which means I'm now convinced she was older than he was.' He pulled forward V's letters. 'I was thinking about it last night. There are two ways of reading "your glass shall not persuade you you are old, so long as youth and I are of one date". Either she took the quote verbatim from her correspondent's letter or she reinterpreted it for the purposes of hers. When I first read it, I assumed it was an interpretation because she didn't put it into quotation marks, and in Shakespeare's sonnet it reads: "my glass shall not persuade me I am old", et cetera, et cetera. Now I'm more inclined to think it was a direct quote and her correspondent was talking about *her* age and *her* glass.' He shook his head at Terry's obvious incomprehension. 'Forget it, sunshine. Just accept that the letter makes more sense if V was older than her correspondent. Youth is eternally optimistic, and age is wary, and V seems to be a damn sight warier of revealing their affair than whoever she was writing to.'

'Which was Billy?'

'Probably.'

'But not definitely?'

'Right. He could have found the letters anywhere.'

Terry whistled appreciatively. 'This is well interesting. I'm beginning to wish I'd asked the old bugger a few more questions.'

'Join the club,' murmured Deacon sarcastically.

Terry demanded an explanation of the lower half of the page. Who were de Vriess, Filbert and Streeter? Why were W. F. Meredith, Teddington flats and Thamesbank Estate included? Deacon gave him a summary of the Streeter connection with Amanda Powell.

'Thamesbank Estate is where Amanda lives and Billy died,' he finished. 'Teddington is where she and James were planning a development of flats and W. F. Meredith is the firm she works for. Its offices are in a converted warehouse about two hundred yards from yours.'

'So, are you saying Billy was this Streeter guy?'

'Not unless he had some pretty radical plastic surgery.'

'But you reckon there's a connection?'

'There has to be. The odds against one woman being associated with two men who both dropped out of their lives are so high they're not worth considering. There are a thousand garages between the warehouse and Amanda's estate, so Billy *must* have had a reason for going all the way to hers.' He ran a thoughtful hand around his jawline. 'I can think of three possible explanations. First, some of the letters he liberated from the bins were hers and he found out her address and who she was by reading them. Second, he saw her coming out of the Meredith building, recognized her as someone he'd known in the past and followed her home. Third, somebody *else* recognized her and followed her, then handed that information on to Billy.'

Terry frowned. 'The second one can't be right. I mean, if he recognized Amanda, then she'd've recognized him. And she wouldn't've come round asking about him if she already knew who he was, would she?'

'It depends how much he'd changed. Don't forget, you thought he was twenty years older than he actually was. It may have gone something like this. Out of the blue, Amanda finds a dead wino in her garage who's known to the police as Billy Blake, aged sixty-five. She's sorry but not unduly concerned until she learns that his name was assumed, his age was forty-five, he was dossing near her offices and there was a good chance he had chosen her garage deliberately, at which point she pays for his cremation and goes to great lengths to find out something about him. What does that suggest to you?'

'That she thought Billy was her old man.'

Deacon nodded. 'But she must have realized she was wrong the minute she got hold of the police photographs. So why is she still obsessed with Billy?'

'Maybe you should ask her?'

'I have.' He threw the boy a withering look. 'It's not a question she wants to answer.'

Terry shrugged. 'Maybe she can't. Maybe she's as puzzled by it all as you and me. I mean, she told us she didn't know he was there till he were dead, so he can't have spoken to her. And, see, you've not explained why he went there. If he *did* recognize her, why should that make him want to die in her garage? And if he *didn't* recognize her – well, why'd he want to die in a stranger's garage? Do you get what I'm saying?'

'Yes, but you're assuming she told you the truth. Supposing she was lying about not speaking to him?' Deacon stretched his hands towards the ceiling, easing the muscles of his shoulders. He watched the boy for a moment out of the corner of his eye. 'He must have been in a pretty bad way to die as quickly as he did, so why did you let him go off on his own like that?'

'You can't blame me. Billy never listened to anything I said. In any case, he was okay the last time I saw him.'

'He can't have been, not if he was dead of starvation a few days later.'

'You've got that wrong. None of us'd seen him for about three, four weeks before he pegged it.' The memory seemed to worry him, as if he knew that it was his own apathy that had killed Billy. *Just as Deacon's apathy had killed his father.* 'He buggered off in May some time, and the next we knew was when Tom read in a newspaper that he'd turned up dead in this woman's garage.'

Deacon digested this surprising piece of information in silence for a moment or two. For some reason he had always assumed that Billy had gone directly from the warehouse to the garage. 'Do you know where he went?'

'At the time we thought he was probably banged up in one of the London nicks, but thinking about it after' – he hesitated – 'well, like Tom said, no nick would have let him starve himself, so I guess he was holed up in a place where he just stopped eating.'

'Had he done that before?'

'Sure. Loads of times when he was depressed or he'd had enough of the likes of Denning. But it was never for more than a few days and he always came back. Then I'd get him down to a soup kitchen and feed him up again. I used to look after him pretty damn well, you know, and I was gutted about the way he died. There weren't no need for it.'

'Do you know where he might have gone?'

Terry shook his head. 'Tom reckoned he went out of town, seeing as no one saw hide nor hair of him.'

'Do you know why?'

Another shake of his head.

'What was he doing before he left?'

'Got rat-arsed, same as always.'

'Anything else?'

'Like what?'

'I don't know,' said Deacon, 'but something must have persuaded him to up stumps and vanish for four weeks.' He cupped his hands and beckoned with his fingers. 'Talk to me. Was he begging that day? Did he speak to anyone? Did he see someone he recognized? Did he do anything unusual? Did he say anything before he left? What time did he go? Morning? Evening? *Think*, Terry.'

'The only thing I remember that were different,' said Terry, after obliging Deacon with several seconds of eye-screwing concentration, 'was that he got pretty excited about a newspaper he found in a bin. He used to flick through them, looking at headlines, but this time he read one of the pages and gave himself a headache. He were in a bloody awful mood for the rest of the day, then he passed out on a bottle of Smirnoff. He were gone by the next morning and we never saw him again.'

Chapter Thirteen

AS NEAR AS TERRY could remember, Billy had left some time during the week beginning the fifteenth of May. Having prised this piece of information out of him, Deacon bundled him into the car and drove to the *Street* offices. Terry grumbled the entire way, complaining that pubs and clubs were supposed to be the order of the evening, not looking through newspapers . . . Deacon's trouble was he was so old he'd forgotten how to enjoy himself . . . The fact that he hated Christmas didn't mean everyone else had to be miserable with him . . .

'ENOUGH!' roared his long-suffering host as they approached Holborn. 'This won't take long, so for Christ's sake, shut it! We can go to a pub afterwards.'

'All right, but only if you tell me about your mother.'

'Does the word "silence" make up part of your vocabulary, Terry?'

''Course it does, but you promised to answer my question about not giving her a chance to stop your dad killing himself.'

'It's simple enough,' said Deacon. 'She hadn't spoken

to him for two years, and I couldn't see her starting that night.'

'Didn't they live in the same house?'

'Yes. One at each end. She looked after him, did his washing, cooked his meals, made his bed. She just never spoke to him.'

'That sucks,' said Terry indignantly.

'She could have divorced him and left him to fend for himself,' Deacon pointed out mildly, 'or even had him institutionalized if she'd tried hard enough. That sort of thing was easier twenty years ago.' Briefly, he glanced at the boy's profile. 'He was impossible to live with, Terry – charming to people one day, abusive the next. If he didn't get his own way, he became violent, particularly if he'd been drinking. He couldn't hold down a job, loathed responsibility, but complained endlessly about everyone else's mistakes. Poor old Ma put up with it for twenty-three years before she retreated into silence.' He turned down Farringdon Street. 'She should have done it sooner. The atmosphere improved once the rows stopped.'

'How come he had all this money to leave if he didn't work?'

'He inherited it from his father who happened to own a piece of land that the government needed for the M1. My grandfather made a small fortune out of it and willed it to his only child, along with a rather beautiful farm-house which has a six-lane motorway at the bottom of its garden.'

'Jesus! And that's what your mother's nicked off of you?'

Deacon turned into Fleet Street. 'If she has, she earned it. She sent me and Emma away to boarding school at eight years old so that we wouldn't have to spend too much time under the same roof with Pa.' He drove down the alleyway beside the offices and parked in the empty car park at the back. 'The one reason he and I were still speaking at the end was because I had less to do with him than either Ma or Emma. I avoided the place like the plague, and only ever went home for Christmas. Otherwise I stayed with school and university friends.' He switched off the engine. 'Emma was far more supportive, which is why Pa left her only twenty thousand. He grew to hate her because she took Ma's side.' He turned to the youngster with a faint smile, visible in the backwash of the headlamps. 'You see, none of it's the way you thought it was, Terry. Pa made that second will out of spite, and the chances are he was the one who tore it up anyway. Hugh knows that as well as I do, but Hugh's in a mess and he's looking for a way out.'

'Are all families like yours?'

'No.'

'Well, I don't get it. You sound as though you quite like your mother, so why aren't you speaking to her?'

Deacon switched off the headlights and plunged them into darkness. 'Do you want the twenty-page answer or the three-word answer?'

'Three-word.'

'I'm punishing her.'

*

'What's up with everyone tonight?' asked Glen Hopkins as Deacon signed in. 'I've had Barry Grover here for the last two hours.' He studied Terry with interest. 'I'm beginning to think I'm the only person whose home holds any charms for him.'

Terry smiled engagingly and leaned his elbows on the desk. 'Dad here' – he jerked a thumb at Deacon – 'wanted me to see where he worked. You see, he's pretty choked about the fact Mum's been on the game since he kicked her out, and he wants to show me there are better ways of earning a living.'

Deacon seized his arm and spun him round towards the stairs. 'Don't believe a word of it, Glen. If this git carried even one of my genes, I'd throw myself off the nearest bridge.'

'Mum warned me you'd get violent,' whined Terry. 'She said you always hit first and asked questions later.'

'Shut up, you cretin!'

Terry laughed, and Glen Hopkins watched the two of them vanish up the stairs with a look of intense curiosity on his usually lugubrious face. For the first time that he could remember, Deacon had looked positively cheerful, and Glen began to imagine similarities of bone structure between the man and the boy that didn't exist.

Barry Grover was equally curious about Terry, but he had spent a lifetime masking his true feelings and merely stared at the two from behind his pebble glasses as they barged noisily through the door into the cuttings' library.

He made a strange sight, isolated as he was at a desk in the middle of the darkened room with a pool of lamplight reflecting off his lenses. Indeed his resemblance to some large, shiny-eyed beetle was more pronounced than usual and, with an abrupt movement, Deacon snapped on the overhead lights to dispel the uncomfortable image.

'Hi, Barry,' he said in the artificially hearty tone he always used towards the man, 'meet a friend of mine, Terry Dalton. Terry, meet the eyes of the *Street*, Barry Grover. If you're even remotely interested in photography and photographic art, then this is the guy you should talk to. He knows everything there is to know about it.'

Terry nodded in his friendly fashion.

'Mike's exaggerating,' said Barry dismissively, fearing he was about to be made to look a fool. He had already suffered the humiliation of Glen's knowing looks and poorly disguised curiosity when he arrived. Now he turned his back on the newcomers and pushed the photographs of Amanda Powell under a sheaf of newspaper clippings.

Terry, who was largely insensitive to undercurrents of emotion unless they had a basis in paranoid schizophrenia or drug addiction, wandered over to where Barry was sitting while Deacon got to work on the microfiche monitor in search of newspaper files from May 1995. This was not an environment Terry knew, so it didn't occur to him to question why this fat, bug-eyed little man with his pernickety gestures should be closeted alone in the semi-darkness of a large room. If he and

Deacon were there, then presumably it was quite natural for Barry Grover to be there, too.

He perched on the side of the desk. 'Mike told me you were the best in the business as we were coming up the stairs,' he confided. 'Says you've been trying to work out who Billy Blake was.'

Barry drew away a little. He found the youngster's casual invasion of his work space intimidating, and suspected Deacon of putting him up to it. 'That's right,' he said stiffly.

'Billy and me were friends, so if there's anything I can do to help, just say the word.'

'Yes, well, I usually find I work better on my own.' He made sweeping gestures with his hands, as if to clear the desk of obstruction, and in the process uncovered an underexposed print of Billy's mugshot in which the eyes, the nostrils and the line between the lips were the only clearly defined features.

Terry picked it up and examined it closely. 'That's clever,' he said with frank admiration in his voice. 'No fuss means you can see what you're looking for.' He picked up another similarly underexposed print and laid the two side by side. They were very alike, with only minor variations in the spatial relationships between the features. 'That's amazing.' Terry touched the second photograph. 'So who's this geezer?'

Barry took off his glasses and polished them on his handkerchief. It was an indication of mental torment. He couldn't bear to have his painstaking efforts pawed by this shaven-headed thug. 'He's a lorry driver called

Graham Drew,' he snapped, moving the photographs out of Terry's reach.

'How did you know he looked like Billy?'

'I have his photograph on file.'

'Jesus! You really *are* something else. You mean, you can remember all the pictures you've got?'

'It would be irresponsible to rely on memory,' Barry said severely. 'Naturally, I have a system.'

'How does that work?'

It didn't occur to Barry that the youngster's interest might be genuine. He assumed, because he had come with Deacon, that he was more sophisticated than he was and interpreted his persistent questioning as a form of teasing. 'It's complicated. You wouldn't understand.'

'Yeah, but I'm a fast learner. Mike reckons my IQ's probably above average.' Terry hooked a spare chair forward with his foot and dropped into it beside his new guru. 'I'm not promising anything but I reckon I'd be more use helping you than helping him.' He jerked his head towards Deacon. 'Words aren't my thing – know what I'm saying? – but I'm good with pictures. So, what's your system?'

Barry's hands trembled slightly as he replaced his glasses. 'On the assumption that Billy Blake was an alias, I'm working through photographs of men who have avoided police capture in the last ten years. One is looking,' he finished pedantically, 'for people who felt it necessary to change their identities.'

'That's well brilliant, that is. Mike said you were a genius.'

Barry pulled forward a folder from the back of the

desk. 'Unfortunately, there are rather a lot of them, and in some cases the only record I have is a photofit picture.'

'Why're the Old Bill after this Drew bloke?'

'He drove a cattle truck containing his wife, two children, thirty sheep and £2 million of gold bullion on to a cross-Channel ferry, and vanished somewhere in France.'

'Shit!'

Barry tittered in spite of himself. 'That's what I thought. The sheep were found wandering around a French farmer's field, but the Drews, the gold and the cattle truck were never seen again.' Nervously, he opened the folder to reveal prints and newspaper clippings. 'We could go through these together,' he invited, 'and sort them into those that are worth a second look and those that aren't. They represent the hundred or so men sought by the police in 1988.'

'Sure,' agreed the boy cheerfully. 'Then what do you say to coming out for a drink with me and Mike afterwards? Are you game or what?'

Deacon spun his chair round an hour later. 'Oi! You two! Shift your arses! Come and read this.' He cocked both forefingers at them in triumph. 'If this isn't what made Billy go walkabout, I'll eat my hat. It's the only damn thing in the news during the first half of May that makes a connection with what we've got already.'

MAIL DIARY Thursday, 11th May, 1995

Nigel offers small consolation

Following her divorce from restaurateur Tim Grayson, 58, Fiona Grayson is believed to have returned to her first husband, entrepreneur Nigel de Vriess, 48. According to her friend, Lady Kay Kinslade, Fiona is a frequent visitor to Halcombe House, Nigel's home near Andover. 'They have a lot in common, including two grown-up children,' said Lady Kay. She drew a discreet veil over the bitter divorce ten years ago when Nigel abandoned Fiona for a brief affair with Amanda Streeter, whose husband, James, later vanished with £10 million from the merchant bank that also employed Nigel de Vriess. 'Time heals everything,' said Lady Kay. She denied that Fiona is having money problems.

Nigel, who once described himself as 'the man most likely to succeed', has had a chequered career. He made his first million by the age of 30, but after disastrous losses in a failed trans-atlantic airline venture, he joined the board of Lowenstein's Merchant Bank in 1985. He left in 1991 'by mutual consent' after entering the computer software business through the purchase of Softworks, a small, underfunded company with hidden potential. He renamed it DVS, recruited a new workforce with new ideas, and turned it round in four years to become a major player in the lucrative home computer market.

Less successful in love, Nigel has been married twice and his name has been linked with some of Britain's most beautiful women. But Fiona clearly remembers him more fondly than most. One of his ex-lovers, actress Kirstin Olsen, described him memorably as: 'undersized, tight-fisted and performs better on top'. Kirstin Olsen's new romance is Arnold Schwarzenegger look-alike Bo Madesen, voted 'the sexiest hunk in the world' by readers of *Hello!* magazine.

Deacon read it aloud for Terry's benefit and chuckled when the boy laughed. 'It probably serves him right, but I feel sorry for the poor bastard. He obviously didn't compensate Ms Olsen adequately for the effort she put into her orgasms.'

'Hell has no fury like a woman scorned,' quoted Barry ponderously.

'I know that one,' said Terry. 'Billy taught it me.' He fell into his imitation of Billy's voice and declaimed theatrically: '"'*Heav'n* has no rage like love to hatred turned, nor *Hell* a fury like a woman scorn'd.' How-*ever*, Terry, that doesn't mean *fury* as in anger, it means *Fury* with a capital eff, as in the winged monsters sent by the gods to create *hell* on earth for sinners."' He beamed at the two men and returned to his own mode of speech. 'Billy reckoned they came after him every time he got pissed. It was one of his punishments, to have Furies claw at him whenever he was off his head.'

'He had a passion for hurting himself,' Deacon explained to Barry. 'He'd thrust his hands into a fire to cleanse them whenever they offended him.'

'The Furies sound more like DTs,' said Barry.

'Yeah, well, it was him used to claw himself, but he always said he was fighting off the Furies when he was doing it.' Terry pointed a finger at the monitor screen. 'So are you reckoning Billy went looking for this Nigel geezer? Why'd he want to do that?'

Deacon shrugged. 'We'll have to ask Nigel.'

'I expect this is too simplistic,' said Barry slowly, 'but could Billy just have wanted Amanda Streeter's address?

If he didn't know she was calling herself Amanda Powell, how else would he find her?'

'That's gotta be right,' said Terry admiringly. 'And that means Billy must've known James, seeing as how Amanda didn't know Billy. Know what I'm saying? So all you've gotta do now is find out the names of blokes that James knew and you'll have Billy sussed.'

Deacon shook his head in mock despair. 'We could work out who he was in five minutes if we knew how to access the information you already have in your head.' He arched an amused eyebrow. 'The man was clearly educated, he was a preacher, he was a fan of William Blake, quoted Congreve, knew his art, his classics, had views on European politics, believed in a code of ethics. Above all, he seems to have been a theologian with a particular interest in the Olympian gods and their cruel and arbitrary meddling in people's lives. So? What kind of man has those characteristics?'

Barry removed his glasses and set to work on them again. His self-loathing had become a physical pain in the pit of his stomach, and he was afraid of what he might do this time if Deacon abandoned him. He knew the other man well enough to know that if he divulged Billy's identity now, what little interest Deacon had in him would vanish. Deacon would set off with Terry in hot pursuit of Fenton, leaving Barry to the terrible confusion that had reigned in his soul for twenty-four hours. He thought of what awaited him at home, and in despair he clung to the hope that his hidden knowledge offered him. Deacon didn't need to know who Billy was

– *not yet anyway* – but he did need to know that Barry would deliver eventually.

'My father was fond of misquoting Dr Johnson,' he murmured nervously, as if fearing he was about to make a fool of himself. '"If patriotism is the last refuge of the scoundrel," he used to say, "then theism is the last refuge of the weak." I could be wrong, of course, but—' He hesitated, glanced at Terry and fell silent.

'Go on,' Deacon encouraged him.

'It's not fair to speak ill of the dead, Mike, particularly in front of their friends.'

'Billy was a murderer,' said Deacon evenly, 'and it was Terry who told me about it. I doubt he could have shown a greater weakness than that, could he?'

Barry replaced his glasses and peered at them both with a look of immense satisfaction. 'I thought it must be something like that. You see, his character was flawed. He ran away. He was a drunk. He killed himself. These are not the attributes of a strong man. Strong men face their problems and resolve them.'

'He might have been ill. Terry describes him as a nutter.'

'You told me he'd been living as Billy Blake for a minimum of four years.'

'So?'

'How could a mentally ill man maintain a false identity for four years? He would forget the rationale behind it every time he hit rock-bottom.'

It was a good point, Deacon admitted. *And yet . . .* 'Doesn't the same logic apply to a drunk?'

Barry turned to Terry. 'What did he say when he'd been drinking?'

'Not much. He usually passed out. I reckon that's why he did it.'

I define happiness as intellectual absence . . .

'You told me he used to rant and rave when he was drunk,' Deacon reminded him sharply. 'Now you're saying he passed out. Which was it?'

The boy's expression was pained. 'I'm doing my best here, okay? He ranted when he was half-cut and passed out when he was paralytic. But half-cut doesn't mean he didn't know what he was saying. That's when he got going on poetry and the day sex machine crap—'

'The what?' demanded Deacon.

'Day – sex – machine,' repeated Terry with slow emphasis.

'What's that supposed to mean?'

'How the hell should I know?'

Deacon frowned while his mind tried to make sense of the sounds. '*Deus ex machina?*' he queried.

'That's it.'

'What else did he say?'

'A load of bull usually.'

'Can you remember his exact words and how he said them?'

Terry was becoming bored. 'He said hundreds of things. Can't we go and have a drink? I'll remember better once I've had a pint. Barry wants one, too, don't you, mate?'

'Well—' The little man cleared his throat. 'I'd need to put things away first.'

Deacon looked at his watch. 'And I need to make a photocopy of this piece on de Vriess. How about giving us ten minutes' worth of Billy in a rant, Terry, while Barry and I finish off? Then we'll go pubbing and forget about it for the rest of the evening.'

'Is that a promise?'

'That's a promise.'

Terry's performance was a *tour de force* which Deacon captured on a tape cassette. The youngster had an extraordinary talent for sustaining a different voice from his own but whether it sounded anything like Billy was impossible to tell. He assured Deacon it was a perfect imitation until Deacon replayed the first thirty seconds and Terry collapsed in heaps of laughter because he sounded like an 'upper-class twit'. The content of the speech was largely irrelevant, in so far as it was a repetition of Billy's belief in gods and retribution together with the few snippets of poetry that Terry had already recalled for Deacon. Also, and disappointingly, Terry left out any reference to *deus ex machina* because, as he said afterwards, he'd never really understood what Billy was talking about, so it made it more difficult to remember the words he'd used.

Deacon, who had been thoroughly entertained by the entire proceedings, gave him a friendly punch on the arm and told him not to worry about it. However, Barry, to whom most of it was new, had listened with grave attention, and rewound the tape to isolate a small passage which followed a listing of gods.

'*. . . and the most terrible of all is Pan, the god of desire. Close your ears before his magical playing drives you insane and the angel comes with the key to the bottomless pit and casts you down for ever. You will wait in vain for the one who descends in clouds to raise you up. Only Pan is real . . .*'

'Couldn't "the one who descends in clouds to raise you up" be Billy's *deus ex machina*?' he suggested. 'Think of pantomimes and the good fairy emerging from dry-ice vapour to wave her wand and effect a happy ending.'

'And if it is?' Deacon prompted him.

'Well' – Barry marshalled his thoughts – 'Pan was a Roman god, but if I remember correctly "the angel with the key to the bottomless pit" comes from the Book of Revelation, which is of Judaeo-Christian inspiration. So Billy seems to have believed that it was the *pagan* gods who ensnared men into sin, but the *Judaeo-Christian* God who exacted punishment. Which must have left him very confused about where salvation lay. Should he placate the pagan gods, as he seems to have done with this business of burning his hand, or the Christian God through his preaching?'

'Where does "the one descending in clouds" fit in?'

'I think that's his symbolic view of salvation. He talks about waiting "in vain", so he obviously doesn't believe in it – or not for himself anyway – but if it does happen, it will be in the form of a *deus ex machina*, a sudden amazing apparition who reaches into the bottomless pit to raise him up.'

'Poor bastard,' said Deacon with feeling. 'I wonder what sort of murder it was that made him think he was beyond the pale of salvation?' He shivered suddenly and noticed that Terry was rubbing his hands in an effort to keep warm. 'Come on, it's damn cold in here. Let's go and get that drink.'

Barry watched Terry play the fruit machines with money supplied by Deacon. 'He's a nice lad,' he said.

Deacon lit a cigarette and followed his gaze. 'He's been living on the streets since he was twelve years old. It sounds as if he has Billy to thank for the fact that he's as straight as he is.'

'What will you do with him when Christmas is over?'

'I don't know. He needs educating but I can't see him agreeing to going back into care. It's a bit of a poser really, one of those bridges you only cross when you come to it.' He turned back to Barry. 'Was he helpful on the photographs?'

'A little quick to discard the improbables, but it doesn't seem to register with him that Billy was much younger than he looked. I had to rescue one or two.' He took an envelope from his pocket which contained various prints. He spread them across the table. 'What do you think of these?'

Deacon isolated a high-quality photocopy of a young fair-haired man staring directly into the camera. 'I recognize this one. Who is he?'

Barry tittered happily. 'That's James Streeter, taken twenty-odd years ago when he graduated from Durham University. He was brought up in Manchester so, out of interest, I applied to the local newspapers and one of them produced that. It's extraordinary, isn't it?'

'He's a dead ringer for Billy.'

'Only because he was thinner and appears to have had his hair bleached.'

Deacon took out his print of Billy and laid it beside the young James Streeter. 'Have you compared these two on the computer?'

'Yes, but they're not the same man, Mike. It's a closer match because we're looking at a similar relationship between camera angle and subject, but the differences are still obvious. Most notably the ears.' He picked up the cigarette packet and placed it across the bottom half of Billy's face with the upper edge touching the bottom of an ear lobe. 'It *is* all about angle, of course, but Billy's lobes are larger than James's and their bottom edge is roughly in line with his mouth.' He moved the packet to the other photograph and placed it in the same position. 'James has hardly any lobe at all and the bottom edge is in line with his nostrils. If you synchronize the eyes, nose and mouth on the computer, the ears immediately part company, and if you tilt the angles to synchronize the ear lobes then the rest parts company.'

'You're pretty good at this, aren't you?'

Pleased colour tinged Barry's plump cheeks. 'It's something I enjoy doing.' He nudged the other prints, artfully isolating a profile shot of Peter Fenton. 'Do you recognize anyone else?'

Deacon shook his head. He took a last look at James Streeter, then pushed the photographs aside. 'It's a wild-goose chase,' he said dispiritedly. 'I'm beginning to think Billy's a side issue anyway.'

'In what way?'

'It depends what Amanda Powell's agenda was when she told me about him. She must have known I'd find out about James, so whose story am I supposed to be investigating? Billy's or James's?' He drew thoughtfully on his cigarette. 'And where does Nigel de Vriess fit in? Why would he give Amanda's address to a complete stranger?'

'Perhaps he doesn't like her,' said Barry, tacitly disclosing his own prejudices.

'He did once. He left his wife for her. In any case, however much you dislike someone, you don't give their address to any old nutter who turns up.' He eyed Barry curiously. 'Do you?'

'No.' Barry looked uncomfortably at the photograph of Peter Fenton. 'I suppose it's possible they knew each other from before.'

Deacon followed his gaze. 'Nigel and Billy?'

'Yes.'

He looked sceptical. 'Wouldn't he have told Amanda who he was? Why talk to me if Nigel could have given her his name?'

'Maybe they're no longer in contact.'

Deacon shook his head. 'I wouldn't bet on that. She's not the type a man could forget very easily. And de Vriess likes women.'

'Do you like her, Mike?'

'You're the second person to ask me that' – he held the other's gaze for a moment – 'and I don't know the answer. She's out of the ordinary, but I don't know whether that makes her likeable or ruddy peculiar.' He grinned. 'She's damn fanciable. I'll say that for her.'

Barry forced himself to smile.

Chapter Fourteen

TERRY HAD TURNED on the overhead light in Deacon's bedroom and was prodding the slumbering man's shoulder aggressively. Deacon opened one eye and looked with extreme disfavour on his protégé. 'Stop – doing – that,' he said slowly and clearly. 'I am not a well man.' He rolled over and prepared to go back to sleep again.

'Yeah, right, but you've got to get up.'

'Why?'

'Lawrence is on the phone.'

Deacon struggled to a sitting position and groaned as his hangover hit him behind the eyes. 'What does he want?'

'Don't ask me.'

'Why didn't you leave the machine to take a message?' growled Deacon, glancing at his clock and seeing that it was six fifteen in the morning. 'That's what it's for.'

'I did, the first four times, but he just kept ringing back. How come you didn't hear it? Are you deaf or what?'

With muttered imprecations, Deacon stumbled through to the sitting-room and picked up the receiver.

'What's so important that you have to wake me at the crack of dawn on Christmas Eve, Lawrence?'

The old man sounded worried. 'I've just been listening to the radio, Michael. I sleep so little these days. I'm guessing that either you or I or both of us can expect a visit from the police shortly. I know Terry's there because he answered the telephone, but can you vouch for his movements last night?'

Deacon rubbed his eyes vigorously. 'What's this about?'

'Another incident at what I assume is Terry's warehouse. Look, find a news bulletin on your radio and listen to it. I may be completely wrong, but it sounds to me as if the police are looking for your lad. Call me back as soon as you can. You may need me.' He rang off.

It was the top story, with details breaking as the newscaster was on air. Following an attempted murder and the arrest of a suspect on Friday afternoon, further trouble had erupted among the homeless community in a docklands warehouse in the early hours of Christmas Eve when several men had been doused with petrol and their clothes set alight. The police were looking for a youth, five feet eleven inches tall, shaven-headed and wearing a dark coat, who was seen running from the warehouse following the incident. Although they had not released his name, the police were looking for a known suspect who was believed to hold a grudge against the warehouse community following the attempted murder on Friday.

For all Terry's surface bravura, he was only fourteen years old. He stared at the radio in tearful panic. 'Someone's grassed me up,' he stormed. 'What am I gonna fucking do? The Old Bill'll crucify me.'

'Don't be an idiot,' said Deacon sharply. 'You've been here all night.'

'How would you know, you bastard?' demanded Terry angrily, his fear sparking further aggression. 'I could have gone and come back without you knowing anything about it. Shit, you didn't even hear your phone ringing.'

Deacon pointed at the sofa. 'Sit down while I phone Lawrence back.'

'No chance. I'm out of here.' He bunched his hands into fists. 'I ain't gonna let the fucking pigs anywhere near me.'

'SIT DOWN,' roared Deacon, 'BEFORE I GET **REALLY** ANGRY!' Afraid that Terry would bolt if he left the room to search out Lawrence's number, he switched to the loudspeaker, pressed 1471 to give him a voiced number recall of the last person who had phoned him, then pressed 3 to dial that person back. 'Hi, Lawrence, it's Michael and Terry on the amplifier. We can both hear you and both talk to you. We think you're right. We think the guys at the warehouse have grassed Terry, and we think the police will come knocking. So what do we do?'

'Can you vouch for his movements?'

'Yes and no. We got back here about two o'clock in the morning, courtesy of a taxi. I abandoned my car in Fleet Street because I was over the limit. We were with a chap called Barry Grover until about one fifteen a.m. We were pissed as rats. The last thing I remember is telling

Terry to stop giggling like a schoolgirl and go to bed. I crashed out immediately and the next thing I knew was Terry giving me grief because you were on the phone. I can't swear he was here between two and when he woke me' – he squinted at his watch – 'which means four and a quarter hours are unaccounted for. It's a hypothetical possibility that he went out, but a practical no-no. He could hardly stand when I pushed him into his bedroom, and I am one hundred per cent certain that he's been there ever since.'

'Can you hear me, Terry?'

'Yeah.'

'Did you leave Michael's flat after you got back to it at two o'clock this morning?'

'No, I fucking didn't,' said the boy sullenly. 'And I've got a fucking headache, so I'm not answering fucking questions about what I didn't fucking do.'

Lawrence's dry laughter floated into the room. 'Then I'm sure we're worrying unnecessarily – perhaps there are two shaven-headed youths known to the police after Friday – but I do urge you to purify the flat. Our friends in the police force tend to react unfavourably to anything that requires chemical identification. Let me know if you run into trouble, won't you?'

'Why can't he speak English occasionally?' asked Terry ungraciously as Deacon put the phone down. 'What was he saying? That I'm guilty of something?'

'Yes. Possessing a class-C drug. How much cannabis have you got left?'

'Hardly any.'

'None' – Deacon banged the table – 'as of now. It's

going straight down the bog.' He fixed the boy with a gaze that would have pinned butterflies to a board. 'Do it, Terry.'

'Okay, okay, but it cost me a fortune, you know.'

'Not half as much as it's going to cost me if it's found here.'

Terry's natural ebullience resurfaced. 'You're more scared than I am,' he said with a knowing leer. 'Ain't you never wanted to live a little? See how much bottle you've got when the cops've got you pinned to the canvas?'

Deacon chuckled as he made for his bedroom. 'I tell you what, Terry, I'm more interested to see how much bottle you've got. You're the one they'll be using for target practice, so I wouldn't give them too much to aim at if I were you.'

They were fully dressed and eating breakfast when the police arrived half an hour later in the shape of two detective sergeants, one of whom was DS Harrison. When Deacon answered the door and agreed that he did know where Terry Dalton was – sitting at his kitchen table, as it happened – Harrison expressed surprise that they were up so early on a Sunday morning.

'It's Christmas Eve,' said Deacon, taking them through the flat. 'We're visiting my mother in Bedfordshire, so we wanted to make an early start.' He resumed his place and tucked into his cereals again. 'What can we do for you, sergeant? I thought Terry gave you a statement on Friday.'

Harrison glanced at the boy, who was happily engaged

on his third bowl of cornflakes. 'He did. We've come about a different matter. Can you tell us where you were at three o'clock this morning, Mr Dalton?'

'Here,' said Terry.

'Can you prove that?'

'Sure. I were with Mike. Why d'you want to know anyway?'

'There's been another incident at the warehouse. Five comatose men were saturated with petrol, then set alight. They're all in hospital and two of them are critical. We wondered if you knew anything about it.'

'Not fucking likely,' said Terry indignantly. 'I ain't been near the place since Friday night. Ask Mike.'

Harrison turned back to Deacon. 'Is that right, sir?'

'Yes. I invited Terry to spend Christmas with me after he made his statement to you. We stopped off at the warehouse on our way home on Friday to pick up a few of his things, and he's been in my company ever since.' He frowned. 'When you say you wonder if Terry might know something, are you suggesting he was involved?'

'We're not suggesting anything at this stage, sir, just making enquiries.'

'I see.'

There was a short silence while Deacon and Terry continued with their breakfast.

'When you said you were with this gentleman last night,' Harrison asked Terry, 'what did you mean exactly?'

'What d'you think I meant?'

'Let me put it another way, sir. If you and Mr Deacon shared a bed last night, then it's doubtful you could have left the bed without him noticing. Is that what you meant when you said you were with him?' The sergeant's expression was neutral but there was a look of amusement on his colleague's face.

A stillness settled on the boy which Deacon interpreted as anger, but when Terry raised his head there was cunning in his eyes. 'I reckon it's down to Mike to answer that,' he said off-handedly. 'This ain't my pad. He's the one calls the shots around here.'

Deacon located the youngster's naked toe under the table and ground his metal-tipped shoe heel into the unprotected flesh. 'Sorry,' he murmured as Terry yelped, 'did I hurt you? My foot slipped, sweetheart.' He pursed his lips into a rosebud and prepared to blow a kiss in Terry's direction.

'Bog off, Mike!' He glared from Deacon to the two policemen. ''Course we didn't share a sodding bed. I'm no pillow biter, and he's no sausage jockey. Got it? He were in his bed and I were in mine, but that don't mean I buggered off in the middle of the night to go torching the guys at the warehouse. We didn't get back here till round two, and I was out like a light the minute I hit the sack.'

'We've only your word on that.'

'Ask Mike. He's the one pushed me through the door of my room. Ask Barry, if it comes to that. We said goodnight to him at past one, and he'll tell you I was too rat-arsed to go looking for the warehouse in the middle of the night. And while you're about it, ask the taxi driver who gave us a ride. He only brought us back because it was on his way home and Mike paid up front and over the odds in case him and me puked all over the sodding seats. Which we didn't.' He drew breath. 'Shit! Why'd I want to set fire to anyone anyway? The old geezers there are looking after my mattress.'

'Who's Barry?'

'Barry Grover,' said Deacon. 'He works for the *Street* magazine and lives in Camden somewhere. We were with him from eight thirty to one fifteen.'

'Was it a black cab or a minicab?'

'Black cab. The driver was about fifty-five, grey-haired, skinny and wearing a green jumper. He picked us up on the corner of Fleet Street and Farringdon Street.'

'You were lucky,' said Harrison drily. 'Black cabs are usually pretty thin on the ground at Christmas time.'

Deacon just nodded. He didn't think it necessary to mention that he'd climbed on the taxi's bonnet at the traffic lights and refused to budge until the driver agreed to a fifty-quid fee. It was a rip-off but preferable to passing out in the gutter.

'Do you mind if we look around your flat, sir?' Harrison asked next.

Deacon eyed him curiously. 'Why would you want to do that?'

'To satisfy ourselves that your beds were slept in last night.'

'You should make them get a search warrant,' Terry said.

'What on earth for?' asked Deacon.

'The Old Bill aren't allowed to go poking round people's private things just when they fancy it.'

'Well, I've no objection at all to them looking at my

room, but if you've got a problem—' He broke off with a shrug.

''Course I ain't got a problem,' said Terry crossly.

'Then what are you bellyaching about?' Deacon stood up. 'This way, gentlemen.'

The two sergeants accepted a cup of coffee and relaxed enough to join Deacon and Terry in a smoke. 'Terry fits the description of a youth seen running from the scene after the incident,' Harrison told them.

'So do a million others,' said Deacon.

'How would you know, sir?'

'We heard the description on the radio.'

'I thought you might have done. May I ask who alerted you?'

'My solicitor, Lawrence Greenhill,' said Deacon. 'He heard the bulletin and warned us to expect a visit from you.'

'So you were lying when you said you were visiting your mother?'

'No. We'll be leaving as soon as you've gone, but I will admit we were woken rather earlier than I'd intended. If you hang around, my alarm will go off in approximately' – he consulted his watch – 'thirty minutes.'

'When do you expect to be back?'

'This evening.'

'And you're happy for us to check your story with Barry Grover and the taxi driver?'

'Be our guests,' said Deacon. 'You can do more.

Check that we were in the Lame Beggar until ten thirty, and then at Carlo's in Farringdon Street until one in the morning when we were finally thrown out.'

'Your mother's address please, sir.'

'I don't want to see your mother,' said Terry morosely, hunched in the corner of the passenger seat as they set off for the M1 after collecting Deacon's car from the *Street* car park following yet another taxi ride, 'and she won't want to see me.'

'She probably won't want to see me either,' murmured Deacon, calculating that he'd shelled out a fortune in incidental expenses since Terry had moved in. He was coming to the conclusion that teenagers cost more than wives. Terry's appetite alone – he'd eaten enough breakfast to sink a battleship – would beggar most people.

'Then why are we going?'

'Because it seemed like a good idea when I first thought of it.'

'Yeah, but that was just an excuse for the Old Bill.'

'It's good for the soul to do something you don't want to do.'

'Billy used to say that.'

'Billy was a wise man.'

'No, he weren't. He were a bloody pillock. I've been thinking about it, and d'you know what I reckon? I reckon he never starved himself to death at all but let someone else do it for him. And if that ain't stupid, I don't know what is.'

Deacon glanced at him. 'How could someone else do it for him?'

'By keeping him permanently pissed so he didn't think to eat. See, food were only important to him when he was sober – like when he were in the nick – otherwise he'd forget that it's eating that keeps you alive.'

'Are you saying someone kept him supplied with booze for four weeks so that he'd drink himself to death?'

'Yeah, I mean, it's the only thing that makes sense, isn't it? How else could he've stayed rat-arsed long enough to starve? He couldn't've bought the sodding stuff because he didn't have no money, and if he'd been sober, he'd've come back to the warehouse. Like I said, he used to bugger off from time to time, but he always came back when the booze ran out and he started to get hungry again.'

DS Harrison had rung the bell of the Grovers' terraced house in Camden several times before it opened a crack and Barry's sweaty face peered through it. 'Mr Grover?' he asked.

He nodded.

'DS Harrison, sir, Isle of Dogs police station. May I come in?'

'Why?'

'I'd like to ask you a few questions about Michael Deacon and Terry Dalton.'

'What have they done?'

'I'd rather discuss this inside, sir.'

'I'm not dressed.'

'It'll only take a minute.'

There was a pause before the security chain rattled and Barry opened the door wide. 'My mother's asleep,' he whispered. 'You'd better come in here.' He opened the door of the front parlour, then closed it quietly behind them.

Harrison sniffed the cold, musty air and looked about him. He was in a time capsule from a forgotten era. Drab velvet curtains hung beside the windows with pale stripes where the sun had bleached their colour, and ancient wallpaper showed a tide mark of rising damp from the ground outside. Photographs of a man in First World War uniform crowded the mantelpiece, and a portrait of a young woman in Edwardian dress smiled sweetly above it. The furniture had the dark and heavy imprint of the Victorian age, and the atmosphere was heavy with the weight of years, as if the door of the room had been closed on a day in the distant past and never reopened.

He rested a hand on the back of a mildewed chair, feeling its dirt and its dampness soil his palm, and he thought unquiet thoughts about what sort of people chose to inhabit so oppressive an environment.

'You mustn't touch anything,' whispered Barry. 'She'll go mad if she thinks you've touched something. It's her grandparents' room.' He pointed to the photographs and the painting. 'That's them. They brought her up when her own mother ran away and abandoned her.'

He smelt of sickness and stale drink, and presented a pathetic picture in a worn towelling dressing-gown that barely met across his fat stomach and striped pyjamas. The sergeant was torn between sympathy towards a fellow traveller – Harrison had been on too many jags himself not to know the pain of the morning after – and a strange flesh-crawling antipathy. He put it down to the bizarreness of the room and the man's unpleasant smell, but his sense of revulsion remained with him long after the interview was over.

'Michael Deacon says you'll confirm that you were with him and a youth called Terry Dalton from eight thirty last night until approximately one fifteen this morning. Are you able to do that?'

Barry nodded carefully. 'Yes.'

'Can you tell me what they were doing when you last saw them?'

'Mike stopped a taxi by climbing on the bonnet, then he and Terry got into it. There was a bit of a row because the driver didn't want to carry drunks, and Mike said it was obligatory as long as the customer could pay. I think he gave the driver the money in advance, and then they left.' He pressed a queasy hand to his stomach. 'What's happened? Were they in an accident or something?'

'No, nothing like that, sir. There was some trouble last night at the squat Terry Dalton's been living in, and we wanted to assure ourselves that he wasn't involved in it. How would you describe his condition when you saw him off in the taxi?'

Barry wouldn't meet his eye. 'Mike more or less had to drag him into the cab and I think he was lying on the floor when it left.'

'And how did you get home, sir?'

The question clearly alarmed Barry. 'Me?' He hesitated. 'I took a taxi, too.'

'From Farringdon Street?'

'No, Fleet Street.' He took off his glasses and started to polish them on his dressing-gown hem.

'A black cab or a minicab?'

'I phoned for a minicab from the *Street* offices. Reg Linden let me use the phone in reception.'

'And did you have to pay in advance as well?'

'Yes.'

'Well, thank you for your help, sir. I'll see myself out.'

'No, I'll see you out,' said Barry with an odd little giggle. 'We don't want you turning the wrong way, sergeant. It wouldn't do at all if you woke my mother.'

Deacon drove through the farmhouse gates and parked in the lee of the red-brick wall that bordered the driveway. The drone of motorway traffic was muted behind the baffle and the house slumbered in the winter sunshine that had emerged from the clouds as they travelled north. He peered up at the façade to see if their arrival had been noticed but there was no sign of movement in any of the windows that looked their way. There was a car he didn't recognize outside the kitchen door (which he rightly attributed to the live-in nurse), but otherwise the place looked exactly the same as when he had stormed out of it five years before, vowing never to return.

'Come on then,' said Terry when Deacon didn't move. 'Are we going in or what?'

'Or what probably.'

'Jesus, you can't be that nervous. You've got me, ain't you? I won't let the old dragon bite you.'

Deacon smiled. 'All right. Let's go.' He opened his car door. 'Just don't take offence if she's rude to you, Terry. Or not immediately anyway. Hold your tongue till we're back in the car. Is that a deal?'

'What if she's rude to you?'

'The same thing applies. The last time I came here I was so angry I damn nearly wrecked the place, and I never want to be that angry again.' He stared towards the kitchen door, recalling the episode. 'Anger's a killer, Terry. It destroys everything it touches, including the one it's feeding on.'

'Looks like we've caught our arsonists,' said Harrison's partner as he re-entered the station an hour later. 'Three subhumans by the names of Grebe, Daniels and Sharpe. They were picked up thirty minutes ago still reeking of petrol. Daniels made the mistake of boasting to his girlfriend about how he and his mates had done the local community a service by getting rid of undesirables, and she rang us. According to her, Daniels heard about the trouble at the warehouse on Friday and decided to go in and torch it last night. He says all homeless people are scum, and he's buggered if their kind should be allowed to infect the streets of the East End. Charming, eh?'

'And I've just wasted six hours chasing after Terry Dalton,' said Harrison sourly, 'ending up with the weirdest bloody bloke you've ever seen in Camden.' He shuddered theatrically. 'You know who he reminded me of? Richard Attenborough playing Christie in the film *10*

Rillington Place. If it comes to that, the house reminded me of a flaming film set.'

'Who's Christie?'

'A nasty little pervert who killed women so that he could have sex with their corpses. Don't you know anything?'

'Oh, *that* Christie,' said his partner solemnly.

The live-in nurse was an attractive Irish woman with soft grey hair and a buxom figure. She opened the kitchen door to Deacon's tap and invited them in with a warm smile of welcome. 'I recognize you from your photographs,' she told Deacon, wiping floury hands on her apron. 'You're Michael.' She shook his hand. 'I'm Siobhan O'Brady.'

'How do you do, Siobhan.' He turned to Terry who was skulking in his shadow. 'This is my friend Terry Dalton.'

'I'm pleased to meet you, Terry.' She put an arm around the boy's shoulder and drew him inside before shutting the door. 'Will you take a cup of tea after your journey?'

Deacon thanked her, but Terry seemed to find her mothering instincts overpowering and was bent on extricating himself from her embrace as soon as he decently could. 'I need a piss,' he said firmly.

'Through the door to your right, then first left,' said Deacon, hiding a smile, 'and mind your head as you go. There isn't a doorway in this house higher than six feet.'

Siobhan busied herself with the kettle. 'Is your mother expecting you, Michael? Because she hasn't said a word to me if she is. She's a little forgetful these days, so it may have slipped her mind, but there's nothing to worry about. I can find a little extra to feed you and the lad.' She chuckled happily. 'How did we manage before the deep-freeze? That's what I'm always asking myself. I remember my own mother pickling eggs to tide us over the lean periods, and nasty-looking things they were too. There were fourteen of us and it was a struggle to make any of us eat them.'

She paused to spoon tea into the pot and Deacon seized the opportunity to answer her first question. She was a garrulous woman, he thought, and wondered how his mother, who was the opposite, put up with her. 'No,' he said, 'she's not expecting me. And please don't worry about lunch. She may refuse to speak to me, in which case Terry and I will leave immediately.'

'We'll keep our fingers crossed then that she does no such thing. It would be a shame to come so far for so little.'

He smiled. 'Why do I get the feeling that you *were* expecting me?'

'Your sister mentioned the possibility. She said if you came at all, it would be unannounced. I think she was afraid I'd ring the police first and ask questions later.' She poured boiling water on to the tea-leaves and took some mugs from a cupboard. 'You'll be wanting to know how your mother is. Well, she's not as fit as she was – who is at her age? – but, despite what she's claiming, she's nowhere near death's door. She has impaired vision, which means she can't read, and she has difficulty walking because one of her legs is packing up. She needs constant supervision because her increasing immobility has caused her to take shortcuts on her diet, which, of course, means she could pass out with hypoglycaemia at any moment.'

She poured a cup of tea and passed it to him with a jug of milk and the sugar bowl. 'The obvious place for her is some sort of nursing home where she can retain her independence *and* be given round-the-clock care, but your mother is very resistant to the idea. We have all tried to explain to her that she could live for another ten years, but she has a bee in her bonnet about being gone in a couple of months and is determined to die here.' She fixed him with a knowing eye. 'I can see from your expression that you're wondering what business this is of mine – why is the nurse siding with Emma and Hugh? you're thinking, when they're only after getting shot of their debts – but, my dear, the truth is I can't bear to see a patient of mine so unhappy. She sits day after day in her sitting-room, with no one to visit her and no one to care, and her only companion is a talkative, middle-aged Irish woman with whom she has nothing in common. It breaks my heart to watch her struggling to be civil to me in case I up my stumps and leave. Almost anything would be preferable to that. Would you not agree, Michael?'

'I would, yes.'

'Then you'll try to persuade her to be sensible?'

He smiled apologetically and shook his head. 'No. If her mind's all right, then she's capable of making her own decisions. I'm damned if I'll interfere. I wouldn't begin to know what's sensible and what's not. I can't even make rational judgements for myself, let alone for someone else. Sorry.'

Siobhan seemed less troubled by this answer than he expected. 'Shall we find out if your mother will see you, Michael? Either she will or she won't, and there's little sense in putting it off.'

Cynically (and accurately) he guessed that Siobhan's complacency was based on her knowledge that Penelope Deacon would do the exact opposite of anything her son suggested.

Chapter Fifteen

AMANDA POWELL'S elderly neighbour looked up from where she was preparing lunch and was alarmed to see a man fiddling with the lock on Mrs Powell's garage. She knew the house was empty because Amanda had told her earlier that morning that she was spending the Christmas holiday with her mother in Kent. Shortly afterwards, she had driven away. The woman hurried through to the sitting-room to alert her husband, but by the time they returned to the kitchen window the man had gone.

Her husband sallied forth – somewhat reluctantly, it must be said – to discover where the would-be intruder had gone. He tried the garage door, but it was firmly locked. The same was true of the front door. He glanced up and down the quiet road, then with a shrug rejoined his wife.

'Are you sure you didn't imagine it, darling?'

'Of course I didn't imagine it,' she said crossly. 'I'm not senile. He'll have nipped across the gardens at the back and be trying somebody else's house by now. There'll be quite a few of them empty this weekend. You must ring the police.'

'They'll want a description.'

She paused in her peeling and stared out of the window, picturing the scene. 'He was about six feet tall, thin, and he had on a dark coat.'

Muttering that it seemed unkind to trouble the police on Christmas Eve, and anyway every house had an alarm system, her husband nevertheless made the call. But as he put down the telephone after receiving an assurance that a patrol car would be sent to check the house, it occurred to him that he had seen a man fitting that description once before.

When he had stood outside Mrs Powell's garage and watched the police lay a dead tramp on a stretcher . . .

He decided not to mention that to his wife.

'I don't know why we're bothering,' she said as he went back into the kitchen. 'It's not as though she ever does anything for us.'

'No,' he agreed, peering through the window. 'But then she doesn't like people very much, does she?'

There was a surreal quality to the scene that met Deacon's eyes as he and Siobhan approached the open sitting-room door. Far from being marooned in a chair as Siobhan had described, his mother was upright, leaning on Terry's arm, and peering at a painting on the wall. 'Of course, I can't really see it now,' she was saying, 'but if I remember correctly, it's a George Chambers Junior. Can you make out the signature in the bottom left-hand corner?'

Terry made a pretence of reading the artist's scrawl. 'You've got an amazing memory, Mrs D. George

Chambers Junior it is. Did he always paint the sea then?'

'Oh, I'm sure he must have done other things, but he and his father were famous marine artists of the last century. I bought that years ago for £20 in a down-at-heel gallery in south London somewhere, and I had it valued at Sotheby's a week later for hundreds. Goodness only knows what it's worth now.' She urged him to move on. 'Do you see a portrait of me in the alcove? A big, bold one with lots of rich colour. Read the signature on that,' she said triumphantly. 'He's a wonderful artist and it was such a thrill to be painted by him.'

Terry stared in agony at the canvas.

'John Bratby,' said Deacon from the doorway.

Terry flashed him a relieved smile. 'Yeah, well done, Mike. It's a John Bratby all right. Mind you, Mrs D., considering how beautiful you are, do you really reckon he's done you proud? It's bold, like you said, but it ain't pretty. D'you know what I'm saying?'

'Yes, I do, but my character isn't pretty, Terry, and I think John captured that perfectly. Can we turn round?'

'Sure.' He assisted her to face her son.

'Come in, Michael,' said Penelope. 'To what do I owe this unexpected pleasure?'

He smiled uncomfortably. 'Why do you always ask the hardest questions first, Ma?'

'Terry seemed to find it easy enough. When I asked him who he was and what he was doing here, he said you and he had a visit from the – er – Old Bill this morning and it seemed like a good idea to get out of London for a while. Was he lying to me?'

'No.'

'Good. I'd rather you came because you're on the run from the police than because you've been talking to Emma. I won't have any more browbeating, Michael.' She nudged Terry in the ribs. 'Take me back to my chair, please, young man, and then go and sort out some drinks for us in the kitchen. There's gin, sherry and wine but if you'd rather have beer, I expect there's some in the cellar. Siobhan will help you find it.' She resumed her seat. 'Sit down where I can see you, Michael. Did you shave before you left?'

He took a chair, facing the window. 'Afraid not. I didn't have time before the police came, and forgot about it afterwards.' He rubbed his jaw thoughtfully. 'The eyesight's not that bad then?'

She ignored the remark. 'Who is Terry and why is he with you?'

'He's a lad I interviewed for a story on homelessness, and when I discovered he had nowhere to go for Christmas, I suggested he stayed with me for a few days.'

'How old is he?'

'That has nothing to do with why the police came this morning, Ma.'

'I don't remember saying it did. How old, Michael?'

'Fourteen.'

'Dear God! Why aren't his parents looking after him?'

Deacon gave a hollow laugh. 'He'd have to find them first.' He was shocked by how much his mother had changed. She was an older, smaller, thinner shadow of herself, and the piercing blue gaze had dimmed to grey. He had been prepared for a wounded dragon who could still breathe fire, but not for one whose fires had gone out. 'Don't waste your sympathy on him, Ma. Even if he knew where his parents were, he wouldn't go back to them. He's far too independent.'

'Like you then?'

'Not really. I was never as self-sufficient at his age. He has social skills that I still don't possess. I could no more have walked into this room at fourteen and struck up a conversation with a complete stranger than fly over the moon. What did he say to you, as a matter of interest?'

A faint smile hovered round her lips. 'I called out when I heard him tiptoeing along the corridor. I said: "Whoever that is, will they please come in here?" And when he came in he said: "Have you got ears in the back of your head or what?" Then he took great trouble to assure me he wasn't a burglar but that, if he were, there were some "well brilliant" pictures that might take his fancy. I gather this house resembles a palace while your flat is as boring as a men's public lavatory. What are you going to do with him when Christmas is over?'

'I don't know. I haven't thought about it yet.'

'You should, Michael. You have a nasty habit of taking on a responsibility lightly and then discarding it when it bores you. I blame myself. I should have forced you to face up to unpleasantness instead of encouraging you to avoid it.'

He looked at her. 'Is that what you did?'

'You know it is.'

'No, I don't. What I know is that I watched you martyr yourself for no good reason, and I made up my mind that nothing on earth would induce me to go down the same route. Julia and I loathed each other, never mind what she said afterwards. Believe me, she was as glad of the divorce as I was. Okay, I was the one who had the affair, but you try sleeping with a woman who doesn't want sex, doesn't want babies and makes it abundantly clear that she only got married in the first place because Mrs Deacon was a preferable title to Miss Fitt.' He stood up and walked restlessly to the window. 'Haven't you ever wondered why she never remarried, and why she continues to call herself Julia Deacon?' Briefly he glanced back at her. 'Because getting out from under her parents was all she was interested in, and I was the sap who helped her do it.'

'And what was Clara's reason for getting married? How long did that one last, Michael? Three years?'

'At least she gave me a bit of warmth after eight frigid years with Julia.'

Penelope Deacon shook her head. 'So why didn't she produce any children?' she asked. 'Perhaps, after all, it's you who don't want them, Michael?'

'You're wrong. She didn't want to lose her blasted figure.' He pressed his forehead to the glass. 'You've no idea how much I envy Emma. I'd give my right arm to have her daughters.'

'No, you wouldn't,' said Penelope with a dry laugh. 'They're perfectly revolting. I can only tolerate them for a couple of minutes before their simpering starts to annoy me. I did hope you'd give me a grandson. Boys aren't so affected as girls.'

*

DS Harrison raised his hand in greeting to two uniformed policemen who were getting out of their car as he exited the station. 'I'm off,' he said. 'Five days' hard-earned leave, and I'm planning to enjoy every damn minute.'

'You jammy bastard,' said the driver enviously, opening the rear door of the car and grabbing the occupant by the arm. 'Come on, sunshine. Let's be having you.'

Barry Grover emerged blinking into the sunlight.

Harrison paused. 'I know this guy,' he said slowly. 'What's the story?'

'Acting suspiciously in a woman's garden. More accurately, wanking his little heart out over a photograph of the occupant. What name do you know him by?'

'Barry Grover.'

'How about giving us ten minutes then, sarge? He's claiming to be a Kevin Powell of Claremont Cottage, Easeby, Kent. Says he's related to the Mrs Amanda Powell who owns the house. We thought it pretty unlikely, seeing what he was doing to her photograph but, according to her neighbours, she does have relations in Kent. She drove down there this morning to stay with her mother.'

Harrison looked at Barry in disgust. 'His name's Barry Grover,' he repeated, 'and he lives with his mother in Camden. Jesus Christ! I hope to God wanking's the least of his crimes or we'll be digging out bodies from under his floorboards.'

*

'My son and I have never seen eye to eye,' Penelope Deacon told Terry, 'so much so that I can't think of a single decision he's made in life that I've agreed with.'

'You were thrilled when I said I was marrying Julia,' murmured Deacon from his position by the window.

'Hardly thrilled, Michael. I was pleased that you'd finally decided to settle down, but I remember saying that Julia would not have been my first choice. I always preferred Valerie Crewe.'

'You would,' he said. 'She agreed with everything you said.'

'Which shows how intelligent she was.'

'Terrified, more like. She used to quake every time she came into the house.' He dropped a wink in Terry's direction. 'Ma viewed every girl I brought home as potential marriage material, and she used to put them through the mill to find out if they were suitable. Who were their parents? Which school did they go to? Was there a history of insanity in their family?'

'If there had been, it would have been pointless your marrying them,' declared Penelope tartly. 'Both sets of genes would have been so tainted, your children wouldn't have stood a chance.'

'We'll never know, will we?' said Deacon equally tartly. 'Every time you brought up the so-called insanity on our side, the girls did a runner. It probably explains why Julia and Clara baulked at having children.'

Terry grinned. 'That can't be right, Mike. I mean, okay, I've only lived with you for a couple of days but it don't take that long to see you're not a nutter.'

'Who asked you to interfere?'

Terry was sitting on the floor, stroking an ancient, moth-eaten cat that had been around so long no one knew how old it was. It purred with raucous pleasure at Terry's ministrations, which Penelope said was unusual because senility had made it irritable with strangers.

'Yeah, but you need your heads knocking together,' said the boy. 'I mean, you should listen to yourselves. Argue, argue, argue. Don't you never get tired of it? There might be some sense if it were going somewhere, but it isn't, is it? Me, I think Mrs D. probably said a load of things she shouldn't've done about you killing your dad, but you've got to admit she weren't far off in what she said about your wives. I mean, they can't have been much cop – either of them – or you'd still be married to them. Know what I'm saying?'

The contents of Barry's pockets and the envelope he'd been carrying were spread out in front of him on the table of an interview room, and sergeants Harrison and Forbes stared at them in perplexity. There were the prostitutes' cards and a stiffened condom that told them, without benefit of forensic analysis, what it had been used for. There were a dozen head shots of different men, some fully exposed, some underexposed, a paperback entitled *Unsolved Mysteries of the Twentieth Century*, and a folded newspaper clipping. There was the sodden photograph of Amanda Powell, now discreetly wrapped in cellophane to preserve the evidence of Barry's shame, a leather wallet containing money and credit cards, and a dog-eared snap of Barry cradling a toddler in his arms.

The tape had been running for fifteen minutes, and Barry hadn't said a word. Tears of humiliation ran from his eyes, and his flaccid cheeks wobbled pathetically.

'Come on, Barry, for God's sake talk to us,' said Harrison. 'What were you doing at Mrs Powell's house? Why her?' He poked at the photographs. 'Who are all these men? Do you wank on them as well? Who's this child you're holding? Maybe you've got a thing about kids? Are we going to find pictures of children all over your walls when we go searching your mother's house? Is that what you're so worried about?'

With a sigh, Barry slid off his chair in a dead faint.

The police doctor accompanied Harrison into the corridor. 'He's certainly not dying,' he said, 'but he's scared out of his wits. That's why he fainted. He says he's thirty-four but I suggest you take twenty years off that to get an approximation of his emotional age. My best advice is to ask a parent or a friend to sit with him while you ask him questions, otherwise he'll probably collapse again. Work on the basis that you're dealing with a juvenile, and you might get somewhere.'

'His mother's not answering the phone and, judging by the shrine she's made to her grandparents in the front room of their house, she's barking mad anyway.'

'Which would explain his delayed development.'

'What about a solicitor?'

The doctor shrugged. 'My professional opinion, for what it's worth, is that a solicitor will terrify him even more. Find a friend – he must have some – otherwise you'll end up with a false confession. He's the type, Greg, believe me, so don't expect me to stand up in court and say anything different.'

The telephone rang in the kitchen. A few seconds later Siobhan popped her head round the sitting-room door. 'It's for you, Michael. A Sergeant Harrison would like a few words.'

Deacon and Terry exchanged glances. 'Did he say why?'

'No, but he made a point of stressing that it has nothing to do with Terry.'

With a shrug in the boy's direction, Deacon followed the woman out.

'Michael seems to be developing quite a relationship with the police,' Penelope remarked drily. 'Is this a recent thing?'

'If you're asking is it my fault, then I guess it is, sort of. The Old Bill wouldn't even know his name if it weren't for me. But you don't need to worry about *him* getting into trouble, Mrs D. He's a good bloke. He don't even drink and drive.' He watched her out of the corner of his eye. 'He's been well kind to me, bought me clothes and such, taught me stuff I didn't know. A hundred other guys wouldn't've given me the time of day.'

She didn't say anything and Terry ploughed on doggedly.

'So I reckon it wouldn't do no harm to show him you're pleased to see him. I remember this old geezer I used to know – he were a bit of a preacher – telling me a story about a rich bloke who took half his dad's loot, spent it all on women and gambling and ended up on the streets. He was really poor and really miserable until he remembered how nice his old dad had always been to him before he left home. Then he thought, why am I bumming crusts off strangers when Dad'll give them to me with no questions asked? So he took himself home, and his dad was that pleased to see him he burst into tears because he thought the silly bastard had died years ago.'

Penelope smiled slightly. 'You've just related the parable of the prodigal son.'

'D'you get the point, though, Mrs D? Never mind what sort of mess the bloke made of his life, his dad was over the moon to see him.'

'But for how long?' she asked. 'The son hadn't changed, so do you think his father would still be pleased to have him around when he started making a mess of his life again?'

Terry thought about it. 'I don't see why not. Okay, maybe they'd have the odd spat now and then, and maybe they couldn't live in the same house, but the dad wouldn't never be so unhappy as when he thought his son was dead.'

She smiled again. 'Well, I'm not going to burst into tears of joy, Terry. First, I'm far too crabby to do anything so sentimental and, secondly, poor Michael would be appalled. He can't cope with weepy women, which is why both his wives walked off with so much of his money despite the fact neither of them had children.

Certainly Julia knew how to turn on the waterworks when it mattered, and I've no doubt Clara was equally adept. In any case, I think you'll find he already knows I'm pleased to see him, otherwise he wouldn't be talking as freely as he is.'

'If you say so,' said Terry doubtfully. 'I mean, you seem like two straight-up types to me and, let's be honest, if I were looking for a mum – which I *ain't*,' he pointed out carefully, 'I'd as soon have you as the nurse out there who can't keep her paws off of me. Plus, she don't half talk a lot. Yabber, yabber, yabber. I reckon I heard her entire life history while I was looking for the gin.' He laid a gentle hand on the cat's head and drew forth another rumbling purr. 'What's a pickled egg anyway? It sounded right horrible.'

Penelope was laughing as Deacon came back into the room and he was surprised to see how young she looked. He remembered a Jamaican friend telling him once that laughter was the music of the soul. Was it also the fountain of youth? Would Penelope live longer if she learned to laugh again?

'We have to go back to London,' he told Terry. 'I'm a bit hazy on details, but Harrison says Barry's been arrested for acting suspiciously in Amanda Powell's garden. Barry won't say a word, and they want to know if I can shed any light on some photographs he has in his possession.' He frowned. 'Did he say anything to you about going to see her?'

Terry shook his head. 'No, but if he don't want to talk, that's his business. Don't see why we have to go stirring things up just because the Old Bill says jump.'

'Except there's something very odd going on and I want to know what it is. According to Harrison, they had to call in a doctor because Barry collapsed in a dead faint the minute they started asking him questions.' He turned to his mother. 'I'm sorry about this, Ma, but I do need to go. It's a story I've been working on for weeks. It's how I met Terry.'

'Ah, well,' she said with a sigh of resignation. 'It's probably for the best. Emma and her family are due some time this afternoon, and I've no doubt there'll be a terrible row if you're still here when they arrive. You know what you and she are like.'

Nobly, her son bit his tongue. More often than not it was Penelope's stirring that had set her children at each other's throats. 'I'm a reformed character,' he said. 'I stopped arguing with my nearest and dearest five years ago.' He stooped to peck her on the cheek. 'Look after yourself.'

She caught his hand and held on to it. 'If I sell this house and move into a nursing home,' she said, 'there'll be nothing for you when I die, particularly if I live as long as the doctors say I'm going to.'

He smiled. 'You mean, the threats of disinheritance if I married Clara were hogwash?'

'She was a gold digger,' said Penelope bitterly. 'I hoped they'd put her off.'

'They might have done if I'd ever repeated them to her.' He gave her hand a quick squeeze. 'Is this the only thing that's stopping you from moving?'

She didn't answer directly. 'It worries me that Emma will have had so much and you will have had so little.

Your father always intended you to have the house, and I made that clear to Emma when I set up the trust. Now she's pressing me to sell the wretched place, and put aside a similar amount for you as she's already had, and use the balance to pay for a nursing home.'

'Then do it,' said Deacon. 'It sounds fair to me.'

'Your father wanted you to have the house,' repeated Penelope stubbornly, withdrawing her hand from his in irritation. 'It's been owned by Deacons for two centuries.'

He looked down on her fluffy white hair and had a sudden urge to bury his nose in it as he had done as a child. He suspected he had just heard the nearest thing she would ever make to an apology for tearing up his father's will. 'Then don't sell it,' he said.

'That's hardly helpful.'

'Sorry,' he said with an indifferent shrug, 'but it's no skin off my nose if you bankrupt your daughter and spend the rest of your life with a series of nurses so that I can flog the place the minute you're gone. Let's face it, I've never shared your passion for living on the motorway, so I'd use the money to buy myself somewhere decent in London.' He dropped another sly wink at Terry. 'If anything's pissed me off about my divorces it's ending up in a miserable rented flat after losing two perfectly good houses.'

'Which is a very good reason *not* to let you have this one,' said Penelope, rising obligingly to the bait. 'Easy come, easy go. That's your philosophy, Michael.'

'Then take that into the equation when you decide what to do. If you want another two centuries of

Deacons living here, Ma, then you'd better leave the house to the Wimbledon branch of the family. I seem to remember they gave birth to a son about ten years ago.' He glanced at his watch. 'We really must go, I'm afraid. I promised the sergeant we'd be there in under two hours.'

She smiled a little bitterly. 'As I said, easy come, easy go.' She held out a hand to Terry who had stood up. 'Goodbye, young man. I've enjoyed meeting you.'

'Yeah, me too. I hope things work out for you, Mrs D.'

'Thank you.' She raised her eyes to look at him and he was startled by how blue they suddenly became in the sunlight shafting through the window. 'What a pity your mother is lost to you, Terry. She'd be proud of the man her son is becoming.'

'Do you think she's right?' Terry asked after several minutes of subdued thought in the car. 'Do you think my mum would be proud of me?'

'Yes.'

'It don't make no difference, though, does it? She's probably dead of an overdose by now, or banged up in a nick somewhere.'

Deacon stayed silent.

'She'll've forgotten all about me anyway. I mean, she wouldn't've got rid of me if I mattered to her.' He looked despondently out of the window. 'Don't you reckon?'

Yes, thought Deacon, but he said: 'Not necessarily,'

as he drove up the slip road on to the motorway. 'If you were put into care because she went to prison, that doesn't mean you didn't matter to her. It only means she wasn't in a position to look after you.'

'Why didn't she come searching after she got out then? I were there for nigh on six years, and she can't have been banged up that long, not unless she killed someone.'

'Perhaps she thought you were better off without her.'

'I could go looking for her, I suppose.'

'Is that what you'd like to do.'

'I think about it sometimes, then I get frightened she and me'll hate each other. I just wish I could remember her. I don't want some old tart with a drug problem whose frigging door's always open to any man as wants a shag.'

'What *do* you want?'

Terry grinned. 'A rich bitch with a fast Porsche, and no one to leave it to.'

Deacon laughed. 'Join the queue,' he said, moving into the fast lane and putting his foot down, 'but I don't want mine for a mother.'

Amanda Powell opened the door of Claremont Cottage and frowned enquiringly at the Kent policeman on the doorstep. The frown deepened as she listened to what he said. 'I don't know anyone called Barry Grover and I've no idea why he had a photograph of me. Did he succeed in breaking into my garage?'

'No. According to the information we've been given,

he was arrested in your garden but there were no signs of forced entry to any of the buildings.'

'Are the London police expecting me to go back and answer questions about this?'

'Not unless you want to. We were merely requested to pass on the information.'

She looked worried. 'All I told my neighbours was that I was spending a few days with my mother in Kent, so who gave you this address?'

The policeman consulted a piece of paper. 'Apparently Grover gave his name as Kevin Powell of Claremont Cottage, Easeby, when he was first arrested. We were asked to check the address and we discovered that a Mrs Glenda Powell lives here. It seemed likely she is your mother.' He frowned in his turn. 'He does seem to have a lot of information on you. Are you sure you don't know who he is?'

'Quite sure.' She pondered for a moment. 'Why might I know him? What does he do?'

He checked the paper again. 'He works for a magazine called the *Street*.' He heard her indrawn breath and looked up. 'Does that mean something to you?'

'No. I've heard of it, that's all.'

He wrote on a page of his notebook and tore it out. 'The investigating officer in London is DS Harrison and you can reach him on the top number. I'm PC Colin Dutton and my number's the bottom one. There's probably nothing to worry about, Mrs Powell. Grover's in custody, so he certainly won't be bothering you for a while, but if you're worried at all, then phone Sergeant Harrison or myself. Happy Christmas to you.'

She watched him walk past her BMW to the gate, and smiled brightly when he turned for a last look at her. 'Happy Christmas, constable,' she said.

'What's wrong?' called her mother on a note of anxiety from the sitting-room.

'Nothing,' said Amanda calmly, taking the brooch from her lapel and driving the pin under her thumbnail. 'Everything's fine.'

Deacon shook his head when Harrison finished. 'I really don't know much about Barry,' he said. 'I don't think anyone does. He never talks about his home life.' He looked in distaste at the besmirched photograph of Amanda Powell which had been cast like an island into the middle of the table. 'As far as I know, his only connection with Mrs Powell was when he developed some film after an interview I did with her. One of our photographers took some shots' – he jerked his chin at the table – 'and that was the best of them.'

'Why did you interview her?'

'I was writing a piece on the homeless and she was in the news in June when a man called Billy Blake died of starvation in her garage. We thought she might have general views on the subject, but she didn't.'

Light dawned in Harrison's eyes. 'I knew her name was familiar but I couldn't place it. I remember that incident. So why is Barry still interested in her?'

Deacon lit a cigarette. 'I don't know, unless it's something to do with the fact that he's been trying to help me identify Billy Blake.' He took one of his own prints of the dead man from his inside pocket and handed it across. 'That's him when he was arrested four years ago. We think Billy Blake was an assumed name and that he may have committed a crime in the past. He used to doss in the warehouse with Terry Dalton and Tom Beale.'

Harrison lifted an envelope from the floor and emptied its contents on to the table. 'So these headshots are your possible suspects?' He isolated the underexposed print of Billy's mugshot. 'And this is the dead guy?'

Deacon nodded.

Harrison unfolded a photocopy and flattened it on the table. 'This one's pretty close.'

Although Deacon was looking at it upside down, he knew Billy's face like the back of his hand and the shock of recognition was enormous.

Shi-it!

It was an enlarged copy of the picture of Peter Fenton that had accompanied Anne Cattrell's piece.

The little bastard had been holding out on him!

'It's close,' he agreed, 'but you need a computer to be sure.' *He'd fucking KILL Barry if the police got the story before he did!* 'Do you remember James Streeter?' Harrison nodded. 'We're more interested in him.' Disingenuously, he turned the graduation picture of James to face Harrison, and lined it up beside Billy's mugshot. 'That's probably why Barry's so interested in Amanda Powell. She was Amanda Streeter before James stole £10 million and left her to face the music alone.'

The sergeant's smile would have done credit to a cat. 'It's the same bloke.'

'Looks like it, doesn't it?'

'So what are you saying? James came back with his tail between his legs, and she starved him to death in her garage?'

'Could be.'

Harrison pondered for a moment. 'It still doesn't explain why Barry was in her garden wanking on her photograph.' He fingered idly through the prostitutes' cards. 'Guys with this kind of thing in their pockets worry me. And why does he carry a picture of himself with a kid? Who was the child and what happened to it?'

Deacon ran his thumbnail down the side of his jaw. 'You say he hasn't opened his mouth since he got here?'

'Not a dicky bird.'

'Then let me talk to him. He trusts me. I'll persuade him to give you what you want.'

'Even if it means he gets charged?'

'Even if it means he gets charged,' agreed Deacon rather savagely. 'I don't like perverts any more than you do, and I certainly don't want to work with one.'

Chapter Sixteen

BARRY'S SPECTACLES had been removed, giving him a naked look. He sat on the cell bed, head hanging forward, shoulders slumped in defeat. Deacon was told later that there was a fear he might break the lenses and try to cut his wrists – he was deemed a suicide risk – which also explained his lack of belt and shoelaces. He peered blindly towards the cell door when it opened, more like a sad-faced clown than a cockroach, and his plump little body shook with dread.

'Visitor for you,' said the custody sergeant, ushering Deacon in and leaving the door open. 'Ten minutes.'

Deacon watched the policeman walk away, then lowered himself on to the bed next to Barry. He expected to feel his usual antipathy but found himself pitying the man instead. It wasn't hard to imagine the sort of nightmare Barry was going through. There was precious little dignity to be found in a police cell at the best of times, none at all when your first experience of it was after committing a lewd act in public.

'It's Mike Deacon,' he said, wondering how much Barry could see without his glasses. 'Sergeant Harrison phoned me, told me you were in need of a friend.' He fished out his cigarettes. 'Are you going to let me smoke?' He watched the other's eyes fill with tears and punched him lightly on the shoulder. 'Is that a yes?'

Barry nodded.

'Good man.' He bent his head to the lighter. 'We haven't much time, so you're going to have to talk to me if you want my help. Let's start with the easy stuff first. You had a photograph of a man holding a child. The sergeant thinks the man's you, but I think it might be your father holding you as a toddler. Who's right?'

'You,' whispered Barry.

'You could be his double.'

'Yes.'

'Okay, next question. Why do you carry prostitutes' cards in your pocket? Is that how you spend your time when you're not working?'

Barry shook his head.

'Then why were they in your pocket?' He paused for an answer, but went on when he didn't get one. 'Talk to me,' he said kindly. 'You're not the first man in the world to be caught wanking, Barry, and you certainly won't be the last, but the police are putting the worst interpretation on it because they think you spend your time sniffing round toms.'

'Glen Hopkins gave them to me on Friday,' whispered Barry.

'Why?'

'He said there was no shame in paying for it.' Distress flowed in waves from the quivering body. 'But I *was* ashamed. I didn't like it.' He started to weep.

'I'm not surprised,' Deacon said matter-of-factly. 'I

suppose she had one eye on the clock and the other on your wallet. We've all been there, Barry.' He smiled slightly. 'Even the Nigel de Vriesses of this world have to pay for it. The only difference is they call their toms lovers and their shame becomes public property.' He sat forward with his hands between his knees, matching Barry's own body language. 'Look, does it make you feel any better if I tell you Glen tosses those cards about like bloody confetti? He gave me some a couple of months back when he decided my bad temper was due to lack of sex. I told him to ram them up his arse, where they belonged.' He glanced sideways. 'He caught you on a bad day, and you got ripped off. My best advice is to put it down to experience, and tell Glen to get stuffed the next time he tries it on.'

'He said it was – unhealthy – ' it clearly hurt him to say the word – 'looking at photographs. He said the real thing was more fun. But—' His voice tailed off.

'It wasn't?' suggested Deacon, offering him a handkerchief to dry his tears.

'No.'

Deacon reflected on his first sexual encounter at the age of sixteen, when he had fumbled his way through the act of intercourse without caring too much about satisfying the girl because his own arousal was so intense that every thought in his head was concentrated on not ejaculating before he got inside. To this day, he couldn't think of his and Mary Higgins's loss of virginity without embarrassment. She had claimed it was the worst experience of her life and never spoke to him again.

'You're not unusual,' he said sympathetically. 'Most

men find their first time pretty humbling. So what happened this morning? Why did you go to Amanda's house?'

The story was muddled but Deacon made what he could of it. After Barry's humiliation at the hands of the prostitute his anger, which should have been directed against Fatima – or even Glen – became fixated on Amanda instead. (There was a strange logic to it. He had been studying pictures of her when Glen had accused him of unhealthy practices, and in his mind's eye she had assumed the proportions of a Jezebel.)

Had he known less about her, it wouldn't have mattered, but his interest in Billy Blake and James Streeter had led him to build up a file of press cuttings on her. The reasons why he should have wanted to go out to her house and confront her were obscure, but they seemed to lie in his total confusion about whether he had hated or enjoyed the sex act. He wouldn't have gone at all had Deacon and Terry not filled him with Dutch courage on Saturday night. Tight as a tick, he had waved them off in a taxi, then called one for himself and told the driver to take him to the Thamesbank Estate.

He wasn't very sure now what his intentions were – certainly he hadn't expected to find her lights on – but at two o'clock in the morning he had stood in her garden and watched through her open curtains as she made love to a man on her sitting-room carpet. (Deacon asked him if he recognized the man, but Barry said no. Interestingly, he described him in detail but he barely mentioned Amanda.)

'It was exciting,' he said simply.

Yes, thought Deacon, it would have been. 'But illegal,' he said. 'I'm not sure if you can be charged with voyeurism, but you can certainly be charged with trespass and indecent behaviour. Why did you go back this morning anyway? It was broad daylight, so you were bound to be spotted.'

The simple explanation was that Barry had put the envelope of photographs on the ground the night before (to leave his hands free, Deacon guessed) and forgotten them. The more complex explanation seemed to concern his extraordinarily ambivalent attitude to living with his mother ('I don't want to go back,' he kept saying), his barely remembered love of his father and a half-understood desire to rekindle his excitement of a few hours earlier. But the house was clearly empty, and the only excitement left to him was to desecrate Amanda's photograph. 'I'm so ashamed,' he said. 'I don't know why I did it. It just – happened.'

'Well, if you want my opinion, it's a good thing the police caught you,' said Deacon bluntly, squeezing the burning tip out of his cigarette. 'Maybe it'll persuade you to wise up to the facts of life. You've got more going for you than to end up as some grubby little man who can only get a hard-on outside a window. Admittedly I'm no psychiatrist, but I'd say there are a couple of areas you need to sort out pretty damn quick. One, get out from under your mother and, two, come to terms with your sexuality. There's no sense in directing your anger against women if your preference is for men, Barry.'

Helplessly, Barry shook his head. 'What would my mother say?'

'A hell of a lot, I should imagine, if you're silly enough to tell her.' Deacon clapped him on the back. 'You're a grown man, Barry. It's time you acted like one.' He smiled. 'What were you planning to do, as a matter of interest? Wait till she was dead before you could be the person you wanted to be?'

'Yes.'

'Bad plan. That person would have died long before she did.' He stood up. 'Are you going to let me tell the sergeant what you've told me? Depending on what he says, you may want a solicitor with you when he questions you. And you'd better be prepared for the fact that Glen Hopkins will be asked to confirm that he gave you those cards on Friday. Are you ready for all that?'

'Will they let me go if I tell the truth?'

'I don't know.'

'Where will I go if they do? I can't go home.' His eyes welled again. 'I'd rather stay here than go home.'

God almighty! Just don't say it, Deacon. 'You can use my sofa while we sort something out.' *We-ell . . . It was Christmas . . .*

And . . .

. . . Barry knew who Billy Blake was . . .

Harrison was sceptical. 'You're being naive. I know the type. It's the classic profile of a sex criminal. A repressed loner with an unhealthy appetite for spying on people. Lives with his mother but doesn't like her. Can't make adult relationships. First offence is exposing himself in public. We'll be banging him up for rape and/or child molestation next.'

'On that basis you'll be locking me up as well,' said Deacon with a friendly smile. 'I'm a loner. I disliked my mother so much that I didn't speak to her for five years. I can't make successful adult relationships – as evidenced by my two divorces – and the worst offence I ever committed, judging by the thrashing I received, was when I bought a pornographic magazine at the age of twelve and attempted to smuggle it into my house with the intention of admiring my erections in front of a mirror.'

The sergeant chuckled. 'It's a serious point, though. You were twelve, Barry's thirty-four. You were going to practise in your bedroom, he was practising in somebody else's garden. At twelve, the damage you can do to someone else is hopefully limited by your size. At thirty-four, you're likely to be very dangerous indeed, particularly if you're thwarted.'

'But you can't charge him with what he *might* do. At worst, you've got him for trespass and indecency, and that's not going to keep him off the streets for long. Look,' he said persuasively leaning forward, 'you can't label a man a pervert for one aberrant episode. It wouldn't have happened if Glen Hopkins had kept his stupid ideas to himself, or if Barry had had more sense than to try something he wouldn't enjoy. The poor guy's hopelessly confused. He loved his father, who died when he was ten, he's terrorized by his mother and he'd just paid a hundred quid to lose his virginity to a woman who treated him like a lump of meat. On top of all that, Terry and I got him drunk – for the first time in his life as far as I can make out – and he found himself watching live sex inadvertently.' He gave a low laugh. 'Then you turned up on his doorstep this morning and scared him out of his wits because he thought Amanda must have seen him. He only went back for his photographs, for God's sake, and had a quiet wank in her absence because he was still aroused. Is this *really* the profile of a classic sex criminal?'

Harrison tapped his pen against his teeth. 'He was trying to break into Mrs Powell's garage. Where does that fit in?'

Deacon frowned. 'You haven't mentioned that before.'

'It's how we caught him. Her neighbours reported a possible intruder, and we sent out a patrol car.' He pushed a piece of paper across the table. 'It's all there in black and white.'

Deacon read the incident report. 'This man's described as six feet tall, thin and wearing a dark coat. Barry's about six inches shorter, fat and the only coat I've ever seen him in is a blue anorak. It's in his cell at the moment.'

The sergeant shrugged. 'I wouldn't rely on that description. The neighbours are in their eighties.'

Deacon studied him with amusement. 'God help you if my mother heard you say that. Surely you can see there were two different men? You've nicked the easy one –

the wally. My best advice, if you want a result, is to look for the tall guy.'

'If he exists,' said Harrison cynically.

Terry was bored to distraction by the time Barry and Deacon emerged from the inner recesses of the police station. 'You've been two hours,' he said crossly, pointing to the clock in the waiting area. 'What did Barry do then? It must have been something pretty bad if it took this long to sort.'

Deacon shook his head. 'He was watching Amanda's house, and got nicked in mistake for a man who tried to break into her garage half an hour earlier. It's taken all this time to establish that he doesn't answer the description of a tall, skinny bloke in a dark coat.'

'No kidding! You want to get Lawrence on to it. He'd soon sort these bastards out. That's harassment, that is, banging up a bloke for no reason. You all right, Barry? You don't look too good.'

Deacon shoved him through the front door into the freezing evening air before the desk sergeant could set him straight. 'Barry's coming home with us,' he murmured in Terry's ear. 'His family kicked up rough because we sent Harrison round there this morning, so I've said he can sleep on the sofa for a day or two. Do you have a problem with that?'

'Why would I?' asked the boy suspiciously.

'It'll be crowded with three of us.'

'Do me a favour,' he said scornfully. 'The warehouse was *crowded.*' He looked expectantly at Barry, who had followed them out. 'I hope you can cook, mate, because Mike's sodding useless. He can't even boil an egg without burning it.'

Barry looked nervous. 'Only self-taught, I'm afraid.'

'Yeah, well, me and Mike ain't been taught at all, so you get the job.' He jerked his head impatiently towards the car. 'Let's get going then, shall we? I'm starving. You realize we ain't had nothing to eat since seven o'clock this morning?'

While Terry escorted Barry into the kitchen and kept him captive there until he cooked something edible, Deacon took the telephone into his bedroom and made a call to Lawrence. 'I'm sorry to keep bothering you,' he said, 'but I need some advice and I don't know who else to ask.'

'I'm honoured,' said Lawrence.

'You haven't heard what the problem is yet.' As briefly as he could he related the details of Barry's arrest. 'I persuaded them he deserved a second chance, so they gave him one hell of a bollocking and released him. As long as nothing else comes to light, he's in the clear.'

'So what's the problem?'

'I said he could stay here with me and Terry.'

'Dear, dear. A latent homosexual who performs acts of gross indecency living cheek by jowl with a disturbed adolescent who will probably have no compunction at all about leading him on in order to blackmail him. You certainly have an appetite for trouble, Michael.'

Deacon sighed. 'I knew I could rely on you to be

objective. So what do I do? Barry's under strict instructions not to tell Terry why he was arrested, but Terry's no fool and he'll have worked it out for himself by tomorrow.'

Lawrence's happy laugh rippled down the wire. 'Start praying?'

'Ha! Ha! How about this? Come to Christmas lunch tomorrow and help me keep the peace. Being a lonely old Jew without family who rarely feels useful, you can't possibly be doing anything. Can you?'

'Even if I were, my dear chap, I couldn't resist so charming an invitation.'

DS Harrison was shrugging on his coat when a colleague popped his head round the door to say there was a Mrs Powell to see him. 'Tell her I've gone,' he growled. 'Dammit, I've already lost six hours' leave because of her blasted trespassers.'

'Too late,' said the colleague with a jerk of his head. 'Stewart told her you're here and she's waiting down the corridor.'

'Damn!' He followed the other man out.

'Detective Sergeant Harrison,' he introduced himself to the woman. 'How can I help you, Mrs Powell?' She was quite a looker, he thought, a great deal more attractive in the flesh than in her photograph, and he wasn't surprised that watching her make love on her carpet had set Barry's hormones racing.

She gave an uncertain smile. 'I'm frightened to go home,' she said simply. 'I live alone' – she gestured unhappily towards a window – 'and it's dark. This man you caught in my garden? He is locked up, isn't he?'

Harrison shook his head. 'We've released him pending further enquiries. But our understanding was that you wouldn't be home until after Christmas, and we asked Kent police to inform you of our decision together with our reasons for doing it. There's obviously been a breakdown in communications.' He wiped a hand over his face in irritation. 'I don't think you've anything to fear, Mrs Powell. In our opinion, the man acted out of character after getting drunk and won't be troubling you again. He's currently staying with a friend of his, Michael Deacon, whom I think you know, and we don't anticipate any further trouble.'

Her eyes opened wide in alarm. 'But Michael Deacon forced his way into my house only four days ago when *he* was drunk.' She shivered suddenly. 'I don't understand. Why did no one talk to me about any of this? I've never heard of this man Barry Grover, but if he's a friend of Mr Deacon's—' She caught at Harrison's sleeve. 'I *know* someone's been watching me,' she said urgently. 'I've seen him at least twice. He's a short man with glasses and he wears a blue anorak. He was standing outside my house about ten days ago when I turned into my drive, and he walked away when he saw me. Is that the man you arrested?'

Harrison frowned uncomfortably. 'It certainly sounds like him but he claims he didn't go near your house until Saturday night.'

'He's lying,' she said flatly. 'I saw him again about a week ago. It was very dark but I'm sure it was the same person. He was standing under a tree at the entrance to the estate and his glasses caught my headlamps as I drove in.'

'Why didn't you call the police?'

She pressed trembling fingers to her forehead as if she had a headache. 'You can't report every man who looks at you,' she said. 'It only becomes frightening when they start to behave oddly. According to the policeman who came to tell me about the arrest, he was exposing himself over a photograph of me.' Her voice rose slightly. 'If that's true, why aren't you prosecuting him? He's not going to stop now, not if he's been allowed to get away with it. By letting him go, you've given him the right to terrorize me.'

Harrison turned back to his office and opened the door for her. 'I'll need a statement from you, with details of when and where you saw him previously. And you'd better include this incident with Michael Deacon.' He checked his watch surreptitiously and stifled a sigh. His wife would not forgive him for this.

Terry took his silver-foil wad out of his pocket. 'Who wants a spliff?' he asked.

'I told you to get rid of that,' said Deacon.

'I did. Up my arse till the heat was off.' He glanced at Barry. 'Barry wants one, don't you, mate? Matter of fact, he deserves one after that meal,' he told Deacon. 'Bloody brilliant, it was. Knocks spots off anything you've managed to produce.' He set to work splitting the tobacco out of Deacon's Benson and Hedges. 'So what were you doing round Aye-mander's place, Barry? I don't buy that cobblers you and Mike gave me earlier. Even the fuzz don't take six hours to tell the difference between a short, fat bloke and a tall, skinny one.' He paused momentarily to fix his pale – and intimidating – gaze on the man opposite. 'You looked shit-scared when you came out.'

Barry's small bubble of confidence over the success of his cooking shrank away. His fear of being thrown out of the flat if this adolescent boy found out what he'd done was greater than his fear of the police. 'I – er—'

'He had every reason to be scared,' said Deacon coldly, levelling a finger at Barry's face. 'He's worked out who Billy is – he's even carrying a picture of him in his pocket – and he knew I'd rip his head off if the police got that information before I did.' His voice hardened. 'Jesus, you're such an arsehole, Barry. I still can't believe you'd jeopardize all the work we've put into this sodding story just for the sake of seeing what that silly bitch looks like in real life.'

'Leave off,' said Terry, peeling cigarette papers from a Rizla packet. 'How could he know the Old Bill was going to turn up? Come on then, Barry, who was he? Anyone I've heard of?'

Barry held Deacon's gaze for a moment, and there was a look of gratitude in his over-damp eyes. 'I wouldn't think so,' he said then. 'He went missing when you were seven years old.' He took off his glasses and started to polish them. 'You saw the photograph?' he asked Deacon. 'And you're sure it's Billy?'

'Yes.'

'But I showed another version of him to you yesterday, Mike, and you didn't even give him a second glance.'

Deacon took a carving knife out of the table drawer and balanced it in the palm of his hand. 'I wasn't joking when I said I'd rip your head off,' he murmured. 'Are you going to tell me who he is before Terry and I start wiping you off the floor?'

The WPC put her arms around a weeping Amanda and looked accusingly at the sergeant. 'Be fair, sarge, you swallowed that scumbag's story hook, line and sinker. He said he watched her making love on her carpet and you believed him, but he was bound to say that or something similar. For your average pervert, a woman semi-clothed or naked in her own house is justification for anything. "It wasn't my fault, guv, it was the woman's fault. She didn't pull her curtains. She knew I was out there and she wanted to excite me." It sucks, for Christ's sake.' She sounded very angry. 'I'm sick to death of men trying to excuse themselves by smearing women. In any case, it doesn't make a blind bit of difference whether Amanda was having sex or not that night. It's still no reason for inadequate little men to jerk off afterwards over their photographs.'

Wearily, Harrison held up his hands. 'I agree. All right? I agree.' He closed his eyes. 'I was merely trying to establish some facts, and I am sorry if Amanda took offence at anything I said.' When a man was wedged between a rock and a hard place, the only way out was to exploit a weakness.

Deacon read what Barry had on Peter Fenton, finishing with Anne Cattrell's piece, then propped his chin on his hands and stared in frustration at the cover of *Unsolved Mysteries of the Twentieth Century*. 'It's all here – a hundred reasons for a man to abscond and live the rest of his life in torment – but no damn reason at all for choosing Amanda Powell's garage to die in.' His own collection of notes was lying on the table beside him and he picked out the cutting on Nigel de Vriess. 'Why should this get him excited? Where's the connection between the Streeter story and the Fenton story?'

'Maybe there isn't one,' said Barry. 'You're only guessing that's what Billy read before he left the warehouse because you want to establish a pattern, but I keep asking myself why Mrs Powell told you Billy's story if she had anything to fear from what you might find out.' He placed Billy's mugshot beside the photograph of the young James Streeter. 'Superficially, there's a pattern here, but it takes a computer to show you there isn't.' He smiled apologetically. 'Perhaps it's a case of truth being stranger than fiction, Mike.'

Terry, dreamily engaged on smoking the joint that the other two had rejected in favour of another bottle of wine, spoke through the blue haze that surrounded him. 'That's the biggest load of crap I've ever heard. You're talking through your arse, mate.'

'What's your theory?'

'Well, look at it this way. What happens to the average wife whose husband dumps her in the shit and vanishes with all the loot? She don't bloody come up smelling of roses, that's for sure.'

'This one does,' said Deacon thoughtfully. 'Reeks of the damn things, as a matter of fact.'

'There you are then,' said Terry owlishly, not too clear what Deacon was talking about.

'So what?'

'Means she's scored, doesn't it? Means she ain't no pushover.' He sought to express himself. 'Means she don't reckon men too high. Ah, shit!' he said, looking at their bewildered faces. 'Don't you understand nothing?'

'We might if you spoke in words of more than two syllables,' said Deacon drily. 'Man has not spent centuries developing sophisticated language to have it reduced to grunts, glottal stops and endless double negatives that convey absolutely nothing. Work out what you want to say and try again.'

'Jesus, you're a poncy git sometimes,' said Terry scathingly, but he made an effort to collect his thoughts. 'Okay, try this. Even when he were drunk, Billy had reasons for what he did. They may not have been *good* reasons, but they were reasons. Do you understand that?'

The two men nodded.

'Right, next point. Amanda's done pretty well for herself, never mind her husband's a criminal and dropped her in it. That makes her a clever bloody bitch. Do you understand that?'

Two more nods.

'So put those two together, and what do you get? You get Billy going to Amanda's house for a reason, and Amanda using her brains afterwards.'

Deacon ground his teeth. 'Is that it?'

Terry sucked the cannabis deep into his lungs. 'My money's on Amanda. If she's cleverer than you and Billy put together, she's going to win, isn't she?'

'Win what?'

'How the hell should I know? You're the one who's playing the game with her, not me. I'm just along for the ride.'

Chapter Seventeen

WHEN THE DOORBELL rang unexpectedly the three men showed varying degrees of alarm. None of them doubted it was the police. Terry bolted for the lavatory and belatedly flushed his guilt into the sewers; Deacon flung open the kitchen window and sought frantically for an air freshener; but Barry, showing more composure than either of them, turned the gas up under the dirty frying pan, crushed garlic into the sizzling fat and started chopping onions. 'I've been expecting them,' he said in resignation. 'I'll not forgive myself if they arrest you, too, Mike. None of this is your fault.'

Harrison grew tetchy when it seemed clear that Deacon intended to keep him indefinitely on the front step of the flats. 'If you carry on like this,' he warned him, 'I'll be back in half an hour with an arrest warrant for the whole damn lot of you. Come on, let me in. I need to talk to Barry again, and you're just making me suspicious with these delaying tactics. What the hell's going on up there? Is Barry shafting that little boyfriend of yours?'

Deacon let him pass. 'Maybe it's time you retired,' he

said dispassionately. ‘Even I wouldn’t stoop so low as to make a remark like that, and I’m a journalist.’

Harrison surveyed him with weary amusement. ‘You’re an amateur, Mr Deacon. A raw recruit could get past you.’

The smell in the flat was revolting, a mixture of burnt fat, garlic, onions and, overall, the exotic reek of Jazz aftershave which Terry had sprinkled liberally over Deacon’s sofa. The kitchen door was shut and Terry and Barry were sitting, none too relaxed, watching the television in the corner.

The sergeant stood on the threshold for a moment, then took out his cigarettes and offered one to Deacon. ‘Interesting atmosphere,’ he said mildly.

Deacon agreed. He accepted a cigarette with some relief. ‘DS Harrison has a few more questions for Barry,’ he announced to the room in general. ‘So maybe Terry and I should make ourselves scarce for ten minutes.’

Harrison closed the door of the flat. ‘I’d rather you stayed, Mr Deacon. I have some questions for you, too.’

‘Not Terry, though.’ Deacon took five pounds from his pocket and jerked his head at the boy. ‘There’s a pub on the corner. We’ll join you there when we’ve finished.’

Terry shook his head. ‘No way. What’ll I do if you never turn up?’

‘Why wouldn’t we?’

Terry flicked a suspicious glance at the sergeant. ‘He ain’t come round to pass the time of day, Mike. My guess is he’s going to arrest Barry again over that Powell woman. Am I right, Mr Harrison?’

The sergeant shrugged noncommittally. ‘I want some

answers to a few more questions, that's all. As far as I'm concerned, you're not involved, so you can go or you can stay. I'm easy either way.'

'But I'm not,' said Deacon firmly, reaching the spare key off a shelf by the door. 'Come on, lad, hop it. If we don't join you in half an hour, you can let yourself back in.'

'No,' said the boy stubbornly. 'I'm staying. Billy were a mate, same as you and Barry are, and you don't walk out on mates when they need you.'

'Let's get on with it,' said Harrison impatiently, lowering himself into a chair and leaning forward to stare at Barry. 'Mrs Powell tells a different story from you, my friend. According to her, you've been stalking her for a couple of weeks, and you're terrifying her out of her wits. She's seen you on at least two occasions, described you down to what colour shoes you wear and denies absolutely that anyone was with her last night or that she was making love on her sitting-room carpet at two o'clock in the morning. She wants you locked up because, until you are, she's too frightened to stay in her house.' He switched his gaze to Deacon. 'She has also described in meticulous detail how your friend here forced his way in on Thursday night and refused to leave. She says he was drunk, violent and abusive, and refused to explain at any point why he was there. So? What the hell's going on with you two and this woman?'

There was a short silence.

'She's very beautiful,' Deacon said slowly, 'and I *was* very drunk, but she's relying on the fact that I told her the next morning I couldn't remember anything.' He strolled across to the television and switched it off before leaning his back against the wall beside it. 'It was true at the time, but not after a decent breakfast and several cups of coffee. She can almost get away with saying I forced my way in, because I leaned on her door when she opened it and it would have been difficult for her to shut me out at that point. But I wasn't violent and I wasn't abusive and there was nothing to stop her calling the police if she was afraid of me. We had a brief conversation before I passed out on her sofa, and the next morning she made me drink a cup of coffee before she let me go. I said sorry so many times that it started to get on her nerves, and when I asked her if I'd frightened her, she said she was long past being frightened by anything.' He smiled slightly. 'She can accuse me of lousy timing and lousy technique' – his eyes narrowed – 'but she can't accuse me of anything else. I hardly ever become aggressive under the influence of alcohol, sergeant. Merely embarrassing.'

'That's true,' said Terry. 'He told me and Barry he wanted babies when he got drunk last night. He were weeping all over the bloody shop.'

Deacon looked at him with disfavour. 'I was not weeping.'

'Near enough,' said Terry with a wicked smile.

Harrison ignored this exchange and turned to Barry. 'You swore you hadn't been near Mrs Powell's house before last night.'

Barry flushed guiltily. 'I hadn't.'

'I don't believe you.'

The little man shook with nerves. 'I hadn't,' he repeated.

'She described you in detail, told me where you were standing when she saw you. How could she do that if she didn't see you?'

'I don't know,' said Barry helplessly.

'Did she say when she saw him?' asked Deacon.

'She's not sure of the exact dates, but the first occasion was about ten days ago, and the second two or three days later.' He took a notebook from his pocket and flipped over the pages. 'She described him as a short man with glasses, wearing a blue anorak, grey slacks and light-coloured shoes which were probably suede. She said he was standing outside her house when she approached it in her car, but walked away when she turned into her drive. Do you still deny that it was you, Barry?'

'Yes.' He looked in desperation towards Deacon. 'It can't have been me, Mike. I never went there before.'

Deacon frowned. 'It sounds like you,' he pointed out, wondering if he had been wrong and Harrison right. 'It's one hell of an accurate description.'

'Jesus, it's a good thing I didn't go for that drink,' said Terry scornfully. 'You two'd be lost without me.' He turned aggressively on Barry. 'What was it I said to you in the kitchen? Sad people wear anoraks, but *really* sad people wear suede shoes. And what did you say to me? It's a pity you didn't meet me on Thursday because that's when you bought the shoes. I told you that bitch was clever. She's got one of those coppers to give her a description of you and fed it back to Mr Harrison here.

If you paid for those shoes with a credit card, mate, you're in the clear, ain't you? There's no way you could've been wearing them ten days ago.'

Barry's sad face brightened. 'I did,' he said. 'I've even got the receipt. It's in my room at home.'

'And how many other pairs of suede shoes do you own?' asked Harrison, unimpressed by Terry's reasoning.

'None,' said Barry with rising excitement. 'I bought these as a Christmas present to myself because all my shoes are black. Mike knows that. He's the one who told me black shoes were boring.'

'Yes,' said Deacon thoughtfully, 'I did.' He bent to flick ash into the ashtray on the coffee table, using the pause for some rapid thinking. 'Give me a description of the man she was with last night, Barry,' he said, 'the one she's denying was there.'

'I've already told you,' said Barry uncomfortably.

'Tell me again.'

'Fair, good-looking . . .' he petered out in an embarrassed silence, unwilling to revisit his shameful voyeuristic excitement. The thrill of the experience had long since vanished for him.

'The description Barry gave me this afternoon,' Deacon told Harrison, 'was tall, slim, blond, tanned and with a tattoo or birthmark on his right shoulder blade. He didn't recognize him, and I don't recognize the description, but let's say I can prove to you that such a man exists and that Amanda Powell is well acquainted with him?'

Harrison wasn't against the proposition. He still smarted from the drubbing he had received when he dared to question her denial. *But* . . . 'What difference would it make?'

'It might persuade you to ask her why she's lying about him being there.'

'I repeat, what difference does it make? There's no law against her having a man in her house, and Barry could have seen him on one of the other occasions she says he was there. In itself, the man's existence proves nothing.'

'But, just for the moment, assume Barry's telling the truth. Accept that he hadn't been to Mrs Powell's house before and that he did see a man there last night. Aren't you curious about why she's lying? I know I am.'

Harrison held his gaze for a moment. 'Mrs Powell is very' – he sought for a word – 'convincing.' He looked as if he were about to say something else, then thought better of it.

'Too convincing?' Deacon suggested.

'I didn't say that.'

Deacon stubbed out his cigarette, then moved to the telephone and consulted the address book beside it. He dialled a number. 'Hello, Maggie, it's Mike Deacon here. Yes, I know it's late, but I really do need to talk to Alan rather urgently.' He waited, then smiled into the receiver. 'Yes, you old buzzard, it's me again. How are you feeling?' He laughed. 'She let you have a Bell's? Things are looking up then. A small favour over the phone, that's all. I'm going to switch over to the loudspeaker because there are three other people in the room, and they're all interested in what I hope you're about to say.

I want you to describe Nigel de Vriess for me.' He pressed the loudspeaker button and replaced the handset.

'What he looks like, you mean?' barked Alan Parker's gravelly voice.

'Yes. You might just confirm that you've never given me a description of him before.'

'Only if you tell me what this is all about. I may be on my last legs, but I'm still a journalist. What's the oily toad been up to?'

'I'm not sure yet. You'll be the first to know after me.'

'And pigs might fly.' Alan chuckled. 'All right, I've never given you his description before. To the best of my recollection he's about my height – which is five eleven – and has blond hair which he dyes to cover the grey. He's always impeccably dressed in dark suits, probably from Harrods. Wears a white carnation in his buttonhole. Good-looking, suave. Think of Roger Moore as James Bond and you won't go far wrong. Anything else you want to know?'

'We were given a description of a man I believe to be him.' Deacon's grin reflected itself in his voice. 'But he was bollock-naked at the time, so how he dresses doesn't help us much. He was described as having an all-over body tan and a tattoo or a birthmark on his right shoulder blade. Can you verify either of those facts?'

'Hah! I can't speak for the tan, but he certainly has a birthmark on his shoulder blade. Legend has it, put about by him, of course, that it's shaped like the devil's number – 666 – which is why he was a millionaire by the age of thirty, the devil looking after his own and all that twaddle. But one of his floozies described it as looking more like a dog's pizzle. Never seen it myself, so can't say either way.' His voice took on a wheedling tone. 'Come on, Mike. What *is* all this? I'll have your hide if DVS is on the skids, and you've kept it to yourself. I've got shares in the bloody thing.'

'To the best of my knowledge, this has nothing to do with his business, Alan.' With renewed promises to keep his old friend posted, Deacon cut the line and lifted an eyebrow in Harrison's direction. 'Amanda's in-laws have been claiming for five years that she and Nigel de Vriess conspired to defraud Lowenstein's Bank of £10 million, then made a scapegoat of her husband by murdering him. No one, including the police, has ever taken the claims seriously because there was no evidence that Nigel and Amanda had anything to do with each other after she married James.'

Harrison digested this in silence for a moment. 'There still isn't,' he pointed out. 'Everything your friend said is presumably in the public domain. What was to stop you or Barry looking it up and then using it to compromise Mrs Powell?'

'Nothing at all,' said Deacon evenly, lighting another cigarette. 'In fact, that's exactly what I was planning to do after Christmas. The first opportunity I had, I intended to make an appointment to interview de Vriess. You'll have to take my word for it that the only research I've done on him so far was to treat Alan Parker to a drink last Sunday and ask him how de Vriess funded the purchase of his mansion in Hampshire, which is the area that's been exercising the brains – and curiosity – of the Streeter family.'

'And I never even knew of him before last night,' put in Barry tentatively.

Deacon retrieved his notes from the kitchen, and shut the door hurriedly on the heavy fetid air that seeped out of it like sump oil. He handed the *Mail* Diary piece to Harrison and explained briefly why he'd been looking for it, or something like it. 'We're after anything that might connect Billy Blake to Amanda Powell,' he finished.

'Have you found a connection?'

Deacon's expression was neutral. 'We're still working on it. As I told you this afternoon, the most likely explanation is that Billy was her husband. But we can't prove it.'

There was a long pause while Harrison considered the implications of what Deacon had told him.

'If Billy was James, then her in-laws are wrong,' he pointed out. 'She and de Vriess couldn't have murdered him five years ago if he was still alive in June.'

Deacon grinned. 'Even we amateurs worked that one out, so I'm beginning to think it's the crux of the whole thing. It's so blindingly obvious, after all.'

He resumed his position against the wall and told Harrison at length how he believed Amanda had seized upon the fortuitous death of a strange man in her garage, who bore an odd resemblance to her husband, to clear herself of lingering suspicions of murder and at the same time formalize her position as a widow. 'My only role, as

I see it, was to be the objective observer who generated official interest,' he finished. 'But she must be very worried now if she thinks Barry saw her and Nigel together. She can't afford doubts being raised about her relationship with him.'

Harrison clearly found the arguments convincing and asked if he could borrow the photographs of Billy's mugshot and the young James Streeter. 'How would you expect her to react when I show her these?' he queried, tucking them into his coat pocket.

But Deacon shook his head. 'I've no idea,' he said honestly, remembering how her nails had dug into his chin when he had made the suggestion himself.

'Why didn't you tell Mr Harrison about Billy being this Fenton geezer?' asked Terry after the DS had gone.

'Do you know what a scoop is?'

'Sure.'

'That's why I didn't tell him.'

'Yeah, but you just gave him a load of bull instead. I mean, Amanda ain't stupid, is she? She can't never have thought it'd be that easy to have James declared dead. The Old Bill'd need loads more proof than a couple of snapshots.'

Deacon grinned. 'She called me a clever man when *I* put the theory to her.'

'Do you fancy her?'

'What on earth makes you think that?'

'Why else'd you want to pass out on her sofa?'

Deacon rubbed his jaw. 'She has the same blue eyes as my mother,' he said reflectively. 'I felt homesick.'

Harrison dropped in at the station before going on to Amanda's house. He made a few enquiries of his colleagues, then put through a call to PC Dutton in Kent. Had Mrs Powell been informed of Barry Grover's release? Yes. And how much information had Dutton given her about him? A full description was the answer, and details of when he had been outside her house. Was this wrong? There had been nothing on the faxed information requesting confidentiality, and Mrs Powell had pointed out quite reasonably that she needed to know who to look for in case he troubled her again.

Harrison had worked himself into a fine fury by the time he reached the Thamesbank Estate.

The WPC who was minding Amanda pending Harrison's return from re-interviewing Barry answered the door. 'Where is she?' demanded the sergeant, pushing past her.

'In the sitting-room.'

'Right. I want a witness to this. You'll make notes of everything she says, and if you bat one eyelid at what *I* say, you'll damn well wish you hadn't. Have you got that?' He shouldered open the door to the sitting-room and sat himself squarely on the sofa facing Amanda. 'You've been lying to me, Mrs Powell.'

She drew away from him.

'There *was* a man in this house last night.'

She leaned forward to sift the rose-petal pot-pourri, scattering the scent through her slender fingers. 'You're quite wrong, sergeant. I was on my own.'

Harrison ignored this. 'We've tentatively identified your' – he chose the next word carefully – '*companion* as Nigel de Vriess. Will he also deny being here?'

Something shifted at the back of her eyes, and he felt his vestigial hackles rise in response. She reminded him suddenly of a bad-tempered Siamese cat his grandmother had once owned. As long as it was left alone, it was beautiful; touched, it clawed and spat. When it tore deep tramlines in her face one day, his grandmother had it put down. 'Beauty is as beauty does,' she had remarked without regret.

'I would imagine so,' Amanda remarked.

'When did you last see him?'

'I've no idea. It's so long ago I couldn't possibly say.'

'Before or after your husband went missing?'

'Before.' She shrugged. 'Long before.'

'So if I ask his partner where Nigel was last night, she'll probably say he was at home with her?'

The tip of her pink tongue played across her lips, moistening them. 'I wouldn't know.'

'I *will* be asking her, Mrs Powell, and I'm sure she'll ask me why I'm asking.'

She shrugged again. 'I have no interest in either of them.'

'Then why were you so determined to discredit Barry Grover earlier?'

She didn't answer.

Harrison dipped a hand into his pocket. 'Tell me

about Billy Blake,' he invited. 'Did you recognize him when you found him in your garage?'

She took the change of tack with only the mildest of frowns. 'Billy Blake?' she echoed. 'Of course I didn't recognize him. Why would I? He was a stranger.'

He produced the borrowed photographs, and aligned them carefully on the coffee table. 'The same man?' he suggested.

Her shock was so extreme that he couldn't doubt it was genuine. Whatever else she might be guilty of, he thought, it had clearly never crossed her mind that Billy Blake might be mistaken for her missing husband.

But then Deacon had omitted to mention that she'd heard that very same theory on Thursday night.

Deacon replaced the telephone receiver with a gleam of amusement in his dark eyes. 'Harrison's pissed off with being sent on wild-goose chases,' he remarked. 'Apparently Mrs Powell looked poleaxed when he showed her the photos.'

'I'm not surprised,' said Terry. 'Like Barry said, if you forget the difference in age, it takes a computer to tell them apart. Maybe she's shitting bricks right this minute because she's suddenly clicked that it might've been James after all.'

'No,' said Deacon slowly, 'she didn't blink an eyelid when I suggested it to her. She's always known it wasn't him, so why throw a wobbly for Harrison?' He looked at his watch. 'I'm going out,' he said abruptly. 'You two can watch a late movie till I get back.'

'Where are you going?' demanded Terry.

'Never you mind.'

'You're planning a Peeping Tom act like old Barry, ain't you? You're going to sneak into her garden and drool while she gets rogered by Nigel.'

Deacon stared down at him. 'You've got a grubby little mind, Terry. Unless Sergeant Harrison's blind as a bat, Nigel de Vriess is long gone.' He levelled a finger at the boy. 'I won't be more than a couple of hours, so behave yourself. I'll skin you alive if you try anything on while I'm out of this flat.'

Terry flicked a thoughtful glance in Barry's direction. 'You can trust *me*, Mike.'

The traffic was thin at that time of night, and it took only half an hour to drop down through the City and head east along the river to the Isle of Dogs. He kept a wary eye on his rear-view mirror, regretting his decision to open the second bottle of wine. Lights blazed in Amanda's house and he toyed with the idea of acting out Terry's fantasy by sneaking round the back and peeping through her sitting-room windows. The idea was more attractive than he liked to admit, but he abandoned it for fear of the consequences. Instead he fulfilled one of Billy's prophecies. '*You will never do what you want because the tribe's will is stronger than yours.*'

He rang the doorbell and listened to the sound of her footsteps in the hall. There was a brief silence while she put her eye to the spy-glass. 'I'm not going to open this door, Mr Deacon,' she said from the other side, 'so I suggest you leave before I call the police.'

'I doubt they'll come,' he said, stooping to smile amiably into the pinhole. 'They're bored with the both of us. At the moment they can't decide which of us is telling more lies, although you seem to have the edge. Sergeant Harrison's deeply put out by your refusal to admit that Nigel de Vriess was in this house last night.'

'He wasn't.'

'Barry saw him.'

'Your friend's sick.'

He leaned his shoulder against the door and took out a cigarette. 'A little confused, perhaps, like me. I had no idea I'd frightened you so much on Thursday night, Amanda, not when you were so charming to me the next morning.' He paused, waiting for an answer. 'Sergeant Harrison's surprised you didn't call the police when I passed out on the sofa. It's what most women would have done when faced with a violent and abusive intruder.'

'What do you want, Mr Deacon?'

'A chat. Preferably inside where it's warmer. I've found out who Billy was.'

There was a long silence before the chain rattled and she opened the door. The light in the hall was very bright and he was taken aback by her appearance. She seemed unwell. Her face was drawn and colourless, and she looked nothing like the radiant woman in the yellow dress who had dazzled him three days ago.

He frowned. 'Are you all right?'

'Yes.' She was staring at him rather oddly, as if she expected to see a reaction in his eyes, and relaxed visibly when he showed none. She stepped back. 'You'd better come in.'

He looked around the hall and noticed a suitcase at the bottom of the stairs. 'Going somewhere?'

'No. I've just come back from my mother's.'

'What's wrong?'

'Nothing.'

He followed her into the sitting-room and noticed immediately that the scent of roses was absent. Instead, the window was open and the rotten smell of the exposed river banks seemed to be drifting in on the night air. 'The tide must be out,' he said. 'You should have kept one of the flats in Teddington, Amanda. There's no tide above the locks.'

What little colour remained in her face leached out of it. 'What are you talking about?'

'The smell. It's not very pleasant. You should shut your window.' He lowered himself on to the sofa and lit his cigarette, watching her as she sprayed the room with air freshener before fluttering the pot-pourri between her fingers to disperse its scent.

'Is that better?' she asked him.

'Can't you tell?'

'Not really. I'm so used to it.' She took the chair opposite. 'Are you going to tell me who Billy was?'

The tic was working furiously at the corner of her mouth, and he wondered why she was so agitated and why she looked so deathly pale. Whatever he may have told Harrison, it would take more than Barry's chance sighting of her with Nigel de Vriess to give credence to the Streeters' theory of conspiracy to murder. She had impressed him as a woman of cool composure, and he was puzzled by her lack of it now. The paradox was that he found her infinitely less attractive in despair – so much so that he wondered why he had ever lusted after her – but a great deal more likeable. Vulnerability was a quality he recognized and understood.

'His name was Peter Fenton. You probably remember the story. He was a diplomat – believed to have been a spy – who vanished from his house in 1988 and was never seen again. Not as Peter Fenton, anyway.'

She didn't say anything.

'You don't seem very impressed.'

She pressed her hands to her lips for a moment, and he realized that her silence owed more to the fact that she couldn't speak than that she didn't want to. 'Why did he come here?' she managed at last.

'I don't know. I hoped *you* would tell *me*. Did you or James know him?'

She shook her head.

'Are you sure? Do you know everyone James knew?'

'Yes.'

Deacon took the *Mail* Diary piece on de Vriess from his pocket and handed it to her. 'Billy read that three weeks before he ended up dead in your garage. Let's say he went to Halcombe House with the intention of getting Amanda Streeter's address out of Nigel because he didn't know you were calling yourself Amanda Powell or that you lived and worked within a mile or so of where he was dossing.' He thought for a moment and, in the absence of an ashtray, tapped ash into his palm. 'The fact that he arrived here meant Nigel must have told him how to find you, which makes your lover a bit of a bastard, Amanda. First, for giving out your address to any old drunken bum who asks for it, and secondly for not telling you to expect a visitor. He didn't, did he?'

She licked her lips. 'How do you know Billy read this?'

Deacon lied. 'One of the men at the warehouse told me. So what's it all about? Why should Peter Fenton be so intent on finding Amanda Streeter? And why would Nigel help him? Did *they* know each other?'

She rubbed her temples with trembling fingers. 'I don't know.'

'Okay, try this. What might Peter have known about you that sent him chasing after you when he read your name in the newspaper? Maybe he had something on you *and* Nigel, and Nigel wriggled out by persuading him it was you he needed to talk to?'

She withdrew into her chair and closed her eyes. 'Billy never spoke to me. I didn't know he was here until he was dead. I don't know who he was or why he came to my house. Most of all, I don't know why—' She fell silent.

'Go on.'

'I feel ill.'

Deacon glanced towards the window. 'Tell me about Nigel,' he prompted. 'Why would he give your address to Peter without telling you he'd done it?'

'I don't know.' She gave a troubled shake of her head.

'Why do you think he knew him as Peter Fenton? It was Billy Blake who died in my garage.'

'Okay. Why give your address to Billy?'

'I don't know,' she said again. 'What sort of man was he?' Her eyes opened wide, and Deacon feared she was about to vomit.

'If you mean Billy, he was a fine man.' He took a handkerchief from his pocket. 'I find it's easier to hold on,' he said with a faint smile, 'but you know where the lavatory is if you need it.' He waited till her gagging ceased. 'A psychiatrist who had three sessions with him described him as half-saint, half-fanatic. I've read a transcript of part of their interview. Billy believed in the salvation of souls and the mortification of the flesh, but he felt himself to be personally damned.' He studied her for a moment. 'From my own experience of him, through the medium of Terry Dalton – a youngster he befriended and cared for – I'd say Billy was a man of honour and integrity despite being a drunk and a thief.'

'Why should any of that make him want to come here?'

Deacon got up and went to the window to toss his dog-end into the garden. The air that blew in was sweet and clean and smelt faintly of the sea. He turned back to the cloying atmosphere of her spare, minimalist surroundings and he began to understand why her car was always parked in her driveway, why she drenched the room in rose-scented spray and, ultimately, why six months after Billy's death she had been so desperate to find out who her uninvited guest had been. He had had an inkling of it once before, but hadn't believed it. He held the back of his hand to his nose, and he saw recognition in her eyes because he was reacting the way she had expected when he first entered the house. 'What did you do to him, Amanda?'

'Nothing. If I'd known he was there, I'd have helped him as I helped you.'

She had put on a hell of a performance for Harrison in the last few hours, but was she acting now? Deacon didn't think so, but then he was no judge. 'Why did you lie to Harrison about me and Barry?' he asked, opening all the windows to let in the freezing air. Anything was better than the sweet, sickly smell of death.

She shook her head, unable to cope with the sudden switch of direction.

'Are the Streeters right? Did you and Nigel work the fraud and then murder James?'

She lowered the handkerchief. 'James worked the fraud. Everyone knows that except his family. They were so proud of the success he made of his life that they forgot what he was really like. He loathed them, never went near them in case their penny-pinching poverty rubbed off on him.' She sounded very bitter. 'He was always on the make, always after insider knowledge of stocks that might double in value overnight. I've never been less surprised about anything than when the police told me he'd embezzled £10 million.'

'Where did he get the knowledge to bypass the computer system? Did Marianne Filbert help him?'

Amanda shrugged. 'She must have done. Who else was there?'

'Nigel de Vriess?' he suggested. 'It's too much of a coincidence that he bought out Softworks after James and Marianne disappeared.'

She rested her head against the back of her chair. 'If Nigel was involved,' she said wearily, 'then he covered his tracks extremely well. He was investigated along with everyone else, but all the evidence pointed to James. I'm sorry the Streeters can't see that but it is the truth.'

'If you dislike James so much, why are you still married to him?'

'I didn't want any more publicity. And why get divorced if you don't want to marry again?' Unexpectedly she smiled. 'There's a simple explanation for everything, Mr Deacon, even this house. Lowndes, the company that developed the Teddington flats, also built this estate. I negotiated a straightforward exchange. I gave them full title to the Teddington property in return for full title to this house. And they did rather better out of the deal than I did. Converting the school was easy because I'd already done the drawings and obtained planning permission, and the flats were sold even before they were finished. Lowndes had far more trouble shifting these houses because they'd overpriced them, and the housing market was in the doldrums in 1991. You may not believe it, but I did them a favour by taking this one off their hands.' Her voice took on its bitter note again. 'If the bank hadn't threatened to pull the rug out from under me because of the uncertainty over James, I'd have made a great deal more by seeing the development through than by accepting this house in lieu.'

Were explanations ever that simple? Why hadn't she

fought harder to see her project through? She was no pushover, in all conscience. *And once she'd cleared herself of involvement in the fraud* . . . 'You told me Billy liked to doss down as near the river as possible,' he said, 'but the same is true of you. Teddington's on the river. This house is on the river. Your office is on the river. Could the river be the connection between you?'

She raised the handkerchief to her mouth. There was still no colour in her face except the blue of her eyes, which followed every movement he made. 'If I knew the answer to that—' She paused. 'I thought – well, I hope it's enough just to identify him. If I can put the right name on his plaque—' She fell silent.

'He'll rest in peace?'

She nodded. 'It's not always like this, you know.' She gestured unhappily towards the window. 'It's been worse since you came to the house.'

'Has he ever spoken to you?'

'No.'

'I think I heard him,' Deacon said matter-of-factly. 'Either that or I was dreaming. "Devourer of thy parent, now thy unutterable torment renews,"' he explained. 'I heard that.'

'Why would Billy say that?'

'I don't know. He was obsessed with religion. I think he may have murdered somebody and that's why he believed he was damned. Both he and his wife seemed to see hell as their inevitable destiny.' *'My own redemption doesn't interest me . . .' Whose then? Verity's? Amanda's?* He eyed her curiously. 'He preached repentance to others but seemed to see his own salvation in terms of a divine hand reaching down into the bottomless pit to pull him out. He said there's no way out of hell except through God's mercy.'

Her fingers tightened round the handkerchief, compressing it into a tight ball. 'What does that have to do with me?'

Or me, thought Deacon. *Why do I get the feeling that my fate is inextricably linked with Billy's . . .? He said London was full of shit . . . I've watched men die violently . . . The water reminded him of blood . . . She sends her shit along the river to infect the innocent places further down . . .*

'I need to talk to Nigel de Vriess,' he said abruptly. 'If he gave Billy your address, then Billy may have explained why he wanted it' – he paused to reflect – 'although it doesn't explain why Nigel didn't warn you to expect him.' He smiled slightly. 'I would have said he didn't like you, Amanda, if Barry hadn't witnessed what you and he were up to last night.'

She shrugged indifferently. 'Your friend's quite capable of coming up with sick fantasies about what he saw through my window. What he did to my photograph was disgusting. Even you must recognize he's an unreliable witness.'

Deacon drew his coat about him. It was very cold although Amanda seemed unaffected by it. 'I don't. He's totally reliable when it comes to anything visual. Is the Streeters' conspiracy theory right? Is that why it's so important to keep denying that Nigel was here?'

'You've already asked me that, and I've already given you my answer.'

'Do you have de Vriess's telephone number?'

'Of course not. I haven't seen him in five years.'

He gave a low laugh. 'Then for your sake, I hope he's as good a liar as you are. You're too elegant to end up with egg on your face.' He raised a hand in farewell. 'Happy Christmas, Amanda.'

'Happy Christmas, Mr Deacon.' She held out his handkerchief.

'You keep it,' he said. 'Something tells me you'll be needing it more than I do.'

Terry Dalton (14)
Lived with Billy from 1993

Cadogan Square
Geoffrey Standish's house?

Paris
Embassy? Peter Fenton

Tom Beale (68)
Lived with Billy from – ?

m. (1956)

m. (1980)

Verity
(1937–1988)

Anthony & Marilyn

The warehouse
(How long derelict?)

HELL

SUICIDE

Peter Fenton/Billy Blake (45)
(Winchester, Cambridge, Foreign Office)
(1950–1995)
(Vanished 3 July 1988)
Geoffrey Standish died 10.3.71 – 20 mls from Cambridge

IDENTITY

The Thames

MURDER

Nigel de Vriess (48)
(Softworks/DVS/left
Lowenstein's – 1990)

Amanda Streeter-Powell (36)
m. (1986)
James Streeter (44)
(Vanished 27 April 1990)

MONEY

W.F. Meredith (architects)
Teddington flats (*c.* 1900)
Thamesbank Estate
(Amanda moved 1991)
(From where?)

Lowenstein's Bank

Marianne Filbert
(Left UK for USA – 1989)
(Vanished April 1990)

Where was Billy in April 1990?

Chapter Eighteen

'I RECKON YOU and Mike take me for a mug,' said Terry, opening another can of lager and sprawling on the sofa again. 'I don't swallow this bullshit about you wanting to know what Amanda looked like. I've seen the way you watch Mike, and I've seen the way he watches you, and my guess is you're panting for him to do some uphill gardening, and he don't fancy the idea.'

Barry wouldn't look at him. 'I don't understand what you're talking about,' he said.

'Sure you do. You're a faggot, Barry. So what were you after when you went round Amanda's? And what did the Old Bill nick you for?' He put a cigarette between his lips and rolled it from side to side with the tip of his tongue. 'Know what I think? I think you got well worked up having a drink with me and Mike, and then went out to do some damage to the competition. I bet it really sticks in your gullet that he fancies Amanda more than he fancies you. Am I right or am I right?'

Barry reached forward to switch up the volume on the television. 'I don't want to talk to you,' he said.

'Stands to reason. You might hear something you don't want to hear, like Mike ain't so unavailable as he's making out.' His lips thinned to a cruel line as he lit his cigarette. 'He's pretty fucking keen on me, that's for sure.'

Barry didn't say anything.

'How about you then? You keen on me, too, are you? You were getting mighty close last night when we were going through them photos.' He propped himself on one elbow and drank noisy mouthfuls of lager.

'You shouldn't be talking like this.'

'Why not?' said the boy with a sneer. 'It makes you excited, doesn't it?'

Barry doubted anything would excite him again. Fear was the only emotion he understood now. He should have trusted his first impression that Terry was a shaven-headed thug, then he could have saved himself this terrible disappointment. He took off his glasses and stared blindly at the screen. 'If I were a different kind of man – a braver one,' he said after a moment, 'I'd stand up to you. Not for me, but for Mike. It doesn't matter what you say about me, I've had people talk about me behind my back all my life, but Mike deserves better. The sad thing is, he thinks you're a decent lad.' He squeezed the bridge of his nose between his fingers as if trying to hold back tears. 'But he couldn't be more wrong, could he?'

'Yeah, well, it ain't your place to lecture me about decency, being as how you most likely got arrested for *in*decency.'

'Did you abuse Billy's friendship the way you're abusing Mike's?'

'If I knew what it meant, I might be able to tell you.'

'Yes, I forgot. You're ignorant as well as despicable.'

Terry grinned. 'You want to be careful what you say to me, Barry. I ain't scared of no queer.' He blew a stream of smoke disdainfully in Barry's direction.

'Don't do that,' said the fat little man in a stifled voice. 'I suffer from asthma.'

'Jesus wept. If you weren't such a girl, you'd've hit me. Ain't you got no bottle at all?'

He was quite unprepared for the speed with which Barry launched himself at his throat, and equally unprepared for the little man's deceptive weight and strength. As his lungs started to struggle under the combined constriction of his throat and Barry's solid knee in the centre of his chest, he realized he'd tried the rape scam on the wrong person. He looked despairingly into Barry's unseeing eyes and saw only madness.

'Where's Terry?' asked Deacon as he let himself back into the flat.

'In his room.'

'Asleep?'

'Probably. He's been in there half an hour. Can I get you something, Mike? Coffee? A drink?'

Deacon looked around the room, noticed Terry's abandoned cigarettes on the floor and the stain on the carpet where his lager had fallen over. 'What's been going on?'

Barry followed his gaze. 'I'm sorry about that. He knocked the can over accidentally. He's tired, Mike. Don't forget he's only fourteen.'

'Did he try something on?'

'I'd rather you asked him.'

'Okay. How about a coffee? I'll check on him while you're making it.' He watched the other man go into the kitchen then went down the side corridor and tapped lightly on the spare bedroom door.

'If that's you, you murdering bastard,' said Terry's suspicious voice from the other side, 'you can bog off. I ain't coming out till Mike gets back.'

'It is Mike.'

'Jesus,' said the boy, pulling the door wide, 'am I pleased to see you. Barry's round the fucking twist. He tried to kill me.' He pointed to his throat. 'Look at that. Fucking finger prints.'

'Nasty,' said Deacon, looking at the red marks on the boy's neck. 'Why did he do it?'

'Because he's a nutter, that's why.' Terry poked his head nervously round the door jamb. 'By rights I should have the law on him. He's well dangerous, he is.'

'What's stopping you?' Deacon's eyes narrowed. 'You weren't so backward when Denning went mad.'

'That were different.'

'Meaning Denning didn't have a reason to attack Walt but Barry had a damn good reason for attacking you? You're a fool, Terry. I warned you to behave while I was out. Frankly, if you're not prepared to treat Barry with respect, you'd better leave now.'

'How do you know it weren't him started it?'

'It's the law of the jungle. Rabbits never attack weasels unless they're cornered. Plus, you're still alive, which you wouldn't be if Barry was a nutter.' He started to walk away. 'You've got two choices, sunshine,' he said over his shoulder. 'Apologize or go.'

'I ain't apologizing to no pervert. It's him tried to kill *me*.'

Deacon turned round. 'You didn't learn a damn thing from Billy, did you?' he said wearily. 'He put his hand in the fire for you to teach you the dangers of uncontrollable anger, be it yours or anyone else's, but you were too stupid to understand the message. I think I'm wasting my time with you, just as he did. You'd better start packing.'

It was a subdued Terry who joined them in the kitchen ten minutes later. There was a revealing redness about his eyes, and his walk was less cocky than usual. Deacon, who was reworking his chart, glanced up briefly, expression neutral, then returned to what he was doing. Terry thrust his bony hand at Barry. 'Sorry, mate,' he said. 'I were well out of order. No hard feelings, eh?'

Barry, who had been sitting in an uncomfortable silence while Deacon ignored him, took the hand in surprise. 'I think – ' he looked at the marks on Terry's neck – 'well, it's I who should apologize.'

'Nah. Mike's right. It were me pushed you into it. You're braver than you think. You said you'd stand up, and you did. It were my fault.'

Barry looked as if he was about to agree with him until he caught Deacon's gaze on him and changed his mind. The only thing Deacon had said to him since he'd returned to the kitchen was: 'I don't care what he said to you, Barry, but if you ever lift a hand against a child again, I'll take you apart at the seams.'

Now Deacon pointed to an empty chair as he pushed the chart to one side. 'Sit down,' he invited, listening to the distant sound of bells ringing out for midnight mass. 'Perhaps we should have gone to church,' he said, nodding towards the window. 'We always used to go to midnight mass when I was a child and it's the only time I can remember us functioning as a normal family.'

Terry, accepting this for what it was – a truce – perked up again. 'Did you go the night your dad shot himself?'

Deacon smiled slightly at Barry's horrified expression but the horror was for Terry's insensitivity, he thought, and not his father's messy death. 'No. If we had, he wouldn't have done it. We stopped going to church when he and Ma stopped talking.'

'Billy said the family that prays together stays together.'

Deacon didn't reply because he didn't want to disillusion the boy. He often thought it was the accruing disappointment of the thousand prayers that went unanswered that had led his family to disintegrate. *Please God, let Pa be nice to my friends . . . Please God, let Pa be ill so that he won't come to sports day . . . Please God, let Pa die . . .*

'My father was an atheist,' said Barry apologetically, as if he, too, didn't want to disillusion the boy.

'What happened to him?' asked Terry.

'He died of a heart attack when I was ten.' Barry sighed. 'It was very sad. My mother changed afterwards. She used to be such a happy person, but now, well, the trouble is I look so like my father – she resents that, I think.'

The conversation lapsed and they listened in silence to the pealing bells. Deacon regretted stirring memories, however good the cause. In twenty years he had not rid himself of the terrible sight of his father's blood-spattered study and the shapeless huddle that had once been Francis. Suicide, he thought, was the least forgivable of deaths because there was no time to prepare for the shock of bereavement. Whatever grief he had felt had been subsumed in disgust as he had wiped his father's blood and brains off walls, paintings, shelves and books.

It led him to think of that other suicide. 'I wonder why Verity hanged herself,' he murmured.

'I don't reckon she did,' said Terry. 'I reckon it were Billy killed her.' He gripped the air as he had done beside the brazier the first time Deacon had met him. 'That'd be more than enough to send him off his rocker.'

Deacon shook his head. 'That's the first thing the police would have looked at. The evidence of suicide must have been very convincing to persuade them otherwise.'

'Surely Anne Cattrell's right,' said Barry. 'If Verity found out by accident that she'd married her husband's murderer, wouldn't that be reason enough to kill herself?'

'I don't see why. She hated Geoffrey.' Deacon tapped his pencil against his teeth. 'According to Roger Hyde's book, her son thought she was having an affair.' He ringed Verity's name and drew a line down to James Streeter. 'How about that? Think how alike James and

Peter were. She'd have been attracted to James on looks alone. It's one explanation for Billy's interest in Amanda's address.'

'Meaning he was after revenge?' queried Terry doubtfully. 'I don't see that, Mike. First off, he'd be taking revenge on the wrong person and, second off, the dish wouldn't just be cold, it'd be fucking freezing.'

Deacon chuckled. He would never tell the boy how much he admired the guts he'd just shown in that handshake with Barry, but it didn't mean the admiration wasn't there. *Shades of his relationship with his mother? In the end, perhaps love was stronger for being disguised. Clara had never ceased declaring her love right up until the day she left him.* 'All right, hot shot, give me a better idea.'

'I ain't got one. I just reckon it's all to do with fate. See, Amanda could've talked to any journalist, but she picked the one who'd get hung up on it enough to keep going. You said yourself you and Billy are linked by fate.'

'She didn't pick me,' said Deacon. 'I picked her or, more accurately, my editor picked her and sent me off against my will to interview her. Depending on what she was expecting to achieve, she was either lucky or unlucky that events in Billy's life have faint echoes in mine.'

But Terry was not to be dissuaded. 'And then there's me. I weren't never going to phone you about Billy, but then I had to because of Walt. And if Mr Harrison hadn't recognized Tom, I wouldn't have been worried about him dropping me in it, and if you hadn't met old Lawrence and persuaded him to come and hold our hands, then he wouldn't've stuck his nose in about good parenting' – he paused for breath – 'and I wouldn't be here now. Plus, Barry wouldn't've got pissed and taken himself off to gawp at Amanda and none of us would know that Nigel was still shafting her. That's fate, that is,' he finished triumphantly. 'Ain't that right, Barry?'

Barry ducked his head to take off his glasses. He was so tired after the emotional buffeting of the last twenty-four hours that he was finding it increasingly difficult to follow the conversation. 'I suppose it depends on whether you think, as my father did, that everything happens accidentally,' he said slowly. 'He believed there was no purpose to life beyond the furtherance of the species, and that you could either suffer your pointless existence or enjoy it. But to enjoy it you had to plan ahead in order to minimize the threat of unpleasant accidents.' He smiled ruefully. 'Then he died of a heart attack.'

'Do you agree with him?' asked Deacon curiously.

'Oh, no, I agree with Terry. I think fate plays a part in our destinies.' He replaced his spectacles and sheltered nervously behind them like an inexperienced knight preparing for battle. 'I can't help feeling that it doesn't really matter why Verity hanged herself, or not as far as Amanda Powell is concerned anyway.' He put a fat finger on Deacon's chart where it said: *Where was Billy in April 1990?* 'This is Billy Blake's fate, not Peter Fenton's. Peter Fenton died in 1988.'

Far away, the bells fell silent as Christmas Day began.

*

Such strange dreams inhabited Deacon's mind that night. He put them down to the fact that he opted for the sofa in order to have Barry and Terry securely shut in bedrooms with himself as a physical barrier between them. But he sometimes thought afterwards that it was too easy to say it was a bad night, coupled with subconscious fears of homosexual rape scams and memories of his father, that led him to dream about James Streeter covered in blood.

He started out of sleep in a threshing frenzy at four o'clock in the morning with his mind full of the knowledge that *he* was James and that he had woken seconds before the final crushing blow that was going to kill him. His face was awash with sweat – *blood?* – and his heartbeat hammered in the silence of the night. *And when the heart began to beat, what dread hand and what dread feet* . . . Was this a dream? *My mother groaned, my father wept, into the dangerous world I leapt* . . . Who am I? *Devourer of thy parent, now thy unutterable torment renews* . . .

It soon became clear that the old adage 'Too many cooks spoil the broth' was a true one. Barry began patiently enough but, faced with Deacon's and Terry's natural incompetence in the kitchen, he progressed rapidly through irritation to outright tyranny. 'My mother would have your head for this,' he remarked acidly, pushing Deacon away from a bowl of saturated stuffing and transferring it to the sink.

'How am I supposed to get it right if I don't have a measuring jug?' asked Deacon sulkily.

'You use your intelligence and add the water a little more slowly,' said Barry, pressing the soggy mess into a sieve and squeezing out the excess liquid. 'It may come as a surprise to you, Mike, but you're not supposed to *pour* the stuffing into the turkey, you're supposed to *stuff* it in. That's why it's called stuffing. If you poured it in, it would be called pouring.'

'All right, all right, I get the message. I'm not a complete idiot.'

'I told you he couldn't cook,' said Terry self-righteously.

Barry turned his indignation on the boy and lifted a tiny sprout from the meagre pile on the draining board. 'What's this?' he demanded.

'A sprout.'

'Correction. It *was* a sprout. Now it's a pea. When I said take off the outer leaves, I meant one layer, not two centimetres' worth. We're supposed to be eating these, not swallowing them with a glass of water.'

'You need a drink,' said Deacon's shaven-headed incubus prosaically. 'You aren't half ratty when you're sober.'

'A drink?' Barry squeaked, stamping his little feet. 'It's nine o'clock in the morning and we haven't even got the turkey in yet.' He pointed a dramatic finger at the kitchen door. 'Out of here, both of you,' he ordered, 'or you can forget lunch.'

Deacon shook his head. 'We can't do that. I've invited Lawrence Greenhill over. He'll be very disappointed if there's nothing to eat.' He watched fury rise like a red tide in Barry's face and flapped his hands placatingly as he backed towards the kitchen door. 'Don't panic. He's a great guy. You'll like him. I'm sure he won't mind waiting if the meal isn't ready on the dot of one o'clock. Look, here's an idea,' he said, as if he was the one who had thought of it, 'why don't Terry and I make ourselves scarce so that you can get on with things? We'll be back at midday to lay the table.'

'That's good,' said Terry, raising two thumbs in salute. 'Cheers, Barry. Just make sure you do loads of roast potatoes. They're my favourite, they are.'

Deacon caught him by the collar and hoicked him through the door before their chef vanished in a puff of spontaneously combusted smoke.

'Where are we going?' asked Terry as they climbed into the car. 'We've got three hours to kill.'

'Let's muddy some waters first.' Deacon reached for his mobile and dialled Directory Enquiries. 'Yes, the number of N. de Vriess, please, Halcombe House, near Andover. Thank you.' He took a pen from his inner pocket and wrote the number on his shirt cuff before switching off the telephone.

'What are you going to do?'

'Phone him and ask him what he was doing at Amanda Powell's house on Saturday night.'

'Supposing his wife answers?'

'The conversation will be even more interesting.'

'You're cruel, you are. It's Christmas Day.'

Deacon chuckled. 'I shouldn't think anyone will answer. It'll be his secretary's number. Guys like de

Vriess don't make their private numbers public.' He squinted at his cuff as he punched the digits. 'In any case, I'll hang up if Fiona answers,' he promised, putting the phone to his ear. 'Hello?' He sounded surprised. 'Am I speaking to Nigel de Vriess? . . . Is he there? . . . He's away? Yes, it is important. I've been trying to contact him on a business matter since Friday . . . My name's Michael Deacon . . . No, I'm phoning from a mobile . . .' A long pause. 'Would it be possible to speak to his wife? . . . Can you give me a number where I can find Nigel? . . . Then perhaps you can give me an idea of when he'll be back? . . . My home number? Yes, I should be there from midday onwards. Thank you.' He gave his telephone number at the flat, then disconnected and frowned thoughtfully at Terry. 'Nigel's gone away for a few days and his wife is too unwell to speak to anyone.'

'Jesus, what a bastard! I betcha he's ditched the poor cow for Amanda.'

Deacon drummed his fingers on the steering wheel. 'Except I'd put every cent I've got on that being a policeman who answered the phone, and you don't call in the police just because your notorious husband is shagging another woman.'

'What makes you think he was Old Bill?'

'Because he was too damn efficient. He cut me off after I gave my name in order to see if it meant anything to whoever was in the room with him.'

'Could've been a butler. You're likely to have a butler if you live in a mansion.'

Deacon fired the engine. 'Butlers speak first,' he said, 'but there was silence on that line till I asked for Nigel de Vriess.' He drew out into the road. 'You don't think he's done a bunk, do you?'

'Like James?'

'Yes.'

'Why'd he want to do that?'

'Because Amanda warned him that Barry saw him in her house and he's decided to run.'

'Then why hasn't she gone, too?'

Deacon recalled the suitcase that he'd seen in her hall. 'Maybe she has,' he said rather grimly. 'That's what we're going to find out.'

They drove into the Thamesbank Estate and parked across the road from Amanda's house. It had a deserted look about it. The curtains were open but, despite the greyness of the morning, there were no lights inside and the car was gone from in front of her garage.

'She could be at church,' said Terry without conviction.

'You stay here,' Deacon said. 'I'm going to have a look through her sitting-room windows.'

'Yeah, well, just don't forget what happened to Barry when he did that,' said the boy morosely. 'If the neighbours see you, we'll be carted off to the flaming nick to answer more bloody questions, and I ain't going without my lunch two days in a row.'

'I won't be long.' True to his word, he was back in five minutes. 'No sign of her,' he said, easing in behind the wheel and fishing out his cigarettes. 'So what the hell do I do about it?'

'Nothing,' said Terry firmly. 'Let the Old Bill work it out for themselves. I mean, you're gonna look a right plonker if you go steaming in with stories about Nigel and Amanda scarpering when all that's happened is they've holed up in a hotel somewhere to hump each other. You've got a real thing about her, except I can't decide whether you fancy her something rotten or think she's a hard-nosed bitch. On balance, I reckon you fancy her because you sure as hell don't like the fact she's still fucking Nigel.' He cast a mischievous glance at Deacon's profile. 'You look like you're sucking lemons every time the subject comes up.'

Deacon ignored this. 'All these houses are identical and hers is the tenth. Why did Billy choose hers?'

'Because the garage door was open.'

'Number eight's open now.'

'So what? It weren't open when Billy came here.'

Deacon looked at him. 'How do you know?'

There was a momentary pause before Terry answered. 'I'm guessing. Look, are you planning to sit here all day or what? Barry ain't gonna like it one little bit if Lawrence turns up and we ain't back.'

Despite Terry's protests, Deacon dropped in at the police station to request Sergeant Harrison's home telephone number. Sir was joking, of course. Did he think private numbers were given out to any Tom, Dick or Harry who asked for them? Had he forgotten that it was Christmas Day and that policemen, like ordinary mortals, welcomed the peace and quiet of the precious little time they spent with their families? Deacon persisted, and finally compromised on the officer's promise to phone Harrison 'at a reasonable time' to relay the message that Michael Deacon needed to talk to him on a matter of urgency regarding Amanda Streeter and Nigel de Vriess.

'It's ten thirty,' said Deacon, tapping his watch. 'Why isn't this a reasonable time?'

'*Some* people go to church on Our Lord's birthday,' was the sharp response.

'But most people don't,' murmured Deacon.

'More's the pity. A God-fearing society has fewer criminals.'

'And so many whited sepulchres that you can't believe a word anybody says.'

'Do you want me to make this phone call, sir?'

'Yes, please,' said Deacon meekly.

When they were within a mile of the flat, Deacon drew the car into a kerb and killed the engine. 'You've been lying to me,' he said pleasantly. 'Now I'd like the truth.'

Terry was deeply offended. 'I ain't lied to you.'

'I'll hand you back to social services if you don't start talking pretty damn quick.'

'That's blackmail, that is.'

'Exactly.'

'I thought you liked me.'

'I do.'

'Well, then.'

'Well, then, what?' asked Deacon patiently.

'I want to stay with you.'

'I can't live with a liar.'

'Yeah, but if I told the truth, would you let me stay?'

It was a strange little echo of what Barry had said yesterday . . . 'Will they let me go if I tell the truth?' . . . But what was truth? . . . Verity? . . .

'You mean, heads you win, tails I lose.'

'I don't get you.'

'Presumably you've spent the last three days trying to weasel your way in by not telling me the truth.' Deacon toyed with the idea of revisiting Terry's behaviour of last night, but thought better of it. He knew from his own experience that post-mortems were bitter affairs which achieved little beyond continuing warfare.

'I reckoned you needed time to get to know me. It took Billy a couple of months before he realized I was the next best thing to sliced bread. Anyway, you can't kick me out. Not yet. I ain't learnt to read, and I want to earn that money you promised to pay me.'

'You've already cost me a fortune.'

'Yeah, but you're rich. Your ma's house alone has gotta be worth a bob or two, so you can easily afford another mouth to feed.'

'I told her to sell it.'

'She won't, though. She's well gutted about tearing up your dad's will and giving your fortune away to your sister. When the time comes – which is the few months she's given herself – she'll fade away. She's made up her mind to it, and there ain't nothing you can do to stop it unless you make it worth her while to stick around a bit longer.'

'And how do I do that?'

A sort of ancient wisdom glimmered in the boy's pale eyes. 'Billy said it's curiosity that keeps people alive, being as how we all want to know what happens next. And them that kill themselves or lie down and die before they need to reckon there's nothing left to be curious about.' He spoke seriously. 'You and your ma ain't got nothing to talk about except the stuff that made you angry enough to walk out on her, so you've got to give her something else to think about. Like me. She'd be well excited if you told her you was gonna keep me. She'd be on the phone all the time, sticking her nose into our business.'

'That's enough to put me off the idea for good.'

'Except if you don't give her a reason to talk to you, then another five years'll go by. And you don't want that any more than she does.'

'Are you sure you're only fourteen?' Deacon asked suspiciously. 'You talk like a forty-year-old sometimes.'

Terry looked injured. 'I'm mature. Anyway, I'm nearer fifteen than fourteen.'

'Social services won't allow you to stay with me,' said Deacon handing him a cigarette. 'If I expressed even mild interest in taking care of you, they'd label me a paedophile. It's dangerous these days for men to like anyone under the age of sixteen.' He held a match to the tip. 'Also, I'm irresponsible. I shouldn't let you smoke these damn things for a start.'

'Give over. I didn't get none of this grief from Billy. He just took me on board like I was his long-lost kid. I ain't asking you to adopt me, and chances are I'll be off out of it in a couple of months. Look, I just want to stay for a while longer, learn to read, meet Mrs D. again. It's a free country, and if you ain't doing nothing wrong, 'cept giving a homeless bloke a bed, why should the bastards at social services interfere?'

'Because that's what they're paid for,' said Deacon cynically, staring through the windscreen. 'How much is it going to cost me to keep a six-foot-tall teenager in food, clothes, beer and cigarettes for weeks on end?'

'I'll go begging. That'll help out.'

'No way. I'm not having a beggar in my flat or an illiterate with an impoverished vocabulary. You need educating.' *Don't say it, Deacon* . . . 'You're going to bankrupt me, probably land me in prison, and at the end of it all you'll bugger off leaving me to wonder what the hell came over me.'

'I ain't like that. I stood by Billy, didn't I? And he weren't half as easy to like as you are.'

Deacon glanced at him. 'If you put one foot out of line and drop me in it with social services or the police, I'll come after you with an axe the minute I'm out of prison. Is that a deal?' He held out his hand, palm up.

Terry gripped it excitedly. 'It's a deal. Now can I phone Mrs D. and wish her happy Christmas?' He reached for the mobile. 'What's her number?'

Deacon gave it to him. 'You really like her, don't you?' he said curiously.

'She's an older version of you,' said Terry matter-of-factly, 'and I ain't never met two people who treated me straight off with respect. Even old Hugh was okay, so maybe you're none of you as bad as you like to make out. Have you ever thought of that?'

Chapter Nineteen

WHAT TERRY HAD withheld was that he *had* seen Billy again before he died, just once, at the warehouse. It was early in the morning and the boy had been sitting on the scrubland at the back, staring out over the river. There had been a dawn mist over the water, which the warming sun had begun to burn off. He described himself as feeling 'fucking depressed'.

'Life weren't the same when old Billy weren't around. Okay, he were a pain in the butt most of the time, but I'd kind of got used to him. Know what I mean? Lawrence got it about right. It were like having a dad about the place – nah, more like a granddad. Anyway, I turned round at one point and the bastard was sitting next to me. It gave me a shock because I hadn't heard him coming. Matter of fact, I don't know how I didn't have a heart attack.' He paused to reflect. 'To be honest, I thought he were a ghost,' he went on. 'He looked about as bad as I'd ever seen him – with white skin, and lips that looked as if there was no blood in them.' He shuddered at the memory. 'So I asked him what he'd been doing and he said, "Toning."'

Deacon waited. 'Did he say anything else?' he asked when Terry didn't go on.

'Yeah, it didn't make much sense though. He said, "untoned sin's the invisible worm."'

Pensively, Deacon stroked his jaw. 'I should think he said "*a*toning" and "un*a*toned". The atonement of sins is the same as repentance.' He brooded for a while, searching through his memory for word associations. 'Blake wrote a poem called "The Sick Rose",' he said at last. 'It's about a beautiful rose that's dying inside because an invisible worm is eating away at its heart.' He stared out at the windscreen. 'You can interpret its symbolism any way you like, but Billy presumably interpreted the worm as unexpiated sin.' He paused again. 'He can't have been talking about his own atonement because he was torturing himself for his sins,' he said slowly, 'which leaves only Amanda. Do you understand all that?'

'Sure, I'm not totally dumb, you know, and you said she reeked of roses. In any case, it was her place he made me take him to.'

'How do you mean "*made*"?'

'He just set off. All I could do was follow. He didn't say a word the whole way, then just walked in her garage and shut the door behind him.'

Deacon regarded him curiously. 'Did you know it was her house?'

'No. It was just a house.'

'How did Billy know the garage door would be open?'

Terry shrugged. 'Luck?' he suggested. 'None of the others were.'

'Did he say anything before he went into it?'

'Only goodbye.'

Deacon shook his head in bewilderment at the boy's apparent acceptance of Billy's bizarre behaviour. 'Didn't you ask him what he was doing? Why he wanted to go there? What it was all about?'

''Course I did, but he didn't answer. And he looked that ill, I thought he'd peg out on me at any moment, so I weren't keen to make matters worse by pestering. You couldn't never stop Billy doing what he wanted to do.'

'But weren't you worried when he didn't come back to the warehouse? Why didn't you go and fetch him?'

The injured look reappeared on Terry's face. 'I did, sort of. I went and hung around the entrance to the estate the next day, but there weren't no sign of him, and I was too scared to go in there two days in a row in case the cops came down on me like a ton of bricks for casing the joint. Anyway, I was afraid of getting Billy in shit if he were holed up somewhere cosy. So me and Tom talked it over, and we'd got to the point of thinking we'd go round and suss the place out when Tom read in a newspaper that Billy'd snuffed it in Amanda's garage.' He shrugged. 'And that were the end of it.'

'Can you remember which day you took Billy there?'

Terry looked uncomfortable. 'Yeah, but Tom reckons I was stoned on cannabis most of that week and got everything muddled. It ain't true, but it's the only thing that makes sense. Me and him went all the way to the cemetery after Amanda told us she'd done the honours for Billy, just to make sure she weren't lying about it, and it was there in black and white. Billy Blake, died June twelfth, 1995.'

Deacon flicked through his diary. 'The twelfth was a Monday, and the pathologist estimated he'd been dead five days when the body was found on the following Friday. So which day did you see him?'

'The Tuesday. And it was the Wednesday I hung about outside the estate, the Thursday me and Tom talked it over and the Friday we reckoned we'd go round to take a butcher's. It were about eight o'clock at night, we was on our way, Tom lifts an *Evening Standard* from a bin, and there's this steaming great headline saying: "Homeless man starves to death." So he reads it and goes: "Jesus, you're an arsehole, Terry, the bastard's been dead for days and you've suckered me into looking for a corpse."'

Deacon was silent for so long that Terry eventually spoke again.

'Yeah, well, maybe Tom was right. Maybe it was the Tuesday before, and I was so stoned I let a whole week go by before I did anything.'

'According to the police he went into the garage on Saturday, the tenth.'

'It weren't a Saturday when I saw him,' said the boy decidedly. 'Saturdays are good tourist days, so I'd've been out begging.'

Deacon felt for the key in the ignition. 'How long after Billy died did Amanda come asking questions?'

'A few weeks. She'd paid for his cremation by then because she told us about it.'

The engine fired and Deacon put it into gear. 'Why didn't you tell her Billy was still alive on the Tuesday?'

Terry stared despondently out of the window. 'For the same reason I didn't tell you. I don't reckon he was, see. Matter of fact, I don't like to think about it too much. I mean, *d'you* believe in ghosts?'

Deacon recalled the smell of death that had been in Amanda's house and wondered uneasily about the nature of Billy's *deus ex machina.*

. . . I believe in hell . . .

. . . I have nightmares sometimes where I float in black space beyond the reach of anyone's love . . .

. . . Only divine intervention can save a soul condemned for ever to exist in the loneliness of the bottomless pit . . .

. . . Please, please, don't stay away longer than is necessary . . .

DS Harrison slept badly. At the back of his mind all night was the disturbing knowledge that he had missed something. He was temporarily distracted by the mayhem of Christmas morning, as his excited children opened their presents and his wife set to work on the lunch preparations, but shortly after eleven o'clock a call came through from the station relaying Deacon's message.

'He refused to explain what this matter of urgency was,' said the desk sergeant, 'and, to be honest, I didn't take it too seriously. But this name, Nigel de Vriess, has now come up in another connection. Hampshire and

Kent are alerting forces across the South to watch out for him. Apparently, his Rolls-Royce was reported abandoned last night in a field outside Dover. What do you want me to do about it? Pass this Deacon's number on to the DCI?'

'No, I'm coming in. Tell the DCI I'm on my way.'

'Amanda must've done something pretty bad to get Billy worked up like that,' said Terry suddenly. 'I mean, he didn't rate stealing and drugs too high, but he didn't lose his rag overly much at the guys who did them. Do you get what I'm saying? It were murder that made him go ape-shit and stick his hands in the fire and talk about sacrifices. Like the time Tom took the geezer's coat off of him and the geezer froze to death in the night. That's when Billy spent the night in the nude to take the blame on himself. He damn near died for it. It were only because Tom got really upset about what he'd done that we were able to get Billy back in his clothes again. So do you reckon she killed Billy by letting him starve to death?'

'No,' said Deacon, whose thoughts had been following similar lines. 'Barry's right. She wouldn't have told me Billy's story if she was afraid of what I'd find out. In any case, I can't see Billy caring too much about his own death.'

. . . My own redemption doesn't interest me . . .

'Whose then?'

. . . I'm still searching for truth . . . There's no way out of hell except through God's mercy . . . I'm still searching

for truth ... Why enter hell at all? ... I'm searching for Verity ...

'Verity's?' suggested Deacon.

Terry shook his head. 'Verity murdered herself.'

... You and I will be judged by the efforts we make to keep another's soul from eternal despair ... Do you enjoy suffering? Yes, if it inspires compassion. There's no way out of hell except through God's mercy ... I'm searching for Verity ...

'James's?'

'Yeah.' Terry nodded. 'I reckon the bitch murdered her old man, and Billy watched her do it. He mentioned once that he dossed west of London before he came to the warehouse. But I didn't pay no mind. It weren't important then. It makes sense now, though, doesn't it?'

'Yes,' said Deacon slowly, thinking of the river above Teddington, where the water level remained constant because the lock gates held back the tides.

Harrison telephoned through to a Chief Superintendent Fortune in Hampshire. 'I have a possible sighting of de Vriess on Saturday night,' he told him. 'He was with a woman called Amanda Powell, previously known as Amanda Streeter. She's the wife of James Streeter, who absconded in 1990 with £10 million. According to my information, she and de Vriess have been intimately acquainted since the mid-eighties.'

'Who's your informant?'

'A journalist called Michael Deacon. He's been investigating the Streeter disappearance.'

There was a momentary silence. 'He phoned de Vriess's house this morning claiming to be a business colleague. We're sending someone up to question him. What's he like?'

'I think he's protecting his story. Look, I suggest your officer talks it through with me here first. The situation's fairly complicated, and it'll probably help to have me there when you question Deacon. He's not the only one involved.' Briefly he recounted Barry Grover's part in the proceedings. 'He hasn't positively identified the man as Nigel de Vriess,' he warned, 'but he described him as having a birthmark on his shoulder, and that's mentioned as a distinguishing characteristic in your bulletin.'

'Where can we find Grover?'

'He's staying with Deacon.'

'What about Amanda Powell? You say she was in her house last night. Is she still there?'

'We're not sure. We've had a car in position across the road for about thirty minutes, but there's been no movement inside. We've also suggested that Kent police stake out her mother's house in Easeby. She was there most of yesterday and only returned to London in the late evening.'

'How far is Easeby from Dover?'

'Twenty miles.'

'Right. There'll be two of us coming up.' He reeled off a number. 'I'll keep that line open for you. The traffic shouldn't be too bad, so expect us between one and one thirty.'

*

Barry was in fine good humour when Deacon and Terry returned. Left to his own devices and with a clear goal in view, he had brought order to the proceedings and appetizing smells drifted from the oven. He beamed at them happily as they came through the door, and Deacon was struck by how different he seemed from the unhappy man who haunted the *Street* offices.

'You're a genius,' he said honestly, accepting a glass of chilled white wine.

'It's not so difficult, Mike. I remembered reading once about cooking turkeys in very hot ovens, and that's what I've chosen to do. It's important to keep the flesh moist, so I've stuffed bacon and mushrooms under the skin.'

He used the same slightly overbearing tone as when talking about his talent with pictures, and Deacon felt sorry for him because he realized that Barry's self-esteem was so fragile that he could blossom only when he could prove to himself that he was better than his peers. On balance, he preferred Barry bossy to Barry in tears, so he kept to himself that Lawrence was Jewish and that bacon might prove difficult.

'And I've made extra roast potatoes for Terry.'

'Wicked,' said the boy admiringly.

'And if you'll pardon the liberty, Mike, I used your telephone to call my mother. It occurred to me she might be worried about what had happened to me.'

'And was she?'

Barry's pleasure was unmistakable. 'Yes,' he said. 'She's been worried out of her mind. It surprised me a little. She never shows any concern when I stay late at the office.'

Deacon wanted to warn him – *Be objective . . . Mother love is jealous . . . As loneliness becomes a memory for you, it becomes a reality for her . . . She's using you* – but he suspected that much of Barry's renewed confidence stemmed from his conversation with his mother, and he held his tongue.

Terry, untrammelled by tact or sensitivity, jumped in with both feet. 'Jesus, she's a two-faced bitch, isn't she? Doesn't lift a finger for you when you're in bother and then goes lovey-dovey on you when your mates help you out. I bet she's hopping-mad Mike's offered you a bed. I hope you told her to bog off,' he finished severely.

'She's not that bad,' murmured Barry loyally.

'I don't suppose mine is either,' said Terry, 'but you wouldn't know it from the way she's treated me. I like Mike's mum the best. She's a bit of an old dragon but at least she's straight.' He took himself off to the bathroom.

Deacon watched the little man toy unhappily with the laid cutlery on the table. 'Everything's black and white with him,' he said. 'He takes people at face value and assumes that what he sees is what he gets.'

And all too often it worked, he thought. Terry's conversation with his mother on the telephone had been a revelation. ('*Hi, Mrs D. Happy Christmas. Guess what? I'm going to stay with Mike for a while. I knew you'd be pleased. Yeah, of course we'll come and see you. How about next weekend? Sure thing. We'll have a New Year's Eve party.*' And his mother to him afterwards: '*For once in your life, Michael, you've made a decision I agree with, but I shall be very angry if you're making promises that you can't keep. That child deserves better than to be tossed aside when something more attractive comes along.*')

'Do you think he's right about my mother?' asked Barry. It was years since she had spoken to him with such warmth, and he longed for Deacon to hand him a straw of comfort.

But Deacon could only think of the little man's ambivalence in the police station when he had expressed fear and hatred of the woman in one breath, then wept for her in the next. Indeed, Harrison had been so concerned by Barry's peculiarity on the subject that he had sent a patrol car to check that Mrs Grover was still alive.

'I don't know,' he said honestly, clapping a friendly hand on Barry's shoulder, 'but natural law determines that offspring must make their own way in life, so I'd keep your mother dangling if I were you. Apart from anything else, if she's this keen to see you after one night away, she'll be eating out of your hand if you make her wait a week.'

'I've nowhere else to go.'

'You can stay here till we sort something out.'

Barry turned away towards the oven, releasing himself from Deacon's comforting hold. 'You make it sound so simple,' he said rather wretchedly, opening the door and peering at the turkey.

'It is,' said Deacon cheerfully. 'Goddammit, if I can put up with Terry, I'm sure I can put up with you.'

But Barry didn't want to be 'put up with'; he wanted to be loved.

*

'Frankly, we thought it more likely we were dealing with a kidnap,' said Superintendent Fortune. 'Neither de Vriess's wife nor his business colleagues report money problems, there's no history of depression and, while he has a fairly murky reputation with the ladies, the general view is that he hasn't strayed since his ex-wife returned to him in May. You can't put much reliance on her word, of course – her husband was hardly likely to keep her up to date with his affairs – but she's adamant that he's had no contact with Amanda Powell in the last seven months.'

'Until Saturday,' said Harrison. 'Mind you, his wife's probably right about the seven-month abstinence. It's not that long if he was trying to make a go of it with his wife.'

'So why break out on Saturday?'

Harrison shook his head. 'I don't know, unless Michael Deacon triggered some kind of panic when he pushed his way in there on Thursday night.'

'It's the time scale that worries me,' said Harrison's DCI. 'According to Kent, the Rolls-Royce was first spotted in the field at lunchtime yesterday, but the farmer did nothing about it because he thought it was a courting couple. He only reported it after he saw it still there as it was getting dark and checked to find the doors unlocked and the car empty. But Mrs Powell wasn't informed of the full extent of Barry Grover's Peeping Tom act until approximately five o'clock, therefore the two incidents can't be connected. Put simply, Nigel vanished from his car several hours *before* there was any evidence that he needed to.'

'Assuming the two of them conspired to murder her husband in 1990?'

'Precisely. And there's no evidence that they did.' Fortune pondered for a moment. 'To be honest, gentlemen, I'm not sure where we go from here. Before DS Harrison's phone call I had a man who'd been missing for two days and an abandoned Rolls-Royce in a Kent field. Now I have him in the company of a former mistress thirty-six hours ago and the only motive for him to do a bunk or for her to get rid of him – which is always a possibility, I suppose – is ruled out because the car was abandoned too soon. I can't possibly justify using precious resources on a wild-goose chase. On the pooled evidence, we can't even point to a crime having been committed.'

'There's still Michael Deacon,' said Harrison.

'Yes,' said his DCI. 'There's also Amanda Powell's house. I think our resources will stretch to lawful entry in order to lay official concerns to rest *vis-à-vis* Mr de Vriess's welfare, bearing in mind that was the last place he was seen alive.'

Lawrence arrived with presents and had to be assisted up three flights of stairs when he collapsed in a breathless heap on the doorstep. 'Dear, dear, dear,' he said, gripping Deacon's hand tightly as he lowered himself on to the sofa, 'I'm not the man I used to be. I couldn't have managed on my own.'

'That's what I told Mike,' said Terry, omitting his own refusal to be the supporting arm 'in case the old poofter tries a grope on the way up'. 'Can we open these now?' he demanded eagerly, tapping the presents. 'We ain't got nothing for you, though.'

The old man beamed at him. 'You're giving me lunch. What more could I ask? Won't you introduce me to Barry first? I've been so looking forward to meeting him.'

'Yeah, right.' He grabbed the little man's arm and dragged him forward. 'This is my mate, Barry, and this is my other mate, Lawrence. Stands to reason you two're going to like each other because you're both mates of me and Mike.'

Lawrence, accepting this naive statement at face value, took Barry's hand in both of his and shook it joyfully. 'This is such a pleasure for me. Mike tells me you're an expert on photography. I do envy you, my dear fellow. An artist's eye is a precious gift.'

Deacon turned away with a smile as the ready flush of pleasure coloured Barry's face. Lawrence's secret, he thought, was that he was incapable of sounding insincere, but whether his feelings were really as genuine as they appeared it was impossible to say. 'Whisky, Lawrence?' he asked heading for the kitchen.

'Thank you.' Lawrence patted the seat beside him. 'Sit next to me, Barry, while Terry tells me who made such a wonderful job of the festive decorations.'

'That was me,' said Terry. 'They're good, ain't they? You should've seen this place when I first got here. It was well unfriendly. No colour, nothing. Do you know what I'm saying?'

'It lacked atmosphere?' suggested the old man.

'That's the word.'

Lawrence looked towards the mantelpiece, where Terry had arranged the *objets d'art* from his doss in the warehouse. There was a small plaster replica of Big Ben, a conch shell and a brilliantly coloured garden gnome squatting on a toadstool. He doubted they represented Deacon's taste in ornaments, so attributed them correctly to Terry. 'I congratulate you. You've certainly made it very friendly now. I particularly like the gnome,' he said with a mischievous glance at Deacon, who was returning with the whisky.

'I'm glad you said that,' murmured Deacon, putting the glass on a table at Lawrence's knee and retrieving his own. 'I've been racking my brains for something to give you, and we wouldn't miss the gnome, would we, Terry?'

'Mike hates it,' confided the boy, reaching it down, 'probably because I nicked it out of somebody's garden. Here, it's yours, Lawrence. Happy Christmas, mate.'

Deacon gave his evil grin. 'I tell you what, if there's a mantelpiece in your sitting-room, then that's the place for it. As Terry says, you can't go wrong with spots of bright colour about the place.' He raised his glass to their guest.

Lawrence placed it on the table. 'I'm overwhelmed by so much generosity,' he said. 'First a party, then a present. I feel I don't deserve either. My gifts to you are so humble by comparison.'

Deacon's lip curled. He had a nasty feeling the old buzzard was about to shame them.

'Can we open them now?' asked Terry.

'Of course. Yours is the largest one, Barry's is the one wrapped in red paper and Michael's is in green paper.'

Terry handed Deacon and Barry theirs and ripped open his own. 'Shit!' he said in amazement. 'What d'you reckon to this, Mike?' He held up a worn leather bomber jacket with a sheepskin collar and the Royal Air Force insignia sewn onto the breast pocket. 'These cost a packet down Covent Garden.'

Deacon frowned as the boy thrust his arm into a sleeve, then glanced towards the old man with a questioning look in his eyes which said: *Are you sure?* Lawrence nodded. 'You'd never find that in Covent Garden,' Deacon said then. '*That*'s the real thing. What did you fly?' he asked. 'Spitfires?'

Lawrence nodded again. 'But it's a long time ago, and the jacket has been looking for a home for many years.' He watched Barry finger his package on his lap. 'Aren't you going to open yours, Barry?'

'I wasn't expecting anything,' said the little man shyly.

'Then it's a double surprise. Please. I can't bear the suspense of not knowing if you like it.'

Barry carefully slit the Sellotape, as was his character, and unfolded the paper neatly to reveal a Brownie box-camera wrapped in layers of tissue-paper. 'But this is pre-war,' he said in amazement, turning it over with immense care. 'I can't possibly accept this.'

Lawrence raised his thin hands in protest. 'But you must. Anyone who can tell the age of a camera just by looking at it should certainly possess it.' He turned to Deacon. 'Now it's your turn, Michael.'

'I'm as embarrassed as Barry.'

'But I'm *delighted* with my gnome.' His eyes twinkled mischievously. 'And I shall do exactly as you suggest and put it on the mantelpiece in my drawing-room. It will look very well beside my collection of Meissen porcelain.'

Deacon bit off a snort of laughter and pulled the wrapping from his present. He didn't know whether to be relieved or dismayed, for while the gift had no material value, its sentimental value was clearly enormous. He turned the pages of a closely written diary, spanning many years of Lawrence's life. 'I'm honoured,' he said simply, 'but I'd rather you left it to me in your will as something to remember you by.'

'Then there'd be no pleasure in it for me. I want you to read it while I'm alive, Michael, so that I shall have someone to reminisce with from time to time. As far as you are concerned, I have been entirely selfish in my choice of a present.'

Deacon shook his head. 'You've already hijacked my soul, you old bastard. What more do you want?'

Lawrence reached out a frail hand. 'A son to say Kaddish for *my* soul.'

The smell of decay that poured out like a tide of sewage when the police burst open the door of Amanda Powell's house drove the team of policemen staggering backwards. So thick and putrid was the stench that it stung eyes and nostrils and loosened the contents of stomachs. The very fabric of the house seemed to ooze with the liquid of corruption.

Superintendent Fortune clapped a handkerchief to his mouth and rounded angrily on Harrison. 'What the hell kind of fool do you take me for? There's no way you could have missed this if you were here last night.'

Harrison dropped to his haunches and attempted to keep his guts from turning inside out. 'There was a WPC here as well,' he muttered. 'I asked her to stay with Mrs Powell while I spoke to Deacon. Believe me, she didn't notice it either.'

'It's clearing, sir,' said Fortune's Hampshire colleague, approaching the doorway warily. 'There must be a draught blowing it through.' Gingerly, he poked his head into the hall. 'It looks like the connecting door to the garage is open.'

There was no immediate response from the remaining policemen. To a man they dreaded what they knew they were going to see, for Nature has not endowed its works of beauty with the smell of death. At the very least they expected rivers of blood around a scene of brutal carnage.

However, when they finally found the courage to enter the house and look into the garage, there was a single naked corpse, intact and uncorrupted, propped against a stack of unopened bags of cement in the corner, gazing wide-eyed in their direction. And while no one put the thought into words, they all wondered how something so cold and pure could reek so vilely of corruption.

Chapter Twenty

'I'M BEGINNING TO wish I'd never met you,' said DS Harrison, stepping wearily across Deacon's threshold and introducing his companion. 'Chief Superintendent Fortune of Hampshire police.'

'I left a message for you to phone.'

'Events overtook me,' said Harrison laconically.

Deacon took in their sombre expressions and belatedly removed the paper hat from his head and tucked it into his pocket. The all-too-simple pleasures of getting gently smashed while eating Barry's turkey dinner and reading dire jokes out of crackers palled rather rapidly in the face of official sobriety. 'Is something wrong?'

The superintendent, a lean, somewhat intimidating individual with eyes that had been trained to see more than they gave away, gestured him forward. 'After you, Mr Deacon. If you please.'

With a shrug, he led the way upstairs and introduced them to his guests. 'If you're from Hampshire,' he said to Fortune, resuming his seat, 'then this must be to do with Nigel de Vriess.'

'How much do you know about him?' asked the superintendent.

'Very little.'

'Then why did you phone his house this morning?'

Deacon glanced at Terry, wondering if the boy could be relied on to keep his mouth shut. *Trust me* was the response in his disarmingly innocent expression. 'It occurred to me that the man Mrs Powell's neighbours saw tampering with her garage door yesterday might have been Nigel, so I thought I'd check to see if he ever went home.' He stroked his nose. 'Apparently he didn't.'

'Later you left a message at the station, saying you wanted to contact me on a matter of urgency regarding Amanda and Nigel,' said Harrison. 'What was that about?'

Deacon consulted his watch. 'It's after three. It won't be urgent any more.' He read impatience in Harrison's face and, with an amused smile, outlined his theory that Amanda and Nigel had done a bunk once they knew Barry had seen them together. 'Terry and I drove to the docklands this morning and checked her house,' he explained. 'It seemed empty and her car had gone. I thought it worth passing on that information if I could, but your desk sergeant was reluctant to bother you.'

'We're talking quite an epidemic here,' said Harrison. 'First James absconds, then Amanda and Nigel. Is this a serious theory you're proposing, Mr Deacon?'

Terry grinned. 'I told you you'd look a plonker.'

Deacon offered the two policemen a drink, which they refused. 'I'm sorry to have wasted your time,' he said refilling the glasses of the others. 'Put it down to the fact that I've had missing persons on the brain for weeks.'

'Meaning James Streeter.'

'Among others.'

Lawrence stirred. 'I doubt you'd be here, gentlemen, if you knew where Amanda and Nigel were, so are we to be given an explanation or left in the dark? I should add that I think it's a little unfair to pour scorn on Michael's theory if you have none of your own.'

The two policemen exchanged glances. 'After all, I think I will have that drink,' said the superintendent unexpectedly. 'It's been a bugger of a twenty-four hours.'

Harrison looked relieved, although whether because he needed a drink or because his colleague had shown a weakness, Deacon couldn't tell. 'I wouldn't say no either.'

They chose beer and, as Terry poured it for them, Fortune gave a brief account of the events that had brought him to London to consult with DS Harrison. 'A short while ago we took the decision to enter Amanda Powell's house.' He paused to drink from the glass Terry handed him. 'We found Nigel de Vriess dead in the corner of her garage,' he went on bluntly. 'He was naked and appears to have died from a blow to the back of his head. It's a rough estimate, but we're looking at death occurring approximately thirty-six hours ago, presumably during the hours following Mr Grover's sighting of him in the sitting-room.'

There was a long silence.

Deacon wondered what the reaction would be if he admitted that he had visited Amanda's house the night before. He suspected that theories on the inexorability of fate would go down like a lead balloon with London's and Hampshire's finest, particularly as Harrison already had his doubts about his and Barry's involvement with the damn woman. He thought of her pallor, and the way her eyes had watched his every movement. Was she afraid he would stumble across the corpse? How close had he come to it, for God's sake? *And how the hell could she have been so calm and collected when the body of her dead lover was secreted in her house and on her conscience?*

He rolled the stem of his wine glass between his finger and thumb, turning it in a slow circle on the table cloth. 'If she had a dead body on the premises, then I'm surprised she complained to you about Barry,' he said to Harrison. 'She's either very cool or very stupid.'

'Cool,' said Harrison, recalling his own impressions of a woman who had calmly allowed the police into her house with a dead man in the garage. 'I'm guessing she wanted to find out how much he'd told us before deciding what to do next. Presumably the original idea was to abandon his car in Dover before disposing of the body somewhere else, but she did a bunk when she realized she couldn't discredit Barry's evidence.' He paused. 'It still gives us a logistical problem. Who drove the Rolls-Royce to Kent if its owner was lying dead in a London garage?'

No one answered.

'If Amanda took it there,' he continued, 'how did she get back in time for her neighbours to speak to her at nine o'clock and then watch her drive away to spend Christmas with her mother? She certainly couldn't have done it afterwards because she was in her mother's house at midday when Kent police informed her of Barry's arrest. Which makes the timeframe too narrow to switch cars, drive the Rolls to Dover and return for the BMW.'

'She could have left home at three o'clock in the morning and caught an early train to London from Dover,' Deacon pointed out. 'That would have got her back by nine o'clock, wouldn't it?'

The sergeant shook his head. 'The first train on a Sunday doesn't reach Waterloo until after nine o'clock.'

'She could have hitched a lift.'

'In the early hours of Christmas Eve? In the dark? Right to her doorstep in time to be bright-eyed and bushy-tailed for her neighbours?'

Lawrence was watching him closely. 'What's your theory, sergeant?'

'We think there was someone else involved, sir. Admittedly this is pure speculation, but let's say de Vriess was struck on the back of the head *while* he was making love to Amanda, which is the only sensible explanation for his nudity. Let's say then that it was the accomplice who collected de Vriess's Rolls-Royce from wherever he had left it – it certainly wasn't parked outside her house or her neighbours would have noticed it – and drove the Rolls to Dover. I think you'd agree that's a more likely sequence of events, given what we have.'

Lawrence smiled. 'I'm a lawyer, my dear fellow. You can't expect me to agree any such thing. An equally likely sequence of events is that de Vriess was so aroused by Amanda that he forgot to lock his car and it was subsequently hijacked by joy-riders. Meanwhile, following their satisfactory session on the sitting-room floor, he took a shower, slipped on the tiles and killed himself accidentally. Amanda, appalled at what had happened, hid the body in the garage and has now fled to think things over. Have you any evidence to disprove my version of events?'

Both policemen looked at Barry. 'Perhaps Mr Grover can help us,' suggested Superintendent Fortune. 'How long did you watch what was going on in that sitting-room, sir?'

Barry looked at his hands. 'Not long.'

'You left before they finished?'

He nodded.

'Are you sure about that, sir? Most men in your situation would have waited till the end. You were unobserved. You stumbled on it by accident. You said yourself it was exciting. So much so' – he glanced briefly at the other three, as if wondering how graphic he could be – 'that you went back a few hours later for a second helping. Why leave before you had to?'

Barry licked his lips. 'I thought she'd seen me. She made him get up suddenly and pull the curtains.'

Fortune showed him a photograph of Nigel de Vriess. 'Was this the man?'

'Yes.'

'Why did you think Amanda had seen you?'

'Because he only got up after she looked at the window.'

'Was there anyone else in the room?'

Barry shook his head.

'Did you look in any of the other windows?'

'No. I was scared of being caught. I went straight back to the main road and took a taxi home.'

'You can't have been that scared,' Harrison said bluntly. 'You were there again in under eight hours.'

'He left his folder of photographs behind,' said Deacon reasonably. 'That's why he went back.' He looked thoughtfully across at Barry. 'She drives a black BMW which she always parks in her driveway. Was it there that night?'

Barry shook his head again.

'Then it was premeditated murder and she didn't need an accomplice,' he said matter-of-factly. 'She made two trips to Dover. The first on Saturday in her own car, which she left down there, returning to London by train, and the second early on Sunday morning in the Roller, returning in her BMW.' He fingered a cigarette from the packet on the table, wondering if she'd made the same round trip nearly six years before. 'The interesting question is what was she planning to do with Nigel's body?' He held the lighter to the tip of his cigarette. 'She must have been very sure of her hiding place or she wouldn't have gone to the trouble of leaving his car near a ferry port.'

The superintendent was watching him closely. 'The only problem with that scenario, sir, is that her neighbours recollect her car being outside her house all Saturday.'

Deacon shrugged. 'If Barry says it wasn't there, then it wasn't there.'

'Sounds to me like they're trying to frame him for the murder,' said Terry aggressively. 'I mean, he's a sitting duck if they reckon she had some patsy helping her.' He nudged Lawrence in the ribs. 'You shouldn't let them question him like this. They ain't given him a caution or nothing.'

'Oh, I think you do our police friends an injustice, Terry. They know as well as you and I that Barry would not have told them he'd seen a man in Amanda's house if he were guilty of murdering him.' He frowned slightly. 'It's quite a problem, isn't it? Assuming Nigel was murdered, then one must accept that Amanda was party to the murder. Yet, she's such a lovely young woman.'

'Do you know her, sir?'

'I've seen her once or twice. She and I are distant neighbours and, as Michael will tell you, I like to sit on the riverbank and watch the world go by.'

'Go on, sir,' said Fortune when Lawrence came to a halt.

'Forgive me. I was wondering how far human depravity can sink without its showing. You see, if Michael is right, then Mrs Powell must have encouraged Nigel to make love to her in order to facilitate his murder, and that would make her very depraved indeed.' He smiled a little wistfully. 'By and large, I prefer to think well of people.'

The superintendent smiled politely, hiding his impatience over an old man's ramblings. 'In my experience there's no relationship between how a person looks and how they behave.'

'Normally I would agree with you.' He took the photograph of Nigel de Vriess from Barry and examined it with interest. 'It's a cruel face, don't you think? But then he was a very arrogant man, and arrogance is a dangerous quality. I can say quite truthfully that Nigel de Vriess was one of the nastier by-products of a civilized society.'

'Did you know him, sir?'

'In a manner of speaking. One of my younger partners handled his affairs for several years.' He tapped the photograph. 'The occasion when he refused to act for de Vriess again was when he was instructed to buy off a young woman who had been beaten to within an inch of her life during sexual intercourse. De Vriess put a value of £10,000 on her physical and mental well-being, but my colleague was so shocked by the damage done to her that he severed our firm's connection with him. He described de Vriess as a psychopath, and nothing I have ever read or heard about him leads me to think any differently. Society should never allow a man like this to accrue wealth. When money is in the wrong hands then justice, the bedrock on which our democracy rests, can always be corrupted.'

Deacon's expression was thoughtful as he looked at his elderly friend.

'I'm not sure I understand the point you're making, sir,' said Fortune.

Lawrence looked surprised. 'I'm so sorry. I assumed it was obvious. You see, I can believe in de Vriess's depravity far more readily than I can believe in Mrs Powell's.'

'But it's de Vriess who is dead, sir, and not his ladyfriend.'

Barry cleared his throat nervously. 'She didn't look at all happy,' he confessed. 'He was pulling her round the room by her hair at one point, and then he made her bend over a little table so that he could – well—' He faltered to a halt. 'I think he might have been raping her,' he added in a whisper.

Five pairs of eyes swivelled in his direction.

'Why the hell didn't you tell us this yesterday?' demanded Harrison.

Barry looked terrified.

'You didn't ask him,' Deacon pointed out. But, by God, it explained much of Barry's confused behaviour over the last twenty-four hours. No wonder he had been able to describe the dominant male with such accuracy . . .

Daily Express

27.12.95

Stop Press: Police took the unusual step this afternoon of releasing the name and photograph of a woman they want to interview in connection with the disappearance of missing entrepreneur Nigel de Vriess, whose Rolls-Royce was found abandoned in Dover. She is Amanda Powell of Thamesbank Estate, London E14, formerly known as Amanda Streeter. She is thought to be in hiding somewhere in the UK.

Daily Express

30.12.95

Stop Press: Following a sighting by a member of the public, police have charged Amanda Streeter-Powell with the murder of her one-time lover, Nigel de Vriess. She was discovered last night in a cottage in Sway in the New Forest which is only 40 miles from de Vriess's home in Andover. Neighbours say she was a regular weekend visitor there. Neighbours in London E14 and colleagues at work describe themselves as 'dumbfounded' by her arrest. 'She's a nice woman,' said one. 'I can't believe she's a murderess.'

Telephone message

From: DS Greg Harrison Date: 3.01.96
To: Michael Deacon (Room 104) Dictated to: Mary Petty

Greg Harrison is fed up with your calls. He says he spends more time talking to you than he does to his wife, and he loves her!

Amanda Powell has been charged with murder and is on remand at Holloway, and, no, he can't take you to see her because you'll probably be called as a witness at her trial, along with Barry. In any case it would be a waste of time your talking to her because she has nothing to add to what she told the police almost six years ago about James's disappearance. She spent the weekend of 27th/28th/29th April 1990 with her mother in Kent, and her mother confirms this. Her alibi satisfied the investigating officers then and continues to satisfy them. Without more evidence, there is no justification for wasting taxpayers' money by trawling the Thames at Teddington.

With regard to de Vriess's murder, and for Christ's sake don't quote Greg as this is all *sub judice* and he could get the sack for talking out of turn (Greg asked me to underline that), Amanda agrees with Fiona Grayson. There had been no contact between her and Nigel for months. Amanda claims she had a chance meeting with Nigel in Knightsbridge on Saturday morning (they were both Christmas shopping, apparently), he became very excited about seeing her again and twelve hours later forced his way into her house in order to rape her. Barry's evidence supports this. When Nigel finally released her, she lashed out at his face and he fell backwards on to the brass doorstop. The forensic evidence (bruise on his cheek/traces of blood on the doorstop) supports this. We are still looking for witnesses who may have seen her BMW in Dover during the Saturday, but have found none to date. The neighbours continue to support her statement that it was parked in her driveway (although they're a little less sure than previously, as they are very used to it being left there).

The reason Amanda didn't dial 999 was because she panicked. She says she realized immediately that she needed to put as much distance between her and Nigel's Rolls-Royce as possible, so drove it to Dover, a town she knows well because her mother lives only 20 miles away. She agrees it's ridiculous that she thought getting rid of the car was more important than getting rid of the body, but she was confused and frightened following the rape. She hitched a lift out of Dover with a French lorry driver, arriving home by 8.30 a.m.

At the moment none of this can be disproved, but Greg is working on it.

Communicate by fax in future. Hard-working policemen can't afford to spend hours on the telephone.

Chapter Twenty-One

DEACON PUT THROUGH another call to Edinburgh. 'It's Michael Deacon,' he told John Streeter when the man came on the line. 'I presume you've read that your sister-in-law's been charged with the murder of Nigel de Vriess?'

'Yes.'

'Have you any idea why she did it, Mr Streeter?'

'Not really. I spoke to her the Friday before Christmas, suggesting a truce. She was surprisingly amenable.'

'What kind of truce?'

There was a short silence. 'The kind you suggested,' he said then. 'I told her we now believed she'd been telling the truth and asked her to use her influence with de Vriess to let us search through the DVS personnel files for anything that might lead us to Marianne Filbert. She agreed and asked me to contact her again in the new year with a view to proceeding.'

'Did she seem worried by the suggestion?'

'She was puzzled by it. She asked me why we believed her now when we hadn't before, and I said you'd become interested in James's story and had persuaded us to work with her rather than against her.'

'What was her answer to that?'

'As far as I remember, she said it was a pity we hadn't attracted your interest five years ago before quite so much water had gone under the bridge.'

'Did you ask her what she meant by that?'

'No. I assumed she was saying there'd have been a lot less anguish for everyone if the truth had come out at the time of James's disappearance.'

'Anything else?'

'No. We wished each other a happy Christmas and said goodbye.' Streeter paused again. 'Do you know if the police have questioned her about James?'

'Yes, but her story hasn't changed. She still denies knowing anything about what happened to him.'

There was a sigh. 'You'll keep us posted, I hope.'

'Of course. Goodbye, Mr Streeter.'

With cast-iron guarantees that her part in the story would never be written, Deacon persuaded Lawrence to talk to his partner about the woman who had been offered £10,000 by de Vriess to keep her mouth shut. 'All I want to know,' he told the old man, 'is whether she reported the incident to the police, and if she didn't, why not?'

Lawrence frowned. 'I imagine because the money was an inducement to stay silent.'

'How can it have been if he had time to go to his solicitor? Most women dial 999 the minute their attacker walks out of the door. They don't give him time to get legal advice. That ten thousand sounds more like severance pay than inducement.'

Lawrence phoned through the answer a couple of days later. 'You were right, Michael. It was in the nature of a pay-off, and she did not report the incident to the police. There had been a history of abuse against the poor woman, which ended in the injuries my colleague witnessed. In fact he urged her to prosecute' – he chuckled happily – 'somewhat unethically, it must be said, because he was still acting for de Vriess at the time, but she was too frightened to do it.'

'Of de Vriess?'

'Yes and no. She refused to give any details but my colleague believes de Vriess was blackmailing her. She was a stockbroker and his best guess is that she used insider knowledge to buy shares, and de Vriess found out about it.'

'Why stop? Why pay her?'

'De Vriess claimed it was a one-off incident when he'd acted out of character because he was drunk. The woman said it was the culmination of a series of such incidents. My colleague believed her and promptly severed our firm's connection with a man he considered to be extremely dangerous. His view is that de Vriess realized he'd gone too far – he broke her arm and her jaw – and decided to release her with a lump sum. His instructions were to offer the woman £10,000 on the clear understanding that there would be no further contact between the two parties.'

'Did she ever get paid?'

Another chuckle. 'Oh, yes. My colleague screwed £25,000 out of de Vriess before refusing any further business from him.'

'You realize this would help Amanda's case considerably? It proves Nigel had a taste for rape.'

'Oh, I don't think so. It wouldn't suit her book at all to have it demonstrated that Nigel blackmailed women in order to make them party to their own rape. As I understand it, her defence is that this had never happened before, that Nigel forced his way into her house in a state of high arousal and that his death was an accident when she lashed out after managing to get free of him.'

'She's lying.'

'I'm sure she is, my friend, but she's fighting for her life, poor creature.'

'Will she get off?'

'Undoubtedly. Barry's witness evidence alone will persuade a jury to acquit.'

'She wouldn't have been arrested but for him,' said Deacon, 'and now she's looking to him to save her. As Terry would say, that's well ironic.'

Lawrence tittered. 'How's his reading coming along?'

'Faster than I expected,' said Deacon drily. 'He's discovered the joys of looking up dirty words in the dictionary, and he's sending me round the bend by reading the definitions out loud.'

'And how's Barry?'

There was a long pause. 'Barry's decided to be honest about his feelings,' said Deacon even more drily, 'and, unless he puts a sock in it pretty rapidly, I'm planning to do the job for him by ripping his balls off and stuffing them in his mouth. I'm a tolerant man, as you know, but I draw the line at being the object of someone else's fantasies.'

FACSIMILE TRANSMISSION DATED: 4.01.96

THE STREET, FLEET STREET, LONDON EC4

From: Michael Deacon
To: DS Greg Harrison

Nota bene: You're not the only person I've been telephoning!

1. John Streeter called Amanda the week before Christmas (on my advice), asking for a truce and saying that the Friends of James Streeter were planning to approach Nigel de Vriess in the new year with a view to searching through the Softworks/DVS personnel files to try and get an angle on Marianne Filbert.
2. Wise up! It's about as likely that Amanda met Nigel by chance in Knightsbridge on the Saturday before Christmas as you or I winning the lottery. The odds against it are phenomenal. For Christ's sake, the world and his wife would have been there looking for last-minute presents. She made an arrangement with him to come to her house for some Christmas jollies. See below.
3. Who owns the cottage in Sway? Amanda or Nigel? If Nigel, then his wife knew nothing about it, and her evidence that there was no contact between Nigel and Amanda doesn't hold water. I'm betting Amanda was required to get herself down there whenever Nigel said

'jump'. (He *knew* she'd murdered James, and was using her as his personal punchbag whenever he felt like sex. Lawrence has told you what a bastard Nigel was, and Barry says he was *raping* her – what more proof do you need that Nigel had a hold over her?)

4. How did she know where Nigel had left his Rolls if it wasn't outside her house? Did he pause in mid-rape to tell her where he'd parked it?
5. If her car *was* parked in her driveway, why didn't she reverse into her garage, load Nigel into the boot and dump him somewhere before getting rid of the Rolls? The fact that she didn't is the best proof you've got that the BMW wasn't there.
6. How does she explain the sacks of cement in her garage when we have photographic evidence that the garage was empty at the beginning of December?
7. Why have rumpy-pumpy in London when they could have gone to Sway, considering she was going there anyway and it was only 40 miles from Halcombe House? Because the disappearing act would have been harder to work from Sway, that's why! It *had* to be London for easy access to Dover; and it *had* to be somewhere he wasn't known. So she phoned him and persuaded him to come to *London* for a change!

This was premeditated murder, which would have worked if Barry hadn't thrown a spanner in the works. While Kent & Hampshire police were running around like headless chickens looking for a kidnapped/absconded entrepreneur she would have been spending a quiet Christmas with her mother (who gives solid alibis!). The only risk was leaving the body in her garage over the holiday, but she didn't have time to dispose of the Rolls *and* Nigel all in one night, so she probably thought it was a risk worth taking. It was never going to be as easy as disposing of James. If she'd tipped Nigel over her garden wall he'd be sitting on a mudbank when the tide went out, and someone would want to know what was in the concrete overcoat. You really *must* trawl the river beside the Teddington flats. I guarantee you'll find a bag of bones weighted down with hardened cement, and you can use John Streeter for DNA comparison. I've met Amanda's mother, by the way, and the alibi's lousy. The poor old thing's been arthritic for years and knocks herself out every night with sleeping pills. Amanda could have murdered half of England and Mrs Powell Snr wouldn't have known a damn thing about it.

Best Wishes

Mike

METROPOLITAN POLICE ISLE OF DOGS FACSIMILE 10.01.96 09.43

From: Greg Harrison
To: Michael Deacon

1. Hearsay evidence. Amanda denies John Streeter said any such thing. Her version is that he verbally abused her as he has done every Christmas since James vanished.
2. We can't prove she didn't meet him in Knightsbridge.
3. The cottage in Sway belongs to a Mrs Agnes Broadbent. The lessee for the past five years has been Amanda Powell.
4. She told Nigel she didn't want to see him and said she would call a taxi. He said: 'Don't bother, I'm going. The Rolls is parked in Harbour Lane.' Then he attacked her. A witness remembers seeing a Rolls-Royce in Harbour Lane that night.
5. She thought about lifting Nigel into the boot of her car but he was too heavy for her. She only just managed to drag him into the garage.
6. She is planning to have the patio relaid in the garden. Some of the stones have worked loose.
7. Sway doesn't enter the equation. De Vriess's only intention was to rape her, so he forced his way into her house to do just that. His death was an accident. (You understand I don't necessarily believe this, but am merely quoting her.)

Have you any idea how much it *costs* to trawl rivers? We've no more reason to search the Thames at

Teddington than any other stretch of water. We need evidence that a body is there. You seem to have it in for Amanda. Why is that?'

Yours

Greg.

PS. You're placing a lot of trust in Barry and Lawrence. Their evidence of Nigel's 'brutality' towards women is very slight. Are you looking for trouble with his family?

THE ECHO

FACSIMILE TRANSMISSION DATED: 15.01.96

THE STREET, FLEET STREET, LONDON EC4

From: Michael Deacon
To: DS Greg Harrison

Lawrence and Barry have no reason to lie, unlike Nigel's family. And far from 'having it in' for Amanda, I'm trying to help her so, as Terry would say, I'm 'well gutted' about the assistance I gave you in finding her. I should have protected her story as assiduously as I'm protecting Billy's, then I'd have been able to interview her. Why the hell didn't you charge her with manslaughter, on the grounds of provocation, and agree to bail instead of having her banged up in the nick? That way I could have effected a chance meeting. I guarantee I'd have got more out of her than your lot ever will.

In passing, are you to blame for my being designated a potential witness? Get real! What did I ever see? Okay, I was in her house on Christmas Eve, but as far as I was concerned the poor bitch was trying to cope with the smell that you lot have seen fit to put down to Nigel. Listen, even I, a humble journalist, know that bodies don't go off that badly after 36 hours in the middle of a cold winter. That was Billy Blake who has been her constant companion since June in a so far vain attempt to force her into an admission of murder. Okay, I know it sounds crazy, but 'there are more things in heaven and earth than are dreamt of in your philosophy', my friend!

Do yourselves a favour, trawl the river by the flats at Teddington and find James. That's her real crime: losing her temper and striking out at a two-timing bastard who was about to skedaddle off to his mistress with £10 million in a numbered Swiss bank account. Not that I blame her, particularly. The more I learn about James, the less I like him, and she's certainly paid her dues by being Nigel de Vriess's plaything for the past six years.

As to that garbage you sent me last week:

John Streeter's wife heard his side of the phone call, so there's independent proof of what he said; search Nigel's bank accounts for the rent payments on Sway; Amanda will have told Nigel to park in Harbour Lane; if Amanda managed to get Nigel atop the sacks of cement, she could get him into her boot (she's an architect, therefore must know something about the mechanics of lifting); no one relays patio stones in the middle of winter – frost cracks cement. Go with your gut instincts. Ask yourself why Nigel raped Amanda. BECAUSE SHE WOULDN'T REPORT HIM. Why not? BECAUSE THE BASTARD HAD A HOLD OVER HER?

I'm guessing that the James scenario went something like this:

- James Streeter was a thief and a liar. He began a mini-fraud in 1985 to fund his stockmarket dreams. When he met Marianne Filbert in '88, he learned how to cream millions and the fraud became more sophisticated.

- In the meantime he'd married Amanda, whom he met through Nigel de Vriess. I can only explain this marriage in terms of escape for her as she must have discovered by then what Nigel was really like. It's harder to say what James's motives were. A bit of social-climbing perhaps (i.e. if Amanda was good enough for the boss, then she was worth having). His father describes him as 'status-conscious'.
- The marriage was a stormy one and James was soon casting around for someone more amenable. Meanwhile, he encouraged Amanda to pursue the Teddington flats project, possibly to legitimize some of his 'dirty' money. (The title deeds were registered in her name only – for tax purposes? – which was why she had no trouble exchanging the property for the house in Thamesbank.)
- As soon as the fraud came to light, Nigel, from his position on the Lowenstein board, guessed that James was responsible. He may even have sussed him through the Marianne Filbert/Softworks/DVS connection – the bank's inhouse investigation will have unearthed the abandoned Softworks security report. Either way, there's a good chance he took a cut in return for tipping James off about when to run.
- I think he also tipped off Amanda out of spite because she certainly learned that James was about to vanish and leave her to face the music alone.
- She killed James in anger, then sheltered behind the fact that all the evidence pointed to him

absconding. Her problem was that Nigel knew what she'd done and held the knowledge over her. I'm guessing he *did* tip Amanda off and *did* take a cut off James and Marianne. When Marianne contacted him to say that James had failed to arrive, he realized that James had never left the UK. After that he put two and two together, worked out that Amanda had disposed of James in the river, weighted down with bags of cement from the building site, and threatened to go to the police. (The MO was so effective, she was going to repeat it with Nigel.)

- The evidence for all of this lies in Nigel's treatment of Amanda, as witnessed by Barry. How could a man like de Vriess afford to do what he did unless he knew she wouldn't go to the police? Dammit, he had everything to lose if she screamed rape the minute he left the house.

Best wishes,

Mike

Mike

THE STREET, FLEET STREET, LONDON EC4

Amanda Powell
HM Prison
1X Parkhurst Road
Holloway
London N7 ONU

15th January 1996

Dear Amanda,
I have no idea if Billy's views on hell and damnation have any validity. He described purgatory as 'a place of eternal despair where love is absent'. However, he saw it not as an eternity of ignorance but as an eternity of terrifying awareness. The condemned soul knows that love exists, but is condemned for ever to exist without it. I believe he was so appalled by this vision that, as Billy Blake, he set out to save sinners from the dangers of unredeemed sin.

For others, he thrust his hands into the fire or subjected himself to intense cold. For you, he died. That is not to say you should carry his death on your conscience because death was what he wanted. Without it, he had no hope of rescuing his much loved wife, Verity, from the loneliness of the bottomless pit to where, as a suicide, she would have been banished. He believed there was no salvation from that terrible place except through divine compassion, and he hoped that if he led a life of extreme penitence before dying voluntarily of self-neglect, he could achieve the miracle of plucking Verity from hell through God's merciful intervention.

You can argue that his mind was completely unhinged by shock, grief, alcohol abuse and persistent malnutrition. Certainly, some of his friends believe he was an undiagnosed schizophrenic. But I agree with the sentiments you expressed the first time I met you. 'We're in terrible trouble as a society if we assume that any man's life is so worthless that the manner of his death is the only interesting thing about him.' Billy's worth was in the efforts he made to save you, because the only reason he sought you out was to persuade you to pay in this life for the murder of James, rather than postpone your suffering into eternity.

The irony is that you were prepared to give an unmourned derelict the dignity in death that you have denied to James, and perhaps that was Billy's intention all along. It's what brought me to see you, after all. Billy must have known that walking to Andover in the middle of a hot summer to learn your address from Nigel de Vriess (although Nigel was abroad at the time, and it was Fiona who told him how to find you) would destroy what little reserves of energy he had. This meant that his death in your garage would be the inevitable consequence of his actions. As you said yourself, he could have attracted your attention, or eaten food from your freezer, but he did neither, just quenched his thirst on ice-cubes and quietly died. He wasn't interested in judging you, you see – he was a murderer himself – he was only interested in reminding you of that other man who had gone unburied and unmourned.

I enclose a summary of what I think happened, which I have sent to DS Greg Harrison. I have omitted Billy's part in the proceedings because he never reported it at the time and because I doubt the police will accept a dead man's witness. But I am confident he was watching in the shadows when you killed James. Neighbours in Teddington remember a squatter in the old school, and Tom Beale from the warehouse tells me Billy mentioned 'dossing upriver from Richmond' before he moved to the Isle of Dogs.

You may ask why he didn't come looking for you sooner. The simple answer is he only knew you as Amanda Streeter, the woman who bought the school where he was squatting, and when you reverted to your maiden name and moved house he lost sight of you until he read your name in connection with Nigel de Vriess. But the real answer is that he wasn't ready. An elderly woman talked to me once about suicide. She said: 'Have you taken into account that there may be something waiting for you on the other side, and that you may not be prepared yet to face it?' Billy understood better than anyone, I think, that he needed to be prepared, and his preparation came through suffering. He always said he hadn't suffered enough.

I don't intend to do any more than I have done already – which is to leave justice to the authorities – except to tell the Streeters that their son *was* murdered. None of us is all bad, Amanda, and we each deserve to be mourned. Billy's salvation I leave to you. My own view is that it makes no difference if he was mad or sane. He believed that saving another soul from hell would earn God's compassion.

You asked me to prove that Billy's life had value, but I'm sure you realize now that you're the only person who can do that. It is in your hands whether, through your own redemption, you also redeem him and Verity.

With best wishes,

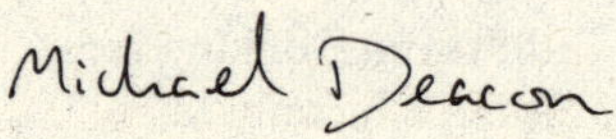

Michael Deacon

PS. Please don't think there is any animosity behind this letter. I have always liked you.

METROPOLITAN POLICE ISLE OF DOGS FACSIMILE 19.01.96 16.18

From: DS Greg Harrison
To: Michael Deacon

Amanda Powell has come clean about James. We start trawling tomorrow at 08.30 am. See you at Teddington!

Yours

Greg.

Greg

Chapter Twenty-Two

AS DEACON ROUNDED the corner of the converted school building, he was reminded of the first time he had visited the docklands warehouse. This was another bleak landscape, enlivened by people in shapeless, dark overcoats. A group of men stood in a huddle a few feet from the riverbank, staring out across grey water, coat collars raised against the biting wind. They were younger and more uniform in their dress, but the cold pinched their faces no less fiercely than it had pinched the faces of the warehouse derelicts. Beyond them, police divers in wetsuits bobbed beside a dinghy which was holding station against the current some yards out from where a twenty-foot stretch of lawn sloped down towards the river, ending at a wooden walkway that formed a towpath along the front of the property. The lawn was planted with shrubs and flowerbeds, curving in to give a framed perspective across the water, and Deacon wondered if this had been Amanda's vision when she drew up the plans for the conversion.

He noticed her suddenly, dressed in black, standing slightly apart with a prison officer and staring as intently at the river as the policemen were. She turned to look in

Deacon's direction as he approached across the grass, a faint smile of recognition lifting the corners of her mouth. She raised a hand in greeting, then let it drop, afraid perhaps that she'd put herself beyond the pale of human sympathy. He raised his own hand in acknowledgement.

DS Harrison peeled off from the group to steer him away from contact with Amanda. He glanced at the camera in Deacon's hand and shook his head. 'No photographs this time, old son,' he said.

'Just one?' murmured Deacon, nodding towards the woman. 'For my personal collection and not for publication. She looks great in black.'

'She would,' said the sergeant. 'She kills her lovers after copulation.'

'Is that a yes or a no?'

He shrugged. 'It's a "be it on your own head". She's trouble, Mike.'

Deacon grinned. 'You're a red-blooded male, for Christ's sake. Haven't you ever wanted to live a little? Don't you think the quid pro quo for the male black widow getting eaten is the best fucking sex he's ever had in his life?'

'It'll be the *only* sex he ever has,' said Harrison sourly. 'In any case she'll be an ugly old woman by the time she's served two life sentences.'

A wetsuited diver lifted a glistening, seal-like head above the surface of the river, and made a thumbs-down gesture to the watchers on the shore. The scene was both colourless and beautiful. Grey sky over grey water, with the black silhouette of the dinghy against a white winter sun. Before Harrison could stop him, Deacon raised his camera and recorded the moment for posterity. 'Nothing in life is ugly,' he said, swivelling the lens towards Amanda and using the zoom to bring her close, 'unless you choose to see it that way.'

'Wait till we pull James out. You'll think differently then.' He offered Deacon a cigarette. 'You were right about de Vriess tipping her off,' he said, cupping his hands around a match, 'except that at the time she didn't know where the information had come from. He sent her a photocopy of the original brief for the bank's in-house investigation, with James mentioned as a suspect. It arrived on the morning of Friday, the twenty-seventh of April, and she spent the day in a panic.' He broke off to light his own cigarette. 'She was due at her mother's that evening but she rang James at his office and asked him to meet her here at the school at six o'clock, ostensibly to discuss one or two problems that had arisen over the conversion plans. She says her only intention was to find out the truth, but it turned into a fight when James started boasting about how clever he'd been. They were inside the school, and she pushed him down a flight of stairs. She thinks he must have broken his neck on the way down.'

He paused as a second diver surfaced. 'According to her, the body's wedged under the boardwalk. That was the obligatory first phase of the construction. Rebuilding the dilapidated towpath in return for the right to convert the school. Supports were driven in to carry the pathway, and she put James in behind them.'

'At six o'clock on an April evening?' said Deacon in disbelief. 'It would have been broad daylight.'

'She didn't do it then.' Harrison drew heavily on his cigarette, sheltering it from the wind with his coat lapel. 'She left James dead at the bottom of the stairs and drove to Kent in a state of shock, expecting the police to be waiting for her when she got there. When they weren't, she began to calm down and realized she'd either have to confess to the murder or get rid of the body. She came back at two o'clock in the morning while her mother was asleep and disposed of it then.'

Deacon was watching Amanda while Harrison spoke. 'How? She's no Arnold Schwarzenegger, and she must have been working in the dark.'

'She's a resourceful woman,' said Harrison, 'and she brought a torch with her from her mother's house. As far as I can make out, she rolled him on to an old door and used the lever principle and a pile of breeze blocks to raise the door high enough to slide him into a wheelbarrow. The plan was to tip him off the boardwalk into the river and hope that when his body washed up further down, his death would be put down to a tragic accident. But she was tired, couldn't control the barrow properly and the whole thing tipped over this side of the walkway.' He gestured towards the shrubs on the left-hand side. 'Five years ago there was a two-yard gap where the bank had eroded, so rather than go through the whole palaver with the door and the breeze blocks again, she launched the body head-first through the gap, assuming it would be sucked out into the main stream.'

'But it wasn't?' asked Deacon when he didn't go on.

Harrison shrugged. 'He never surfaced, so she thinks he must have got snagged on one of the supports, and was then buried under the ballast and cement that the builders tipped in to fill the gaps along the board-walk.'

'Wouldn't they have seen the body?'

'She says she came back on the Monday morning to check, and there was no sign of it. After that, she thought it was just a matter of time before one of us knocked on her door and told her that, far from absconding, James had been dead for weeks.'

'But it never happened?'

'No. She's a jammy bitch.'

'If he's under a ton of ballast, what are the divers expecting to find?'

'Anything to indicate she's telling the truth. They're looking for metallic objects, his Rolex watch, belt buckle, shoe studs, buttons, even his fly. If they find them, we start digging out the ballast looking for the poor sod's skeleton.'

Deacon glanced across at Amanda again. 'Why wouldn't she be telling the truth?'

'No one understands why she's suddenly decided to come clean. She has every chance of walking away from the de Vriess murder because Barry's evidence of rape means she can plead self-defence. We're still working on proof of premeditation but we're having very little success. There's no record of any phone calls, no trace of her car in Dover, and if Nigel ever visited Sway, then no one saw him there.' He jerked his chin towards the river.

'So why give us this for free? What does she expect to achieve by it?'

'A clear conscience?' suggested Deacon.

Harrison dropped his butt to the grass and ground it out with his toe. 'You're a romantic, Mike. This is the end of the twentieth century, and people don't have consciences any more. They have clever solicitors instead. Do you seriously think Amanda would have told us about James if she hadn't been charged with Nigel's murder?' He shook his head. 'The pressure's been building up on her to account for James's disappearance, and she can't afford two separate trials for two separate murders. She might be found innocent once, but never twice, and the last thing she wants is for us to unearth James *after* she's beaten the de Vriess verdict. I'm betting there won't be enough of him left to show how he died, and she wants an assurance before she goes to court that there'll be no more charges pending. What price conscience then, eh?'

Deacon didn't answer immediately, and they stood in silence watching the police industry in the river. 'How did she find out it was Nigel who sent her the photocopy about the fraud?' he asked then.

'He rang to offer his sympathy after James disappeared, and mentioned it then. He said he wanted to warn her that James might be arrested but couldn't do it officially because of his position on the board. She denies your theory about him having a hold over her,' he went on. 'She says Nigel knew nothing about James's death, and claims their relationship had always been amicable until he forced his way into her house and raped her.'

Deacon gave a low laugh which was whipped away by the wind. 'She can't say anything else, not if she wants to plead self-defence.'

Harrison eyed him curiously. 'Why are you so keen to prove it wasn't?'

'I'm not any more.'

'I don't follow.'

Deacon trod his own butt into the ground. 'I'm only interested in her admission that she killed James. As far as Nigel's concerned, I'd say he got what he deserved whether he raped her once or a hundred times.'

'But you're damn sure it was the latter.'

'Yes.' He thrust his hands into his pockets to keep them warm. 'I think he owned her body and soul because he knew she'd murdered her husband. I've spoken to Lawrence's partner and he describes de Vriess as an animal. He says Nigel wouldn't have hesitated to abuse a woman he had a hold over.' He lifted an amused eyebrow. 'Look, there had to be some reason for the bastard's murder. *You* may believe she killed two men in accidental self-defence, but I don't. I think she's probably been planning how to get rid of Nigel for the last five years, but when John Streeter phoned to announce a change of tactics it was the push she needed. It's one thing to be the butt of libellous press releases that no sensible editor has ever touched with a barge pole, quite another to sit idly by while people you fear form alliances on the advice of a journalist.'

Harrison pulled a wry face. 'Where's the evidence? Justice isn't served by idle speculation.'

'It is in this case,' countered Deacon amiably. 'Justice

was served the minute she admitted to killing James, and you can thank Billy Blake for that. He's the one who persuaded her to talk.'

'You're not going to tell me she killed him as well?'

'No. Billy died of self-neglect.'

'What's your theory on why Nigel gave Billy her address?'

'He didn't. Nigel was abroad the last two weeks in May.' He thought back to the bitter woman who had spilled her heart out to him a few days before. 'It was Fiona who told Billy how to find Amanda.'

God knows, I hate her . . . She's ruined my life . . . Nigel and I were divorced because of her, and now she's killed him . . . Yes, I did tell that old tramp where she lived . . . He was completely mad . . . He said he was an instrument of God . . . And then he asked for her address . . . Did it worry me that I was sending a madman after her? . . . Not in the least. It amused me . . . Oh, I've always known where she was and what she was calling herself . . . I'd have been mad not to . . .

There was sudden activity in the water as a diver surfaced and gestured excitedly to the watchers on the bank. Harrison moved forward with a group of policemen, leaving Deacon to cross the twenty-yard gap that separated him from Amanda Powell. She was watching him, not the river, and he felt the pull of her attraction just as he had the first time he met her.

He often wondered why he didn't go to her.

Instead, he retraced his steps up the slope without a backward glance.

THE STREET, FLEET STREET, LONDON EC4

Lawrence Greenhill
23 Wharf Way
LONDON E14

22nd January 1996

Dear Lawrence,
What can you tell me about the following? I came across it last night in your diary.

London – 19th December 1949: A new client, Mrs P., a war widow, came to me today, seeking advice about her 13-yr-old daughter's pregnancy. Should she seek to prosecute the man in question or keep quiet for the sake of her child? At 7+ months the pregnancy is too advanced for abortion – dear God, the poor soul thought it was puppy fat and my heart bleeds for her. She welcomed GS into her home as a friend. He is 27, only five years younger than she is, and she was flattered by his attentions. Her confusion is the greater because she clearly entertained hopes of marriage herself and is devastated to find that he was more interested in seducing her daughter, V. I have advised silence and adoption, and given her the address of a convent in Colchester where her daughter can retreat before her condition becomes noticeable to friends and teachers. The nuns will find suitable parents when the time comes. But I am at war with myself tonight. What sort of world are we living in where innocent children, orphaned by war, become the prey of monsters? Surely such a man should be prosecuted, even if at the expense of his wretched victim's reputation?

Terry says it's fate. Is it? Or is this your God at work? I should have put you at the centre of my chart, and not Billy Blake, for it was you who held the key to both stories. Billy was 'still searching for truth' while you have always known it.

Yours ever,

Michael Deacon

P.S. I've taken your advice and sent Barry home to his mother after he got drunk for the third night on the trot. It's Terry's fault. He teases the poor little sod unmercifully. That being said, I can't take any more protestations of love!

Wednesday, 7 February 1996 – 9.00 p.m. –
Cape Town, South Africa

The young waiter shrugged expressively, and jerked his head towards the figure at the window table. 'She's been crying ever since she got here,' he said. 'I don't know what to do. She won't order, and she won't go.'

The older man approached the table. 'Are you all right, Mrs Metcalfe? Is there anything I can do for you?'

She raised drowned eyes to his face, then rose unsteadily to her feet. 'No,' she said. 'I'm fine.'

As she walked away, he looked down at the English newspaper that she'd taken from the hotel rack when she'd arrived. But he was none the wiser for the banner headline.

DNA proves bones in river were
James Streeter

A Parable of Our Time
by Michael Deacon

THE tragic story of Verity Fenton's suicide and Peter Fenton's subsequent disappearance is well known. Unknown until recently is what happened to Peter, because the truth was buried in a suicide's grave.

'BILLY BLAKE – died 12 June 1995 of starvation.' So says the plaque at a London crematorium which commemorates the death of a homeless man. It should read: 'PETER FENTON OBE. Born 5 March 1950 – died 13 June 1995 of mortification.'

It's hard to conceive how a man like Peter Fenton, so prominent in the twin environments of Knightsbridge and the Foreign Office, could walk out of his house and vanish into thin air unless one understands why he did it. At the time, it was assumed he had run away, so the search was concentrated abroad. What never occurred to anyone was that he had chosen the life of a penitent by embracing poverty in the gutters of London.

Is it any wonder he vanished so successfully when none of us looks too long on the destitute in case eye-contact proves dangerous or embarrassing?

But transformations take time, and Peter, a handsome, darkhaired 38-year-old, should have been recognizable for weeks until poor hygiene and diet reduced him to the skeletal figure of Billy Blake, well-known to the police as a 60-year-old human derelict and street preacher. How could he have changed so radically and in so short a time? The answer, I think, is that the shock of Verity's suicide destroyed him. He was already aged beyond recognition when he entered the anonymous world of the vagrant.

It would be true to say that Peter Fenton died on 3 July 1988 when he walked out of the family home in Cadogan Square. Certainly, he had no interest in being that man again. Peter Fenton was a professional diplomat, an assured and confident man with an enviable intellect and no obvious vices. By contrast, Billy Blake was a tortured individual, who delighted in self-inflicted pain and preached damnation to anyone who would listen. He was an unrepentant alcoholic, thief and beggar, but he strove, often at terrible cost to himself, to protect others from the evil that he had done himself. The irony was that Billy, destitute, was a good man and Peter Fenton, advantaged, was not.

Peter was a murderer who went on to seduce and marry the wife of his victim, Geoffrey Standish. There can be no doubt that he knew exactly who Verity was when he first made love to her, for even if Geoffrey Standish was a stranger when Peter killed him, he will have learned about the man from newspaper reports afterwards. We can speculate that this knowledge added to the thrill of Verity Standish's seduction or we can take a kinder view and say that Peter simply fell in love at first sight with a frail and vulnerable woman whose suffering at the hands of her brutal first husband had left its indelible imprint.

She was a tiny, fine-drawn woman with huge doe eyes, and Peter was by no means the first man to offer her protection. He was, however, the youngest, and Verity, after years of abuse by Geoffrey, who was fourteen years her senior, saw safety in a relationship with a younger man. Nevertheless, she wasn't keen to publicize her love for a toyboy. There is evidence that she didn't want to legitimize the affair because she was afraid of what people might say. But, while she may have married Peter against her better judgement, her fears about the inappropriateness of the match were quickly laid to rest. Their marriage has been described by friends as 'an idyll', 'the greatest love since Abelard and Eloise', 'sweet to watch', 'so intense that it was close to idolatry', 'it's hard to say who adored the other more'.

How tragic then that, obsessed with love of Peter,

she began to ignore the two children she'd had with Geoffrey. It's easy to understand why. At the time of her marriage, her daughter Marilyn, 20, was at university and her son Anthony, 14, was at boarding school. She was no longer so important to them, and her role as Peter's wife took her overseas.

'They always paid for us to fly out in the holidays if we wanted to go,' says Marilyn, 'but it was no fun playing gooseberry for weeks on end. It was harder for Anthony because he was younger. Not that he ever blamed Peter. It was Mother he resented because she never made a secret of how much she'd hated our father. In the end, when Anthony became depressed after his girlfriend walked out on him, his resentment boiled over and he put that advertisement in *The Times*. He knew Mother would read it, and he wanted to jolt her out of her complacency. We'd both heard the rumours that she'd had Father killed, and Anthony wanted to remind her of them. You see, he was only five in 1971, and he never believed that Geoffrey was as bad as everyone said.'

Anthony Standish was 22 years old in 1988. He was an unhappy young man, whose depression over a failed love affair became confused with a long-standing resentment of his mother's coolness towards him. His bitterness found expression in the following advertisement:

'**Geoffrey Standish**. Will anyone knowing anything about the murder of Geoffrey Standish on the A11 near Newmarket 10.3.71 please write to Box 431.'

Anne Cattrell first put forward the theory that Peter had murdered Geoffrey in her article 'The Truth about Verity Fenton' (*Sunday Times*, 17 June 1990). She argued that Peter and Verity may have met much earlier than they ever admitted, and that Peter was Verity's avenging arm. There's no evidence of that, but there is a wealth of evidence to show that Geoffrey and Peter had something else in common in 1971. Which was gambling.

As Billy Blake, Peter confessed to killing a man, and it's reasonable to assume that that man was Geoffrey Standish. Billy's penance was too long and too tortured for his victim to have been unconnected with Verity's suicide. But as Billy Blake, he also preached against the dangers of sudden and uncontrollable anger which leads men to commit acts of violence that they later regret. This would suggest that Geoffrey's murder was the result of a similar anger, making it an unplanned act and not a premeditated one.

We can only speculate twenty-five years after the event, but university friends of Peter talk about his 'illicit Friday-night card games at a private house somewhere in Cambridge' which allowed him to pursue his goals of 'money' and 'the good life'. It is certainly possible that Geoffrey, who was on his way to Huntingdon on Friday, 9 March 1971, learned of such a card game and gained entry to it after phoning his hosts to say he would be delayed. It is also possible that a fight broke out over money and ended, tragically, in death.

There must have been other people present who witnessed what happened. Indeed Peter may not have been alone in the killing, which would explain why it was so successfully disguised as a road traffic accident. More likely, perhaps, is that Geoffrey attacked first – his aggressiveness is well documented – which would have exonerated the other participants, at least in their own minds, of murderous intent. Whatever the truth, the decision was made to protect everyone involved by dumping the body as far as possible from the illegal gambling house and make the death look like a hit-and-run accident.

While there is no evidence to support this theory above any other (except perhaps Peter's abrupt decision to give up gambling 'some time in '71', according to friends) it makes it easier to understand how Verity could have married Peter in ignorance of his crime. For, as Anne Cattrell argued elsewhere in her article, did Verity kill herself because she learned by accident that she'd married her first husband's murderer?

The answer is that it was not an accident. Peter told her himself, during a bitter confrontation between Verity and Anthony after the advertisement appeared in *The Times*. 'I accused her of killing my father and when she burst into tears Peter got very angry and said *he'd* done it. I know it sounds ridiculous,' Anthony says now, 'but I didn't believe him. I thought he was just trying to diffuse the row. It's what he always did. Every time she and I fell out over anything, Peter would take the blame on to himself. It used to make me so angry. My mother was very childish in many ways. She seemed unable to take responsibility for anything.

'I've lived with the guilt of that row for eight years. I wish I'd waited until Peter had come back from the States instead of attacking her the day before he left. It's one of those terrible truisms, that you only realize how much you love a person when you've lost them. I was hurting very badly after my girlfriend left me, but it's no excuse for what I did. I never really believed that my mother had killed my father, but when she hanged herself I assumed she must have done and that Peter had rejected her as a result. I always hoped he'd come back one day, which is why I've never spoken about this before.'

But if Verity didn't hang herself out of guilt, then why? Was it in sudden revulsion against the man she adored? In panic because she was afraid her husband's crime would catch up with him now that Anthony knew the truth? Either explanation could be true but neither satisfies. For all her frailty, Verity was stronger than that. She had put up with years of abuse from Geoffrey, and it seems unlikely that revulsion or panic would drive her to suicide.

My own view is that something infinitely more terrible pushed Verity over the edge. It was a secret she had kept for forty years, and I learned of it by chance from a lawyer whom Verity's mother, Mrs Isobel Parnell, consulted in 1949 about Geoffrey Standish's seduction of her 13-year-old daughter.

'It was a terrible story,' said Lawrence Greenhill. 'Isobel had hoped to marry Geoffrey herself, and she hated Verity for causing her so much pain. The baby, a boy, was put up for adoption, and Verity was sent away to boarding school. The tragedy was that no one considered Verity's pain. At one stroke Isobel had deprived her of child, lover and mother, and one can only wonder what loneliness the poor girl must have suffered. With the benefit of hindsight, it's obvious she would seek to pay Isobel back by marrying the man who had ruined their lives. How could a disturbed adolescent possibly distinguish between love and lust when the woman who loved her rejected her and the man who seduced her continued to pursue her?'

But there are no neat solutions to this story. Peter was not Verity's long-lost son, nor could she ever have believed he was. It is the Registrar General's job to check for just such anomalies before granting marriage licences, and no questions were raised at the time of Peter's and Verity's wedding.

In her rational mind, Verity must have known there was nothing improper about their relationship, despite the intensity of her love for Peter. But in her irrational mind, alone in the awful silence of their empty house after Peter had gone to America, did she start to brood on the unnatural love she had for the murderer of her first husband and did she begin to question the legality of the adoption papers?

Her suicide note speaks of betrayals, and it's tempting to assume she was thinking of her mother and her adopted son when she wrote it. But perhaps a more likely explanation is that she finally recognized she had betrayed everyone, *even Peter*, through her inability to express love naturally. For it's unlikely Peter would have been forced to betray himself to Anthony had Verity loved him less and Anthony more.

As Lawrence Greenhill suggests, Verity Fenton's

real tragedy was her confusion of love with desire. She couldn't adequately express her love for Anthony because desire for a son is illegal, so she chose to consume her surrogate son, Peter, with all the passion in her nature. But, as she dwelt on the consequences of his admission of murder, alone and isolated in Cadogan Square, did it begin to dawn on her that her worship of the man who'd killed the father of *all* her children was a betrayal too far?

And did she decide to kill herself because she realized it made no difference, and that she would want this man to possess her as long as she lived – be he father-slayer *or* son?

(Extracts taken from *Oedipus* by Michael Deacon, to be published by Macmillan, 8 November 1996)

Epilogue

THE FLAT WAS empty when Deacon returned to it, for which he was grateful. He was in no mood for Terry's cannabis-inspired inanity, having had his third row in as many days with the new editor of the *Street*.

Who could have believed he would ever regret JP's departure?

'Different times, different customs, Mike,' JP had said as he left. 'Anodyne's the word I'd use for the new management. You won't be chasing prostitutes any more, just sound bites from trained politicians.'

'I can live with that,' Deacon replied.

'Don't be too sure,' JP had warned prophetically. 'You may not have shared my ideas on what made a good story, but you were always free to write it in any way you chose.' He picked up Deacon's copy on Peter Fenton, which was lying on the desk, and isolated the final two pages which discussed why Billy Blake had died in Amanda Powell's garage. 'I can guarantee you won't get these last seven hundred words into print. I know you want to go public on why and how the poor bastard died, but there's no way the new lot will risk being sued, and particularly not by a prisoner on remand. It's too damned contentious. It almost certainly infringes the *sub judice* rules and it's bound to damage Amanda's right to a fair trial for the murder of de Vriess. And that's not to mention the trouble you'll have from the DV's family when you accuse him of being a multiple rapist.'

'Would you have risked it?'

'Of course. I'd argue that the matter isn't *sub judice* yet because Amanda hasn't been charged with James's murder.' His expression grew cynical. 'And won't be, unless the boffins can come up with a cause of death. Is it true she's withdrawn her confession?'

Deacon nodded.

'Even more reason to publish and be damned then, and if and when we raised enough steam to force a prosecution, I'd make hay out of the fact that our efforts resulted in her being convicted of *both* murders instead of walking away scot-free as she looks like doing at the moment.'

'And if the magazine got taken to the cleaners for libel?'

'We'd have served a kind of justice, on both her *and* that bastard de Vriess.' JP chuckled. 'It's why they've kicked me out, of course. It's all about profit these days, and social consciences like mine come expensive.'

Deacon pressed the 'messages' button on his answer phone. 'Barry's been arrested again,' said Greg Harrison's unemotional voice. 'Drunk and disorderly right on our doorstep this time. His mother's adamant she won't have him back, so he wants to give your address in case he's bound over. You're going to have to sort this, Mike. He says he only gets drunk because he's in love with you.' There was a short pause. *For laughter?* Deacon wondered sourly. 'Look, call me back when you can.'

Lawrence's voice next. 'I'm so sorry, my dear fellow. I see your article has had its teeth drawn. How very disappointing for you. I know how much you wanted to demonstrate that Billy's life had a purpose. Is it any consolation to think of him as Terry's mentor? In the end, surely, that is where Billy's true value lay.'

As the messages came to an end, the emptiness of the flat began to make itself felt. Picasso's *Woman in a Chemise* had gone, along with the television and the stereo that Terry had moved from the bedroom into the sitting-room. Big Ben and the conch shell no longer stood on the mantelpiece, and Turner's *Fighting Téméraire* was just a memory on a blank wall. Deacon went into the kitchen and inspected the biscuit jar. It contained a folded piece of paper.

Cheers, mate. I reckon I've earned what I've taken by learning to read and write. Anyway, it's a lot less than the five hundred quid I could have had off you at the beginning. Give my love to Lawrence and Mrs D. They're good people. You, too. I'll look you up some time. Your friend, Terry.

P.S. Tell that editor to get stuffed and concentrate on book-writing. Do your own thing, mate. I mean, like Billy always said: any man who dies in chains probably deserves to.